Divided

Disclaimer: The themes surrounding this novel adhere to the idea that a person is shaped strictly by the traits related to their zodiac sign. Under no circumstances does portrayal of the zodiac signs in *Divided* mean any derogatory connotation.

ISBN Number: 979-8-9906448-0-9

First paperback edition: June 2024

Edited by Krista Vitola, Lara Allen, and Adrienne Kisner
Proofread by Carol Trow
Cover art by Shirley Tran
Layout by Ava Frechette and Shirley Tran
Printed by IngramSpark in the U.S.A

Dedicated to Boden Frechette
My first and most treasured beta reader

Author's Note

I was not a very popular child.

Shocking, I'm sure.

I was the principal's daughter, so I wasn't too well-loved by the masses in elementary school, and I was a theatre kid, which made me a pariah in my teenage years, obviously.

This doesn't mean I didn't have my friends, and I was as happy as an anxious pre-teen could be considering the circumstances.

The circumstances in question, of course, being a global pandemic.

It felt as though I had no direction. We were stuck indoors, and I grew up in a small town, so there was little to do in a general sense. I thought I had tried everything to pass the time during lockdown: making trick shot videos with my little brother; letting my sister boil the inside of a Sharpie and dye my hair pink (don't ask); and even coining my 'hot girl walks' with my two dogs, doing loops around our neighborhood for miles.

Nothing felt *good*, and nothing felt right. And then I started writing.

It was not a lightbulb, genius moment where everything seemed to fall into place. No, it was me sitting in my sister's room while she aggressively practiced French-braiding my hair and I simply reminded her of our nanny's rapidly approaching birthday.

My sister, being thirteen and obviously far superior to me in true teenager fashion, rolled her eyes and said, "Yeah, I *know* her birthday is tomorrow. She's a Gemini queen."

Interesting, I thought, but not because I suddenly had a brilliant idea but instead because I didn't really know many Geminis who fell under the 'queen' category.

Up until that point, I had a very basic level of astrological knowledge. I knew what every fourteen-year-old knew, which was my sun sign and nothing else, and I defended the Cancer ideals as if it were my job, even though I knew as well as everyone else that most Cancers were sensitive jerks, myself included, sometimes.

Suffice to say, I didn't know a lot. Certainly not enough to write a book (much less four) about a world ruled by the zodiac.

But I had nothing but time on my hands and a strong Wi-Fi network that I didn't have to pay for, and thus, the Googling commenced.

That same evening, I had a note on my iPhone about the length of Magna Carta, and a Google Doc that was as blank as the inside of my brain.

The hardest part, I soon came to realize, was *starting*. Did I think it would get easier as I continued the series, and wrote Book Two, then Book Three, and finally Book Four? Yes.

Did it?

Of course not.

After four years of writing and revising and failing and wanting to quit and falling in love with the process time and time again, *Divided* was finally done. It was one of those times where I finished a full revision, sat back, and said to myself, "That fourteen-year-old girl would be proud of this."

That's how you know it's ready to hit the shelves, I guess. When the quirky high school freshman with raggedy pink hair tells you in some sixth-sense communication that your most important piece of work is ready to be viewed by the world.

Writing *Divided* was not easy by any means. Writing *anything* is not easy by any means, and anyone who has tried to write a novel will tell you that. I was rejected by agents and editors time and time again, and eventually, after four long years, I realized that self-publishing was the option I needed to take going forward. Pursuing self-publishing taught me so much about the literary industry, and it made me feel so connected to my work in a way I didn't experience when I first wrote it. My advice for everyone who chooses to pursue writing or self-publishing is that you absolutely can succeed, as long as you remain devoted to your story and art, and never let your passion for writing wane in the face of difficulties.

There are multiple people who helped me in this process that I couldn't have succeeded without. My parents, Aimee and Justin, who never quite understood *why* I'd choose a career path such as this but ardently supported me nonetheless. My two siblings, who never thought of me as strange or less than and always ensured I had two constant best friends. The team of editors and designers who helped me bring *Divided* from words on a digital page to a real-life book. And, maybe most importantly, I send my deepest gratitude to Diana, Peter, Cameron, and Kiara, the characters who became so deeply *real* and were always around when I needed them most. Many authors say their characters are almost like shadows of real people, but these four are more human than I ever thought they could be. I like to think that I didn't make up their story, I just helped them to tell it.

Thank you for reading *Divided,* and proving to that fourteen-year-old girl that her dreams could come true.

Prologue: The Beginning

Year: 2086

In the depths of North Carolina, in a large house at the top of a hill, a young girl sits at one of the tables in the library, flicking through the pages of a magazine.

Inside, the house was grand and well-furnished. Doorknobs were gilded, walls were a stark white, and all the chairs in the library were upholstered in shining leather. When beams of light cut through the tall windows in the foyer, dust particles illuminated the air.

A man is standing before the girl, frame pulled to his full height. He's tall, skinny, and the way in which he leaned on his elaborately carved cane was odd, to say the least. It wasn't unusual for people to do a double-take when they passed him on the street.

The cane was mahogany, slender, pointed at the end. The carvings were deliberate and delicate: a butterfly here, flying under a weeping willow tree there, blanketed by a sky full of stars.

The rest of the man was no less confounding. His shoes were nearly as glossy as the seal on the invitation he was holding, his brown, carefully tailored jacket went down to his knees, his ascot tie was patterned with green flowers. His mustache was long and curled up at the ends, the same dark color as his gelled and slicked-back hair. Resting atop his nose were a pair of tortoise shell glasses: ones with fake lenses that merely made him look richer.

The girl was, quite frankly, a carbon-copy of the man. She was also tall, but unlike her father she filled out her frame slightly better. Today, her jet-black hair was pinned back from her face in loose ringlets, revealing her large, dark eyes.

"You can't be serious," Barbara Oswald says as she tosses the thick cardstock invitation her father had just been holding onto the table in front of her.

"Believe it or not, Babs, I'm perfectly serious," her father replies, pulling off his leather gloves and setting them gently on the table, right on top of her magazine. "The nation must be united once this ends, and it's time we started making plans."

"Plans for me or for you?"

"Is there a difference?"

Barbara scoffs and rises from her seat. "I want to be at the meeting tomorrow."

"Great. George and Damian will be there, and we can finalize the ceremony."

Barbara rolls her eyes, crossing her arms defensively over her chest. "I won't go along with this. Not quietly."

Orion Oswald pauses in removing his jacket and looks her up and down, gaze softening ever-so-briefly. "Oh, Babs," he whispers, voice full of an emotion she hasn't heard since her mother died. After a moment, he clears his throat and his tone grows stiff again. "You don't have a choice."

The next day, fourteen people file into a dark, furniture-less room, deep in the Oswald's basement. Discretion was necessary for the revolutionaries in question. Three weeks ago, the United States, or 'New America', as it was so affectionately dubbed by the First Twelve, had successfully sunk their first target: Canada.

Almost thirty-eight million people were dead. History, preserved in that Northern territory for over one hundred and fifty years, was lost beneath cold waters.

But that didn't matter.

"First on the agenda," a man says, pulling out a manilla folder. He was Damian Henderson, thirty-eight years old, father to George Henderson. Both Henderson boys were tall, handsome, and finely-manicured: short blonde hair combed neatly, bright green eyes and muscled limbs. But the Hendersons were different from the Millers, or the Lees, or especially the Oswalds: the two boys were nearly dirt poor. Nobody would know based on their pressed suits, and shined shoes, but those suits were secondhand, and the shoes were polished by them. Up against young Barbara Oswald and her satin dresses, fifteen-year-old George and his reused clothes were nothing to look at twice.

Next were the Oswalds. Led by Orion Oswald, a dark-haired man with many a hidden secret, the Oswald family consisted of himself and his daughter Barbara. Fifteen as well, she was thin, tall, and had raven hair that curled down around her shoulders. She was witty and sharp but kept out of these newborn politics because of her youth. Not to mention, standoffish Barbara Oswald could not care less if the discussion did not concern her. Unfortunately, however, for this meeting, there was something on the docket that featured both herself and George Henderson.

Damian Henderson continues. "We need to make a choice about which country we sink next. We have the weapons stock for a smaller one, nothing too powerful."

A woman pipes up, one Barbara recognizes from the occasional soiree as Isabella Garcia. "Argentina?" Her long lashes flutter as she blinks. "We may as well begin to target South America. And sinking from the bottom up is easiest, to avoid Mexico."

"No, no," Anthony King interjects, "I say the United Kingdom. They're far too much trouble already, and they're most likely to fight back. So, I say we get rid of them now."

"Agreed," Orion Oswald says, nodding. He leans forward on his cane, bracing both hands on its polished head. A chill runs down Barbara's spine, and whether it be from the cold basement air or the topic of discussion she doesn't know.

"I *don't* agree," Damian Henderson interrupts. He and George are leaning against the wall, looking far too comfortable and scarily similar in the dingy light. "I say Mexico."

"Mexico is much too large, Mister Henderson," Orion argues, beginning to walk towards the other man. His cane clacks uncomfortably on the cement. "And besides, the United Kingdom *is* our biggest enemy. King is right."

"Who cares?" Damian says, pushing himself off the wall to get face-to-face with Orion. "If we have the weapons, I say we get New America isolated as quickly as possible. Mexico is the next country to put out of their misery."

"Have we decided yet how to organize the people?" Margaret Miller questions, anxiously pushing her silver bracelets up her wrist, the jangling sound setting Barbara's nerves further on edge.

"I'm saying we split three ways. The Appalachians and Rockies are the borders, leaving the midwest as one big section," Henderson says.

Orion scoffs. "Leaving the west coast small and frail? I disagree. We need to split by occupation. For example, the south must be a farming district."

"No, that would never be sustainable-"

"What about by star sign?" Barbara interjects. The adults fall quiet, and all eyes turn to the girl, who had been previously occupied with picking at her manicured nails to distract herself from listening.

"I'm sorry?" Orion says, turning to face his daughter. His expression is unreadable, at least to Barbara.

"Split the people by zodiac. People of a similar sign have similar traits, right? So, there you go. Twelve sectors, twelve signs," the girl says.

"I like that," a voice pipes up from the wall. George Henderson stands up straight, his green eyes piercing in the dim light. "But what do we do about the powers, *Babs*?" he asks, his voice teasing.

Barbara rolls her eyes. "It's *Barbara*. And it's simple; we watch them. One powerful being for each of the twelve here. And when we take over, we take them on."

George nods, pausing a few inches from Barbara. The two study each other carefully, until a woman named Celina Myers speaks. "I believe the next order of business is the betrothal."

Barbara's head snaps to face her. "I don't want it."

"Nor do I," George says, taking a step back from her.

"I believe we have no choice," Orion says. "It will unify the country."

"By marrying the children of two revolutionaries who destroyed all these Americans hold dear?" Barbara says through clenched teeth, "I won't do it."

"My dear, you don't have a choice," Damian Henderson says, crossing to the young girl and taking her by the arm.

Without a word, Barbara slaps him across the face, yanking herself from his grip. "Don't you dare touch me, and don't tell me what to do, either."

"Barbara Helena Oswald, do not speak to Mister Henderson in that tone," Orion says, voice sharp. He's warning her, less on Damian's behalf and more for her own sake.

"I will speak to him however I feel fit, father," Barbara replies, turning her chin up and raising one neatly plucked brow. "He is trying to force me and George into an arrangement that *neither* of us have agreed to!"

"Don't you dare speak for me, Oswald," George Henderson sneers. Barbara turns a little too close to where he's standing and finally gets a good look at him in the dimly lit room.

He's handsome, very much so. Apart from his straw-colored hair and green eyes, he had a chiseled jawline and thick eyebrows, a few shades darker than his hair. Barbara had always seen him as beneath her, she always *assumed* he'd be beneath her, but now she saw him as something more, practically a clone of his father, both inside and out. George was cold, and calculating, and radical to say the least. He was dangerous, Barbara knew. Maybe not now, but someday.

She finally takes a breath, rooting herself to her spot and willing her body to stand tall. "Don't speak for you? So you're saying you'd *like* to spend the rest of your life tied down to me? Watching our parents rule this backwards nation that will be handed to us one day, all broken pieces and angry people?!" She swallows down a lump that had been rising in her throat. "You *want* to fix that mess?"

George crosses to Barbara, getting right up in her face and gripping her wrist tightly, pinning her hand to her side as his knuckles grow white. Her skin flashes with pain as he speaks through gritted teeth. "You're so naive, Barbara. I've had *nothing* my whole life, while people like you have been handed whatever the hell you want. You think if I wanted a dress like the one you've got on, I could just have it? Or if I wanted a fancy pair of gloves or a cane like your father's? I can say with certainty that the day this country is passed to me, the day this *'mess'* is passed to me, I will *revel* in the fact that *nobody* will have any authority over me, or tell me what to do. This includes you, Barbara, my wife or not."

"Really, George. I would think you have some shred of human decency to think of me as more than a trophy. But Lord knows the only reason you'd marry me at all is for money."

George releases Barbara with a hard shove, putting a finger in her face. "Watch your tone, you selfish-"

"Do not ever speak to my daughter that way, you self-righteous prick of a boy!" Orion Oswald howls, pushing George away from Barbara. His gaze cuts into both teenagers, daring them to speak again. Neither does, and the room hangs in a tense silence. Finally, he addresses the adults in the room, tone low. "This wedding will go to a vote. All in favor, say yes," he glances towards the kids once more. "Excuse us, children."

The twelve adults gather closer in the center of the room, leaving George and Barbara on the outside of their tight huddle, as per usual. Eventually they emerge from their group with a final vote. It takes every ounce of

Barbara's self-control to avoid looking at George as Damian and Orion study both children.

"The betrothal is canceled," Damian Henderson says, his gaze cold upon the two teenagers. "But on the other hand, we've agreed that the two of you were right on one thing." He looks around the room, studying every person in turn. Finally, he takes a deep breath and raises his chin up, uttering the words that would change New America's history forever, though none of them knew it then.

"Split the people by zodiac."

Orion Oswald steps forward. "We never put it to a vote."

Damian just laughs, the sound bouncing ominously off the walls of the basement. "You'd be a fool to vote against it, Orion. Think about it: if everyone has the same traits, we won't have any conflict. And if we don't have any conflict, *we-*" he motions to the adults in the room, "-don't get the boot from the Capitol."

The two men regard each other carefully, neutrally, and Myers speaks again after a long beat of icy silence. "But who will lead?"

Henderson sighs. "Barbara was right there too. We each take one of the powerful beings, and establish sectors based on sign."

Anthony King pipes up, rubbing his hands together as a chill passes through the basement. Barbara's teeth chatter, and she wraps her arms around herself. "But what if we aren't one of each sign?"

Damian glares at him, one thick eyebrow raised. Finally, after a long moment, he turns to the woman next to him. "Isabella?"

She turns to face him. Her dark hair is pulled into a neat ponytail at the base of her neck, and she smirks, red lips quirking with the movement. "Virgo."

Damian targets the next person. "Anthony."

"I'm a Pisces."

"Myers?"

"Scorpio," she replies.

Barbara watches in amazement as Damian moves around the room, and one by one, each of the twelve zodiac signs are muttered by each of the twelve adults. Finally, Henderson reaches Orion, regarding him with a passive-but-not-quite-kind glance before speaking. "And you, Oswald?"

Orion glances over at his daughter before turning his gaze back down to Damian. His chest is rising and falling slowly, and Barbara knows he's nervous. About what, she couldn't say, but the way in which his cane was slowly twirling tiny circles on the floor indicated that her father wasn't his normal picture of tranquility.

Orion swallows before answering. "Aquarius."

"And you, George?" Damian says, turning to his son, who has once again retreated to his previous spot on the wall as if the earlier confrontation had never happened.

George smiles that winning, slightly unsettling grin. "Aries."

"Barbara," Henderson commands.

"I'm an Aquarius, too."

"Great," he looks at the other eleven adults, letting himself turn his back on Orion Oswald. "Your children will take over your roles, when you pass. So plan accordingly," Anthony King is the only one who chuckles. "Anyways, meeting adjourned, for now. I'll see everyone tomorrow at seven."

As they file out of the room and back up the stairs, Barbara feels a cold hand tug her around the corner. She nearly yelps until the hand in question comes back up over her mouth. Her eyes adjust to the dim light and she sees George Henderson in front of her, his chest pressed against hers, green eyes darker because of the musty basement but somehow more alert than she'd ever seen.

Slowly, George removes his hand from her mouth, gripping her forearms instead. "You did it, Babs. You just screwed us all over."

Barbara rolls her eyes. "Quit it, George."

"No, I'm serious." Unconsciously, he pushes further into her, making her heart pound against its will. The basement, now without the presence of the adults, is eerily quiet apart from their joined breathing. "Our lives will never be the same again. Do you get that? Did you ever think that there might be people who don't share a sign with their entire family, like you and me? You're pulling the country apart."

Barbara tries to ignore the sting his words cause and instead pushes back, nudging their legs together and making them wobble. A low sound escapes George's throat and he shoves her back into the wall, leaning into her ear. Barbara's breath escapes her throat in a shaking gasp, and her whole body shivers when George's hair brushes her cheek and she hates herself for it. "I want you to remember today. When I'm leading this country, remember this moment, when you decided you would forever engrain yourself as *fourth*. Remember who's first, Barbara Oswald."

With that, he pushes off her and disappears up the stairs.

Year: 2137

The best thing about the future is that it is uncertain.

The worst thing is that, eventually, you will find out what it holds.

Over the course of fifty-one years, New America had changed, and now, in the present, society is much different than the one that existed Before.

But one thing that remained unchanged about America was elitism. Money and popularity still reigned, and whoever climbed higher on those ladders had immense power that could not and would not be challenged by anyone who suffered below.

Leo and Aries and Aquarius, they could afford to design their children, to use their absurd funds to ensure their babies were the same as them and would return to their open arms after a twelve-year hiatus at school. Sometimes, the lucky Libra or Gemini could do the same.

Leo and Aries and Aquarius, they were popular. They had sway in taxes, laws, and reform, and those like Pisces, Cancer, and Virgo were just voices lost in the din of a dystopian nation.

Hierarchy. The best form of nationalism to ever exist.

In school, children learned everything about the past. Old, dead men called 'presidents', who had ruled alone over Old America. Giant cities long forgotten, called all kinds of names: New York, Chicago, Los Angeles. Animals, like 'dogs' and 'cats', extinct for so many years.

But mostly they learned about people. Looks. Traits. Colors and hair and eyes. People were different before New America, their teachers would say. No one wore the same color. No one had the same traits. Everyone was different.

But this was Before. Before people wore colors that were assigned to each of them. Before they were transported across the country for the sake of The Split. Before they turned twelve and were torn away from their friends, crying and kicking and screaming, begging not to be taken away from the only people who made them whole.

But everyone gets older, don't they?

Now she wears only 'Forest Green', and lives only in Sector Seven. She cannot leave. She cannot see her sister Maya, or her friends Kiara, or Peter.

Her name is Diana. No last name anymore, as far as she knows. They took that away too. She's sixteen. Or so she's told, there's no more traditional calendar. And one day, she did something. *They* did something. Something that would destroy New America as they knew it.

Part One: the Taurus

Diana

"Name."
"Diana."
"Number."
"904."
"Sign."
"Taurus."
"Sector."
"Seven."
"Age."
"Sixteen."

Diana is shoved along the wall, shoulder-to-shoulder with a young boy who looks about twelve. He's crying, not used to this annual treatment. Diana regards him warily as the scratchy drywall rubs against her back. And despite the whirring of the ceiling fan overhead, her hair sticks to her forehead and sweat beads near her collarbone.

Today was the day every year where BOZ members traveled to their sectors and inventoried the information of each person. They did it to keep the citizens safe, but more people in the country would die at the hands of aggressive guards today than from any sickness ever seen in New America.

That was part of the charm, she supposed.

The guard inspecting Diana's group goes down the line, eyebrow raised as he takes in the Taureans gathered in front of him. He pauses in front of Diana and the boy, and she watches out of her peripheral vision as the huge man grabs the boy by the chin. Suddenly, the air seems to crackle, and the dusty smell of the town hall is stronger than it was. Diana's skin prickles with energy, and suddenly, she feels more alive than ever.

"Name."

"Andrew," the kid whimpers.

"Number."

"411."

The guard stops short, eyes narrowing. He motions behind him, beckoning another guard closer. They speak in whispered tones, and the second guard leaves, returning momentarily with a man dressed in Forest Green.

He's tall and aging, with graying hair to match his wrinkles. His suit is pressed, and his shoes are shined so thoroughly that the buzzing lights in the town hall glare off their surface. Diana, although her face is neutral, suppresses a shiver of anxiety.

The boy is happy to see the man in Forest Green. "Mister Davis!" he gasps, racing to the BOZ leader. He throws his arms around the man's legs, and the guard who was taking their information grabs the child and yanks him away from the leader. The boy, Andrew, starts to cry, screaming for him to let go. The guard just grips him tighter, knuckles white around the boy's scrawny arms. The screaming makes Diana cringe as the noise pierces through the echoey room.

"What do we do with him, sir?" they ask the Taurus leader.

Mr. Davis doesn't even blink, instead, he looks up and down the line of his people, dressed in the same earthy hue. Everyone, including Diana, stands at a rapt attention, knowing the consequences of stepping out of line, especially on a day like today.

Finally, and without looking away from the row of people, Davis speaks. "This is a warning. Discipline him, not here, but watch the extent of his abilities." He turns to glare down at the young boy, whose cheeks are puffy and red. "Andrew, listen to these men. Okay?"

The boy nods, under some trance inflicted by the BOZ leader that hadn't befallen the others. "Yes, sir," he responds, his voice barely above a hoarse whisper. "Yes."

The guards haul him away, out the door of the town hall, which slams dramatically behind them. Mr. Davis looks down the line one more time, and, in an act of silent defiance, Diana holds her chin up rather than turning it downwards like the others surrounding her. The BOZ leader meets her gaze and smirks.

"Awfully familiar, this one," he says to the guard flanking him. His hollow eyes never leave Diana's. "Her name?"

"Diana. 904," the guard responds, hand resting on his holster just in case.

"Diana," Davis repeats, stepping closer. His eyes travel her face, studying her every feature. "Ah. I know your sister," he says finally, taking a miniscule step back.

Diana's eyes widen, but she says nothing, instead clenching her teeth and staring past the leader at the blank wall opposite them.

Davis laughs coldly at her lack of response. "Not as talkative as she is. I'll tell you, she was a fun one to break."

She can't take it anymore.

But one step towards the man has Diana wrestled to the ground by two more guards, gripping her arms and legs and pinning her to the worn hardwood. Mr. Davis just laughs at the blood trickling from her busted lip, knocked against one of the metal shoulder pads on the guard holding her. "Boys, calm down. Let her go."

"But she was going to attack you, sir," a guard states plainly.

"I said release her," Davis responds, his voice low and chilling. He looks down at Diana, who is still lying on the floor, pushing herself up. "She's going to be important, like her sister. And I'd like to take care of her myself, if need be. So let her go for now," he steps right into Diana's space, looking down at her menacingly. "I know who you are, Diana. And I certainly know your family. It would be a shame if something happened to Maya, so stay in line, yes?"

Diana lets out a shuddering breath, wiping the blood from her chin. "Yes," she whispers back, hating the way her heart thunders within her ribcage.

"Good," Mr. Davis responds. He motions to the guards, standing at stoic attention. "Let's go."

As the town hall doors slam behind them and the headcount resumes, Diana steps back in line, ignoring the whispers and nervous glances. All she can do is pull her injured lip between her teeth and wonder what the hell he meant.

Diana stretches as she heads up the stairs, rolling her head to crack her neck. She sighs as she reaches for the closed door of her room, pausing before she enters. She rubs her foot once, twice, along the shag carpet on the floor, into the bubble in the rug.

It's been there since she moved in. And no matter how much she vacuumed, or flattened the carpet, or pushed down on the spot, the little bump in the carpet stayed right in front of her door. When she was fourteen, Diana even called in the Sector Seven housing team to replace the carpet in the upstairs hallway. To her utmost glee, the bump went away. But one morning, as she was exiting her room, she looked down to see that it had mysteriously appeared again.

So, she adapted, and now the rug bump was more of a friend than any of her acquaintances in Sector Seven. Diana sighs again and pushes the door open, listening to the little *swooshing* noise the carpet made as the door slid over it.

The house is devoid of people and noise. She lives alone. She's been alone since she was twelve, actually. Her room is nice enough, considering it's the same furniture she's had since she moved here four years ago. A queen-sized bed sits on one wall, a vanity on another, and a big dresser to the left of the door. Compared to the other sectors, Seven at least supplied their kids with nice houses, if nothing else. The walls are bare, painted a Forest Green that matches the earthy tone of her clothes. She goes to the dresser and takes out a plain shirt and sweatpants, moving slower than a snail. Then, she moves to the vanity and brushes her hair out, running her fingers gently through the knots and sending a tingle over her scalp. The routine is monotonous and boring, but it's just that: routine. And Diana honors routine more than anything. She stares herself down in the mirror, smiling half-heartedly at the dark circles under her eyes and the small cut on her lip from yesterday's events at the town hall. She glances at her alarm clock on the nightstand, reading the glaring numbers there.

Diana has been putting off sleeping lately, which sounds absurd, but it's for good reason. It's because every time she closes her eyes, she sees the tall, skinny frame of his body or the gentle curls of his dark hair. Peter was taken the year before Diana was, three years after Maya left her. He was shy towards the kids in his grade, but not to Diana. They hit it off right away, spending every waking moment together in their secret hideaway out past the school, deep in the forest. The dream that plays through

Diana's head every night is the scene where he was taken from her, dragged from her, ripped from her.

Diana catches herself yawning in the mirror, and she crosses to the door, pushing her finger against the lock and feeling a little bit of relief when it clicks into place, buckling under her finger. She pulls the covers back from her bed, clicking off her lamp and letting the light from the stars and the moon filter into the room. She climbs into bed, relaxing slightly into the mattress. Her fingers pull the covers up to her chin, rolling over onto her side and staring wide-eyed at the wall.

The last thought Diana has before she closes her eyes is: *See you soon, Peter.*

They run through the underbrush, the ghostly sounds of the rustling trees blending with their melodic giggles.

"Come on, Diana!" Peter whisper-shouts, running ahead, his voice the same wispy tone as the rustling of the leaves.

"I'm coming!" Diana says, her young legs struggling to match his pace, "hold on!"

An eleven-year-old and a twelve-year-old running through the woods, away from the school that rested menacingly in the Plaza.

Running from their lives.

They stop, out of breath, and Peter sits back against a tree. The world around them is dark with shadows, and the trees stretch their long limbs down towards them, safe and inviting. Peter smiles as Diana approaches.

"You need to slow down for me, Peter," Diana says, panting in a weak attempt to catch her breath.

"You just need to get faster, Di," he says back, motioning for Diana to sit next to him.

They recline in a wonderful silence. Finally, Diana speaks.

"They're going to come for us," she says solemnly, "They're going to come and they're going to make us Split."

Peter turns to look at her. "No, they won't. They're not fast enough to catch us."

"Come on, Peter. You've seen the size of those guards."

He turns toward her, a bundle of adrenaline and excitement, and grabs Diana's shoulders, forcing her to look at him.

He had dark hair which fell over his eyebrows. His eyes were hazel, and they looked like an amber stone when he would gaze into the sun. He was thin, and shy around everyone.

Everyone except Diana.

"We're gonna take a little break right now, but then, when it gets night, we can cover ourselves in mud so we blend in." He closes his eyes, as if imagining some beautiful scene. "And then we can get a boat and travel the ocean until we find somewhere Old America forgot to destroy. And we'll make it our own private country, and we can live in a treehouse and be best friends forever," he says, as if it were written in the stars and he was their prophet.

Diana stares at him, not entirely sure if she liked the plan or thought he was crazy. Peter catches her gaze and blushes.

"Or," he says, choosing his words carefully, "we could have our own country... and like, get married or something."

Now it was Diana's turn to blush. "I don't know, Peter. It seems... impossible."

At her words, his face falls. She opens her mouth to console him, but as she does, guards come charging through the brush, aggressively, angrily, disturbing all the peace of this sacred environment. Someone screams; it's Diana. She reaches out her hand to his, and Peter latches on like she was the only thing keeping him from floating off into the sky.

A guard grabs him. The other grabs Diana.

He's crying, which Diana has never seen before, and his hair, his brown mop of hair is falling over his hazel eyes and then Diana is crying and then they rip him from her like a piece of paper being torn in half. His fingers are scratchy like sandpaper, torn up from flipping book pages and running them through the dirt. As her fingers slip from Peter's grip, Diana yells out again, her voice strangled as if the guard's hands were around her throat rather than her waist. As she breathes in to scream again, the air tastes flat and bitter, a stark contrast from the sweet scent of the forest that used to make her feel so calm and safe.

"Peter!" she screams, her lungs raw, empty.

"Diana!" he yells, as they drag him away from their sacred hideaway. "Come find me!"

"Come find me!"

Come find me.

Come find me.

Diana sits straight up in bed, gasping, chest heaving. Her hands roam her face, and she registers that it's wet with tears as her fingertips flit over her cheeks. She wipes her eyes and scrambles out of her bed, looking around her small room as if to make sure everything was still real, make sure nothing here would shimmer out of existence like Peter did every night. She leans against her vanity, studying herself in the mirror just as she did hours before. Her blonde hair is a rat's nest, her eyebrows need plucking, her chin has a speckling of teenage acne. Her green eyes have lost their sparkle.

But *that* part wasn't new.

"Not again," she whispers to no one in particular.

It's not like Diana misses him. She can't anymore. It's been four years, Peter is probably dead, buried beneath Sector Five like so many others. Diana had caught wind of the disease that was spreading through the marshy air and weak Cancers down south, and she could only assume he'd fallen victim to it like so many others.

It's not the longing to see him again that hurts. It's the guilt that she feels every time she has this dream that cuts her to the core.

He was her best friend. Of course she feels guilty that she wasn't there to save him from the mess that is New America.

But she couldn't save him. She *didn't* save him.

Diana glances up at her closed blinds, smiling gently as sunlight beams through the cracks. Her chest warms with something called comfort at the idea that the daytime was here, even briefly, to deter the nightmares. Seating herself at her vanity, Diana plucks her eyebrows and French braids her hair to save her poor neck from the hot Sector Seven sun, desperate to please the only person she had left to impress: herself. Sector Seven used to be a part of Old America made up of the states called 'Texas' and 'Oklahoma', and a small sliver of the eastern part of a state called 'New Mexico'.

In school, Diana excelled at history, especially old geography. She can still name every one of the Old States, not to mention the countries that had once surrounded them. Every ocean has a name, every mountain has a peak, and every season has a cycle. Routine, again, ruled supreme on the surface of every map, and Diana respected that. Now, she lives in the 'general South', and she knows everyone's distance from her in regards to their sectors. Peter to the East, Maya to the West. Her mom is six feet under Sector Six, probably a couple miles from where Maya sleeps and eats, dead of disease two years prior.

She dresses in her usual outfit: leggings, high-top sneakers, and an oversized t-shirt tied up at the bottom of her belly button.

All Forest Green, of course.

Diana decides that today she'll go to the Plaza to talk to Maya, and she grabs her Tracker out of her pocket to send her older sister a meeting invitation.

Trackers are sort of like smartphones, except people can't send personalized messages to each other. They're small and have a clip on the back to hook to a waistband, but most people keep them tucked away in their bags or pockets, to try and ignore the shame of being tracked like an animal. The government uses Trackers to, as the name implies, track citizens, and you get charged a fine if you leave it behind when you leave your house. On the devices, people only have the choice between three buttons:

"Meet me in the Plaza today" (to send to any friends or family one has left),

"To call Sector Train, press here" (to get a monorail to the Plaza),

And, Diana's personal favorite: "To access help from a Guard, please press here."

Only kidding.

Diana presses the first button and sends it to her second out of two contacts: MAYA- SISTER. Her other contact is Kiara, a girl from school who was shipped off to Sector One when they turned twelve, about a month before Diana was off to her own sector. She chose Kiara instead of Peter, because back then, the guards who brought her to her new home down south told her he was "unavailable". Diana, being so young, hadn't questioned it, because those decisions are typically made under duress by a barely-informed twelve-year-old.

She should've, looking back.

Next, she presses the second button, and a few minutes later, she gets an alert that the monorail has shown up at the station in her neighborhood. Monorails are how people travel, soaring through the air on almost-invisible tracks that go from sector to Plaza and back again. The citizens can't cross sectors, but they can take the monorails to the Plaza, where they all head into the same giant station, where people of all colors are dumped into the central hub of America.

As Diana walks down Main Street, she looks around at the other Taureans starting their days. A dad, dressed in a prim Forest Green button-down, hugs his curly-haired daughter goodbye in the driveway before he walks off, lugging a briefcase. Diana swallows against the lump in her throat as the bitter thought of luck creeps into her head. It just wasn't fair. She pictures this father, waiting at the station for his daughter on her twelfth birthday, giddy with anticipation to see her again. And he *got* that chance. She was like him, he was like her. He got the slim chance to twist the odds in his favor, manipulate the scales just so in order to get his way.

So they got each other, and Diana got nobody.

She quickly glances across the street to avoid watching the family. An old woman, hair white as the clouds rising above them, prunes a hedge along the side of her lawn. Everywhere Diana looks is Forest Green, whether it's the grass, the clothes, the treetops, or the houses around her. Stopping in the middle of the sidewalk, she looks up into the blue sky, letting the comforting color swallow her up.

"Just breathe, Diana," Peter used to tell her. When she got scared, he would remind her to pull the air into her lungs and then let it go slowly. When she got nervous, he would remind her to ground herself, his voice always a low whisper in her ear that reassured her more than anything else ever could.

Diana sucks in a deep breath, counting to three before letting it out. She straightens her shoulders and continues to walk, and as she reaches the modern-looking station at the end of the street, she climbs the plexiglass loading dock and starts the count again.

About forty minutes later, Diana arrives at the Plaza. Following the herd of other people, she enters the building where you can 'visit' people from other sectors, and she suddenly remembers how bleak this place is. Picture a prison visiting room, and that's about it, all metal walls and tables and cement floors. The Visiting Center sits on the outskirts of the Plaza, perpendicular to the BOZ high-rise. That's where all the members lived, alone, in their own sort of solitary confinement, just as their citizens did, although they lived far more affluently than their charges. Directly across from the train station is the Capitol, intentionally designed so the BOZ could keep a watchful eye on the people coming and going.

They're only allowed to visit the people on their Trackers, and a year ago, Diana tried to contact the second girl on her Tracker- Kiara- but she never showed up. Maybe she was busy, or just struggling, or even dead. She wouldn't be the only one.

One day, Maya told Diana in school that their mother had spoken to her. Diana's mom decided she didn't want to visit with her when she found out Diana was a Taurus and not a Gemini like her and Maya, and she never knew her dad, so there Diana was, with no parents to love her like they did Maya, because Maya was the same as them. Diana had been born too prematurely, and so Carla Monroe's seemingly perfect plan of having two Geminis was ruined. Someone needed to be blamed, and a sickly, infant Diana was the perfect option.

Unlike their mother, Maya always showed up for Diana, despite the distance and difference in signs, so the sisters visit about once a week. There are always guards in the room, they're always cuffed, and visitors only get ten minutes.

Diana signs in, sits down at one of the tables, and waits for Maya. She swings her feet under the metal table, and allows the guards stationed in the room to cuff her wrist to the table leg, the metal digging uncomfortably against her skin. They have to keep her from running away from a room full of heavily armed guards somehow, right?

The handcuffs were only new this year. According to the other Taureans in the neighborhood, a man had traveled from Sector Eleven to the Plaza to speak to a woman from Sector Eight (a woman whom the neighborhood gossips assumed to be a lover from years past). The guards used to be stationed outside the room, but when the woman left, the metal detectors outside the building went off. Inside her pockets wasn't a knife, or a gun, but it *was* something the Sagittarius man had given her.

An engagement ring.
But that didn't matter.

She was shot down within *thirteen seconds* of leaving the building. And later that day, in the streets of Sector Eleven, the man was tracked down and beaten to death by a regiment of seven guards. He was unarmed and walking home from the doctor's office.

Naturally, people weren't happy. In fact, Sagittarius protesters lined the streets of Sector Eleven for three days after the incident. The leader of the sector, Ms. Victoria Brewer, refused George Henderson's advice to send in troops, and she even allowed some of her own cabinet members to join the protests, although she did not. Diana knew it didn't concern her, as a Taurus, and she tried not to get involved as best she could. It simply was not her business.

But as the sharp metal cuff locks into place against her wrist, she can't help but feel resentful towards the leaders who let it all happen this way.

Five minutes later, Maya shows up, snapping Diana out of her daydream.

"Finally," Diana says.

"Hello to you too," Maya says back, sitting down across the table from Diana. The guards repeat the cuffing process for her, and she smiles as she playfully rolls her eyes. Leave it to Maya to maintain her positive attitude while she's being handcuffed. Every muscle in Diana's body wants to jump up and hug her, but she knows there would be 'consequences' if she did.

"So, I had another one of those dreams," Diana says to her.

Maya nods, chewing her bottom lip and running her fingers over the silver locket she always wears around her neck with her free hand. She takes a second to glance at the guards, then makes eye contact with her younger sister. She glances quickly at her feet, and Diana knowingly follows her gaze. Diana looks down just as Maya starts to move her feet in a series of *left/right* movements that follow the secret code they made when they were younger, trying to hide small secrets from their teachers at school.

What did he say at the end of the dream? she motions.

Same thing as usual. 'Come find me,' Diana shuffles back.

"Weather's awfully nice today, huh?" she says aloud.

"*So* super great," Diana says back. Small talk meant no suspicion from the guards.

Well, I think you know what you need to do. You can't keep going on like this, she says with her feet.

Shocked, and more than a little confused, Diana snaps her head up to look at her right as one of the guards knocks his fist on the table.

"Time to go, 762," he says, referencing Maya's serial number, the one branded into her arm, the one peeking out from under her short sleeve.

"Maya, wait-" Diana says, but Maya's already being shuffled out the door. She glances back over her shoulder and winks at Diana, mouthing *I love you.*

"I love you too," Diana says back in a small voice.

With nothing left to say or do, Diana leaves the visiting center and goes back to the main part of the Plaza. It's nice outside, air thick with morning heat, light creating a shimmering pattern over the horizon. It was almost beautiful. Diana walks to a fountain at the center of the circular area, and glances inside at her reflection, swallowing hard at the difficult memory that seemed to sit eternally in the front of her brain.

"Think, Diana," she whispers to herself. She was good for nothing else. "Think."

Peter wouldn't want to see her after all this time. He probably hates her, if she's being entirely honest.

Right?

But there could be another version of the story. Peter might be elated to see Diana again, and maybe he'll still want to be her friend after everything. Maybe he has more answers. Maybe he has some idea of what's going *on* in New America. She would put money on the fact that *anyone* knew better than her.

Probably not, though.

But maybe he also still misses her the same way she misses him. Maybe he wants his best friend back. Or maybe he still wants to run away, and "get married or something".

Diana sits on the edge of the fountain, gazing across the vast Plaza. She loved her life, she had no choice. She was luckier than others, she knew. At least she wasn't in the Virgos' Sector Twelve, so unpopular that they missed government representation more than once and had no voice in political issues. Or at least she wasn't a Scorpio, so poor that the citizens slept in the snowy streets and died by the masses. But still, deep down, some part of Diana just wanted everything to be *normal.* Even though she didn't know what normal meant, she would guess that normal wasn't being prohibited from walking with your own sister in the open air of the Plaza.

If she had been born fifty years earlier, maybe she could've had a chance. Now, though, she was one of many forced to accept that life had to be this way.

But some small part of her knew that her life was different. *She* was different; she was told so by Jasper

Davis just yesterday. And those who were different were those who made an impact.

The sun beats down on Diana's shoulders, and a single bead of sweat trickles down the back of her neck, disturbing her senses. She dips her hand into the fountain, allowing the cool, superficial water to soothe her nerves. One sentence rings clearly in her brain.

"Come find me."

Life is fleeting, is it not?

Without thinking, Diana races towards the bathroom built into the side of one of the high-rises, walking as fast as she can without drawing suspicion across the large tiled floor, her eyes trained on the sign reading 'Women' on the door.

She screeches to a halt as she reaches for the door handle. Her clothes. They're Forest Green. She won't get anywhere dressed like this.

Come on, Diana. You have to think harder than that.

Patient, hardworking, logical. Patient, hardworking, logical. That's what she was, that's all she was. *Something* there had to be of use.

As she spots a woman in Red walking with a guard, logic comes up to bat. There was one person Diana knew would help her, one young Aries girl who would stop at nothing to reunite their childhood friend group. One girl who never answered her Tracker, one who Diana remembered from school as the strongest person she knew.

Aries 333: 'Kiara'

Positives:

–Adaptable

-Brave
-Generous

Negatives:
-Impulsive
-Self-Willed
-Impatient

Diana can't legally buy clothes that don't match her color, so she has no way of getting on the Aries train unless she's bathed in Red.

But no one said she couldn't steal Red clothes from somebody else.

Diana stands about forty yards away from the motley duo, watching them head suspiciously towards an alleyway. As they disappear around the corner, Diana smirks.

Now, Taureans are toward the bottom of the zodiac social ladder, meaning they fly under the radar far more often than the other signs. So some hard-to-do girls began... *meeting* with guards to keep them off their tails, so they could sneak alcohol for a late-night party or get a discount on new clothes. Of course, nobody has done anything as risky as meeting up with them in the middle of the Plaza, but Aries are a different breed, Diana supposes.

She heads in the direction they went, walking fast so she doesn't get stopped. As she rounds the corner, she nearly gags at the sight in front of her, but she regains her composure and ducks around the corner of a wall, so the lovers can't see her.

Alright, Diana thinks to herself, *ready for the best acting job of your life, Diana?*

She races around the corner, mustering up fake tears and throwing herself to the ground, wailing. The Aries girl and the guard leap apart, and the guard barks gruffly at Diana.

"What is going on?!"

"Please!" Diana shrieks, "I was jumped near the station! It was... it was a Leo boy, my age. Please, get him!"

The guard scoffs, but nods, heading off in the direction of the train station. The Aries woman turns her nose down at Diana, and Diana finally gets a good look at her.

She's tall and thin, with stark red hair and pale skin that's dotted with freckles. She can't be more than three years older than Diana, and she sneers at her from her spot by the wall. "Oh, get up," she huffs, finger-brushing her knotty hair.

Diana rolls her eyes internally and dramatically drags herself to her feet. She glances around quickly to make sure they're still out of the main Plaza's eyeline, and when she's sure they are, Diana crosses to the girl, getting up close in her space.

"Oh my god, get away from-" The Aries starts.

"Okay, shut up," Diana interrupts, "I just saw that you were soliciting that guard. So I'm gonna need something from you if you want me to stay quiet."

"You little-"

"Give me your clothes."

"Excuse me?!"

Diana rolls her eyes, outwardly this time. "I *said,* I need your clothes."

"That's illegal."

"So is what you just did."

The woman sighs. "Fine. But you can't tell anybody."

"I won't."

"What do I get in return?"

These Aries. Diana scoffs. "My silence and also my clothes."

The woman raises an eyebrow. "Why are you dressing as an Aries, anyways?"

"I *am* an Aries. I was helping out the school Headmaster, who put me in Taurus colors. Hurry up."

The woman undresses and Diana does the same, swapping clothes. Diana nimbly plucks the Tracker from the woman's waist, and slips her own into her pocket. The girl's clothes are a little tight on Diana, but she raises an eyebrow and gives the woman, now dressed in Forest Green, a small nod before turning on her heel and heading towards the public restrooms, clutching her new Red shoes in one hand.

As she shuts the bathroom door behind her, Diana hits the light switch and watches in the darkness. If there were any blinking dots, that meant whatever attached to that dot was a camera.

Nothing. Good.

Diana flicks the lights back on and races to the mirror. She grimaces at the bright hue and studies her waist in the reflection. How could a girl learn to love herself in a hot, hatred-filled color such as this one? She sighs and shakes her head, trying to rid herself of the thought, and pulls her hair from their braids, letting her wavy blonde locks fall across her shoulders. She slips the elastics onto her wrist and flings one leg onto the counter, switching shoes quickly and repeating the same process with the other foot. Diana stares at herself in the mirror, her actions not quite registering apart from the steady thump of adrenaline coursing through her veins. She notices that the woman's Tracker is hooked to the waistband of her Red pants, and realizes she'll get straight into Sector One if she keeps it with her. Diana makes up her mind and pulls the lid off the trash can, leaving her own Tracker on top of the used paper towels and receipts. As she looks down at the device, she swallows. She doesn't have much time before the guards realize she's unresponsive, but it's a risk she has to take. Besides, if that Aries woman is caught without a Tracker, maybe that guard she was with would do her a favor.

Diana takes a deep breath and wanders back into the sun. She walks, calmer this time, to the central station. The aggressive shadows that cut across the stones beneath her feet give Diana a flush of cool air, calming her down little by little. As she waits in line, Diana thinks about her plan.

She didn't even want to think about the tortuous punishment she'd be subject to if she were caught.

With help from Kiara, it will make this impossible task a little easier, and it'll make Diana far more confident with someone else on her side. Only once in history had anyone ever escaped New America, and chances were that seventeen years later, this guy was probably dead.

It was a whole scandal when it happened. The guy, a Libra, escaped his sector one quiet night. The whole country was swept by guards, but they never found him, so everyone assumed he had left the country. Diana wasn't born when it happened, but in order to 'properly drill the students' on why one should *never* run from this authoritative country, the disappearance became a whole history unit at school, the 'First and Last Escape from New America'.

As Diana approaches the guard waiting in front of the 'Aries' train, she plasters on her best fake smile. The guard looks her up and down as Diana walks towards him, and stops her in her tracks with a wave of his hand.

"State your business for coming to the Plaza, please."

"Oh, um... I was visiting my sister."

"And your name and number?"

Diana could play this two ways. One, tell them the truth to avoid having to race to make up a fake number and pray he doesn't check the Population Systems, or two, flat-out lie.

"Kiara. Number 333."

The guard raises his eyebrows and waits for her to break. Diana stares him in the eyes, and right when she fears that she's going to either start laughing or burst into tears, he steps over to let her pass.

Oh, thank God.

Diana boards the train and finds a seat by herself, way in the back. No one else boards her train car, and Diana uses the isolation to sit down and think, taking a second to go through her plan.

Step One: Somehow find Kiara when she gets to Sector One.

Step Two: Convince her to help.

Step Three: Find Peter.

Diana looks out the window to avoid thinking about the plan- or lack thereof- and stares at Sector One racing past. This part of the country looks so different than the drylands of Sector Seven, and Diana marvels at the trees and small streams that take up the uninhabited part of this sector. There were a lot of sectors too small to use all their land and depending on the location (and the amount of money each sector had) the places all looked different.

Sector Seven was sitting right in the middle of the economic lineup, so the houses there were smaller and suburban, with solar panels and other environmentally-friendly developments saving Mr. Davis from spending too much on electricity. But there were places like Sector Two, City of the Leos, who had so much money to burn they plated their skyscraper-ridden city in gold and gave their upper-class citizens monthly allowances.

When the train races closer and closer to the central city, Diana notices immediately. The sea of bright Red makes this place so much different than the muted Forest Green that Diana knows. The color reminds Diana of the day she met Kiara, that bright hue reflecting that girl's personality.

"Diana, don't listen to him," Peter says, grabbing Diana's wrist and dragging her away from the cluster of teasing kids on the playground.

Diana wrenches her skinny wrist from his grip and swipes at her eyes, willing herself not to cry in front of them. Unfortunately, one of the bullies, named Evan, notices. He's huge for an eight-year-old, and has always been cruel. He normally doesn't get to her, but Maya had been taken yesterday and school was not *Diana's top priority.*

"Sad, Diana?" he asks, stepping closer to Peter and Diana. "What's the matter? Your stupid sister was taken?"

"Stop, Evan," Diana says in a watery voice. She has no strength to fight with him right now. She didn't ever have the strength, really.

"Oh, please. She deserves it. My teacher says she was a rule breaker anyways," he replies, shoving her hard into Peter's chest. "Why don't you cry about it?"

Diana starts to respond, then swallows, feeling a lump rise in her throat. She scuffs her foot into the wood chips, ducking her head and allowing her hair to fall in front of her face. He pushes her again, and Peter starts to pipe up, clutching her arms and anchoring her scrawny frame to his skinnier one.

"Cut it out, Evan!" Peter says, taking a step forward. Before he can do anything, though, Evan shoves him to the ground. He falls into the wood chips, his boney hands scraping against the splinters.

Evan's cronies start to laugh, the sound jangling Diana's resolve. Some heckle Peter, and Evan, seemingly bolstered by their support, hulks over Diana again. He reaches out as if to push her, when a voice cuts through the tense air hanging over the playground.

"Don't you dare, Evan," a girl says. Everyone turns to face her. She's emerged from behind Evan's friends, and the spring wind is blowing her dark curls off her back. She's short, shorter than Diana, maybe, and her skin is dark and smooth, unlike any of their other classmates. She shoves through the crowd, stepping straight into Evan's space and glaring up at him. He scoffs, turning his head downward to look her in the eye.

"Yeah? Or what?" he asks.

Silence rings out over the playground. Peter scrambles to his feet, coming back up next to Diana. "Let's get out of here," he says.

"No, hold on," Diana says, her eyes stuck on Evan and the girl.

She and Evan are still in a heated stand-off. Both of their hands are balled at their sides, and their gazes are locked on each other. She glances Diana's way, and Evan grins.

"Scared, Kiara?" he asks her.

The girl- or Kiara- rolls her eyes, and without missing a beat, swings her fist into Evan's jaw with all her might.

Both of them stumble backwards, Evan clutching his jaw and Kiara nursing her right hand from the force of hitting him so hard. In a blink of an eye, guards are swarming her, ones who had previously stood idly by as Evan antagonized Diana. One swipes for her, and she ducks under their arms, racing over to Diana and sticking out her hand for a handshake, which Diana hesitantly accepts, jaw slack with shock.

"Nice to meet you. I'm Kiara," she says with a wicked grin. A guard comes over, grabbing her arm roughly, and she gives a two-fingered salute before allowing herself to be dragged away.

When she gets off the train, Diana takes a minute to submerge herself into the world of a strange new zodiac she has never experienced. If she thought Forest Green was overwhelming, Red was even worse. The train station is bustling with people dressed in the hot color. The wood under the platform is different than the plexiglass station in her home sector, and Diana likes the old-fashioned details of this place, never mind how small they were. Signs hang off chains displaying old fares for getting a train, their letters faded from the sun. The houses around here are smaller and older, but the further north she squints, she can see that they spring up into taller, high-rise buildings that seem to be a central city. The station and this old town must rest just on the outskirts. An Aries man spots her staring up at them in wonder.

"Beautiful, isn't it?" he asks.

For a minute, Diana almost asks what he's talking about, but then she remembers where she is and what she's doing.

"Oh, uh, yeah," Diana stumbles. "I love the station."

He shakes his head. "Too bad they're making all these newfangled buildings. I sure hope they don't replace this one."

He leaves Diana with her thoughts. As she watches people exit the station, a familiar thought pricks the back of her brain. What if all the people in the country *were* all together? What if they had been allowed to grow old as friends, to go to college, to move in together? What if they were able to wake up and drive to their parents' house, or fall in love with someone born months away from them? Watch their children grow up and make mistakes, and hug them when they graduate from school? There are a lot of what ifs.

A lot of what ifs that they'll never know the answer to.

A lot of what ifs she needed to stop questioning.

Diana snaps herself out of the trance that had befallen her and looks around. No one she recognizes, not yet. With a sigh of both relief and stress, Diana shakes her head and squares her shoulders, heading towards the busiest street she sees.

Part Two: The Aries

Kiara

"Why are we number One?" the man hollers through a bullhorn.

"We're Aries!" the crowd of thousands screams back.

No, Kiara was not at some major league sporting event. She was at the annual Influx Meeting, which actually was more of a rally than a civil sit-down. Every year, when the last of the new twelve-year-olds were shipped in, George Henderson traveled from the Capitol to Sector One to instill a little patriotism in the first of the zodiacs.

They were all gathered in a big field, where Henderson had just broken ground on what would soon be a new skyscraper complex for the kids and a couple of lucky Aries who would be chosen at random. Now, the almost-dictator was standing on a pop-up stage with a bullhorn, face flushed and neck taut from screaming into it.

Kiara would be the first to fight that her sign was the best. Anyone with any brain would, for their own safety over anything else. But something was suspicious about this new ritual of the Influx Meeting.

In the past, these meetings ended with Henderson reading the numbers of all the new kids, so that the older citizens could help them if they needed to, since everyone in Sector One was apparently one big, happy family. It was their job as Aries to raise their own, after all. But this year was different. This year, their leader was raising them above *the other signs, rather than hammering in their moral obligation to help lead the other eleven. Before, they were equals. Now, they were better.*

"*Fletcher, Aries eight-hundred and eighty-six!*" Henderson screams.

A small boy walks across the stage, in baggy Red clothes. His expression is one of fear, and his big brown eyes are wide and terrified. Guards station him, roughly, into the beginning of a line, just as Henderson calls the next name.

"*Katie, Aries five hundred!*"

As the red-headed girl begins the trek across the stage, the crowd roars, making her jump. Barely, just barely, her hand flies up in front of her face. Kiara sucks in a sharp breath as the air around her turns cold and electric, goosebumps racing up her arms.

It happens almost instantly.

Guards swarm her, even though she's just standing there, and Kiara watches their strong hands grip her arm. Katie kicks and screams, to no avail, and Kiara watches them drag her away, standing her next to Fletcher but not releasing her as the crowd of Aries scream, the sounds rushing through Kiara's veins in a horrifying mass of pure bestial noise.

Katie's chest is rising and falling heavily, and her eyes sweep the aggregation of people. It's almost as if the little girl is looking through them, and Henderson calls the next name as she slumps into the guard's arms, as if all her energy had been vacuumed away.

After a few more minutes, almost thirty kids are standing in a line across the stage. The people haven't stopped shouting, and all the children are wearing matching expressions of terror. Some are crying, others are looking out, mouths agape. Kiara watches them, heart thumping.

Why were they number One? Because they were Aries, is what everyone echoed. It was their birthright. So why did Kiara feel a sour pit knotting at the base of her stomach?

She stands in that field, packed like sardines against random strangers who are apparently just like her, closes her mouth, and puts her hands over her ears.

After some uprisings in Sector Three, the Scorpios were moved with no access to the Plaza at all, even by monorail, and their sector was shrunk by a few hundred miles due to 'complications' with the border wall closest to them. Stifling for the Scorpios, sure, but not for the neighboring Aries, who got a little more room to breathe, and construction on new housing had finally started because of the new space. A couple of skyscrapers were going up to the North, and Kiara was waiting for the letter that would allow her to move to one of the swanky new places and out of her old house.

It was a warm, late morning, and Kiara had decided that today she would take the long walk home from the library. She *normally* went to self-defense classes today, but the BOZ had shut them down in Sector One with no notice, so there was fifty dollars a month down the drain. She's walking past the park when she realizes just how busy it is. People are crowding the streets and sidewalks, casting wary glances at folks like Kiara, who are steering clear from the large crowds.

"God. Talk about a baby boom," Kiara says aloud. There must be something going on. She's never seen this many people in the sector before, especially not in her tired old neighborhood. She grabs the arm of a guard walking past her.

"Excuse me!" Kiara says, pulling him out of the way of the incoming foot traffic.

"Yeah- yeah, what?" he asks gruffly.

Kiara speaks without looking at him. An added perk of being the most honored sign was that guards answered to *you*- not the other way around. "When was the last Influx?" Every year, the Board of Zodiacs selected a maximum of thirty women in their sectors to have children, and they could agree if they wanted. But these new children trickle in for the most part, and the people in the streets don't look like kids. Kiara watches a group of adults stalk into a nearby alley, dressed in Red and looking over their shoulders with nervous glints in their eyes. Trying to keep her thoughts from running awry, Kiara clears her throat and refocuses on the guard next to her.

Silence. Like, straight up radio silence from this guy. Kiara starts to repeat herself, but then she takes a good look at him. He's young. Really, really young. Maybe a year or two older than her, at most. He's got bright red hair and his face is covered in freckles, and if Kiara stared hard enough, the ghost of one dimple appeared in his cheek. His eyes are the brightest gray Kiara has ever seen, and they're swinging around the street wildly, as if looking for something. Or *someone*. When his great big eyes meet hers, Kiara immediately makes the connection.

This boy is *not* a guard.

There's no chance in hell he's an Aries, either.

Kiara yanks him into a shed in the park behind them so that they're shielded from the bustling crowd. As soon as they're out of sight, Kiara turns on him.

"Who are you and what are you doing here?" she asks, trying and failing to straighten up to his height. Only now did Kiara realize he was tall, too, at least five eleven. He doesn't answer her, just stands there sputtering, refusing to meet her piercing gaze. She takes what she hopes is a menacing step forward and tries again. "I *said*, who are you?"

He throws his hands in front of his face. "Stop!" he commands, voice low but somehow nervous. When it becomes evident Kiara doesn't *really* want to hurt him, he lowers his hands. "You're scary for a five footer."

"I don't like being ignored. And I'm five-one." Realizing she's being too harsh, Kiara sits him down on the shed bench with a strong shove on his shoulders and sits a fair distance away from him, out of arm's reach. It's unclear as to whether that benefits her or him more. "Please answer me."

He glares at her before sighing. "Why should I trust you?"

Kiara groans. "Are you kidding? You could drag me out into the street by my hair and shout for help and ten guards would be on me in a second. Not to mention you've got at least fifty pounds and ten inches on me."

He nods slowly. "Nothing leaves this shed." She doesn't reply, and he raises both eyebrows. "You hear me, you psycho?"

Kiara finally nods. The boy runs a hand through his cropped ginger hair, stares out at the horizon, then turns to face her.

"I'm Cameron."

Scorpio 102: 'Cameron'

Positives:
    -Intelligent
    -Sensible
    -Independent

Negatives:
    -Suspicious
    -Arrogant

-Obsessive

"Kiara," she replies, giving him another trademarked wary look and waiting for him to continue. He doesn't. "Is... that it?" she asks. She looks up at him. "You can trust me. I hate the BOZ as much as you do."

"How do you know I hate the BOZ?" he asks, crossing his arms over his chest and slouching a little. For a split second, Kiara worries she could be wrong, but then she remembers that her first-impression feelings are *never* wrong.

She rolls her eyes. "Everyone does, especially the Aries. They're a stuck-up bunch of dictators who do nothing but lounge in the Capitol and roll over to the leaders of the higher-up sectors." She studies him. "And also, anyone can tell you're not an Aries, so you're gonna be caught no matter what, and it would be a lot easier for you if I didn't go and turn you in–"

"Fine." He breaks at last. "I'm a Scorpio. I and all these other people are here to get away from the uprisings. The government is trying to kill us."

"The influx of people..." Kiara wonders aloud. Cameron follows along, nodding. "You're all refugees. But... how did you do it?"

"We stole clothes, like mine, and others made their own."

"But how did you get past the guard increase?"

Cameron smiles sheepishly, and Kiara notes the single dimple in his cheek finally making a full appearance. "We had to take some... desperate measures."

At this, Kiara recoils in disgust. "You killed them?!" She can't believe what she's hearing, but she also can't say she's surprised. Scorpios were... unhinged, to say the least. Even more unhinged than the Fire Signs.

He laughs, a deep belly laugh that cracks the soft volume of the dugout and Kiara's stony exterior. "God, no! Knocked them out, took their clothes, tied them up. Also hijacked the train so they couldn't track it."

Kiara is actually a little impressed. "How many of you in total?" she asks.

"I dunno. I'd wager about four hundred."

"Wow. That's seriously impressive."

At the compliment, Cameron winces. "Not really. More like seriously necessary. I'd say three-quarters of the escapees are women, elderly people, and children. They were in the most danger." He runs his tongue across his top teeth, mumbling his next phrase. "And we had six hundred to start."

Kiara swallows. "They...?"

"Died, most of them. Didn't make it across, got caught. Anything was dangerous that night."

Kiara pauses before attempting to change the subject. "Yeah. I heard the Capitol was pushing back at you guys pretty hard."

He snorts sarcastically. "Hard. Right. Hanging innocent children in the city square definitely qualifies as 'pushing hard'."

Kiara stops and stares at him. He's looking at his hands, expression passive. "I'm so sorry."

"Don't be," he looks at her, gray eyes meeting brown ones.

"Why did they increase your security anyway?" she asks, scuffing her foot in the dirt, splaying her fingers over the Red wooden bench, and trying to avert her eyes.

Cameron shrugs, casting another look towards the horizon, as if the walls of Sector Three would come racing forward and lock him up once again. "Your guess is as good as mine. Our representative on the BOZ, Gerard Myers, was on thin ice with the rest of the board. Myers was the one who said his sector should be cut off, and no one knows why. Two hours after we escaped to come here, he was kicked off the BOZ."

Kiara nods, standing up and brushing her hands down her pants. "Okay. Let's go."

He studies the girl quizzically. "Go where?" Kiara doesn't fail to note the way his hand flies to his pants pocket, and she leans forward quickly and plucks the knife out of it, sliding it smoothly into her waistband. His eyes go wide, and he scooches further back on the bench. "Hey, watch it."

Kiara smirks. "I already said I'm not gonna hurt you, but you never made the same promise." He bites his lip, obviously realizing that she's right, and Kiara continues. "Anyway, we're going to my house. I can't have you wandering the streets. If you get caught and tortured, the first name you're going to blab will be mine."

Cameron jumps up, pulling Kiara with him ...and gives her a *handshake?* "Oh, thank you!"

Kiara gently peels her hand away. "You're welcome. This way."

With that, they head out. Kiara leads the way to her house, passing through the wide streets and getting more than a few glances from suspicious people.

"Ugh, your outfit is drawing way too much attention for my liking," she mumbles.

"Sorry," he whispers, "they were the only pants long enough. Everything else was in women's sizes."

Kiara snickers, and leads him to her front door. She lives in a *delightful* little bungalow that sits right off the road. A white picket fence sits decrepit across her lawn, the mailbox long since torn out. Her front porch is old, the chains from the swing stolen and leaving it looking more like a bench. Kiara bends down and pries up one of the porch planks, fishing around for her key. Her fingertips brush the dirt below, and she huffs, pulling her hand out and coming up empty. Kiara digs around a little more, turning her shoulder so Cameron couldn't watch.

"I think it might be counterintuitive to hide the place your key is when you're bringing me into your house anyways," he says, chuckling softly.

Kiara rolls her eyes. "Well, I *can't* let you in if I don't have my key."

Cameron crosses to her, crouching down and reaching between the planks in the porch. Kiara watches him, tongue poking out of the corner of his mouth, and waits a moment, then two. Finally, Cameron rises to his full height, holding something gold and shiny towards Kiara. He grins. "It was under some dirt."

Kiara smirks and takes the key, pulling it from Cameron's grip. "Thanks." She unlocks the door, one hand on the knob, and pushes it open with a loud creak. "It's not much," she warns, waving him inside. Kiara leaves her shoes on as the pair crosses the threshold, holding out her arms and turning in a slow circle. The room is cold and dark, the furniture is old and well-worn, and the kitchen tap drips steadily.

Cameron smiles a little, running his hand over the back of the couch and leaving a little dust in his wake. "It's... charming," he says quietly, studying the bare mantle. "Certainly better than I had when I was twelve."

"Are you saying that to be nice, or do you actually think that?"

He smiles again, and Kiara likes the sight. She doesn't think anything of the fact that he doesn't actually answer.

She heads down the hall, brushing off the air of mild awkwardness, knowing Cameron is following her, and enters her bedroom. It's small, with a closet built into the wall so she doesn't have to take up space with a dresser. Kiara motions to the bed, covers unmade and pillows overturned.

"You can stay here. I'll sleep on the couch," as she turns to leave, Cameron takes her arm and scoffs, startling Kiara with the sudden physical contact.

"Please. I'll go on the couch. It's your house, after all." He goes to the living room. Kiara quickly changes into a Red t-shirt and leggings, studying her brand in the mirror, and when she enters the living room, Cameron is staring out the window.

He looks over as Kiara approaches, studying her as she falls into her routine, washing up a few dishes she had let hang about in the sink. She crosses to the cupboard, removing a glass and filling it with water from the tap. She wordlessly passes it to the absent-faced Cameron, who takes it with a small smile. Kiara seats herself at the dining table, looking up at him expectantly.

He doesn't say anything, and the two stare at each other for a long, silent moment. Finally, a slow grin breaks out across Cameron's face, and he sets his glass down on the counter before looking up at Kiara under his long lashes.

"So, how's the weather been lately?"

Thirty minutes later, Cameron and Kiara are seated at the dining table, across from one another. They are leaning into one another from their seats, their conversation unfluctuating unless one of them was taking a sip of water.

"You're joking," Kiara says breathlessly.

Cameron shakes his head rapidly, suppressing a grin. "Nope. He fell so hard, he broke his ankle."

"Off the roof!?"

"Off the roof! You should've seen it, he was drunk, trying to do a cartwheel, and the idiot slipped."

Kiara laughs. "Scorpios are *crazy*."

Shaking his head with a chuckle, Cameron rises from his seat, crossing to the sink to refill his glass. As he does, however, Kiara watches his gaze catch on something outside the window, a confused expression passing over his face as the water in the cloudy glass spills over the rim.

"What are you looking at?" Kiara asks, wandering over to him. He's staring at a young blonde girl walking down the street, in a Red outfit that would look normal if she wasn't gazing with awe at every blade of grass.

"She looks like she might be a Scorpio refugee, except I think I'd know if I've seen her. Do you see how out of place she looks?"

Kiara loses her train of thought as her brain clicks the puzzle pieces into place. "Oh my god," she whispers breathlessly.

Cameron looks at her with concern. "Do you know her?" he asks.

Kiara nods rapidly, out of words for the first time. "Oh my god," she repeats. "Diana," and without waiting for Cameron, Kiara bolts from the kitchen and into the street. They notice each other at the same time.

She's grown up since the last time Kiara saw her four years ago. She almost laughs: though she's older, Diana certainly hasn't gotten much taller. She can't be more than five-three. In the midday light, Diana's hair shines like straw-colored silk, and Kiara realizes it's layered in the front, a stark contrast from the pin-straight bob she used to sport in school. And sure, maybe her hair changed, but her bright eyes and smile were exactly the same.

With a giddy grin, Diana runs into the road to embrace Kiara for the first time in four years.

"Ki!" she huffs breathlessly into Kiara's shoulder as the two girls collide.

"Diana, is it really you?" Kiara whispers. Diana nods into her shirt. Regaining her composure, Kiara shoves her away and stares at her, awe turning into anger. "What are you doing here?! Do you know how much danger you're in?"

Diana laughs and nods, taking hold of Kiara's shoulders. Her bright gaze is exactly the same as it used to be. "I came because I need your help-" but before she can continue, Cameron comes out of the house. He stands behind Kiara, and he and Diana size each other up, one threat regarding the other. Cameron raises his left eyebrow, Diana her right, and both have similar body language: crossed arms, tense shoulders, and a less-than-welcoming expression.

"Ki," Diana asks, drawing out the nickname as if hesitant to use it in this stranger's presence, "who's this?" She finally looks at Kiara and lowers her voice. "Listen, if you're hooking up with the guards, I won't make fun of you, but know that a lot of people in Sector Seven did that and-"

"I'm gonna stop you right there," Kiara says hastily, "he's not *actually* a guard."

"Cameron," he says, extending his hand. Diana shakes it with a puzzled expression, and with that introduction over, Kiara grabs both of their arms and drags them into the house, locking the door behind them. Then she yanks the blinds over the windows. She sits them both at the table and they look at her with their matching wide eyes. Kiara decides to question Diana first.

"Di, what on earth are you doing here?" Diana starts to speak, then eyes Cameron, who just laughs.

"If you're going somewhere with Kiara, Miss Diana," he says, "I'm coming with you. She can't exactly leave a Scorpio alone at her house."

Diana's jaw basically hits the floor. She looks at Kiara, then back at Cameron. "A *what?*" she whispers, voice hissing like a snake might.

Cameron says nothing, so Kiara explains his situation first. By the end of her retelling, Diana is grinning.

"Okay, fine," Diana says decisively after a minute of consideration, "Cameron will come too."

Kiara sighs in exasperation. "Where, Diana?" The girls share a look, and for a moment Diana's green eyes glint with unshed tears. Her finger traces the wood grain in the table as she tears her gaze from Kiara.

"I need to find Peter, Kiara," Diana says in a small voice.

Kiara sits across from her and takes her hands, forcing her to look up. "Talk to me."

So she does. Diana tells Kiara and Cameron everything. From the dreams, to her visit with Maya, to her escaping from the Plaza. By the end, even Cameron has been shocked into silence. But, he regains his composure and asks her the one simple question that ended up deciding the future of New America, although none of them knew it yet.

"So," he begins hesitantly. He takes a minute to think to himself, then looks Diana in the eyes.

"What's our next move?"

Part Three: The Scorpio

Cameron

If someone had told Cameron just how much of an impact that one question would have had on their whole operation, he would've said "you're crazy" and left it at that. But sitting around that small dining table in Kiara's dim house, Cameron didn't know the impact that question would have. He just... asked. So, when the two girls stare straight at him, their expressions blank and unknowing, he holds up his hands defensively.

"What?" Cameron asks, "I'm in. You've gotta find your boyfriend, and it's better late than never, right? Besides, a bounty is already out for my head, anyways. I've got nothing left to lose."

Kiara sputters, lost for words. Diana, Cameron thinks her name is, blushes a deep red and mumbles: "He's not my- never mind."

Silence settles over the trio. Finally, Kiara speaks up, keeping her gaze trained on the worn wooden tabletop. "You guys are crazy. We could be killed if we're caught." Shaking her head and pushing away from the table, Kiara hurries away, shutting herself in her bedroom down the hall. Cameron gets up to follow her, but Diana grabs his arm and tugs him back to his seat.

"Don't bother. She'll come around," she says, sounding far more certain than a virtual stranger should.

"Well, let's hope so. I've known her for an hour, and even I don't think there's any coming back from this." With that slip of the tongue, Diana's face falls, and Cameron reaches across the table and grabs her hands.

Diana looks up at him, and Cameron decides to do his best to console her.

"Don't worry. Even if we can't go, I'm sure your friend is fine." Yeah, she doesn't look convinced. "I'm sorry, I'm not very good at consoling people I just met ten minutes ago."

Diana laughs and smiles a brilliant smile that would light up the room if it could. But it quickly fades. "I dunno, actually. Ki was always the person who would stick up for you no matter what. I wonder what happened."

"Well, did anything necessarily need to happen?"

Diana looks at him, raising her eyebrow again. "Something must have happened," she says, her words hammering the air and leading Cameron to believe they were the final judgment on the topic.

"Sorry," he says sarcastically, slouching in his chair.

"That's okay. Thank you." Suddenly intrigued, Diana leans towards Cameron. "What's your deal? Tell me about the escape you pulled off."

Cameron studies the blonde girl in front of him, fighting a smile at the sight of her mischievous expression. He could already tell he'd like this girl, but the bigger issue was the question she was asking. He's gotten it twice today. Does no one understand he doesn't want to talk about it? The last thing he wants to do is relive it; relive the screaming and running and the constant swinging of the gallows in the square.

But Diana asked, and she seemed genuine. And if Cameron is going to help her, she should at least know who he is. *What* he is.

"It was chaos. They…" he can't go on. Diana leans forward and places her hand on Cameron's, wrapping her fingers around his.

"What happened, Cameron?" she asks softly.

Tell her. Tell her what they've done.

"They killed her," Cameron chokes out. Tears flow freely, and yet he's not embarrassed to cry in front of this kind-eyed stranger. Diana doesn't speak. "They killed my baby sister and then took my mother." Cameron gives her hands a squeeze, as if Diana is the lifesaver keeping him from getting swept away into the ocean. He doesn't want to speak anymore, and so he doesn't, looking down at the table and willing himself to at least cry quietly.

Diana's voice pulls him from his dark place, and he relaxes at her modulated tone. Cameron can't help but wonder if she's had practice comforting people. "What was she like?"

Cameron chokes back a bitter laugh that quickly turns into a race to swallow his emotion. "She *was* beautiful. This fiery hair and gray eyes that were the same as mine. She was so… good. So good and so kind, even for a seven-year-old."

Diana smiles. "She sounds lovely."

"She was. So I sent out handwritten letters to all the houses around where I lived. We snuck to the border later that night." He pauses again, looking up at Diana. Her eyes widen, and Cameron feels her fingers begin to shake under his.

Please, Diana. Figure it out. Figure it out so I don't have to tell you.

"The border… Cameron," she drops his hands and puts a distance between them. "Cameron," she repeats. No, she's scared.

"Diana-" Cameron reaches out to her and she stands up so fast her chair knocks over.

"No! Don't touch me." She steps backwards, her back against the wall. She looks him in the eyes and, voice wavering, asks, "How did you get those people past the border, Cameron? You're blocked in on all sides."

She knows. Something in her eyes tells Cameron that she knows, and Cameron's life is over. Literally. She's going to turn him in and they're going to kill him.

"I dropped it," he says meekly. Diana shakes her head, over and over.

"No. No, no, that's impossible. You're- you're like, a mutation or something."

"I know. Please, Diana. I know that. I'm sorry." She's still shaking her head. Cameron continues. Maybe if he keeps talking she'll stop making such a ruckus. "I had some... feeling. And then I touched it, and it just... dropped away. I've never seen anything like it, and I know it sounds insane, but I *promise* it's true. I wouldn't be here if it weren't. I had a power that I could use to help my people, and I couldn't bear to stay after what they did. I'm not going to hurt you. I- I don't want to have to do it again. Please, Diana, you have to understand. I did it to save my people."

Diana stares at him, and then takes a step forward in Cameron's direction. Her whisper is almost inaudible. "I'm not scared of you. I just want an explanation."

"Okay," Cameron whispers back, holding her gaze for one frightening, silent moment.

So he tells her.

Night. Darker than the clothes that hang off the backs of these frightened children. One reaches up and takes Cameron's hand. "Cam," he asks, "what do we do now?"

What do *they do? Just about six hundred people huddled under the cover of darkness waiting to escape their sector. Waiting to be caught. Stuck. Trapped.*

Cameron doesn't answer the child. He can't think. All he can think about is the last two hours and how his life will never be the same now that she has gone.

The light wood of the gallows, like a star against the night sky.

The dirt beneath Cameron's feet darkening with every fallen tear.

The guards sitting her down and taking her shoes off. They should leave them on. Her feet will swell.

Marching her up the stairs. Her toe stubs the step and she winces.

Her waving to Cameron from the crowd. Unaware that they're marching her to her end. No one will tell her.

Cameron rushes towards her. Guards grab him before he gets close.

Cameron screams her name. He's hit in the head by something. Or maybe someone.

She helps them pull the rope over her neck. "Just a necklace," they tell her with wicked smiles. She grins. Another necklace for her meager collection.

Tightened. She frowns. "It's a little tight, sir," she starts towards the stairs, moving to leave-

Then, she's pushed.

Gone.

Cameron feels a squeeze on his hand. The child is looking up at him. "What's wrong?" he squeaks. It's then Cameron realizes he's crying again.

"Nothing," If he says it enough, maybe it will be true. Cameron drops his hand and steps towards the border. A chorus of "no" and "don't touch it" rises up around him.

She was so young. She was so kind. She was so perfect.

And now she's gone.

Cameron presses his hand up against the translucent barrier.

And then it disappears.

Diana stares at him. "Oh, Cameron." She steps towards Cameron again and extends her arms, allowing him to step into them. Her embrace is warm despite Cameron being almost a foot taller than her, and her shaky breaths match his to the point where their chests rise and fall in unison. Cameron's arms stay at his sides, but Diana embraces him fondly, as if she fit naturally there, all tucked up against his chest.

It's been years since Cameron was hugged like this. Years since he was hugged at all. He was so used to being alone that he'd never stopped to relish the moments where someone showed him affection like this, no matter how fleeting the gestures were. So he focuses on his inhale, counting to three before letting his breath out.

With a shaky, choked-up breath, Cameron slowly wraps his arms around Diana's shoulders, returning her hug. Finally, he brings himself to speak, his words muffled by Diana's hair.

"I don't want to do it again. But you have to understand I *can't* go back there. They'll kill me."

"Cameron, hey. I promise you I'm not going to let you go back."

Cameron steels himself and looks down at her. "Okay. Let's go find your friend, alright?"

Diana grins up at him. "Okay."

So they journey into Kiara's room. She's lying on the bed, staring up at the ceiling. When Diana and Cameron enter, she doesn't move a muscle.

"Kiara?" Diana asks.

Kiara doesn't move.

Diana clears her throat and says a little louder: "Kiara?" With no answer, she crosses over to a pillow sitting on the ground, smacking her with it once and letting it drop onto her face.

"Ah! Okay!" Kiara shouts, laughing. Cameron snickers from the doorway, and Diana waves him over to sit next to where she's plopped onto the bed. Kiara stares them down and crosses her arms.

"I know what this is about, you two," she says. She casts a quick glance at Diana. "Give me one good reason I should put my life in danger for a dude we haven't seen in four years."

Well, that was cold. Really cold. And it certainly wasn't angled towards Cameron. He turns towards Diana, who's staring at Kiara with an almost murderous glint in her eye. Diana scoots off the bed and speaks as she paces the room, like her anxiety was manifesting itself into adrenaline.

"One reason? Fine. Because I lost him, Kiara. Peter was counting on me and I pushed him out of my mind like he never existed. Because I left him. Because now that I'm able to go find him, I want to at least try. I can't live with myself dreaming about him every single night and knowing I never got to say goodbye. Or say 'I miss you,' that's why. This isn't like you, Ki. What happened to the girl who would do anything for us? What happened to the girl who was never afraid?"

Kiara's reply seems to come immediately, as if she'd told herself these words before. "I was always afraid. I was just better at hiding it than you." At a look from Diana that could only be described as guilty, Kiara seems to soften. "Diana, there's *so much* that could go wrong. Nobody has ever done this kind of thing before. We're not talking about sneaking into the Plaza, we're talking about *trespassing* in another sector. We could be killed, and we'd deserve it," Kiara responds, throwing her hands up in the air in exasperation. She rises and faces off with Diana, and Cameron bites his lip, stuck between the two on his seat at the foot of the bed. "People are forgotten every day, Di. We're not *meant* to remember each other once we Split, that's the point. You've already broken the rules once, and I couldn't live with myself if Peter is the reason you wind up *dead.*"

"Ki, we could do it. I... I don't know *how*, but we can, we have to."

At this point, the two are face-to-face. It's a brutal standoff from where Cameron is sitting, driven by anger and passion that hasn't been spurred for years. And then Kiara goes and blows up the whole operation with four little words:

"Well, I'm not coming."

Diana opens her mouth to respond when her eyes well with tears, and she turns away, ignoring Cameron's outstretched arm and seating herself on the bed. Kiara's eyes are open as wide as dinner plates, as if she only just understood what she'd done, and she rushes to kneel in front of her friend.

"Di, I'm so sorry. I didn't mean to upset you, I just-"

"*I'm* sorry," Diana interrupts, "I shouldn't have forced you to come. It was stupid anyway. I- I just need to get home before they notice I'm gone."

She rises and heads towards the door. When she reaches the doorway, she turns to face them and manages a shaky smile. "I'm sorry, Ki. Maybe I could see you soon. And Cameron, it was so great to meet you. I hope they don't catch up to you."

And then she leaves.

Kiara sits and stares at the spot where she stood, as if conjuring up her being one more time. Cameron is absolutely incredulous. She's just... gone. Gone, as if she were some kind of supernatural being Kiara and Cameron had dreamed up for an hour or two.

Kiara stands, brushing herself off calmly. Then she turns and leaves.

Out the door.

Down the hall.

And into the street.

Part Four: The Taurus

Diana

Diana trudges down Kiara's porch and past the old fence, hurrying down the sidewalk as fast as she can. The people from earlier have cleared out, probably to hide. It's darkening outside, which is good considering Diana probably looks superbly suspicious walking by herself and crying. She wipes her eyes and turns the corner towards the park, a landmark she remembers from her walk over earlier in the day. It's peaceful here, and quiet, she notices. A pang passes through her heart as she pictures her apartment back home, the smallest and most foolish feeling of homesickness passing through her.

"I'm sorry, Peter," Diana whispers to the sky. "*I'm sorry,*" she repeats, somehow feeling like she's apologizing for more than going back on her promise of finding him.

"Diana!" someone yells from behind her. Diana spins around to see Kiara running to catch up with her. She slows when she comes within a few feet of Diana, putting her hands on her knees as if bracing herself. "God, you walk so fast!"

"Why'd you follow me?" Diana asks, crossing her arms over her stomach against a gust of dry wind.

"Do you think I know?" Kiara says, motioning with her arms out in front of her. "Impulsive Aries, am I right?" She grabs Diana's arms and stares into her eyes. "And because I realized that after I lost my dad, I've had no one. And then you show up, and with you came Cameron, and maybe even Peter. So let's do it."

Diana laughs, a lump of emotion rising in her throat. "I can't thank you enough, Ki."

Kiara laughs with her. "Don't even think about it. Okay. Let's make a plan, yeah? A real one?"

And so they do. They plan everything, gathered once more at Kiara's table.

Operation Rescue Peter (the name was Cameron's idea)

Step One: Travel by foot at night through Sector Two

Step Two: Camp in Sector Two on Eastern border

Step Three: Take monorail to Plaza

Step Four: Find a way through the Plaza and catch a train to Sector Five

Step Five: Hijack someone's Tracker to give Peter coordinates to a meeting point

"Pause," Cameron interjects. "Do any of us know how to hijack a Tracker?"

Kiara shakes her head, but Diana raises her hand apprehensively. "I do. My sister taught me the basics when we were kids, back when we were in school together."

Cameron stares at her, and Kiara is wearing an equally shocked expression. "That's... seriously impressive."

Diana shrugs. "Says the guy who freed four hundred Scorpios."

Kiara taps Diana's wrist to get her attention. "Di, how old were you when you learned this and where the heck was I?"

Diana grins. "I was probably eight, it was a couple months before Maya was taken."

Kiara nods, then smiles. "After this, you *have* to teach me."

"Absolutely," Diana says, smiling back at her. She nods to Cameron. "Where were we?"

Step Six: When Peter comes to meeting spot, Cameron fells border and takes him to the ocean

Step Seven: After reaching a spot far enough away from New America, figure out future plans from there

"Wait," Kiara chimes in. "I don't like these odds. We shouldn't bank everything on finding a new land away from here when we don't even know if anything is even out there."

After a beat of silence, Diana sighs. "When I was younger, I thought that the Americans lied, and everything was just normal. Like, all the countries were just still there, and one day we'd wake up to everything back to how it used to be. Like this was all one sick joke."

It's quiet for another moment, apart from Kiara tapping her foot under the table.

"I used to think that if we were all really well behaved, the BOZ leaders from our sectors would show up and tell us we could leave the country, and we'd go somewhere tropical, some island where we could see our families."

The girls turn to Cameron expectantly. He speaks without looking at them, his breath escaping in a quiet scoff. "Hell, I just wanted to live somewhere where I could walk the street by myself without fearing for my life," he's quiet, solemn, almost. Then he pipes up, tapping at their little list with a pencil. "There needs to be some place where there's a record of whether or not there's other land."

By now, Cameron had made his own Red outfit from an old pair of bedsheets that he dyed and sewed with the girls' assistance. Diana reaches over and rubs his collar between two fingers. "This is incredible, Cameron. How'd you learn to sew?"

"My mom taught me when I was thirteen. We had to patch our clothes pretty often," he responds, glancing down at his shirt.

"Well," Diana says, releasing her hold on him and promptly changing the subject, "Peter's sector is further south than here. What if when we get Peter, we use Cameron's old guard outfit to sneak into the Capitol and steal the maps from the BOZ files?"

Cameron grins. "I like the idea, but they probably keep those under lock and key. Even if they believed that I'm a guard, they wouldn't let me go all the way into the archives."

Kiara raps her hands on the table in an anxious, rhythmic movement. "Well, if we went straight from Sector Five, we could easily get to the Plaza by monorail once we're disguised," she stares pointedly at Diana, her hands stilling for a fleeting moment, "and Diana, who's the one person you know who can sneak just about anything into the Capitol with ease?"

Diana laughs. "Maya."

"Exactly," Kiara states plainly. "What if we call her to us when we get there? And then *she* sneaks us into the Capitol?"

"Who's Maya?" Cameron asks, glancing between Diana and Kiara, who were sharing a conspiratorial smirk.

"My sister," Diana explains, turning to Cameron, "she used to work at the Capitol. She's... resourceful, to say the least."

Cameron shrugs, as if it were perfectly obvious. "Well, she sounds like an ally to me."

Diana nods, bemused by this new idea which she turns over in her head for a moment. Maya was the rogue, the thief who slipped right under someone's nose and was gone in a snap of her fingers. For years she's been sneaking resources to people in poverty in Sector Six. She's average height, weight, looks, and to the naked eye, she's the last person you'd suspect to get into any trouble. She never told Diana much about her escapades, probably to keep her out of the loop in case any repercussions made their way to their family. They never did of course, and eventually, Maya's adventures ceased, but with the right amount of coaxing, Diana was sure she'd do it again.

"I like it," Diana says, standing. "Shall we pack?"

Cameron slumps on the table. "But I'm so tired. I need *sleep*."

Kiara rolls her eyes and smacks the back of his head playfully. "Fine. You sleep. We'll pack in shifts. You have two hours, so make it count."

Cameron pumps his fists in the air. "Thank you, girls. And I will make every *second* count," he gets up and wanders into Kiara's room, closing the door lightly behind him.

Diana studies the closed door he just exited through. "Are we sure we can trust him?"

Kiara nods from next to her. "I'm not entirely sure, but he could be a valuable asset," she turns to Diana with a small smile. "Scorpios *are* notoriously complicated, no?"

"Yeah," Diana allows. "But what if he's out to cause trouble?"

Kiara rolls her eyes. "He's not. He led four hundred Scorpios out of Sector Three, for god's sake."

"True." Diana relents. "I guess he can stay for now."

Dismissing the topic, she turns to walk to Kiara's small broom closet. She pulls out two Black bags: a duffel bag, and one drawstring.

"This is good, I think," Diana says, "I didn't bring anything, so we'll have to pack here," she sticks her hand into the bag and feels around.

"What are you looking for?" Kiara asks.

"A false bottom? A lot of Old American bags had those, right? You know, so they could get weapons through the stations without alerting guards?"

Diana feels around the bottom, moving past folds in the fabric until she finds a small zipper hidden under a loose piece of fabric. She unzips it, and discovers a book-sized hidden pocket in the bottom of the bag. Diana grins up at Kiara and motions for her to look for herself.

"Nice," Kiara says, pulling her hand from the pocket, "perfect for a weapon or two, plus some dyes for our clothes."

They take two utility knives and place them in the hidden pocket. Then they bustle about, filling bottle after plastic bottle with water and packing what little food Kiara has into the top section of the bag.

"We don't have dye," Diana points out. "How are we going to get disguises? We can't *legally* buy any of this stuff, in case we need to make different clothes."

Kiara smirks, tapping her finger against her chin mockingly, then crosses to her kitchen, pulling out a drawer filled with napkins and washcloths. She pulls out a washcloth towards the back of the drawer, unraveling it to reveal a few small vials of dye, bright colors contained in tiny clear bottles.

"Ki!" Diana laughs. "You absolute rebel. How did you get those?"

Kiara starts sorting them by color, setting out the ones they need, and Diana watches her fingers move in rapid rhythm. Gray, Red, Forest Green, Brown, Black, Orange, Navy Blue. One for each sector they might have to visit. "I got them from the Plaza last time I was there. A vendor was selling them behind the visiting center, and I grabbed them before she was shut down. I figured it's better to have them than not have them, you know? She charged a pretty penny per vial, though."

Diana nods, helping her put the vials in a small box, cushioned with meticulously folded paper to avoid them breaking or spilling. They put the box delicately into the hidden compartment, then Diana stands and brushes herself off.

"Should I go wake up Cameron?" Diana asks. Kiara quirks an eyebrow, and points at her clock. It reads 8:54, and Diana grimaces. "Nevermind. Wait another day, then?"

Kiara nods. "I'll take the couch. You can sleep in the bedroom with Cameron."

Diana heads in, seeing Cameron sprawled on the bed, in all of his clothes. She scoffs, and hauls his legs to the other side of the bed with a grunt of effort. Stirring, he grins up at Diana with half-open eyes.

"Hey hey," he says, his voice raspy with sleep.

"Hi," Diana whispers, "is it alright if I crash in here?"

He wriggles over to the side, making just enough room for Diana. She leaves her clothes on but removes the elastics holding her messy bun in place, shaking her fingers through her knotted hair, and flops down next to him. She snuggles under the covers, and Cameron stays on top of the comforter, politely rolling away from her. Diana snorts as she watches him move. "You don't have to freeze on my behalf."

Cameron laughs with her. "I didn't want to get in your space. Don't flatter yourself." He pulls the pillow out from under her head, sticking it over his face as Diana protests. "Also, if you could keep the snoring down, I'd *love* to sleep tonight."

"Fine," Diana says, grabbing the pillow back. They lay in silence for a second. "I'm sorry about your sister," Diana whispers.

She realizes that he might have fallen asleep, and feels a little foolish. Then, he stirs. "It hurts to lose someone you love. Someone you're close to. It's unlike any other pain."

"Yeah," Diana whispers, "I can't imagine how hard it must be."

He nods, and Diana can feel the movement vibrate through their pillows. "It doesn't ever register. It's almost like a really terrible wake-up call, you know? One day, everything is fine, and the next, someone has dragged you from your life and forced you to watch everything crumble to pieces." Cameron turns to face her. "You're lost."

Diana turns her head to catch his gaze. The two examine one another for a moment before Diana finally speaks. "You helped all those people," she whispers.

Cameron's gray eyes sparkle in the darkness. "Because that's what was right."

Part Five: The Scorpio

Cameron

Cameron wakes up next to Diana, closing his eyes against the white light filtering through the window drapes. He takes a moment to let himself sink into the pillows and sheets, reveling in relaxation for the first time in many days. In many months, even. The quiet soon becomes stifling, though, so he rolls over to wake Diana up, shaking her shoulder.

"Diana," Cameron whispers, "we should get a move on."

She mumbles something, still locked in a deep sleep, and her eyebrows knit together, like Cameron's physical intervention was making her upset. Words escape her mouth in a whisper, so quiet Cameron has to lean forward to hear her.

"*Peter!*" Diana is louder now, yelling his name over and over. She winces in her sleep, and says his name again, kicking her legs so hard she flings herself to the other side of the bed, directly into Cameron. Reflexively, he grabs her arms to keep her still, used to having to comfort the little kids in his old group home back in Sector Three who suffered from night terrors.

"Diana! Diana, wake up. It's okay, you're having a nightmare." He wraps his arms around her waist, pinning her arms to her side so she can't thrash anymore. Kiara rushes in from the couch, eyes wild with fear.

"Is everything okay? I heard yelling." She sees Diana settling, and the panic in Cameron's face, and her expression softens a little bit. She comes and sits on the bed, tucking her legs beneath her. "Oh, no. A nightmare about Peter, I'm guessing?"

"Does that happen a lot?" Cameron asks, slowly releasing a now-peaceful Diana. Kiara nods in affirmation.

"Since we were eleven. She used to tell me about them in school, and she seemed so scared. It only started the year we were eleven, the year after he left."

"God, that's awful," Cameron says, trying not to look at Diana. "What do you think will happen when we find him?"

Kiara looks towards her hands, clasped tightly in her lap, lips pursed in consideration. "*If.*"

"What do you mean, 'if'?"

Kiara glances at him. "I don't know, okay? All I know is that this is going to be harder than we think. We're lucky if we make it to him at all."

"Are we sure he's safe to trust?"

"Yes. Positive. He wouldn't endanger me and Di like that." She shoots a glance towards Diana, now sleeping with a small smile on her face, looking as happy as a child with a chocolate bar. Cameron nods in understanding.

"Were they ever together?" he asks, "like... romantically?" Kiara shifts her head from side to side, in a gesture of uncertainty.

"I don't think so. In school, we were far too young to be dating, so it never was definite. But there was definitely... something." She studies Diana. "But now, I think she just wants her friend back." She looks over at Cameron. "Cameron, can I ask you a question?"

"Sure."

She chews the inside of her cheek. "Have you ever... felt like that about someone?" Her hands sit restlessly in her lap. "I mean, *liked* someone in that way?"

He thinks back, then nods. "Yeah, I have. Once. A *long* time ago."

Kiara nods slowly. "Do you want to talk about it?"

"Sure. I was like, fourteen, he was twelve, and we tried 'dating.' I mean, if you can consider two hot-off-the-presses Scorpios holding hands behind their houses 'dating'."

Kiara laughs. "Who was it?"

"You probably don't know him. His name was Max, he was your age, actually."

She gasps. "Max, like, the hopscotch kid?!"

Cameron's eyes widen. "How do you know him?"

"We went to school together. He used to *beg* our teachers to let us go outside and play hopscotch. He never let anyone else play with him, though. After the Split, I never heard anything about him," she motions to Cameron with her hand, "until now, obviously."

He laughs. "That's hilarious. He never mentioned you, or school."

The mood turns serious again with that last word. "Well, what happened?" Kiara asks.

Cameron shakes his head and shrugs sadly. "You know. Not allowed per BOZ standards. 'Same gender, same zodiac' doesn't really sit right with them. Especially because we were so young."

Kiara looks up at him with pity, and Cameron realizes he definitely underestimated how colorful her eyes were, flecks of gold spattered in her tawny irises. "I'm so sorry."

He shakes his head. "I'm okay now. I... I've given up on being with someone, I guess. New America won't ever change, so I have to instead," he shrugs. "That's life."

"...I guess. That really sucks. Maybe someday things will change." Kiara smiles halfheartedly at him. "Anything's possible."

Cameron cracks a genuine grin at this girl who he's known for a day, this girl who knows his two biggest secrets and yet looks at him like he's truly a normal human. Cameron silently wraps his arms around her, and she buries her face in his shoulder, emotions passing through the embrace that they wouldn't normally speak aloud. The two stay that way until Diana stirs.

"What are you guys doing in here?" she mumbles, rubbing her eyes and rolling onto her back.

Kiara reaches down and strokes her hair, pushing the tangles away from her face in a comforting gesture. "We came to grab you, but you were having a nightmare."

Diana closes her eyes and grimaces, as if it physically pains her to think about. "I'm sorry." Her voice is a hoarse whisper, and she raises her hands to push the heels of her palms into her forehead.

Cameron pulls her into the hug. "Don't be. We're going to find him, and then you won't have nightmares anymore."

Diana nods, looking half-convinced. "Kiara, is there anywhere I can brush my hair and teeth?" she asks, changing the subject naturally, as if she'd practiced this before.

"Yeah, the bathroom's down the hall. We should all freshen up, probably."

Something clicks in all their brains at the same time, and the three teenagers look between each other, glaring suspiciously at one another until finally Cameron shouts: "I call showering first!"

The girls groan and mumble curse words under their breath, and Cameron fist pumps the air triumphantly.

They travel down the hall together, squeezing shoulder-to-shoulder to stalk down the narrow hallway. Kiara's whole house is floored with dark hardwood, weathered from years of walking. The walls are painted an eggshell white, and they are bare of pictures or artwork. Cameron catches Diana looking at the bare walls and he wonders what her home looks like, if she misses it. When they reach the bathroom door, Kiara pushes it open with one hand and flicks on the dingy light. She points to the counter and the shower, pulling a few towels off the shelf as she speaks. "Cameron, for the hot water, turn the knob all the way to the right. It says turn it to the left, but don't."

Cameron raises an eyebrow and regards the shower handle warily. "...Oookay."

"Diana, extra toothbrushes are in the drawer below the counter. Toothpaste is in that glass, mouthwash is in the cupboard."

"Perfect. Thank you, Ki."

Cameron grabs a towel from the little stack and turns to Kiara. "What are you going to do?"

Kiara snickers, like it's completely obvious. "Change my clothes. I'm completely taking advantage of my closet being available for me."

Diana, toothbrush hanging from her mouth, spins around and grabs Kiara's forearm. "Can 'oo plesh get me 'cose too?!" Toothpaste spews from her mouth and she doubles over the sink.

Cameron snorts with laughter, and Kiara pats her hand, smirking. "Sorry, can I get that one more time?"

Diana wipes her mouth with a washcloth, now rid of the toothbrush, and clears her throat. "Can you please get me clothes too? I'll give them back after, pinky swear."

"Yeah, of course," Kiara replies, "keep them, if you feel so inclined."

She exits the bathroom, and Diana looks at Cameron through the mirror, where he's messing with the shower knob. "Cameron, I'll be out of your way in a second. I just need to brush my hair."

Cameron shrugs, unbothered. "I don't care. Take as long as you need," he turns on the hot water, pulling his shirt over his head. Diana notices and turns away from the mirror, towards the wall, and Cameron sheds the rest of his clothing and pulls the shower curtain shut behind him.

Hot water pours past his ears and down his face, and he scrubs his hands through his hair as his muscles relax. He shampoos quickly, soaping up his hands and running them down his arms and across his face. By the time he's done washing off, he doesn't want to get out, but he turns off the water and sticks his hand out of the curtain, groping around for the towel he left on the hook. A hand passes it to him, and he thanks whichever one of the girls it is before pulling the towel back through the curtain and wrapping it around his waist.

He pulls back the shower curtain to see that Diana is still in the bathroom, a new set of clothes folded on the toilet seat. She smiles at Cameron, pointing at his head. "Does that always happen when you're in the shower?" She asks.

Cameron crosses to the mirror, wiping the condensation off before studying his reflection. Sure enough, his hair is spiked in multiple different directions.

He brushes it down with his fingers, and turns back towards Diana, who's turning on the shower again. "Only when I'm in a hurry and have five minutes to wash my hair."

She chuckles, and Cameron exits the bathroom, changing back into his Red clothes. He goes to the kitchen, where Kiara is packing up extra water and food in the drawstring bag. Silently, Cameron joins her, and the two fall into a steady rhythm, working as swiftly as a conveyor belt in a factory.

"Thanks for lending your bathroom," Cameron says, not bothering to look at Kiara.

"Anytime," she replies, glancing at him out of the corner of her eye. Her movements slow just barely, like she was hesitant to ask the next question. "Were you in one of those homes? Back in Sector Three?"

Cameron sighs and nods. "Yeah. Luckily, I was. Me and... forty other boys, I think." He chuckles ruefully. "This was the first hot shower I've had in weeks."

"Why?"

He shrugs. "Normally I let the younger boys go before me, so they can have hot water. They're the ones who get pneumonia or flu and good hygiene helps them get better. Usually."

Kiara nods, reaching over and placing a hand on Cameron's wrist and forcing him to look at her. "You're a good person."

She said it plainly, as if it were *true*, and Cameron scoffs before he can stop himself. "I'm a Scorpio, is what I am."

Before Kiara can reply, Diana enters, wet hair pulled into a braid, with her shorter flyways stuck to her temples. Kiara brushes herself off, regarding Cameron and Diana with a passive expression, and smiles, seemingly producing the duffel bag out of nowhere, although Cameron knows it was probably just next to the table. Kiara holds the bags up and tosses the duffel to Cameron. She swings the drawstring on, then throws a map of New America towards Diana, who just barely catches it. "Di, will you navigate?"

Diana grins. "It would be an honor."

Cameron swings the duffel bag over his shoulders like a backpack, then grapples to get his shoes on. "Ready, ladies?" he asks, straightening up to face them.

Diana does a two-fingered salute, and Kiara grins so wide her white teeth shine like the rising sun outside her house. "Ready," they both chime. So off they go.

Part Six: The Aries

Kiara

"I'm just gonna say it. Where *exactly* are we?" Cameron asks.

His question is met with silence. The motley team was standing in the eastern area of Sector One, surrounded by a patch of vast forest, void of people besides the trio. Directly to their right was the barrier separating Sector One and Sector Two. In front of them was the wall separating Sector One and the ocean. Diana hands Kiara the map, pointing to their location.

"We're here, but we're *supposed* to be..." she trails off, scanning her finger around the map and finally landing on a location miles away from where they were, "here."

"So you're saying we walked *away* from the station?" Cameron asks.

Diana doesn't reply, studying the map again. Holding it up to the light, her pale green eyes flit across the page, her lip pulled between her teeth. Finally, she speaks. "No, not technically." She points out a spot on the map, a spot that was, presumably, where the trio was currently standing. "Kiara, your map is wrong. Where did you get this?"

Kiara groans. "Someone in the Plaza sold it to me. It must have been–"

"–A scam," Diana finishes.

"Okay, so what's our next move? We're going to waste too much time going all the way back to where the train *really* is," Cameron says, voice sounding a little more frantic than he probably intends.

Kiara eyes Cameron. "Well, Cameron could drop the border, if he feels comfortable. But that would release any Aries or Leos close enough to this border."

Cameron shakes his head. "There has to be another way."

Diana scuffs the dirt with her foot. "Can we go under?" she asks no one in particular.

"There's no way. There would've been endless escapes if we could just dig," Cameron retorts.

Kiara eyes the tall trees that surround them. "Go over?"

Both of her companions shake their heads. Cameron walks to the farthest back section, the 'crust' of the pie slice that is Sector One, if you will. A tree runs through the border, the translucent wall cutting it in half vertically. It's a tall oak tree, with a thick trunk that's cut straight down the middle by the intimidating wall. Kiara has never seen it this close, and the low hum of the wall sends a barely-detectable vibration through the ground underneath her. Cameron turns to face the girls.

"Do you think this tree cuts the rest of the border off?" He asks.

Kiara catches on quickly. "Like if you dropped the section from the tree all the way to the right - that thirty feet there - would it drop the whole thing or just that section?"

Cameron nods, seemingly relieved Kiara was following his idea. She shrugs. "Wouldn't hurt to try."

Diana stands up straight and nods. "I'm sure that the Aries aren't stupid enough to run into the ocean if it does drop the whole thing, anyways."

Kiara snorts sarcastically. "I wouldn't be too sure about that."

Both of the others stare blankly at her.

She shrugs. "Impulsive and impatient? We'd be the first sign *to* run straight into the ocean, after being holed up in this shithole country for years."

The others ignore her jest, and Cameron approaches the wall, his silhouette outlined by the glow of the border. Diana and Kiara step closer as well, and Kiara studies the wall. A pang of cold fear settles in the pit of her stomach as she tilts her head all the way back to look at it, jutting its way into the sky. Kiara can tell Diana feels it too, because she swallows audibly next to Kiara and takes a subtle step back, as if the border could reach forward and swallow her whole. Cameron, though, seems perfectly fine, and he looks up and down, right and left, a practiced motion. He doesn't shy away, even though Kiara can see the hairs on his arms standing up. He's still inches away from it, a breath's distance, his tall form hunched in focus, then, in a moment evidently debated upon, he reaches his hand out and places his palm against the wall. He seems almost sad, mouth downturned in a frown, his eyes squeezed shut. He gives a gentle push forward, and the wall falls away.

It's the most incredible thing Kiara has ever seen.

Quickly, Cameron steps backwards, staring at the openness. Diana takes a few quick steps back to study the whole scene, leaning to the left to see around the side of the tree. She smiles giddily.

"The rest is still intact," she says. And she was right. The long, almost never-ending stretch of border that separated Sector One from the ocean was still there, a light teal-gray color that went as far as the horizon. The thirty feet from the tree to the eastern wall was gone, though, replaced instead with a small cliff, and outwards of that, a large, vast mass of ocean reached its dark tendrils across the world.

"Wow," Kiara whispers. She stares out at the ocean, entranced by the dark blue that meets a lighter shade on the horizon: sky and sea.

It's like nothing Kiara has ever seen before. She *hasn't* seen anything like it before, she realizes. She's seen skyscrapers rise from the ground, she's seen the vast concrete Plaza stretch before her in the center of the world, but she's never seen this.

Diana walks to the edge. They're about three feet above the top of the water, and occasionally, the sea laps up to wave to them, spilling over the grass where Diana kneels down. Cameron grins at the girl's amazement, and sits to join them. Diana looks at Cameron, the same way children would look at their teacher. "Can I touch it?" She asks.

He shrugs, crouching next to her. "I don't see why not."

So Diana leans over, making sure to keep her weight on the ground, and skims her fingers over the water. She sucks in a sharp breath, then sticks her whole hand in. However, she very quickly yanks it back out. "It's freezing!" She laughs breathlessly.

Cameron stands. "I think I have an idea. What if I drop the Sector Two border really quick, then we hold onto this tree here and swing ourselves around?"

Diana and Kiara share looks of confusion, and Cameron rolls his eyes. "Let me show you." He snaps off a small branch from the tree holding the rest of the wall in place and begins to draw something in the ground. It's a triangle shape, and in the center goes a few rectangles to apparently represent buildings. He puts a big, square building towards the point of the triangle. "Sector Two is set up differently than the rest of the sectors. While the rest of us have a scattered city that unravels into the suburbs, like where Kiara lives, Sector Two is only high-rises."

"Since they're all filthy rich," Diana mumbles.

"Exactly," Cameron confirms. "So, there's little to no risk involved with this far wall-" he motions to the back of the triangle, "-being dropped for a few moments."

"Won't all those people in the skyscrapers see the wall disappear?" Kiara asks, crossing her arms over her chest.

Cameron shrugs. "Maybe. But since nobody is close enough to get there in the time it's down, they'll just think it's a figment of their imagination, since I'll put it back up as soon as we're through. I need thirty seconds, tops."

Diana stands and nods. "We're already in this deep. Why the hell not?"

Kiara's eyes widen. "Wow, Di. Who are you and what did you do with the old Diana?"

She shrugs. "She got left behind in Sector Seven. This one just wants to get out of these godforsaken woods."

Cameron isn't listening anymore, in fact, he's stood up and wandered back to the open wall. He grabs the branch of a nearby tree, holding on so he doesn't fall into the ocean. He sticks his hand against the wall of the Leo's sector, dangling precariously over the ocean, and then uses his momentum to swing out and around into their sector. There are more woods on the other side, so he's disguised under the cover of trees, just like he said he'd be.

"Come on! Before people notice!" he says. Diana grabs the branch with one hand, then Cameron's hand with the other and he pulls her over smoothly, save for

Diana's strangled yelp that escapes her throat. Kiara goes next, and when she's across, Cameron holds his hand over the ground where the border was. In a matter of seconds, the border is back up, locking them into the new sector. They sit, reveling in silence and relief for a moment, listening intently to the woods around them to make sure they've not been found out.

"Can I be honest?" Cameron breaks the silence. The other two nod, catching their breath. "I did *not* think that was gonna work."

The girls huff out short, semi-audible responses, nodding in agreement. Their heavy breathing is the only sound. It's peaceful here, and they're certainly off the beaten path. There's no one in orange anywhere to be seen, and they're deep in a thick, dim forest. The sunlight filters gently through the tops of the trees, now taller oaks with heavier branches.

"Cameron," Kiara says, grabbing his attention from across the clearing, "watch this," she turns to Diana, poking her arm. "Di, pop quiz. What states did this area used to be?"

Diana bites her lip and thinks for a moment, observing the land around her. "Um, this used to be Kentucky, West Virginia, and Ohio."

Cameron gives her a dramatic spattering of applause, looking around to study the forest as if he could see it the way Diana did. "I *wish* I paid that much attention in school."

Kiara leans into Diana, whispering so only she can hear. "And Virginia."

Diana smiles knowingly. "And Virginia," she echoes.

Diana crosses the clearing and sits against a tree with her legs pulled to her chest, breathing silently, letting her head fall against the bark and closing her eyes. Cameron reaches across the little clearing and pokes her leg.

"What're you thinking about, Diana?" He asks.

Diana answers without opening her eyes: "I don't really know. But it was like this the last day I was with Peter." She opens her eyes slowly, seeming to look somewhere else, instead of at Cameron and Kiara. Like she was in a whole new world. "Peaceful. Quiet. A silence almost begging to be broken, you know?"

Cameron and Kiara share a look. Kiara runs some dirt between her fingers and averts her eyes, trying to avoid the subject. Cameron senses the tension and stands, grabbing their hands to pull the girls with him.

"Let's dye our clothes, yeah?" he asks, unzipping the false bottom in the bag and grabbing the Orange vial. He grabs a flask of water and starts to pull off his shirt. He eyes the two girls and swivels his finger, and they comply, turning around so they can't see him. The girls hear him pour the water onto his clothes, then the quiet dripping of the dye soaking into the cotton. Diana sits criss-cross and begins to doodle in the dirt while they wait while Kiara braids together blades of tall grass, and after a few minutes of Cameron holding his clothes in the barrier's heated direction, he shouts towards them:

"Dry and decent. You guys are all set."

Kiara turns around to see Cam wearing his Red pants and a shirt that is definitely Orange, no matter how spotty it may be. "Woah," she says, "show us how."

So Cameron repeats the process with Kiara and Diana looking on, and soon they're outfitted in Orange, brighter than the purest and hottest flame.

Diana makes a face. "This color is *so* gross. Why is it so bright?"

Cameron laughs at her. "Cool it, Forest Green. Not everyone can look like *grass*."

Diana shoves him. "Alright, coal dust. Say what you want."

Kiara rolls her eyes at the two of them. "Can we just go? We have a monorail to catch."

"Ooookay." Cameron mumbles, just loud enough for Kiara and Diana to hear, "Fire hydrant."

Diana snorts with laughter, and Kiara holds up a certain finger in his direction, rolling her eyes and grinning.

Quickly, so as to avoid attention, the group walks through the City of the Leos, "oohing" and "aahing" at the architecture that sprouted up around them as they drew nearer to the main city. Leos were proud and charitable, but they were also wasteful and indulgent, which the three saw firsthand when walking past giant, gold-encrusted buildings surrounded by homeless people begging for anything they had. Truly, it was a magnificent place: a city of gold and glass constructed over time to house one of the most complicated and popular signs.

"Wow," Kiara says, "these Leos know how to *build*."

"Tell me about it," Cameron replies, running his hand across a gold-plated streetlight.

"Peter's mom is a Leo," Diana begins, gaze fixated at the very tops of the gilded skyscrapers, "I wonder if she's still around here somewhere."

"Too bad she didn't rig Peter's birth," Cameron says, sidestepping a well-dressed woman. "He could've lived a perfect life of luxury."

The monorail station, they noticed upon arrival, was no different from all the other buildings: flashy and huge. The railings shone and the platform was glass, with windows arching high above their heads. They approach the door, trying to fight against the crowds of people in silky dresses and Orange suits who pay no mind to these commoners.

"Let's just get in fast," Diana says, trying to muscle past the people and into the station. She's nearly swallowed by the crowd, and Kiara and Cameron push forward to follow. Someone grabs Diana's arm from behind, and all of them jump, spinning around to come face-to-face with a guard.

"What's in those bags?" he asks gruffly. He grabs at Cameron's bag, and the boy sidesteps away, mumbling a curse word or two under his breath.

"Do you need something?" Kiara asks the guard. He grabs at them again, snarling, and the kids shove quickly past him into the station.

"Get back here!" the guard shouts at their retreating forms. "Someone stop those kids!"

Kiara, Cameron, and Diana start to run in the direction of the closest departure sign, blinking in bright lights that read 'To Plaza'. They hear the guard shouting behind them, then a chorus of angry voices, and they pick up the pace, all three striding forward in unison. Kiara's legs start to burn, but they all continue on, dodging through people dressed in Orange silks and suit coats who glare at them as they sprint past. Kiara looks to her left to see Cameron sprinting next to her, but he still manages to shoot Kiara a wink when they make frantic eye contact. Diana is to Kiara's right, clutching her fraudulent maps in an iron vice grip, running so fast her loose hair whips around her face.

The guard's footsteps get quieter behind them, but the monorail is starting to pull away from the loading dock. Cameron scrambles ahead of the girls, grabbing a bar on the side of the train to launch himself into the car. Kiara tosses him her bag and grabs his hand, and Cameron yanks her to safety.

Cameron and Kiara are safely on the moving train, but Diana is running back the way they came, chasing after the retreating vehicle. Cameron shoves the bags at Kiara as the doors start to close, heaving them open again, his hands straining and his teeth clenched.

"Diana!" He yells. "Jump!"

So she does, without hesitation, leaping off the platform and tackling Cameron onto the floor of the monorail. He tumbles to the ground, wrapping his arms around her and rolling further into the train. Cameron quickly sits up, pulling the handle of the car door shut. Kiara looks around to see that they're in a transport car, one that isn't supposed to be open for passengers.

Whoops.

Diana stands, breathing deep, and wraps her arms around Cameron. Kiara rushes towards the two of them, and they pull her into the hug with them, breathing heavily for one relief-filled moment.

"What the-" Diana huffs, "-what was that?"

Kiara speaks from her position against Cameron's chest. "You just jumped onto a moving train, Di. That's what that was."

"I hate this," Cameron begins, trying and failing to catch his breath, "I like you guys, but I hate this."

They separate and take their seats on the floor by the window, and Diana sits between Cameron and Kiara, pulling out her map. She ducks her head towards the paper, twining her hair around her finger, and points towards the Plaza.

"Almost there, guys. I'd say fifty minutes until we get to the Plaza. Any ideas for getting clothes when we arrive?"

Cameron nods. "Dyeing Orange to Gray will be impossible. We'll need to buy them in Sector Five."

"But they aren't gonna let us on the train dressed as Leos," Kiara says.

"We'll have to steal them from somewhere," Diana says quietly. Cameron and Kiara nod. Diana rolls her map up, sticking it in her bag. She tucks the bag protectively under her legs, then slouches and crosses her arms. "Let's make a plan, then."

After about fifteen minutes of bad ideas, Cameron suggests, "What about the school?" At confused looks from the girls, he elaborates. "Like, if we get in there, we can steal from their stock, the stuff they give to the kids when they leave."

Kiara wrings her hands together. "Guys, if we get caught, we'll be killed."

Diana chews her lip. "We've got no other ideas."

Cameron leans his head on the window. "I sure hope Peter is worth it. For all of our sakes."

Part Seven: The Taurus

Diana

Diana gulps as the monorail approaches the giant station at the Plaza, an hour after their chaotic departure from Sector Two. The three of them shuffle out of the transport car and into the main forum, and Cameron grabs Diana's hand from next to her. He yanks her and Kiara out of the way and around the side of a building.

"Okay. Let's split up, walk around, and meet at the schoolhouse in, say, ten minutes," he casts wary looks at the strangers around them, as if any one of them were an undercover guard, "I don't want us walking around all together, just to be safe."

The two girls nod, and they all head out into the main circle. Diana takes a shaky breath, and Kiara catches her eye out of her peripheral vision, shooting Diana a small smile.

"We've got this," Kiara reassures her in a soft whisper.

Diana grins and nods.

Then, they all head their different ways.

After many scrambling minutes, the team races back to the fountain in the center of the Plaza to meet each other. Cameron whispers excitedly to the girls: "I found a way in."

Kiara shrugs. "A window?"

Cameron looks at her, disappointment etched across his face. "You stole my whole thunder."

"Everyone is in class right now," Diana says, glancing over at the large building, cleverly ignoring her friends.

"Right. So the dorms are empty," Cameron confirms.

Kiara sighs. "It's the best idea we have."

"It's the *only* idea we have," Diana mumbles just as she did before.

"Exactly. So why not?"

So the three head toward the school. Kiara and Diana are nailing the "walk like a Leo, talk like a Leo" thing, but Cameron is struggling with the "walk" part.

"Cameron," Diana whispers, glancing around nervously at the strangers who are eyeballing them suspiciously, "straighten your back."

He grimaces. "It's so *hard*. I'm used to hunching my shoulders to avoid being *literally* dragged into the street and beaten."

Kiara snorts with stifled laughter. "Just try."

So he straightens his back and struts like some demented creature. Kiara quickly shoves his shoulders back down and mumbles: "Yeah, maybe not."

While they bicker about Cameron's posture, Diana takes a second to observe their surroundings. It's late morning, and the large circular forum is starting to fill up. The wind is whistling in a gentle breeze, and although the sun is shining, the chill that comes with this late part of the year filters through the air. Long shadows from the high-rise apartments arc over the concrete ground, and the schoolhouse is nestled within these dark contours.

Soon, they're at the front entrance. Diana approaches slowly with Kiara, while Cameron creeps behind them. There aren't guards here, but the three know that there certainly will be inside.

"Guys, I don't know why I'm really, really scared," Diana says.

"Me too," Kiara whispers.

"We have to go in," Cameron says, voice firm with confidence, "even if we're nervous."

The group heads around the back of the building, where the air turns chilly and dark in the shadows of late afternoon. The space is devoid of noise, as if the alleyway was soundproofed. The only sounds are the trio's shallow breathing and the gentle thud of their shoes on concrete.

They all pause by a window, shades drawn over it. The bonus about spending twelve years of their life in one building was that all three knew the place like it was a second home. Which, unfortunately for their racing hearts, it still sort of was.

Cameron messes with the window, hoisting it up a crack. It opens with a gentle splitting noise, and he pushes it up further, swinging himself through it and under the blind. Kiara pushes herself up and follows suit, accompanied by Diana.

They're in a dorm room, outfitted with two sets of bunk beds. It's a boys' room, as observed through the musty smell and clothes strewn across the floor. Cameron goes to the closed door, feet padding across the shag carpet, and reads the sign hanging there.

"Ethan, Liam, Benjamin, and Wyatt," he reads, turning around to face the girls. His face is stony. "Scorpio, Sagittarius, Aquarius, and Scorpio, respectively."

"At least Liam is going to a place with a good leader," Kiara mumbles, walking around the room and tracing her fingers over the surfaces.

"And Benjamin is going to a sector with money," Diana says, leaning against the wall.

Cameron hangs his head. "And let's just pray for Ethan and Wyatt."

Diana scoffs, crossing her arms. "You guys, this is so... wrong. All of this."

Kiara nods, picking up a pillow from the floor and putting it back on the nearest bed. "These boys don't know any different."

"I miss it," Cameron blurts out. The girls stare at him, gaping, and he chuckles sadly. "I do. I miss not knowing what the future held. I miss being able to share a room with boys who weren't Scorpios, I miss being able to eat every day and sleep indoors. I miss it all, no matter how twisted that may sound."

Kiara and Diana are quiet, until Diana nods. "I miss it too, I guess."

"Yeah," Kiara agrees. "I think I do too."

"Do you think there are others who feel the way we do?" Diana asks, her searching gaze leveled at her companions. "Like, do you think that we aren't the only ones who feel so... complicated?"

Cameron and Kiara both hesitate, but then they both nod in tandem, too. "I would put money on it," Cameron replies. "People know that there used to be a time where things weren't so hard. And they'd be foolish to not want to go back to that."

"Even if they don't want to go back," Kiara begins, "they'd be foolish not to want better lives for themselves, at least."

The three revel in that quiet for a moment, the air stale and thick with desolation and something that felt like hope. Finally, Cameron nods to no one, turning back to the door and cracking it open. Kiara and Diana snap out of their funk and cross to look over his shoulders, standing on their tiptoes.

"Coast is clear. Wardrobe is down the hall to the right, if I remember correctly," Cameron says.

"Let's go," Kiara interrupts, ducking under Cameron's arm and heading down the hall.

They walk in silence, casting wary glances around the building. This particular wing was softer and cozier than the others, leading the group to believe it was for a younger age group. It was so unlike the cold, vast halls of the adolescent and teenage wings that it was more jarring than comfortable for outsiders. This meant fewer guards, but it also meant that a group of teenage Leos, who were at least four years out of their school age, looked far more out of place.

They reach a door marked 'Storage' and push it open. Cameron flicks on the light as Kiara closes the door behind them, and the room illuminates, revealing shelves full of clothes. They're piled up to the ceiling, sorted by size and color. Diana finds the Cancer row and begins rifling through it, grabbing a Gray short-sleeved shirt that looks like it could fit Cameron's slim frame and Gray pants that would go over his lanky legs. She grabs two of the same crewnecks for herself and Kiara, and two pairs of Gray leggings that are a size children's extra-large.

"We'll have to squeeze, I guess," she says to the others. She passes out the clothes, and everyone begins to change, throwing discretion to the wind. When she's done, Diana stands uncomfortably in front of the door, trying to stretch the waistband of her leggings.

"Ow. Tight," she says, letting go of the waistband and cringing at the snapping sound it makes as it comes into contact with her skin.

Cameron claps her on the shoulder, smiling at her. "You look great. Shall we go?"

Diana throws her hair up in a ponytail and they head out, one by one, to avoid suspicion. Soon, they regroup at the boys' dorm.

Diana locks the door behind them, turning to face her friends. Kiara's shirt is a little too tight, revealing a sliver of her midsection. Cameron's pants are too short, showing off his socks. But uncomfortable clothes or not, they were dressed, and now they had a one-way ticket to Sector Five.

"Ready?" Diana asks. The others both nod and they start outside back through the window. As they pass a cluster of guards towards the center of the Plaza, one grabs Cameron's arm.

"Wait. Didn't I just see you? A Leo?" He asks Cameron, side-eyeing him angrily.

Cameron doesn't give anything away, only stares at the guard's hand on his arm in disgust. "A Leo? No," he says in an unrecognizable, sloppy Southern accent, "I'm a Cancer. Please, sir, remove your hold on me."

The guard squeezes his arm tightly, glaring down at Cameron, who refuses to break eye contact. After a tense moment highlighted by Cameron's unwavering nonchalance, the guard releases him, and they scuttle out of their line of sight.

"*Way* too close, guys," Diana says to them. Kiara grits her teeth and nods, and Cameron peeks over his shoulder, back the way they came, finally letting out the breath he had been holding.

The team boards the train with no problems, and soon the monorail has lifted and they're soaring above the Plaza. Sector Five covers a lot of land, and the station is right in the middle, so, according to the screen at the front of their train car, they have about an hour of waiting time.

They find a car away from everyone, with a couch for sleeping and floor-to-ceiling windows. Fifteen, maybe twenty minutes pass in silence, and then they enter Sector Five.

It lives up to its dreary reputation. The sky is overcast, and it seems like the whole of the sector is lost in a shroud of fog and sleep. The few scattered buildings that Diana can see are made of cracked and creaky wood, and she quickly realizes that this sector is simply a land of neutral colors. Kiara quickly lies down on the couch, duffel bag under her head, and closes her eyes. Cameron approaches Diana at the windowsill and looks out at Sector Five and the setting sun with her for a peaceful, quiet moment.

Finally, he speaks. "What are you gonna say to him?"

A smile dances quickly across Diana's lips at the thought of finding Peter, although she doesn't pull her gaze from the glass. "I don't know. Any suggestions?"

"Well, what are you feeling right now?"

"I don't know. Excited. I've missed him," she turns to face Cameron, leaning against the windowsill, "but I'm also scared. What if things have changed?"

Cameron studies her for a second, then speaks. "They probably have. It's been years, right? So he's bound to be a little different. You're *both* bound to be different. But I don't think anything he feels towards you has changed. In fact, he's probably feeling stronger towards you than ever. Distance makes the heart grow fonder, right?" He ponders for a moment, then starts again. "Maybe he'll be confused, but that's normal. You can't neglect first impression feelings like that. I say, when we get there, we lay low and you guys just talk. Kiara and I will get out of your way, and you can hash out everything that has or hasn't happened over the past four years. Okay?"

Diana opens her mouth to speak, but nothing comes out. Her eyes well with tears, and she swipes at her eyes as Cameron silently pulls her into his arms, with Diana clutching to him like a shipwrecked sailor to a life raft. He rocks them back and forth gently, tightening his grip on Diana. After a moment, she pulls away.

"I guess that about covers it," Diana sniffles. She rushes forward and hugs him again, and whispers into his shirt: "I'm lucky to have met you, Cameron."

He hugs her tighter and says, "I'm lucky to have met you too. When I was younger, I was never one for friends. But then I met you, and Kiara, and suddenly, I have a purpose again. I'm with you guys all the way. We're gonna be thick as thieves."

Diana lets out a laugh as he gestures towards his stolen outfit and turns to face the window. Cameron does too, and they stare out at the view for a moment. After a silent interlude, Diana grabs his hand gently. She whispers to the window, but she can feel Cameron's eyes on the side of her head. "I'm excited to see him, Cam."

Diana feels Cameron's smile radiate towards her, and he gives her hand a gentle squeeze. "I know."

After an hour, the three disembark on the platform of the Sector Five station. All of them marvel at the buildings, Louisiana-style bayou homes painted uniformly in a flat shade of Gray. They wander down the street, and Cameron grabs the written plan out of Diana's bag.

"Step six, girls. 'Hack a Tracker to get Peter to a rendezvous spot.'"

They pause and look around. The streets are oddly quiet, and after a moment, Kiara fills the silence. "Cancers are summer kids. That's like, a lot of people. Why is no one here?"

She's right. The three are the only souls around, with the muggy intersection devoid of any noise or people.

"Maybe... a breakout?" Diana supplies. Cameron shakes his head.

"The place would be teeming with guards if there was. And they never would've let us in."

Diana wanders forward and grabs a piece of paper typed with a typewriter off a lamppost. She reads aloud, "Danger- refrain from leaving homes and business establishments. Over twenty-thousand Cancers lost to disease so far this year."

They all share a look, and Cameron shrugs. "Better get inside, then."

They head into a bar off the side of the street. The only other person there is a bartender, who barely looks up as the teens enter. The three take a seat at a booth at the far end, facing the front entrance. Cameron leans forward to conspire with Kiara and Diana.

"I see the perfect person to hijack a Tracker from," he says, jabbing a finger towards the barman.

Diana nods as she shifts her weight on the slick leather seat, nose wrinkled in slight disgust. "I'm not gonna be the one to knock him out."

Cameron groans. "I don't want to either, though."

Kiara shoves off of the seat, rolling her eyes. "You two are such drama queens. I'll do it."

Kiara strolls towards the bar, sliding into a stool. She points at the largest bottle on the shelf behind the man and smiles sweetly at him. "May I read the label on that?" she asks. The bartender grunts some kind of approval and hands her the bottle. After studying the contents inside and pretend-reading the label, she quickly hefts it over her head with both hands and brings it down hard on the bartender's head. He crumples to the floor, and Diana springs up and shuts the blinds with one hand while locking the door with the other. Cameron races into the back room, emerging with a thumbs up.

"No back exit," he says. The other two nod, and race to the side of the fallen barman. Kiara checks his pulse.

"Shallow, but there," she says, "although it's only a matter of time before a guard notices his Tracker is unresponsive."

"Nice, Ki," Diana says. She wrestles with his shirt, yanking it up to reveal his Tracker hooked into his belt. She grimaces. "I... don't want to touch that," Diana says.

Cameron shakes his head, then wraps his hand around the man's belt and yanks. The Tracker comes off cleanly, and he quickly punches a few buttons. Diana can't help but wonder if he'd done this for the Scorpios who'd escaped; if his skills were forced by his surroundings.

"Factory settings are shut down," he says. "Who can wire this to get ahold of Peter?"

Diana grabs it away from him. "Gotcha," she says with a grin. She quickly unlatches the back, revealing a tiny panel. Diana frowns, biting the inside of her lip. "I need something small to pull out this wire. Then, I can access the Capitol records of everyone in this sector."

Kiara holds up one finger, then pulls the false bottom out of the bag, revealing her utility knife. She flicks the blade out, and Diana grabs it and wedges it under the wire, pulling it clean away from the device. She plugs in a white wire to a blinking, blue reactor, and the screen lights up with a list titled "Sector Five Citizens."

Diana scrolls down quickly, scanning the faces to see if Peter is on the list. Soon, she spots the familiar mop of hair and pale skin, and quickly clicks on his face. She starts to type a message, when Cameron grabs her arm.

"Wait," he says abruptly, "the Capitol could be watching us right now. We need to be discreet, but also direct enough so Peter understands."

Kiara nods. "Like a code."

Cameron nods his approval. "Exactly."

Diana thinks for a minute. The unconscious bartender stirs, prompting Kiara's frantic whisper: "Anytime now, Di."

"I'm thinking!" Diana says, racking her brain for an answer. She types out, *Teem ta nrehtuos llaw thginot. Llet on eno. -Di*

She hits send before anyone can object. Kiara and Cameron stare at her. "What does it mean?" Kiara asks.

"Meet at southern wall tonight. Tell no one," Diana says, "I reversed the words."

Cameron grins slyly. "You evil genius."

"How is he gonna know what that means?" Kiara asks.

"We used to leave each other codes in the dirt outside the school, so we could arrange meetings. Since he was in the class above us, we started seeing each other less and less as we grew up, so we needed a way to communicate."

Before anyone can respond, Diana quickly stands and crushes the Tracker under her foot. She helps the other two up, then heads for the door, turning to face them. "Let's get to the southern wall, then," she says with a smile. Her eyes catch on the barman, still lying on the floor. "Preferably fast."

Kiara laughs and claps her hands excitedly as Cameron grins.

The three exit the bar hurriedly, heading towards the woods on the outskirts of town.

After walking through the forest for a while, they reach a section of the translucent border wall, slowing their pace. After finding a secluded section away from the main forest, the group hunkers down next to the wall. Diana takes a moment to gaze around her.

It's beautiful here, more beautiful than even Sector Two. It's a forest of magnolia trees, ones so big they put the photos from school to shame. It's not their time to bloom, but there are long, bare, tendril-like branches that are so large Diana thinks she could sleep on one comfortably. Although simple, the trees are spectacular and give this sad sector a glimmer of beauty. The sun will be setting in a few hours, and Diana looks around to see her tired companions starting to slow down.

Cameron takes his Orange clothes out of the bag and lays them at the foot of the huge magnolia tree, lying down on them as if they were a blanket and closing his eyes. Kiara sits next to him, eating a bag of pretzels. She looks up at Diana expectantly.

"You should try to rest, or at least eat something, Di. I'll wake you up when the sun starts to set, if you want."

Diana sighs. "Thanks, Ki. Hand me a snack."

Kiara tosses her a small roll of crackers, and Diana catches them one-handed and slumps down against the tree.

Cameron sighs, not opening his eyes, his freckled hands folded against his stomach. "I could stay here forever."

Kiara raises one eyebrow and looks around. "It's... different from Sector One, that's for sure."

Cameron readjusts, finally opening his eyes, and Diana watches his gray irises scan the forest. "It's so beautiful. And quiet. Nothing ever really slows down in Sector Three, you're always moving, all the time, you have to be. But here, it feels like we're not even in the world anymore."

"It *is* relaxing," Diana agrees.

"More than that," Cameron continues, "it's *warm*." He turns his head a little to look at Kiara. "Ki, when was the last time it was this warm where you live?"

She smiles gently and shakes her head. "Never."

"Never," Cameron repeats. He rolls his eyes up a little to look at Diana, who's looking down at him. "Sorry, Di, you can't relate. I guess that it's always muggy down where you live."

Diana nods her head and smiles. "It's always this hot in Sector Seven. Maybe worse."

They fall quiet, and Diana watches Cameron close his eyes and snuggle further into his makeshift bed. Kiara watches him too, chewing the inside of her cheek. "You know what I realized, Cameron?"

He quirks an eyebrow and slowly opens his eyes. "Hm?"

"You just used mine and Diana's nicknames."

Cameron sits up, looking between the two girls. "Is that... okay? I didn't even realize, I just-"

Diana shushes him with a wave of her hand. "Cameron, do you want to know what Kiara and I always said to each other at school?"

He visibly swallows. "What?"

Diana glances at Kiara, who is struggling to hide a smile. "Ki, if you'd do the honors?"

"Sure, sure," Kiara says, "as soon as we became friends, do you want to know what people called us?"

"Uh, sure?"

"Di and Ki. Never Diana and Kiara, or vice versa. And one day, we told each other that if someone became acquainted with us, and then they referred to us with our nicknames, they were automatically our best friend."

Cameron looks confused, and Diana notices his little forehead wrinkles from his creased eyebrows. "Okay?"

Diana jumps in. "Well, you did just that. And you helped with this crazy adventure."

"And not to mention, saved our lives multiple times already," Kiara adds.

"Ah, right," Diana says sarcastically, counting off on her fingers as she speaks, "getting us into Sector Two, saving me on the train, breaking into the school."

Cameron looks at the pair, smiling mischievously at him. "I can say with one-hundred percent certainty I don't know what you're getting at."

Kiara shrugs and turns to Diana. "Best friend?"

Diana makes a big show out of considering this offer, and then turns to Cameron, sticking her hand out for him to shake it. "Best friends, if you'll have us."

Cameron looks down at her hand and his face slowly breaks into a grin. "I would be honored."

Diana flings her arms around his neck, and if he wasn't sitting, she would've tackled him to the ground. He wraps his arms around her waist, and Kiara crosses to them, joining the hug as well. They stay like that for a second, in the quiet of Sector Five.

"Yeah, Cam, you're right," Diana whispers, nuzzling further into his shoulder.

"About what?" He whispers back, his breath pushing her blonde flyaways off her temples.

"Staying here forever," she responds, closing her eyes and allowing her body to relax into a gentle sleep.

Diana is brutally shaken awake by Kiara a few hours later. It's pitch black, and Cameron and Kiara are squeezed on either side of her. They pull her quickly behind the tree trunk, and that's when Diana notices both of them look absolutely terrified. Their faces are illuminated by the moonlight, and both are breathing heavily, mouths clamped shut to avoid the violent breaths from escaping their lips.

"What's going on?" she whispers. Cameron puts a shaky finger to his lips, and Kiara peeks around the side of the tree, quickly whipping back around.

"Someone's coming," she whispers. "I could hear their footsteps, and they're getting louder."

Diana gulps. "Do you think-?"

Cameron shakes his head. "There's no way he could've gotten here so fast." Some emotion, maybe hope, flickers across his face. "Right?"

They sit with their heads against the trunk, listening intently. Sure enough, footsteps are rapidly approaching. They keep quiet, until it sounds like the person is right on the other side of the tree. Diana closes her eyes, bracing for the impact of a fist, or a bullet. Some part of her wonders if this is the end.

"Hello?" the person whispers loudly.

It's almost as if the entire forest quiets. The branches of the magnolias stop rustling, the wind stops whispering to the dry dirt, even Kiara's audible gulp seems to cut off mid-swallow.

Diana's eyes shoot open. "Oh- oh my god," she whispers. Kiara and Cameron both whip around to look at her, and Cameron peeks out from behind the tree. "Is he alone?" Diana whispers frantically, her hand finding his wrist in the dark.

Cameron squints into the night and it's silent for another beat. He turns back around. "Looks like it," he says with a grin.

Kiara smiles. "He came," she says, her voice lilting as if four years of pressure had just fallen off her shoulders.

Diana leaps up before they can stop her, and she runs around the tree trunk. Sure enough, he's there. His hair is the same, maybe a little longer, but only just covering his ears. His skin is still pale, with his high cheekbones and crooked smile and thin lips. He's taller, not as tall as Cameron, but taller, nevertheless. He's still thin, but healthy, still lanky but muscular at the same time. He's so much older, so much stronger, so much more handsome.

Diana grins widely. "Peter," she manages.

He turns to look at her. Kiara and Cameron are behind her, Diana feels them shift around on either foot, unsure what to do, to move or to stay put. Peter copies her smile. "Diana," he says. His voice holds the same resonance, deeper but still wispy, like his twelve-year-old self is still in there somewhere.

Diana takes a step towards him. He doesn't move towards her, but she takes another step forward and before she can blink he's closed the distance between them, wrapping Diana in his arms. She breathes him in, and he smells like cotton and fresh laundry, exactly the same as he used to. He laughs breathlessly, his chest moving under her as Diana tucks her head into his chest and he buries his face in her hair. After a long moment, Diana steps away.

"Peter," she says again, her eyes searching him over again as if she was unsure that what she held in her arms was real, "you came."

He nods. "Yeah. I figured out your code. Nice throwback, by the way, although it was way less dangerous when we were sneaking around in the schoolyard," he smiles, softening when he looks Diana in the eye. "You have a lot of explaining to do."

Diana shakes her head. "Tomorrow. Tomorrow. But first, I-" she can't go any further, the emotion and adrenaline of the moment catching up to her all at once. She ducks her head, and Peter slowly steps towards her again. He holds Diana at arms' length, each hand on either side of her face. One hand cups her cheek, the other twines its fingers through her knotted hair.

"Please, don't cry. I'm okay. *We're* okay." He hugs Diana again, leaning down and whispering to her. "You need a hairbrush."

Diana laughs against him and squeezes him tighter. She looks up at him. "Should we get some rest?" she asks.

Peter nods and they turn towards the others. Cameron is staring at them, wide-eyed, and Kiara is grinning widely. Cameron raises his hand in an awkward wave.

"Uh, hi, Peter," he says, "I guess we should fill you in, huh?"

It was more awkward than any of them would have imagined. Peter stands against the tree, and the other three are shoulder-to-shoulder about four feet in front of him, simply observing his movements.

Diana can't look away from his eyes, those hazel eyes she's waited so long to see again.

Kiara wonders how he got so tall. And muscular. He used to be so scrawny.

Cameron can't tear his eyes away from the one brunette curl that routinely falls over his forehead.

"Are you guys gonna stop staring...?" Peter trails off, looking between the three nervously.

The others realize their mistake and quickly clear their throats, shifting their weight from one foot to the other.

"It's great to see you again," Kiara says, ever so bravely, stepping forward and hugging him again.

"Yeah, you too, Ki," Peter whispers into her hair.

As they hug, Cameron turns to face Diana. "I get the nickname thing now."

Diana smirks and nods, eyes still stuck on Peter. "Yup."

"Okay," Peter says definitively, pulling away from Kiara. "You guys owe me an explanation."

"Right," Diana says. "What do you want to know first?"

Peter considers for a second, and then his eyes land on Cameron's. "Who is he?"

The two boys make eye contact, and the energy around them grows strange, thrumming with force. Cameron squirms uncomfortably at Peter's ridiculously bright eyes, and without Cameron's knowledge, Peter is actually doing the same thing for the same reason.

"Oh, this is Cameron," Diana says, taking Cameron's arm and snapping them from their staring contest. "He's a Scorpio."

"A *what?*" Peter asks incredulously.

Cameron grins, seemingly pleased with Peter's less-than-enthusiastic reaction. "We're both water signs, at least!"

"No, I got *that*, but, Di, what on earth are you guys doing with a Scorpio *by yourself?*"

Kiara shrugs. "Peter, have you actually *met* a Scorpio?"

"Obviously not," Cameron says, crossing his arms and raising one eyebrow.

"You guys are... sort of similar, actually," Diana says slowly, tilting her head. "Intelligent."

"Check," Kiara says, smiling.

"Dedicated," Diana continues.

"Yes," Kiara replies.

"Sensitive-"

"Okay, I get it," Peter says, cutting her off with a little chuckle. He politely sticks out his hand towards Cameron. "It's nice to meet you."

Cameron hesitates but takes Peter's hand in his and shakes it. "Yeah. You too."

"He's a Best Friend now," Kiara states plainly.

Peter eyes the ginger hesitantly, releasing his hand. "...Okay. I'm trusting you guys' judgment on this one."

Cameron smiles at him, patting his forearm. "Good. Anyway, let's give you that explanation."

Peter smiles back at him and then nods to the girls. "I like him already."

Part Eight: The Cancer

Peter

Peter is pushed into a chair as his left ankle is tightly cuffed to the table leg.

Sitting across from him is Maya Monroe, a girl who he's only barely familiar with. He knew her through his best friend Diana, who Peter hadn't seen in... two years, now.

Maya was eighteen, a Gemini Capitol worker, this enigmatic figure that Peter sometimes wondered if he was imagining. But Peter and Maya were privy to a dangerous secret, one they were forced to speak about at these undercover meetings.

Maya smiles at Peter but says nothing as the guard steps away from them. He looks around conspiratorially before lowering his voice to a whisper and addressing Maya.

"Alright, you kids have ten minutes before someone else gets in here, so make it count."

Maya shoots him that dazzling smile. "Thank you. I really appreciate it."

He nods and gives her the tiniest smile in return. "Anything for a friend of Oliver's."

He leaves, and Maya leans back against her chair, the rattling noise of the handcuffs making the hairs on the back of Peter's neck stand up. "Alright, Peter," she says, crossing one leg over the other, her Yellow clothes glaringly bright in this dark room, "have you thought any more about what I told you?"

She was asking as if she had just asked him for the answers to a homework assignment or something, far too nonchalant for any outsider to believe that in their previous *meeting, Maya had shown Peter an old book with the country's biggest secret and revealed to him that he was somehow a part of it.*

"Yeah, I remember," Peter mumbles, "I still don't want you to tell me any more."

Maya leans forward, her hands resting flat on the tabletop. "Peter, I won't. If you want to live in ignorance about what role you play in this, so be it. But these powers are dangerous, Peter. You have no idea what they can do."

Peter shakes his head. Half of him wants her to stop talking and the other half wants her to go on. "Try me."

"Okay, fine. The Gemini power can warp someone's soul, Peter. They can raise the dead. And, combined with the Libra power, they have the ability to fully bring someone back to life, completely fine. And that's just one example."

Peter's chest heaves with a sharp breath, and he forces himself to swallow. "Maya, you're talking about treason. You're talking about endangering everything."

Her green eyes turn pleading, and suddenly, Peter sees so much of Diana in her. "I know it's crazy, but please, Peter, you have to be with me on this. We can't protect Diana if we don't try."

Peter's chest pangs, and he shoves away the familiar ache he feels when he thinks about that young blonde girl. In the back of his mind, he can still hear her shrill screams from that day two years ago.

With a deep breath of resolve, Peter looks up, meeting Maya's gaze. When he speaks, some part of him feels suddenly different.

"Then we'll try."

When Peter was in school, he never would have believed he could have seen people of multiple zodiacs anywhere together. They were taught that others were dangerous. The Cancers were especially sheltered due to their 'emotional' nature, and these water signs were groomed to believe they as a single zodiac sign had to band together to avoid these much more wild, much more complicated signs.

But, sitting in a forest in the pitch dark with a Taurus, an Aries, and *god forbid* a Scorpio, Peter can picture his school teacher having a brain aneurysm. And then, she would have turned right back around and had a heart attack after listening to their story.

"Wow," Peter says after they fill him in. The others are all sitting a safe distance away from him, even Diana, and Peter can't blame them because his two friends haven't seen him in four years and this other dude has just met him.

Diana nods and smiles. "So, are you coming with us? Our next step is finding Maya, so she can get us into the Capitol."

Peter nods half-heartedly, biting his lip in thought. He tries to fight memories of secret meetings to the back of his brain as he looks around at the others, then regards the ginger-haired boy who towers at least a few inches over him and is staring at Peter warily. "Cameron, right?"

He nods. "Yeah?"

Peter continues: "Tell me again about you escaping with the Scorpios."

Cameron eyes him, obviously gauging his threat level to himself and the girls. "Why?"

Kiara nudges Cameron. "You can trust him." She looks at Peter. "Besides, three against one? We can take him, if we have to," she smirks, glancing at Peter reassuringly, "even though we *won't* have to."

Peter chuckles. At least Kiara hasn't really changed. He looks at Cameron, who starts with a reluctant sigh. "Well, what they were doing was wrong. Splitting us off from our rights and resources is unjust, and on top of that, applying extreme violence to keep an otherwise peaceful sector under control is just the Capitol flaunting its power. I needed to get my people out of there, before something even worse happened."

Peter nods slowly, and the group falls silent. After a moment, Diana pipes up. "Why do you ask, Peter?"

Peter jerks his head up to look at her. Her face is framed by the small flames in the fire they've made behind a big magnolia tree, and her big green eyes seem to look right through him. His heart leaps into his throat and he swallows, suddenly nervous to voice the idea that had been swimming in his head since he was fourteen.

"Well," Peter says carefully, "because. If the BOZ is treating one zodiac that way, what's gonna stop them from doing that to all of us? Look at these rules they've made. Look at the people they're harming, and for what? Because a small child or an older woman is a threat to this 'perfect world' they've created? I'll tell you one thing. This 'perfect world' was created through a series of violent acts that have obviously not changed. Diana, did your class learn about those protests a long time ago in school?"

She looks surprised for a moment, then nods. "Yes, we did."

Peter nods, then clarifies for the others. "The Old American government would be violent towards people protesting, because these people supposedly posed a 'threat' to the government. Then, they destroy the world, basically, and now we're living a better, safer future according to the BOZ. Well, looking closely, these attacks on the Scorpios look an awful lot like those attacks, and the BOZ is set up the same way as parts of the Old

American government. There's one person from each zodiac sign, but through the years, they've dwindled."

Kiara nods. "I remember that. They almost pulled the Libra representative because the rep before her lost 'an object of great importance'."

Cameron snaps his fingers, as if remembering something. "And when they cut the Scorpios out, they pulled our rep too."

Diana's eyes widen. "And they told us in school that those representatives were *against* the BOZ. Remember when we were briefed on the 'consequences' of going against the government?"

All of them nod. Then, it's quiet.

Finally, Cameron gasps. "Peter, I know where you're going with this."

Peter smiles and nods. "I'm glad someone gets it."

Diana looks between the two boys. "I'm confused. What does he mean?"

Peter hesitates, trying to gauge Cameron's reaction. Cameron smiles back at him, so Peter tells the girls: "I think we should take down the BOZ."

Kiara sucks in a sharp breath. Diana just laughs. Cameron looks at Peter and shrugs, as if he knew they would react this way.

"Are you kidding?" Kiara asks, eyebrows raised as if waiting for Peter to tell the punchline of this hilarious joke.

He shakes his head, staying quiet. The girls look at Peter, then Kiara's eyes widen. "Oh, my god, you're not joking."

"I'm not," Peter says, "it's a legit thing to think about. I mean, look at us! We're four totally different zodiacs that are sitting peacefully together without ripping each other's throats out like the BOZ thinks that we might."

Diana tilts her head to the side, lost in thought. "Yeah, but it's only four of us. I *really* don't like our odds of storming the Plaza and hoping we're not shot."

Cameron stands. "Sure. But, I know for a fact every Scorpio knows of what I and the others did, and they'd be with us."

Diana shakes her head. "They can't get *out,* Cameron. How could they be with us?"

Peter chimes in. "Maya could definitely convince some Geminis, too." He crosses towards Diana and kneels in front of her. She looks at him under her long lashes, and Peter speaks as gently as he can. "What do you think?"

Diana looks at him for a moment, eyes searching his face. Then, she pulls back, standing and backing towards the forest. "I need a second to think," she says, before turning and running off.

The three who are left look at each other. Cameron nods slowly to himself, then speaks. "I'm gonna go get her before she gets found out," and then he takes off in Diana's direction before Peter can reply.

Peter looks towards Kiara, who shrugs. "Good to see you again," she says sarcastically. Peter smiles at her, and she crosses and gives him another gentle hug. When she speaks, her voice has turned sincere. "We've missed you."

Peter pulls away from her, walking over to the tree and running his hand along the bark. The coarse dirt crunches beneath his feet, and for a moment, that's the only sound as he lets his head empty of thoughts besides the repetition of the pattern his finger was moving. Peter leans back against the tree, facing the border, and Kiara comes over to join him. They say nothing, staring at the glaring blue, until she finally asks:

"How are you feeling?"

"I'm okay," he replies. Peter doesn't continue, and yet it's almost as if Kiara is seeing into his thoughts, for then she says:

"You're thinking about this plan."

Peter nods.

"And Diana," she says, not looking at him.

Peter nods again. "I missed her."

Now it's Kiara's turn to nod. "Yeah. It's been a while."

Peter laughs a little. "You could say that."

Kiara turns to face him. "Can I tell you something about Diana?"

Peter looks over at her out of the corner of his eye. "Sure."

Kiara takes a deep breath, then continues. "I know you two were really close. And I think now that you're here you could be again. But she's not fragile, and she's not that eleven-year-old you left anymore. I've seen her grow in so many ways, and I've only spent a few days with her at this point. I've seen a different Diana than the one we grew up with. And I think maybe you should take a second to see her too."

Peter turns her words over for a moment, thinking about the change that his best friend could have gone through during their time apart. "I think... I think you're right. I've already seen such a difference in her and I've been here for less than three hours."

Kiara smiles. "Right? I think that all of us are underestimating her."

Peter nods. "Except Cameron. They seem to get along well."

She snorts. "Pack up the jealousy, my friend. Trust me, he's not interested."

"Oh, please," Peter says, chuckling a little and shaking his head, "I'm not *jealous*. I'm glad she has him, and vice versa. It reminds me of our old relationship."

Kiara laughs. "Good. I know she still thinks of you as her best friend."

"Me too." He looks over at her, out of the corner of his eye, "I'm glad I found *both* of my best friends."

She cocks her head. "Well," she says sarcastically, dimples shining through her smirk, "let's not jump the gun on this."

Peter laughs, then trails off, staring at the border. Kiara looks at him quizzically, and Peter can hear her saying his name from somewhere far away, her voice faint and fuzzy. Clearer though, closer, he can hear a faint buzzing sound, and he begins to feel almost *enveloped* by the warmth of the translucent, pale light glowing in front of him. He reaches out his hand towards the wall, wanting nothing more than to touch it, go through it, warp it and control it.

"Peter, no! Don't-" Kiara shouts, and it seems to break the trance he's fallen under.

But it's too late.

His fingers skim the surface-

-and the border warps, twisting a small ball of the glowing matter into his hand the size of a baseball. The rest is intact, but he's *holding* it. Nestled in his palm is a swirling, blue mass of sizzling material.

Peter is holding a piece of the wall that separates them from the rest of the world.

Was this what Maya was trying to tell him?

The glow, illuminating all that is near it, blankets a confused face. *Kiara's* face. She stares at the boy, mouth agape, a mixture of fear and bewilderment written on her face clearer than the black and white text in a newly printed novel.

The buzzing noise from before concedes to Kiara's voice, which cuts through the air like a knife.

"Let go," she says, her voice shaking, "Peter, you're gonna get hurt. Let go of it."

Peter quickly flips his hand upside down, shaking it around wildly, but the ball does not fall out of his palm. He whips his hand as fast as he can to the right of them, inadvertently releasing the ball from his hand, hitting a tree about twenty feet from where they stand. Before the two can blink, the ball expands into a protective forcefield against the tree, surrounding it in a ring of the shimmering matter that looks the same as the wall rising up behind them. Peter looks down at his empty hand, and then back at the tree, whose bark has transformed from scraggly brown to electric blue.

"Woah," Kiara says, her voice no higher than a whisper. They move cautiously towards the tree, the dirt crunching under their feet the only sound, and pause a few inches away. Sure enough, the small border goes all the way around the trunk, and the tree is surrounded by a pillar of the glowing forcefield.

"Is it... protecting the tree?" Peter asks.

Kiara shrugs. "I dunno. You can touch it. Throw something at it, or punch it, I guess."

So, Peter bends down and picks up a rock lying close to his foot. He rolls it once, twice, between his fingers, then looks at the tree, taking a deep breath. He hurls it as hard as he can towards the shield, and it hits the material before rocketing back at him, barely giving him enough time to leap out of the way before it flings past where he had previously been standing. Peter shakily stands up and brushes himself off, then chooses his second option and drives his fist as hard as he can into the wall. It slams against the shield, and he grunts as he gradually shoves his hand through. As his fist finally sinks through the last of the material, Peter grins triumphantly at Kiara, moving to pull his hand out. It won't budge, and he struggles for a moment until she says:

"What is the issue with you?"

He pulls again, harder this time. Still no movement. "My hand is stuck."

"Well, just suck the stuff back into a ball or something," she says, crossing her arms over her chest and cocking her head as she watches him struggle.

Peter sighs in exasperation, turning to look at her and using his free hand to motion to his stuck one. "Do you think I know how to do that?"

"I don't know, Peter! Just try!" she fires right back, her hands flying up in frustration.

So he does, craning his fingers upwards and flexing them towards the border, back in his direction. Slowly but surely, the matter pulls itself back into a compact ball, resting itself comfortably into the center of his palm as if it had fit there his whole life. Peter looks at Kiara, amber eyes wide, and she smirks, nodding her head and letting her lips stretch into a grin.

"Nice, man. Imagine what we could do with some training."

"Oh, so I'm a weapon now?" he replies, raising one eyebrow.

Kiara huffs in response. "Peter, don't do that. Just think. You can warp the borders. Did you know Cameron can drop them, too? You two are a force of nature."

He blinks at her. "What do you mean, he can 'drop them'?"

She sucks her lips in between her teeth and her mouth forms a straight line. "Story for another day."

Peter nods, pondering her mysterious tone for a moment. "I guess you're right. We should tell them, huh?"

Kiara nods, right as Cameron and Diana walk back into the campsite. They stop short when they see Peter holding the ball. Peter watches as Diana's green eyes grow in shock, and he glances at Cameron to see the worry lines creasing his forehead.

"Oh, my god, what the hell?" Diana asks, backing up and promptly colliding with Cameron's chest. He grabs her arms to halt her, but he too looks similarly petrified. "Peter, what are you doing?" Cameron asks, his words curling up at the end.

Peter holds up his hand with a smile, causing the two of them to scurry further backwards, stumbling over each other's feet and ankles. It's only then does Peter realize he's aiming at them, and he closes his fist, swallowing the ball so it diminishes into a glowing light that creeps through his fingers and makes his hand almost seem to glow.

"I can warp the borders. And I can throw them, too."

Diana steps forward, and Peter can see her swallow. "Show us."

So, he opens his hand, revealing the ball. He turns back towards the tree from before, and he rears his hand back to throw-

"Wait!" Kiara interrupts. Peter startles, and the ball disappears from his palm in a quick flash of white light, gone with a *hiss*.

"What?" Peter asks, slightly annoyed, studying the lines on his palm. "I lost it."

She shrugs, unconcerned. "Grab a new one. You've done it before, you can do it again. I interrupted because I think you should shoot at me."

Peter, from where he had moved towards the wall once more, halts in his tracks, and then turns slowly to face her. "Are you joking?"

She shakes her head. "Nope. You didn't incinerate the tree, so I figure you won't char me, either."

He nods slowly, mulling it over, then shrugs. "Okay. Sure."

"Wait, guys," Cameron says, stepping forward to grab the attention of the others. Peter can't help but notice his strangely long eyelashes. "These powers aren't something to play around with. Trust me when I tell you that reining them in is way harder than you think. Someone could get hurt."

Peter pauses and nods, turning to Kiara. "He's right, Ki. Maybe I shouldn't."

Kiara shrugs. "It's fine. Chances are we're not gonna make it through this coup anyway, so why not kickstart the danger?"

From a ways away, Cameron shakes his head. "They've gone mad." Diana nods, eyes still wide as dinner plates.

Peter reaches toward the border and grabs a fistful out of it, easy as that. He can almost *hear* Diana's sharp intake of breath. He turns towards Kiara, who's moved about thirty yards away. Peter raises his eyebrows, silently asking if she's sure. She reads his mind for the second time today and nods, spreading her arms wide, inviting. Peter pulls his arm back, aiming carefully. Diana covers her eyes, and Cameron's eyes widen, transfixed on the scene playing out in front of him. Peter throws the ball in Kiara's direction, and when it makes contact with her stomach, it splits out into a column that shoots up, arcing in a dome over her head to create a protective tube around her.

Diana uncovers her eyes, and her jaw drops when she sees Kiara perfectly intact and still moving inside the shield, which is about three feet wide in diameter.

Peter races towards her, stopping about three feet away. "Are you okay?" He asks.

He can see her nod. "Yep. And I can hear you loud and clear," she turns towards Cameron and Diana, who have moved closer, marveling at this strange new power, "Cam, get me out?"

Cameron nods and complies, resting his hand against the tube. It disintegrates into the air as quickly as it formed, and Kiara steps out, smiling. Peter's eyes go wide at Cameron's power, and his heart picks up at the idea of this kind of magic really existing.

"Woah," Diana says. "Two superheroes."

Cameron and Peter roll their eyes simultaneously, and then catch each other's gaze and share a smile. Diana turns to Kiara, and Kiara faces Diana. "We should train them *together*!" both girls shriek.

Peter and Cameron don't have time to protest, so they spend the next few hours training, with Peter throwing shields around the girls and Cameron racing to drop them. Kiara is their tester, since Diana proclaimed she'd rather be anywhere else than enveloped by the border, and so she times them instead, seeing how quickly they can work as a team to trap Kiara and then free her, while also ensuring the group's solitude every so often. After a while, Cameron and Peter slump against the trees, sitting on the ground and panting. Diana comes up to the two and claps her hands together.

"Okay. Here's what we know. Your best time was sixteen seconds. Peter, you need to work on aiming faster, and Cameron, try to get more comfortable pinpointing the weakest spot that will cause the border to drop the fastest." The boys both nod, and she continues, "Also, in a fighting situation, this is good to trap guards who we can't hold off, since they can't touch it without getting burned. Peter, we should try to see how little of a ball you actually need to make a shield, since we won't have access to much of the borders if we're fighting in the Plaza," she leans over them, grinning at their tired faces. "You guys are too cute. Good job today. Get some rest and we'll work on more logistics tomorrow." She and Kiara head towards the fire pit, making another small fire and pulling out water and snacks, lost in conversation with each other.

Peter turns to Cameron. "Did she just call us 'cute?'"

Cameron laughs. "Yes. Yes, she did." He gets to his feet, stretching his arms over his head. He looks down at Peter and offers him his hand. Peter takes it, and Cameron pulls him up. Peter's sore legs wobble, off balance a little, and Cameron grabs his elbows, steadying him. They look at each other for a moment, and Cameron smirks a little before dropping his hold on Peter's arms and turning to walk back toward the girls. Peter shakes his head, letting out a shaky breath. He walks over to the rest of the group, settling down in between the girls and across from Cameron, who catches Peter's eye and smiles, and Peter grins back, the two of them staying that way until Diana clears her throat.

"Peter? What do you think?"

Peter shakes his head and turns to her. "Hm?"

Diana eyes him, then repeats her question. "I *said,* one of us should take watch while the others sleep."

"Or two," Kiara says, "one person can't fend off a group of guards while the other three are rubbing sleep from their eyes."

Diana nods. "It's settled then. You boys will take the first watch. Wake Kiara and me up when the moon is starting to go west."

They head off towards the magnolia tree, whispering amongst themselves about the events of the day.

"Um, I don't think it's settled- okay," Cameron argues, quickly realizing it's a lost cause.

Peter scoots closer to the fire, his back to the girls and facing out at the openness of the forest. Cameron settles across from him, and Peter notices his back is angled so he can turn quickly if he has to. He wonders if Cameron had to protect himself like that as a child. They sit in silence for a few moments, until Cameron speaks.

"So, powers. How does it feel?"

Peter sighs. "It's fine. A lot more pressure than I was expecting."

"Well, this whole *'vive la France'* thing was your idea. There would've been a lot of pressure on you no matter what."

Peter grins. "Thanks?"

"You're very welcome," Cameron says without missing a beat.

It's quiet again, and Peter can hear Diana sleeping soundly, her breathing audible, but light, as if she's someplace far from here. He turns his head instinctively towards her, and Cameron notices.

"What do you think?"

"About?" Peter answers, turning back to face him.

"I dunno. How do you feel?"

Peter drags his finger in the dirt. "I've gotten that question a lot today."

"Well, you must feel something. Unless you're a superhero *and* a robot."

Peter studies the other boy for a second. "Are you always like this?"

"Like what?" Cameron asks, a small smile dancing across his face.

"Like..." Peter trails off, and Cameron fills the silence instantly, as if his brain has synced with Peter's.

"Rendered you speechless, I have."

Peter rolls his eyes playfully, then points at Cameron. "Like that. Joking. Playful."

"It's the best defense mechanism," Cameron says, smiling at first but then dropping his eyes towards his feet.

"What do you mean?" Peter asks, worried about what he might've churned up.

"I... lost my sister and my mother recently. I lost my home. I lost my people, and I lost my rights as a Scorpio. I've lost a lot, and it happened because I let my guard down. So, from now on it stays up, and people stay out."

"That's a sad way to live."

"Well," he says, meeting Peter's eyes, "our world is a sad place."

Peter breathes deep, reveling in the silence, but Cameron speaks again. "Makes you wonder how we'll be remembered, right? Now... nowadays we're born to be forgotten. Born to work, and comply, and suffer, until the only thing left to do is die, I guess. But if I can do something-" he glances at Peter and shoots him a lopsided smile, "-if *we* can do something to be remembered, maybe other kids after us can have a chance. Maybe even *we* could have a chance."

Peter studies him for a moment, and opens his mouth to speak, to say anything at all. Before he can though, Cameron blurts out a question that quiets Peter's thoughts for a fleeting moment.

"Do you have feelings for her?" Cameron asks. For the first time all night, he doesn't look at Peter, instead staring over his shoulder at Diana. He sounds less like the troubled, diplomatic boy who just spoke of remembrance and rather like a normal teenager.

Peter takes a deep breath, puffing his cheeks and blowing the air out slowly. "I... I don't know."

"You've said that a lot. 'I don't know'."

"Well, I don't."

"Well, you must know something, Peter."

"I haven't seen her in four years."

"So, I'll take that as a 'no', then?"

"It's an 'I don't know'."

"That's not an answer."

"Well, what do you want me to say?" Peter asks, his voice rising. "I don't even know you!"

Cameron looks taken aback for a second, then snarls back at Peter, "You're right. And here I was trying to connect with you since I thought we had a few things in common. But I guess you're not interested in 'connection' right now," he says the word 'connection' with air quotes, as if mocking him.

Peter sighs. "I'm sorry. I shouldn't have snapped at you."

"You're *sorry*?"

Peter looks at him. "There's that defense mechanism again."

Cameron holds up his hands in an act of surrender. "We all have one."

"Really? I don't."

"You do, actually."

"*Right.* You've known me for four hours."

"Your point?"

Peter is stunned silent for a second. Who does this guy think he is? "Fine. Then what is it?"

Cameron smirks. "You rub your thumb across your index finger when you're nervous. So far it's happened when you first saw Di, then when you aimed at us with the ball, then when we were practicing, every time before you aimed at Kiara. And a few minutes ago, when Diana said we'd stay up together."

Peter flushes, then stares at his hands like they've betrayed him. Peter looks back at Cameron, and he's still smirking, knowing he's caught Peter in a corner. There's no point in playing cat-and-mouse with him any longer.

"Okay. You got me."

Cameron crosses his arms. "I know."

It's quiet for a moment, and then Peter speaks. "To answer your question, I'm pretty sure I don't have feelings for her, at least... not right now. I don't know her anymore. She's changed. It's like meeting and getting to know a whole new person. I mean, I know she's still the old Diana, but four years is a long time." He looks up at the dark sky. "And when we were little, we were never apart. She spent more time with me than she did with her own sister. And being reunited feels so, so good, but there's a tension between us that will only go away in time," Peter swallows hard and turns his head to face Cameron, noticing he's been staring at Peter the whole time.

Cameron studies Peter silently, and his eyes trace Peter's face so searchingly he blushes again. "You feel lost, don't you?" Cameron asks finally.

Peter nods before he can stop himself. "I do. I feel like I'm... alone, even though my two closest old friends are here and I have a new... thing to focus on," he waves his hand as a gesture to his powers, "I feel like no one understands what I've been through since we got Split, and no one has bothered to ask. No one else knows me anymore."

Cameron nods slowly, standing up and crossing in front of Peter. He sits down next to the other boy, not speaking, but close enough for Peter to understand. The space Cameron fills makes him feel a little less alone, a little more comfortable. He's trying to tell Peter he's going to be okay, and surprisingly enough, Peter gets the message.

They sit quietly, avoiding each other's eyes. It's easier that way, so they don't have to talk. Peter watches Cameron's eyes trace his arm and land on his hands.

"Stop it."

Peter raises one eyebrow and turns to look at Cameron. "Sorry?"

Cameron quickly lays a hand over Peter's clasped fingers. "Stop moving your thumb."

"I'm doing it again?" Peter pulls his hands out from under Cameron's, fingers now stilled completely.

"Yes. Relax."

"Okay," Peter says instantaneously.

Silence follows again. But this time, Peter is conscious of his still hands. After another minute, Cameron rises and walks over to the girls, shaking them gently to wake them up.

Peter, left alone, watches Cameron and wonders how he said so much with so few words.

Part Nine: The Scorpio

Cameron

"Perfect! Just like that!" Diana shouts from across the clearing to Cameron. Kiara is whispering something in her ear.

He's standing next to Peter, who's holding a ball of the border material. They'd been training all morning, and the girls were in yesterday's clothes and staring at them like they were their test subjects in a lab.

"I don't get it," Peter whispers, turning to face Cameron. Their forearms brush and Peter's eyes flick downwards towards the contact.

Cameron's eyes widen at the blush that's become barely visible at the base of Peter's neck. "Um... me either."

Both boys promptly turn away from each other.

"Okay, wait," Kiara interrupts, "I want to try something."

"What?" Diana asks, backing up a little further on the grass, as if nervous.

Kiara begins to walk towards the boys, who back up simultaneously. "Well, you know how there are some zodiacs that are compatible with one another?" She looks between Peter and Cameron, who both shake their heads even though they know quite well what she's talking about.

"Yes?" Diana responds, crossing her arms and answering for the boys.

Kiara reaches the boys and points to a tree next to them. "Peter, if you would," she commands, ignoring Diana.

Peter, without breaking eye contact with her, releases the ball in the direction of the tree. Cameron is stunned at his confidence, considering he found out his power *yesterday*. Something about the way he commands the power so well lights something up in Cameron, which he fights to ignore. The forcefield goes up around the tree, and Kiara nods with satisfaction.

"Okay. Now Peter, go stand next to that shield. Put your palm up against it, but *don't* reel it back into your hand."

Peter looks confused. "So... just hold my hand there?"

Kiara nods. "Yeah. Trust me," she turns to Cameron, "you can drop it. Peter, when he does, *then* channel the energy back into your hand. But only when it starts to drop away."

Cameron nods slowly. "Okay... what's the end goal here?"

Kiara crosses back to Diana, talking as she walks. "Well, I'm thinking that if the two of you keep the other person in mind while you try your powers, you'll be able to sync them together, because your signs are compatible with one another. So, for example, Peter being nearby when Cameron drops the border will make Peter able to summon it from wherever he's standing, as long as he keeps Cameron's ability in his mind as well."

Both boys nod in understanding, and Peter grins from where he's standing by the wall. "That's *genius.*"

"Just try it," Kiara says, shaking her head at the compliment.

Cameron kneels at the base of the wall, looking up at Peter, who's standing over him. He smiles up at him. "Ready?"

"Ready," Peter responds with a joking smirk. "Just remember to think of me."

Cameron tilts his head sarcastically. "Might be tricky. You're pretty forgettable."

Before Peter can respond, Cameron conjures up the stark image of Peter firing at the tree and places his hand at the base of the wall. He feels the material almost liquidate under his fingers, before it disappears. When he looks back up, Peter is staring down at his hand, hazel eyes wide with shock.

Cameron rises to his feet and grabs Peter's wrist, tugging his hand closer to get a better look. He can hear the girls laughing from further away, and he turns to look over at them.

Kiara and Diana are cheering like little kids, hugging each other and jumping around so that they almost fall over. Cameron looks back down at Peter.

"It worked," he whispers.

Peter nods, still staring at the material that he summoned back into his hand. He looks up at Cameron, studying his eyes, and gently pulls his wrist from his grip. Without breaking eye contact, he backs up a few steps and releases the ball at the tree. "Do it again," he whispers back.

Cameron grins at his command, biting his lip. "Yes, sir."

"Twenty!" Kiara hollers.

"*God,*" Peter whispers, bending over with his hands on his knees and looking up at Cameron with a tired smile, "that's hard."

Cameron nods from his seat on the ground, up against the tree. "Yup."

"Okay," Diana says, approaching the two, "that really works, you guys. But it seems we have a problem." Peter collapses to a sitting position next to her, and she points at him like she was waiting for it to happen. "That. It seems the further away you get, the more tired your powers become."

"The more tired *we* become," Peter huffs.

"Right," Diana confirms, "so I have a solution."

"Just be done for today?" Cameron asks, his voice sounding a lot more like begging than he wanted it to.

"No, instead, I want to-"

Peter cuts her off with a gentle look. "Di, come on. We've been going at this for what, five hours?"

Cameron nods, relieved that Peter said something. "Yeah. We just need a break."

Diana bites her lip, considering. "Okay, fine. We'll be done for now."

Cameron leaps to his feet and wraps her in a hug. "*Thank* you, Di. You're the best."

She laughs. "You're welcome. I don't want you to hurt yourselves on my account."

Just then, Cameron feels something wet hit his nose, and he looks up to see a cloudy sky, a stark contrast to the normal blue projected upon them.

"No," Diana groans. "We have no shelter." Cameron watches as she shifts almost naturally into delegation mode. "Let's get under this tree, you guys."

Kiara, Diana, and Cameron turn to start picking up their belongings, but Kiara pauses as she notices Peter, face turned up towards the sky, gentle smile playing across his lips. "Peter, come on. You're gonna get soaked."

Peter opens his eyes as he turns to look at her. His Gray shirt is speckled with dark spots from the precipitation, and he shrugs one shoulder nonchalantly. "Nah. Rain never lasts long here. So why not enjoy it?"

Everyone pauses where they are, and then Kiara nods slowly. "Rains all the time where I'm from."

"Never in Sector Seven," Diana mumbles.

"Just turns to snow, for me," Cameron says.

All four look at one another. Cameron wrings his fingers together, feeling confused and more than a little awkward. How is it possible that four people could already be so close, but so different? It just didn't feel... normal.

But then again, *normal* usually meant *alone*.

Finally, Peter breaks the silence by standing up as the rain begins to come down a little harder. He reaches for Kiara, grabbing both her hands. "Come here, Ki."

She laughs a little, allowing him to tug her out from under the tree canopy and into the shower with little resistance. "What are you doing?"

He pulls her to the center of the clearing and spins her under his arm, causing her to shriek and dissolve into giggles. "Dancing! Come on, if it rains where you're from, you must've danced in it before."

She shakes her head, allowing him to pull her into a hug as they sway back and forth. "Nobody dances in the rain, you weirdo."

He picks her up and spins her around, all smiles that set Cameron's heartbeat into overdrive. "We do now."

As Cameron watches, he gets an idea, turning to Diana and holding out his hand. "No rain, huh?"

She looks down at his extended invitation, then back up at him with a mischievous grin. "No rain."

He pulls her into the shower as well, twirling her and swaying back and forth. For the first time in a while, Cameron just feels *happy,* and he glances over to see his other two friends grinning just as wide as he was.

"Di!" Kiara shouts. Diana turns to look at her, and Kiara beckons her over. "Remember our handshake from school?"

As they begin to execute a complex handshake, Peter crosses to Cameron, pausing just close enough so their shirt sleeves touch. Cameron glances at him out of the corner of his eye, and the other boy is still smiling towards the clouds. "This was a good idea."

Peter shrugs, now watching the girls. "I just figured everyone could use a little pick-me-up."

"You were right." They stand in silence for a second. Finally, Cameron speaks. "But it was a bold choice to choose dancing."

Peter looks over at him, confused. "Why?"

Cameron begins to shimmy his hips in a chaotic back-and-forth movement, and Peter snorts with laughter. Cameron throws his arms up as well, performing some ridiculous rain dance as he twirls in a circle. "Because I'm a *really* good dancer, and none of you could match my skill."

Peter nods, covering his mouth with one hand, shoulders shaking with laughter. "*Right,*" he says sarcastically, "we could never compete."

Cameron, in a bold and very much not thought out decision, reaches out and grabs his hand, pulling him a little closer. Peter smiles softly at him, and Cameron swears he could feel Peter squeeze his fingers a little tighter. Cameron grins and motions around them, putting a hand out to catch the rain. "Show me your moves, superhero."

The next day, Cameron is woken up by the girls early in the morning. Everyone is already awake, and Cameron can only recall bits and pieces of the past few days. Diana running off, Peter discovering his powers, hours of training, Peter and Cameron staying watch...

Cameron sits up and notices the girls are still standing over him, with Peter hovering a safe distance away. Cameron's surroundings are familiar, the thick trunks of the magnolia trees and rough dirt make up his bed, and the shining border makes for one hell of a nightlight.

"Cameron?" Kiara asks.

"Uh-huh?" he mumbles, rubbing his eyes.

Diana and Kiara share a look, and Diana steps forward to address Cameron, crouching in front of him.

"We're gonna head out. We have to meet Maya at the Capitol as soon as possible."

Cameron stares at her for a second. "Already? But Peter and I..."

"Have more training to do, yeah. Well, we're hoping we can find out more about your... *conditions* in the Capitol records to help us train you better."

Cameron nods. "Okay. Are we ready?"

All three nod.

"Okay," Cameron says again. "Jeez, why did you let me sleep so late?"

Peter pipes up from behind the girls. "Ki said something about... morning anger?"

Cameron's head whips around to face Kiara. "She said *what*?"

"Nothing!" Kiara says, holding out a hand to help him up.

Cameron grumbles half-convincingly. "Are we packed, at least?"

A duffel bag nails him in the stomach.

"Ow!" Cameron shouts, at the same time Diana hollers, "Sorry!"

Cameron laughs and nods, smiling briefly at Peter before turning to the girls. "Let's go, then."

So they head out, making good time trudging through the thick forest. They're still dressed in Gray, so they're probably safe if anyone comes across them, but Cameron can't say the same for their feet and legs as they trek through fallen branches, large logs, and jagged rocks. The dirt under their feet is thick and somewhat swampy, and Cameron cringes as his shoe squelches through the muck.

They walk in a steady formation: Diana at the front, tracing her finger over her non-fraudulent map and occasionally looking around, Peter and Kiara on either side a few steps back from her, and Cameron bringing up the rear. Cameron looks around their surroundings, but his eyes wander to Peter.

He never noticed that Peter's shoulders were that muscular. Or that his hair is longer in the front than it is in the back. Or that his-

"Ouch," Cameron groans as he lands face-first on the ground. The group turns around and rushes over to him, crouching by Cameron's side as he helps himself into a sitting position.

"What happened?" Peter asks.

Cameron clears his throat awkwardly as he takes in Peter's worried, *adorable* expression. "I... don't know?"

Kiara motions to a log, a scraggly one with a long stick-like limb protruding from the side of it. Sure enough, a few pieces of string hanging off the sharp branch prove her silent theory correct.

Diana gasps and turns away, and Cameron looks down to find a large gash running down his ankle. It's sloughing blood, and it's at least two inches long. Cameron grits his teeth. "Damn."

Peter crouches and skims his fingertips lightly over the surrounding skin. He pushes a little too hard, and Cameron jerks his leg away. Peter looks up at him apologetically. "I'm sorry!" he says, frantically.

Cameron can't help but smile a little. "It's okay," he whispers.

Peter gets back to work. "Di. Come here for a second."

She comes over cautiously, crouching next to him. Peter motions to Kiara, pointing towards her bag. She hands the duffel to him, and he grabs the utility knife out of the bottom before handing the bag back to her. Peter places a hand on Diana's shoulder, turning her to face him. Something inside Cameron pangs with jealousy as he watches their close contact, and he can't help but feel guilty about it.

"Di, do you mind if I steal the hood of your sweatshirt?" Diana looks confused, so Peter elaborates. "Like, can I cut it off and use it as a bandage for his ankle?"

"Oh," Diana says, "sure."

So, she turns around, leaning her back into Peter's chest. He carefully cuts through the fabric of her shirt, detaching the hood from the rest of the sweatshirt. When he's done, he turns back to Cameron. Diana stands and scuttles back over to Kiara, away from the bloodshed happening all over Cameron's ankle.

"Okay," Peter says, "Ki, grab some water, will you?" So, Kiara grabs her water bottle from the bag and hands it to him, and Peter takes it wordlessly, beginning to unlace Cameron's shoe.

"What are you doing?" Cameron asks.

"Taking off your shoes and socks before they're bled through."

He can't argue with that, so Cameron stays quiet. He watches Peter work, pulling off Cameron's shoe and sock and rolling up his pant leg a little more. Peter pours some water into the cap of the bottle, and trickles it onto the wound. After some blood is cleared away, he grimaces.

"Uh oh. What?" Cameron asks.

"It's pretty deep, and it tore a lot of skin. I might need to cut some of the torn part off to keep it from infecting, since we don't have antiseptic."

"Ugh. Okay," Cameron says.

Peter looks at him, all seriousness. "It'll hurt."

"I know."

He nods, leaning closer to Cameron's ankle and taking his knife back out. "Don't move."

"Aye aye, captain."

So, Cameron grits his teeth as Peter cuts the first piece of skin off the wound. It's not dead skin yet, so Cameron can still feel it when it gets cut. It takes a total of three minutes, and Cameron is breathing heavily by the time he's done. It's almost like electrical wires have been run up his leg, and Cameron moves his jaw around to unclench it as he tries to catch his breath.

Peter looks up at Cameron, resting the knife on the ground and placing a gentle hand above the cut, which does look slightly better without all of the torn skin. "You alright?"

Cameron nods. "Yup."

"Okay. I'm gonna clean it and wrap it now. This might hurt, but it's only me applying pressure to the top of your wound so it slows the bleeding."

Cameron nods, and Peter dumps a little more water on the wound. Cameron can see it clearly now, and it really is deep. It's torn his pant leg a bit, and gotten through a good few layers of skin. Peter takes the fabric piece, tearing it into rectangular strips and wrapping it around the cut. Quickly, blood starts dotting the light fabric.

"Shit," Peter says. He waves a hand at Kiara, and she rushes over, turning around and letting him cut her shirt too. Peter continues wrapping the wound and tucking the fabric into itself to keep it in place, until Cameron has a thick homemade bandage that's stopping the bleeding, at least for now. Peter rubs his thumb over the bandage, and then gently rolls Cameron's pant leg back down.

Diana pipes up from where she's watching with Kiara. "Peter, where did you learn how to do that?"

Peter smiles, not looking at her and instead continuing to inspect and correct his work. "I took a class when I got shipped to my sector about four years ago. It was mandatory, since this sector has that disease."

"What kind of disease is it?" Diana asks.

Peter shrugs. "I'm not sure. It's killed a lot of Cancers. That's the good thing about the wall, I guess, because it keeps the disease from spreading."

The others all nod, and Kiara speaks after a moment. "Can you stand?"

Cameron opens his mouth to reassure her, but then he realizes he doesn't know the answer to her question. Cameron starts to stand up, but as soon as he puts weight on his ankle, he nearly topples over. He sticks his arms out to steady himself, willing his tree-pose to withstand the injury.

"So, that puts a damper on things," Diana says, "how will we continue? A wound of that size is going to need a little while to heal."

Kiara looks towards the two boys, raising an eyebrow. She opens her mouth, but Cameron quickly cuts her off, reading her thoughts clearly on her face. "Nope. No way. I'm not making him carry me the rest of the way."

"Well, would you rather Di or I try it?"

That shuts Cameron up really fast, and Diana nods, addressing the boys. "She's right, guys. It's still like a day's journey on foot back to the station, and we can keep resting, since we're really on no schedule. Besides, we need to work out what we're gonna do with this whole coup thing."

Peter appraises Cameron carefully. "I can try, if you're okay with it."

Cameron purses his lips, considering his options. After a minute, he swivels his finger around and Peter turns with his back to Cameron's chest. Cameron hops towards him on his good foot, whispering in his ear: "Sorry about this."

Peter chuckles lightly. "It's not your fault, it's that log's."

"Very true."

So, Peter crouches a bit, holding his arms backwards and putting his hands on the inside of Cameron's legs. The girls cross over to them, Diana helping Cameron up and Kiara keeping Peter steady until Cameron is situated on his back. Peter holds his legs, and the girls slowly let go, allowing Peter to successfully stand on his own while perching Cameron on his back.

"Got it?" Peter asks Cameron.

"Yes sir," Cameron replies, "nice view from up here."

"Nicer view from down here. You two look like one big giant," Kiara says, choking back a laugh.

"You're a jerk," Cameron tells her.

"And you're a cripple. Watch yourself before I make you walk."

Cameron rolls his eyes, and they start off again.

"Can we slow down?" Peter asks. He's gasping for breath now, and he has to stop to adjust his and Cameron's little predicament more often than before. They still look like a walking zodiac demon of sorts, dressed all in Gray with Cameron's bright hair shining above Peter's dark curls.

The girls stop and turn around, coming over to help Peter lower Cameron to the ground and prop him against a tree. The sun is setting, and the group hasn't gotten out of the woods yet, quite literally. The trees have started to thin, though, leaving them in a more vulnerable position. Cameron watches Diana analyze their surroundings, her eyes moving around to scan their perimeter. Her eyebrow quirks up as she listens around, and after a moment, she turns towards the others triumphantly. Cameron can practically see the gears turning, and he wonders what dangers she's thinking about that the others aren't.

"I think we're good here for a bit. We shouldn't sleep, in case someone finds us, but we can make plans and rest for a while," she says, the rest of them looking on like students to their teacher. She eyes the other three, raising her eyebrows as if she's really surprised that they have no idea what to do. "*Okay*, fine. Peter?"

He looks up at her quickly. He wasn't paying attention and she knows it. "Yeah?"

"Look at our map and try to estimate how much longer this trip to the Plaza is going to take. Then go through our food and water and see how long we can last."

He nods rapidly. "Okay." He reaches for the bags and the map and engrosses himself in the task. Cameron watches his hazel eyes scan the paper and swallows, forcing himself to look away.

Diana chooses her next victim. "Kiara."

"Present," she says flatly, getting a snort out of Cameron and a glare from Diana.

"Can you help me work out where and when we're going to meet Maya?"

Kiara nods and turns to Cameron, waiting for the command Diana is going to dish out.

"Cameron."

"Yes, ma'am."

"You have some experience with these types of revolts. Can you make us a list of people, places, and things that will help gain a crowd and spread our message?"

Cameron blinks slowly. "That's kind of an important job."

Diana nods. "Well, you're the best person for it."

Cameron smiles, feeling bolstered by her tone. "Okay. I can do it."

Diana smirks confidently. "I know."

And so, they get to work, totally engrossed in their tasks. The space they chose fills with silence, and the only sounds are the quiet rustling of leaves and the crunching of coarse dirt. They're spread over a good area that's far enough away from each other to get things done, but also close to each other in case of an emergency. Kiara and Diana are to the left of Cameron, tucked in an open space and drawing pictures, presumably of the Plaza, in the dirt. Peter is on Cameron's right, about ten feet away, rifling through their bags with vigor. Cameron smiles and takes in the sight, feeling appreciative for the people he somehow just seemed to know.

Cameron breathes out heavily. "Okay," he says to himself, turning to Peter, "is there a pencil and paper in there?"

Peter looks through the bag and then pulls a pencil out. "No paper," he remarks.

"No problem. Toss that over here."

So he does, hucking the pencil in a wide arc over his head in Cameron's direction, and it sails towards Cameron and *whaps* him on the head. Cameron blinks, clearing his vision, and picks it up, looking over to Peter, who is staring back at him with a horrified expression.

"OhmygodI'msosorry," he says, speaking so fast his apology sounds like one big word. Cameron laughs at him, shaking his head and grinning, running his hand over the little achy spot on his head.

"Hey, it's all good. No lasting concussion thus far."

Peter smiles sheepishly and nods, turning back to his job. Cameron does too, tapping the pencil on his leg and looking around for a writing medium. He leans his head back against the tree, closing his eyes to think. He reaches up to scratch his head where the bark scraped his skull, and that's when it hits him. He turns and presses his hand along the dry bark and fits his fingers into a crack, pulling downwards and peeling the bark with his fingers until it breaks off into a piece about the length of a shoe and the width of his hand. Cameron flips it over to the smooth side on the back, the side that sits against the trunk of the tree, and grins triumphantly to himself. He starts to write, drawing two lines that split the bark into three equal sections. One is for 'People', another 'Places', and the last 'Things'. Cameron fills the first one quickly, writing 'Maya's Geminis', 'Scorpios', and 'Libras?' with a question mark since he's never *actually* met a Libra and has trouble thinking they'd believe them. The second box gets the words 'Plaza' and 'Capitol', with Capitol going above Plaza, since Cameron assumes they're going there first. The final box gets 'Trackers', 'Flyers', and 'Word-Of-Mouth'.

Cameron reviews his list once more, then sits and waits for the rest of his team.

Part Ten: The Taurus

Diana

"Run me through that one more time?" Diana asks Kiara.

Kiara nods, pointing to a sketch she made in the dirt with her finger. "Sure. So basically, I think that we skip over the Plaza and go straight to the Capitol. When we're there, we should find the Tracker Controls and pull the plug completely and shut it all down. Then, you hack the system and send the citizens a message about the revolt. Once that's done and we're certain it's been delivered, we get the hell out of there, cover our tracks and wait for the people to start showing up."

Diana nods slowly. "That makes sense. I'd need to see the controls to hack it though. I've never worked on a whole system before."

breathing shakily and tears are threatening to burst from her eyes, and she doesn't know where this onslaught of emotion came from. Kiara looks up from their drawings and gasps.

"What's wrong?" she asks Diana. She sounds scared. "Are you hurt?"

"No. No, I'm not hurt," Diana manages.

"Then what's going on?"

Diana looks at her through wet eyelashes. "I don't *know*. I feel like... this is all a lot."

Kiara stares at her. "Because it is."

"Well yeah," Diana sniffs, "but I mean a lot for me. And you guys, obviously, but I've never done something this big before and I don't want to mess it up. I don't know what my strengths are, but I look around at the rest of you and I see 'Kiara, the kickass warrior Aries who won't hesitate to knock people out', and don't forget the two magical teenage boys over there who have powers literally no one has heard of before. And what am I? 'Diana, the girl who can hack a Tracker to send one text'?" She looks at her friend, truly scared for the first time. "If we mess up, we die. I... I don't want that, as stupid as it sounds."

Kiara takes a deep breath and thinks to herself. "Well, I think that over the past couple days, you've been more in touch with this group than anyone, Diana. I think you're our leader, and you're damn good at telling your team what to do. I've seen you get smarter, and stronger, and become a better friend than I could ever ask for, or even deserve."

Diana studies her for a moment. "Really?" she asks, her voice sounding smaller than she anticipated.

Kiara nods. "Yes! You need to open your eyes and realize your own awesomeness."

Diana laughs, sighing. "I'm gonna hang that on my wall."

"Go ahead. I give you permission."

Diana holds out her arms and Kiara scooches into the hug. "I love you, Di."

"I love you, too. And thank you."

Kiara pulls back and smiles. "For what?"

After a little while, the girls notice that Cameron is starting to doze, so they join him and wave Peter over. Peter leans down and shakes Cameron awake, then plops down next to him. Kiara and Diana sit across from them, and Diana takes a deep breath before launching into the spiel.

"Okay, Peter first. What did you find?"

He opens their duffel. "We probably have enough food for three days, but our water is dwindling badly. I'd give us a full day at most."

Their faces fall. "That's sucky," Cameron says.

"Majorly," Kiara answers.

"Okay," Diana says, trying to diffuse the disappointment. "Cam?"

Cameron hands over his list. "That's everything I came up with."

Diana turns it over in her hands. "And it's on bark because..."

"Because we had no paper and it was dry enough to write on."

Peter looks at Cameron out of the corner of his eye and whispers: "Smart."

Diana nods and smiles. "Wicked smart. Good job, Cameron."

"Thanks," Cameron says, rubbing the back of his neck with a sheepish smile.

"Kiara and I decided we should go to the Capitol first to hack the Trackers and send a message to the whole country. So that should be our next goal."

"And steal some food or water, while we're there," Peter says.

"That too," Diana says.

"Can we sleep now?" Cameron asks, his head lolling back on the tree. Kiara shoves her hand behind his head before it can hit the tree and holds it there while Cameron closes his eyes. They watch him for a minute, and Cameron smiles without opening his eyes. "I know you're all staring at me."

"What do you expect us to do?" Diana asks, giggling at his light attitude.

"I don't know!" he replies. "Let me *sleep*."

"We can't, Cam," Kiara says. "Move your head, my hand is asleep."

"No. You're in it now."

So Kiara yanks her hand away, and Cameron's head smacks back against the tree. Kiara shakes out her hand while Cameron rubs his head, fully awake.

"Mean," he whispers, running a hand through his hair.

"Should we go?" Diana asks. She stands and brushes herself off, and Peter holds a hand out to stop her.

"I want to check Cameron's ankle first. I'm worried it's gonna get infected."

Kiara grimaces. "Ew. I'll get our stuff together, you guys do your thing."

So Diana kneels next to the boys and rolls up her sleeves. "Tell me what to do, Peter."

"Okay. I'm gonna take the bandages off, and you can prop his foot up in your lap."

Diana nods and takes Cameron's foot in her hands. She kneels on the ground and places Cameron's leg in between hers, allowing Peter to unwrap his makeshift bandages. He stares at Cameron's unwrapped leg for a moment, and then starts to whisper, "Huh."

"What?" Diana whispers frantically. Cameron is dozing again on the tree, and Peter is holding his used bandages in a trembling hand. Diana leans over to glance at his ankle, and gasps when she sees the wound. The cut has not changed, but the severed skin has darkened in a stomach-churning infection.

"Can you fix it?" Diana asks.

Peter stares at Cameron's ankle, then at his face. The world seems too eerily quiet for a minute. "No," he says quietly.

"No? So it'll just heal on its own?"

"I..." Peter starts, sighing, "I don't know. It might," he looks at Diana, "but it also might get worse."

"Worse... like how?"

Peter shrugs. "In all my training, I've never seen any infection like this before."

Diana shakes her head. "Will this... kill him?"

Peter doesn't answer, shrugging his shoulders and not looking away from Cameron's face. His expression is vacant, and Diana hopes that his knit brows meant he was thinking, not mourning. He silently leans forward and presses his hand against Cameron's forehead, quickly pulling it away. "He's burning up." Before Diana can answer, Peter stands and kicks at the dirt, "I'm so stupid! How did I not notice this?!"

"Peter, it's not your fault," Diana gently sets Cameron's leg down and stands up to face Peter.

"It is! *I* treated the cut, I could've... I could've..." Peter trails off, staring at Diana.

She looks at him, at her childhood friend, at this boy who she knows all about and knows nothing about at the same time. Diana just nods, even though she can't claim she really understands what's happening and walks forward to hug him. Peter is still for a moment, and then melts into the embrace. He isn't crying, but his lip is quivering; Diana can feel his shallow breaths reverberate through the fabric of her shirt.

"We'll do everything we can," Diana says quietly. She's at a loss. What can she say, what can she do? Something in her chest feels hollow and cold, and she purposefully doesn't look at Cameron.

"I'm sorry. I'm so sorry. I've made everything worse," Peter says in a quavering voice.

"No, Peter. Don't apologize for caring. You are just as much a part of this team as the rest of us, and I promise you, Cameron will be okay." He pulls away from her, nodding. Peter wipes his eyes and Diana nods, rubbing his arms. "I'm gonna go tell Ki we're going to be a little held up."

Peter nods, clearing his throat, and Diana heads over to Kiara. "Hey," she says.

Kiara looks up from where she's zipping up their bag. "Hi."

"Cameron is super sick and we don't know if it's gonna clear up so we're staying here for a while," Diana says quickly.

"Wh–what?" Kiara asks, standing up to face Diana.

"I'm sorry we didn't get you sooner. Peter sort of freaked out."

"No, it's okay. But what are we gonna do? We can't leave Cameron, not now."

"Yeah, I know. I... *we*... don't know. Peter says it has to heal on its own. It's a game of chance at this point, I guess."

"Okay... what about Maya? We need to get to her soon if she's gonna get us into the Capitol."

Diana stares at her. "Didn't you just hear the part about Cameron maybe... dying? We can't leave."

Kiara chews her lip. "Obviously. But can't you see how badly this is going to go if we're briefing her on everything we've done the past few days literally *as* she's breaking us into the most heavily guarded building in the world?"

"So what can we do? We can't go *to* her. She's halfway across the country from us and we're stuck here."

Kiara just shrugs. "I've packed our bags. What if I went to get her?"

"What?! By yourself? Ki, that's too dangerous."

"Isn't everything we're planning on doing dangerous?"

Diana's jaw practically drops to the floor. Kiara sighs and grabs her arms. "I'm not gonna go all the way to her sector, just find some way to contact her and have her meet me in the Plaza. From there we can come back here and stay until Cameron gets better."

"What about clothes? And how are you gonna get a Tracker?"

"I've knocked someone out before, I can do it again. And I'll tell her to find clothes or dye hers before she comes."

Diana chews her lip. She's not liking the sound of this plan. "Fine," she says, "but you need to be careful."

Kiara smiles. "When am I not?"

Part Eleven: The Aries

Kiara

After Diana reluctantly lets her go, Kiara puts some of their food and water into the drawstring bag and heads out, map in hand. She was going to say goodbye to Peter, but he was occupied keeping a now-unconscious Cameron alive, so she skipped over that farewell. Kiara walks through the woods by herself, heading towards the inhabited part of Sector Five. As she walks, Kiara listens to the trees rustle and the dirt crunch. A crypt-like silence hangs in the air, and she doesn't know whether to be freaked out or feel peaceful. She decides on the latter, and continues, increasing her pace just slightly.

After about thirty minutes, the terrain under Kiara's feet changes from dirt to tar, and she squints in the darkness to make out her surroundings. She's made it out of the woods, and Kiara's heart rate speeds up when she realizes just how close to danger the rest of the group is. A guard could stumble onto their camp *by accident,* and she'd be powerless to help them. She takes a deep breath and continues, not concerned about running into anyone because it's the early evening and it's already nearly pitch black out.

Kiara estimates it will be about six-thirty when she gets to the station, and about seven-fifteen when she gets to the Plaza. Once there, she plans on sneaking some unsuspecting pedestrian into a dark alley and knocking them out, then stealing their Tracker and trying to hack it the way Diana did to reach Maya.

Problem is, Kiara doesn't *quite* know how to do that. But she'll figure it out. She always does.

Kiara quickly gets consumed in her own thoughts as she keeps walking, scuttling hurriedly past the bar from the other day and hoping the bartender won't peek out the window and recognize her. Once she's all clear, Kiara goes back to thinking, mainly about Cameron. What will happen if he doesn't survive? Diana will be totally lost, she's barely keeping it together as it is. She thinks back to when she first met Cameron, after his escape from Sector Three. He had seemed so lost, but now he's got the rest of them, and the revolt, and he's arguably the most important person on the team. Cameron is the glue that holds them together, with his witty remarks and unyielding bravery. And not to mention, they wouldn't have even made it out of Sector One if he hadn't done his crazy border-dropping magic.

Needless to say, the only thing Kiara picks out from her turbulent thoughts is that they need him.

Kiara gets to the station quicker than she expected. It's basically deserted, with the guards' Black uniforms blending into the dark sky. She approaches the doors, and they wave her through without giving her a second glance. *Alright,* Kiara thinks, *that works.*

Kiara boards the next train to the Plaza, and paces back and forth in the empty car that she boards at the very back. What is she doing? The panic starts to set in when Kiara realizes that Maya is much, much further than she thought, and now she's caught between an older girl who is a virtual stranger and three people she knows who she's voluntarily leaving behind. But it was worth it, for Diana if no one else. Kiara takes a few deep breaths, but nothing works, anxiety building in her chest and threatening to spill over the edges of her stony resolve.

She walks to the window, letting the buildings zipping by cool down her racing thoughts as she thinks hard. She just has to try to find a Cancer to get clothes from, that's step one. It might even work, as long as she's not spotted. Kiara stumbles and realizes then that she's *exhausted,* the adrenaline of the day finally catching up to her, so she slumps on a bench and loops the straps of her drawstring through her arms, shoving it under her head. She quickly starts to doze, and after a few minutes, Kiara is fast asleep.

"Who knows the answer?" Teacher asks.

The crowd of twelve-year-olds don't answer. Everyone is staring at their tables, except Kiara.

Her eyes are locked on one of the countdown clocks behind Teacher. They dot the wall behind her, hanging in neat rows and counting down 'years, weeks, days, minutes, hours, seconds'. Left to right, the numbers tick down. The clocks were hung in alphabetical order, and while the other kids were avoiding the gaze of Teacher to dodge answering the question, Kiara was locked onto a clock hanging between 'James' and 'Lilian'.

"Kiara."

And there were thirty seconds left on the timer. Once it ran out, guards would burst in and grab her from her seat, without even interrupting the lesson taking place.

Someone else notices Kiara's clock, too. Diana, who had been the topic of a schoolyard tussle Kiara took four years ago that created their little friendship, was seated a few chairs down and glanced her way. Diana meets Kiara's eye, and her worried expression confirms Kiara's fears. Out of all these kids, Diana probably knew this sort of fear. Kiara knew that her best friend, a boy named Peter, had been taken last year, June 29th. It was March 30th now, Kiara's birthday. Diana's was April 22nd, about a month from Kiara's.

Kiara is shocked out of her thoughts when a buzzer goes off. It's a painful, high-pitched screeching, and the kids cover their ears as her countdown clock blinks a bright red. Teacher doesn't even blink, simply walks to her desk and hits a button under a plastic lid. She continues talking, and the air leaves Kiara's body. She is letting them take her and not even thinking twice. As soon as the button is pressed, their classroom is stormed by two guards, who quickly pull Kiara from her seat and grab her by the arms, holding her by the elbows. As they march her past Diana's desk, she turns and reaches out her hand. Silently, Kiara takes it, squeezing it quickly before they pull her from Diana's grip.

They take Kiara down the hallway, until they reach some white doors that are pushed open and Kiara is ushered through. The room they entered was dimly lit and furnished with only a table and two chairs, one of which was filled by a man with stark white hair in a Red suit. He motions silently to the chair across from him, and Kiara sits. The guards close the doors and one stands on either side. Kiara remembers she couldn't see their faces, because they were wearing dark sunglasses and Black clothes that covered just about every inch of skin on their bodies. She turns to the man in the suit, dressed head-to-toe in Red. Undershirt, suit jacket, tie, shoes, socks. Kiara's eyes widen, and she recognizes him as the Aries representative on the Board Of Zodiacs. She clamps her jaw shut and a tremble runs through her body when she realizes just how powerful this man is.

And now he's alone with her.

"Kiara. 333," he says, folding his hands on the table and looking at her. Kiara shifts in her seat, pulling the hem of her White cotton dress down further over her lap.

"Yes," she whispers.

"333, it is March 30th. Your birthday."

"Yes."

"That makes you an Aries."

Kiara just nods.

"333, today you will be sent to your sector. Sector One. You will be given a branding and a default outfit. Then you will be transported by monorail to your sector and put up in a house that will be your permanent placement for the rest of your life. Your lessons at school have prepared you to live by yourself and have given you the resources needed for any assistance." He looks at her, his icy eyes boring a hole into her face. "Do you have any questions?"

Kiara feels her lip tremble, and she bites the inside of her cheek until she tastes blood. "Will I be alone in the house?"

"Yes."

"But what about my father? He told me I would see him when I turned twelve."

He looks at her again. Then he looks to the guards, motioning for them to take a step closer. "Your father is not an Aries."

"I know. He's a Pisces."

"No, you will not see him again."

Kiara swallows hard. "What?"

"I said you will never see him again. You are of two separate signs." His voice was cold, and it rattled through the room, leaving Kiara silent.

"But I'm only twelve. I can't live on my own."

"You don't have a choice."

"But I can't!" she shouts. Her voice is shrill and it doesn't sound like her own. "I can't!"

The man shuts her up with a backhand across the face. Kiara gasps loudly and her hand flies up to touch her *cheek, but the guard to her left reaches out and shoves her hand back into her lap.*

"Get her clothes and get her out of here," George Henderson says.

The other guard pulls out a Red dress, exactly the same as Kiara's current White one, and hands it to her. She sits there, waiting for them to motion her over to a changing room.

"Get dressed," the guard growls.

"I have no privacy," Kiara says resolutely.

"Get. Dressed," the guard says again.

Kiara looks at the Aries man, but the dangerous glint in his eyes has turned into a hungry, triumphant one. So she stands and shrugs out of her dress, trying to stay as covered as she can and trying desperately to ignore the Red Man's prowling gaze. Kiara quickly pulls the Red dress over her head, standing there in silence once she's done. One of the guards grabs her old dress and it disappears into the folds of his jacket, and the other takes her arm and shoves a burning hot iron rod on it with no warning.

Kiara kicks and screams, but it does nothing, for after a few seconds, "333" is burned into her arm, her flesh crackling and smoking as if it were kindling in a fire. She gasps and chokes on her tears, but to no avail, as the Red Man rises and crosses to her.

"Beautiful," he says, his voice a whisper as Kiara attempts to control her emotions. "A special little girl."

His hand finds her cheek, the same one he slapped moments earlier, and Kiara shivers with fear as his thumb drags across her dark skin. "I want to go home," she whispers.

Henderson does nothing but grin. "You have no home anymore, 333," he replies. "That's the point."

With a look to the guards, she's dragged out of the room and shoved into a waiting car right outside the schoolhouse doors. Kiara remembers from classes that only the BOZ has cars, so she's assuming this is the Red Man's personal vehicle.

"We're taking you to the station. There you'll get a house key," the guard driving says.

The one in the passenger seat turns to her. He's holding a small device that Kiara guesses is the Tracker. "Who do you want your two contacts to be?" he asks.

"No," the other guard says.

"What?" the first one responds, sounding confused. "Does she not get one?"

"No. She can't."

"Why?"

The scarier guard, the one who took her dress, looks over at Kiara. He turns back to the other guy and lowers his voice. "In relation to 762. Her sister, at least. Henderson doesn't want 762 connected to anyone right now."

"Probation?"

"Yes. 333 being a Fire Sign makes it too dangerous to be near her."

Kiara listens to them talk rapidly, back-and-forth in what sounded like some sort of secret code, some language Kiara didn't understand but they did. Finally, after a good three minutes of listening, she squeezes herself in.

"Why don't I get to talk to anyone? That's not fair."

The guard in the passenger seat turns around slowly to face her. "It isn't about fair. It's about law."

Kiara crosses her arms. "Who's 762, and why can't I talk to their sister?"

"Because Mister Henderson said so. Stop arguing or you'll regret it."

"You don't scare me."

"We don't have to. Mister Henderson will do that himself."

Kiara stops arguing, breath catching in her throat as her skin burns with hatred from where he touched her. She looks out the window at the Plaza zooming by. "Where are we going?"

"Stop asking questions."

She stops.

The guard driving shakes his head, whispering to the other man just loud enough for Kiara to hear. "I told Mister Henderson we should just get rid of her. But he insisted she stay alive." He glances Kiara's way briefly. "We'll see how that goes."

Part Twelve: The Scorpio

Cameron

"Ugh," is all Cameron can manage. Then, "ow," when something burning and wet hits his forehead.

Cameron opens his eyes slowly, painfully, to see Peter leaning over him, his hand hovering a few inches from Cameron's forehead and dripping water.

"Did that... hurt?" Peter asks, quirking an eyebrow.

Cameron groans. "It's *burning.*" His voice is rasping and he clears his throat against the hot sensation tingling there.

Peter looks at his hand. "It's cold water."

"It's hot."

"No, it isn't," then, quieter: "shit."

Cameron tries to focus his eyes on Peter's face. "What's wrong?" Cameron mumbles.

"Your cut is infected. And you're feverish. I was trying to cool you off, but I guess it's not working."

Cameron nods. Ow. That will not be happening again. Their little clearing looks... empty? He grabs Peter's hand to get his attention. "The girls?"

Peter nods. "Diana is asleep. Kiara is going to the Plaza to bring Maya back here."

Cameron closes his eyes. Sleeping sounds good. "You should sleep, too."

Peter shakes his head, shaking Cameron a little to get him to open his eyes. "No, neither of us should sleep. I can't have you slipping into a coma."

"A coma sounds good," Cameron says, not opening his eyes. Peter reaches forward and grabs his face, his fingers soft and gentle on the back of his jaw. Unsurprisingly, much of Cameron likes that feeling.

"No, Cam! Stay awake!" Peter is shaking his head. He's saying something, something about disease or infection or sterilization, and Cameron's stomach churns at the thought of the bloodied log and dirty knife.

Why? Cameron wonders. *Is it bad?*

Suddenly, Cameron's head is filled with a loud buzzing. He stares at Peter, and Cameron can see his mouth moving. Is Peter... buzzing at him?

"Cameron!" Peter shouts.

The buzzing stops. "What," Cameron says. It was supposed to be a question. Why did it not come out as one?

Peter says nothing, just looks at Cameron and frowns. Cameron thinks he's crying. That, or he spilled water on his face. His expression crumbles Cameron's insides, and he wants to reach out to him, but he knows he wouldn't have the strength to.

"I know you won't remember this because of your fever, but I need you to not die on me. Please. And thank you."

"You're welcome," Cameron says hoarsely.

Peter laughs. "Can you do me a favor?"

Cameron nods. Damnit, he forgot how bad that hurts.

"I need you to survive tonight, okay? Then we can go from there."

Cameron opens his eyes to a blinding light. "Ow, stop that light."

He hears a distant laugh. A girl's laugh. "That's the moon, Cam."

Cameron's eyes fly open, much to the despair of his searing migraine.

"Diana?" he gasps.

She smiles. "Morning, sunshine."

"Where's Peter?"

She exhales dramatically. "Wow. I offer to take care of you for a few hours, and you already want him back."

Cameron chuckles, but it sounds more like a wheeze. "Is he sleeping?"

Diana nods. "Do you want me to wake him?"

"No, it's all right," he mumbles. He looks back to Diana. "Am I gonna make it, Doc?"

She laughs again. "You're still feverish. The verdict is still out on your ankle, too."

Cameron nods, which hurts a little less than before. He bites his lip, feeling somber now, feeling the weight of Peter's words from earlier. "Di, I want you to know that I'm so lucky to have met you. Tell Kiara that when she comes back, too. And tell Maya that I'm sorry I couldn't meet her."

Diana looks at Cameron with wide eyes. "What?" She blinks, and her eyes get wet, shining brighter green than usual. "Please tell me you're not gonna die, like, *right* now."

Cameron coughs. "Not yet, I don't think. But just in case."

She props up his ankle and starts pouring a little water on it. Cameron grits his teeth together against the white-hot pain that flares from his leg.

"And what would you like me to tell Peter?" Diana asks, semi-suggestively.

Cameron chokes on his breath. "What?"

"You've mentioned me and Ki, even Maya, but what would you like me to tell Peter when you *inevitably* pass away?" she says with a joking smirk.

"Um..." he starts. "Tell him... tell him that I'm sorry for dying."

"Right."

Cameron groans before he can make a witty remark. "Ouch." He clutches at his stomach.

"What hurts?" Diana asks.

"My stomach."

So, she pulls up his shirt and raises an eyebrow. She runs her fingers over Cameron's abdomen and he shivers. "Yikes. That is *so* weird." She swivels her head around, still holding up Cameron's shirt with one hand. "Peter?" she yells.

His head pokes around from a tree a little ways away. "Yeah?"

Diana looks back over to Cameron, at his stomach. Cameron can't see it from the angle he's sitting at, but by the look on Diana's face, something isn't right. "Can you come check this out?"

Peter comes over, his neutral expression quickly fading into one of pure dread as he catches sight of Cameron's stomach. Peter kneels down and presses his fingers against Cameron's stomach. After a moment, Peter presses down again. Hard.

"Ah!" Cameron gasps.

"Did that hurt?" Peter asks.

"Uh, yeah!"

"Sorry," he says. He turns to Diana. "It's spreading. But it's not on *top* of his skin anymore, it's spreading to his organs."

"What the hell?" Cameron asks. "I'm right here."

The two of them look up at him. "Right," Peter says. "I think the infection has gotten under your skin and is infecting your organs."

"Then why is everything else getting better?" Diana asks.

"I think I have a theory, actually," Peter says, still staring intently at Cameron's stomach. Cameron wiggles around to try to look. Directly over his navel, the skin is almost translucent, like ice, and below it is a stain of black bacteria that is worming its way across the underlayer of his skin.

"What is it, Peter?" Diana asks.

"My theory is that because Cameron has powers, his normal immune system is weakened or wired differently than yours or Ki's. I think that even a small injury like this one could be detrimental because of it, actually."

"Gross," Cameron says.

"Yeah," Peter looks up at him. His eyes are soft and worried, and Cameron could stare into them forever.

Peter opens his mouth to speak, looking quickly back down at Cameron's stomach. Then back to him.

"Peter," Cameron says, "what is going on? I'm just gonna go ahead and assume I'm definitely on my way out."

Peter snorts with a sarcastic laugh, leaning back into a sitting position. "Honestly? This could kill you."

Cameron nods, smiling faintly. "One can hope."

The joke very obviously doesn't land, and Cameron grimaces as Peter turns to Diana. "Can you grab me some water?"

She nods, returning with their water bottle. Peter pours a little on Cameron's ankle, letting the liquid seep into the wound. The two boys look at one another.

"I'm no nurse, so I apologize in advance for any unconventional cleaning methods," he mumbles, as his fingers play with the hem of Cameron's shirt.

Cameron shakes his head. "Not like I can run away."

Part Thirteen: The Aries

Kiara

Kiara is right on schedule.

As the story goes, she arrives at the Plaza *perfectly* on time. The sky is dark, but bright lights from the buildings around her illuminate the cobblestoned area. Across the way, the Capitol building stands tall, the dome rising above the rest of the architecture and casting an imposing ebony shadow over her. Sitting in between Kiara and the Capitol is a huge fountain, and even despite it being late evening, it's still shooting tall arcs of water into the air. She looks around, and she can feel herself deflate when she realizes just how empty it is here. There are maybe ten people total not counting the guards, and double that when you *do* count the guards. Kiara's no mathematician, but she doesn't like that ratio.

She continues to walk, wandering aimlessly to try to build up her courage. It's only after a minute or so when she realizes her feet are taking her to the school. When she gets there and finds a spot out of sight in an alley, Kiara peeks into a window. Through it is an empty classroom, with the lights out. The teacher and students must have gone to their dorms for the night already. The only light in the room is a wall of clocks, counting down the remaining time of the twenty or twenty-five kids in that particular class. Kiara feels bad for them, staring at their clocks, because they have no idea what their life is going to be like. Sure, they know that they'll go to their sector when they turn twelve, get fun clothes in their very own color, and get their very own Tracker, but they don't know that their every move will be watched, or that they won't have *anyone*, or that the government is feeding them lies. Kiara watches as some clock for a little kid named 'Lila' hits its last five minutes.

Then she knows what she needs to do. The world needs to be better for kids like them. And now, Kiara had the chance to be part of the solution.

"Damnit, Kiara. *What* are you getting yourself into?" she mumbles to herself, turning away from the school and back towards the main atrium. She looks around for a Cancer to take clothes from, but she sees none. The back of her neck starts to sweat, and her body flushes with heat, despite the evening breeze. She heads towards the public restrooms and locks herself in, slumping against the door. That's when she notices it.

A sign, with Cameron's face blown up in a black-and-white photo with the words: "WANTED: 100,000 dollar reward for Scorpio 102."

"No, no, no," Kiara says. She rushes out of the bathroom, almost colliding with a light post. She comes face-to-face with another poster, except this time, Peter's face is on it instead of Cameron's. Then, she spots one by the fountain with her own face. Then, one pinned to a doorway with Diana's.

Everywhere Kiara looks, a poster is there. They've been found out by someone. And whoever they are, they've got money and they want them dead.

Kiara turns in a full circle, squeezing her fists together and trying to calm her racing thoughts. Focus, focus. Okay, she needs to find a Tracker. Problem is, the number of people has dwindled even further, however, there are fewer guards around, too. So, Kiara pinpoints a heavyset man dressed in Pink walking towards the station. No guards are around him, but there are two at the entrance to the monorails. So Kiara needs to catch him before he gets into their line of sight. She hurries forward until she's about ten paces behind him, and she continues to approach slowly until she's literally right behind him. Kiara spots the Tracker on his belt, and she notices that when he steps forward, it shifts further backwards. So, she waits until he's stepped forward again, and she plucks it gingerly from his belt, turning and starting to casually walk back the way she came. As she catches her breath, Kiara tries to remember what Diana did in the bar.

Diana flicks the blade out, and she grabs it and wedges it under the wire, pulling it clean away from the device. She plugs in a white wire to a blinking, blue reactor, and the screen lights up with a list titled 'Sector Five Citizens'.

"Okay," Kiara says, flicking the back of the Tracker off. She uses her fingernail to pull out a black wire, leaving it discarded on the ground, then she shoves a white wire aggressively into a blue blinking thing that she can only assume is the reactor Diana had mentioned. She flips it back over and taps the screen a few desperate times, and twelve sectors pop up. Kiara quickly selects 'Sector Six' and scrolls until she gets to the seven hundreds.

"Seven hundred sixty one... seven hundred sixty two," she selects Maya's photo, and quickly taps out, "Meet me at the Plaza monorail station." Only Diana has time for secret codes. Kiara sends it quickly and throws it over her shoulder, pulling open the bathroom door and locking herself inside.

Kiara waits what she thinks is a half hour, then cautiously peeks her head out of the bathroom. She squints towards the station, seeing a dark figure silhouetted in the facade of the building, hidden from sight, a drawstring bag slung over their shoulder, and Kiara suppresses a smile. Only Maya could hide in plain view like that. Kiara looks both ways, before making a mad dash towards the dark alley in which Maya was hiding. As Kiara reaches her, she notices the familiar face and figure of a girl she met so long ago.

"Guys, come on. She's nice, and I promise you'll like her," Diana pouts, crossing her arms.

"I dunno, Di," Peter says. "She's a lot older than us, and I doubt she even has time to talk."

Peter was right, but Kiara certainly wasn't going to jeopardize her newest position as third musketeer in this motley crew.

Diana was in no position to concede, though. "Peter, my sister and my two best friends have to meet at some point."

Peter sighs, finally relenting. "I guess."

Diana claps her hands. "Good! Let's go."

So, she takes them both by the hand and drags them across the schoolyard, where nearly thirty twelve-year-olds are perched on top of a domed climbing structure. They're talking animatedly about something, and only when one notices the three smaller kids approaching do the voices quiet.

"Hey, Maya," a lanky brunette calls. "Isn't that your sister?"

In the center of the group, a gorgeous blonde-haired girl turns her head down to look at them. She nods, and some of the other older kids chuckle teasingly. Maya is obviously embarrassed by their presence, but she doesn't say anything, instead hooking her legs around the bars underneath her and letting herself fall through the structure, flipping once and landing neatly on her feet in the ground in front of them.

She and Diana embrace, and Kiara notices that the two look scarily similar, blonde hair that lands in the center of their shoulder blades, bright green eyes, and neither were very tall.

"Hey, Di," Maya says, pulling away. She sizes up Peter and Kiara. "Who are they?"

Diana grins, tugging the two of them closer to her side. "This is Peter, and this is Kiara. They wanted to meet you."

Peter waves sheepishly, and Kiara just nods. Maya smiles back at them and then promptly turns back to her sister. "Well, Di, I'm glad you've met some friends."

"Me too," Diana says. She takes her sister's hands and lowers her voice. "How much longer?"

Maya huffs out a sharp breath. "Two weeks."

Diana lets out a sad sigh, and Kiara notices her lower lip quivering. Maya tilts her chin up to face her and hugs her once again. "Don't worry, Di. It'll be okay."

"And you promise you'll pick me to be a contact, right?"

Maya nestles her face in her sister's hair. "Of course I will, silly."

"Okay," Diana says, right as one of Maya's classmates hollers her name.

"I gotta go, Di," Maya says, detaching herself from her little sister. She turns to Peter and Kiara. "It's nice to meet you two."

Peter takes Diana's hand and leads her away from the bigger kids, but Kiara lingers behind for a moment. As Kiara *turns to leave, though, she hears someone call her name softly.*

"Kiara." She turns to see Maya still standing there.

"Yeah?" Kiara asks, feeling uncomfortable and out-of-place around these older kids.

"Just..." Maya trails off, watching Diana walk away, "watch after my sister, okay? Don't let anything happen to her."

Kiara nods, giving Maya a small smile. "I won't."

"Maya!" Kiara gasps after they pull away from a quick hug. "We need your help."

Maya nods. "Tell me everything."

Kiara starts, then hesitates. "This is important. A matter of life or death, really. So can we-?"

"Yes. You know that I would do anything for my sister, and you along with her."

"Okay," Kiara says with resolve. She'd have to take Maya's word for it, she had no other choice. "How much do you know?"

"Nothing, aside from the fact my sister and her boyfriend's faces have been plastered across the Plaza with two other kids I can only assume are you and one of the escaped Scorpios."

"Oh, my god. She didn't tell you anything?" Kiara asks, staring at her, mouth agape.

"No. She's been missing for a week or so, and we normally talk every few days. I was starting to get worried."

Kiara studies her face and the lines etched there from days of worrying about her baby sister. She's right, too. Diana could have been killed and Maya wouldn't have had a clue.

"Okay. So after Diana left the visiting center, she left her Tracker, disguised herself as an Aries, and successfully got on the train to Sector One."

"Holy shit."

"It gets better. She gets to my house, where she finds me and Cameron, the ginger Scorpio on the other poster. He actually led the escape in Sector Three, managing to free hundreds of people after his sister died," Maya winces at that, but Kiara is already going on, "Diana convinces us to help her. So, we walked to the far back of Sector One. Cameron drops the border–"

"He *what?!*" Maya asks.

"Oh, right, yeah, so Cameron actually has powers that allow him to drop and raise the border walls as he pleases. They don't burn him, either."

"So all the Scorpios, just somehow getting released…"

Kiara nods. "That was him. Anyway, Cameron drops the border and we get into Sector Two. We dye our clothes Orange, walk to the monorail station, and ride the train to the Plaza. We steal Gray clothes, get on a train, and go to Sector Five. I knock a guy out and Diana hijacks his Tracker to send a coded message to Peter, and then Peter finds us in the woods and we realize he actually has powers too."

"Let me guess. He can squeeze the border into tiny bullets and shoot them out of a gun."

Kiara snaps her fingers and points at Maya. "Close. He can grab pieces out of the border and turn them into force fields by throwing them at someone," Maya just blinks, and Kiara continues. "So, next we were gonna go find you, since you can get us into the Capitol, but Cameron hurt his ankle and is now basically dying of an infection, and apparently we're on the country's 'Most Wanted' list, so they sent me."

"But why do you need Capitol access?"

Kiara grimaces. "For staging a revolt."

"Oh, I see. You want access to the Tracker systems."

Kiara grins and nods. "And the archives. We want to see how Cameron and Peter got their powers."

Maya smirks. "I actually have an idea about that. But we should tell the whole group," she looks around. "So, next step?"

"We need to get back to Sector Five. That's where everyone is."

Maya nods, pulling a set of Gray clothes out of her bag. There's a crimson stain on the shirtsleeve, but Kiara doesn't ask, instead turning and shielding Maya to allow her privacy to change, and after a moment, they're ready to go, but Maya halts in her tracks after a few steps. "What about your Scorpio friend? Does he need medicine?"

Kiara shrugs. "Yeah. But we don't have any. And it was too dangerous for me to try to steal some alone."

Maya looks down at Kiara. "Well, you're not alone now."

Kiara smiles. "You're right."

Maya motions towards a high-rise, with a pharmacy nestled on the ground floor. They head that way, under the cover of darkness, unseen by any other human.

Except two.

A man stands on the steps of the Capitol building, hidden in the shadow of one of the menacing pillars that ground the power of the building to the stone steps. Next to him, a man bathed in Forest Green studies the scene.

"Is that your missing citizen?" the first man asks.

"No, sir. Her sister," the man in Forest Green says. "Should we stop them?"

The first man grins a wide, toothy grin that brightens the darkness around them. "No. Let them have their fun. We'll be waiting for them when the time comes."

The man in Forest Green disappears into the Capitol building, leaving the other man alone.

"I'll get you soon, 333. I'll get you soon."

He straightens his Red tie and walks back into the Capitol.

Part Fourteen: The Cancer

Peter

"Do you think she's there yet?" Diana asks. She's been pacing past the tree where Cameron is sleeping and where Peter is sitting next to him for the past hour, stressing about Kiara and Maya.

"Di," Peter says from the ground, "come, sit, please."

Diana looks at him, then huffs, plopping down next to him and sticking Peter in the middle of a Cameron-Diana sandwich. He reaches his arms out wordlessly, and she leans into his hug, sighing a shaky sigh.

"I'm sure both of them are okay," Peter whispers.

She pulls away from him. "But I have no way to know."

"None of us does, so we just need to wait it out. If they aren't here by tomorrow night, we keep going as best we can. That's all we can do."

She nods. Her resolve frightens Peter, and he studies her with a puzzled expression. "What?" Diana asks, huffing out a worried laugh.

"Nothing, I just... I just realized we haven't properly caught up at all."

Her eyes widen. "You're right! I don't even know what day it is any more, if I'm being completely honest."

"Okay, how about a game of 'Questions and Answers'?" Peter asks, referencing the get-to-know-you game they used to play at school.

"Sure. You start," she says.

Peter looks around at their dark little campsite. "If you could be in any other sector, what would it be and why?"

Diana smiles. "Good one. I think Sector Six. I'm not like a Gemini at all, and I certainly don't like their color, but I would want to be near Maya."

Peter nods. "Solid answer. Disappointed you wouldn't pick here in the deep south, though."

She shakes her head good-naturedly. "Too hot. Okay, Pete, my turn."

"Not *Pete*. That makes me sound like a middle-aged man."

"You're about there."

Peter shoves her arm. "Diana! I am literally *one* year older than you. Do not start."

"Okay, okay. Here's your question: What has your favorite part of this whole shebang been so far?"

Peter nudges her. "Trick question. Seeing you and meeting the rest of the gang."

Diana smiles. "I'm glad."

Peter dares to hold her gaze for a moment, and Diana does the same. Peter's heart leaps into his throat as his gaze dips to her lips, and something in him just... wants to find out.

She's close, closer than she's ever been to him, so near that he can feel her breath as he closes the distance and kisses her softly on the lips.

Diana, to Peter's abject horror and surprise, kisses him back, and after a beat, they pull away from each other.

They stare at one another for one second, then two.

And then they both burst out laughing.

"Oh, god," Diana starts, touching her lips as if she's not quite sure what happened. "Let's never do that again."

Peter nods rapidly, running a shaky hand through his hair. "Agreed. I just-"

"-Had to know," she finishes.

"I had to know," Peter affirms. He looks her way quickly. "I'm sorry, I shouldn't have-"

"-Peter," she interrupts, "it's fine. Trust me, I... have been wondering as well."

The two pause for a moment, and it's as if the pair were synced, for they both say confidently and resolutely, "Just friends."

Peter laughs before he can stop himself, pulling Diana into a hug. He doesn't know why he's relieved, but some part of him is, and some part of him feels almost changed. Diana hugs him back, and the two stay like that, immersed in that little shred of giddiness, before it fades.

They fall silent as Diana pulls herself from Peter's arms. "Are you scared, Diana?"

She closes her eyes. "God, I'm terrified. The thought that next week we could be dead scares the life out of me."

Peter grimaces. "We've done scary things before. Remember?"

She looks at Peter and nods, and somehow he knows that she's thinking of that same day in the woods. "What are you most scared about for the day we revolt?"

"Hurting someone," he says instantly. "I don't want to have to use my powers for harm, but I also don't want anything to happen to you guys. I don't enjoy the pressure that comes with having these powers, but I also know that it makes me a valuable asset, in battle *and* outside of it.

It's a lot of back and forth, with a lot of unknowns in the middle," Peter looks over at her. "You?"

Diana ponders the question, staring at the ground. "Losing someone. We're throwing a lot of innocent people into the crossfire, along with the group of people I care about the most. I don't want anything to happen to us, but I can't help thinking that something could."

Peter doesn't have an argument for her, so he stays quiet, reaching around to their pack and grabbing the bottle of water out of it. He sets it on the coarse dirt below them, helping himself onto his knees to check on Cameron's condition. Peter lifts up Cameron's shirt, and sees the sight they've been accustomed to for the past day: Cameron's skin now all dotted with black infection, and his breathing is shallow. He sleeps for hours at a time, waking up in a sluggish state to mumble incoherent sentences before falling back asleep.

Peter gently shakes him awake, and Cameron blinks through groggy eyes at Diana and Peter leaning worriedly over him.

"Hi," Peter says. "You feeling okay?"

Cameron closes his eyes again. "Never better."

Peter shakes his arm. "No, Cameron. Stay awake."

Cameron opens his eyes again. His gaze is surprisingly alert, and they stare into Peter's with a fiery intensity. "I *can't*, superhero. Not for much longer."

Peter shakes his head, heart thumping at Cameron's desperate tone. "No, you have to. Remember what we're doing?"

Cameron nods slowly, as if every movement hurts him.

"We're going to fix everything. Okay? Remember your sister. You can't let her go without doing something."

Cameron looks at Peter again. He sucks in a sharp breath, his head lolling back. Diana only just sticks her hand behind his head to keep it from hitting the tree, and Peter reaches around his waist to keep him upright.

"Peter. He needs help *now*," Diana says desperately.

"I know, I know. I can't do anything," Peter says frantically, "I can't. I have no medicine."

"So this is it, then?" Diana asks. Her breath has disappeared, and she's speaking like she just ran a marathon, all heavy and panting.

Peter tries to choke back his panic. He tips the last of the water into Cameron's mouth, and his eyelids flutter open.

"Cameron, please. Please, do not close your eyes," Peter pleads.

Cameron looks at him. "It hurts so bad."

"I know. It *will* get better, though. Please, Cam, do it for me and Di," Peter's voice cracks as he looks at the other boy, and it's all he can do to keep making promises he knows won't come true.

Diana nods rapidly, her hand still bracing Cameron's head. "You're okay."

Cameron shakes his head, leaning back into her hand. He grips their hands weakly, whispering "I'm sorry," before closing his eyes.

The clearing falls silent. "No," Peter whispers. It feels like someone has ripped the air out of his lungs, and Diana slumps forward, curling into herself. Her shoulders shake with silent sobs.

Quiet all around them.

But something is not right.

Peter places his two fingers on Cameron's throat. "He's still breathing," he whispers.

Diana's head snaps up. "What?"

Peter looks at her, then back to Cameron. "His pulse. It's still there."

"Well, what can we do?"

Silence once more.

Peter sits back on his heels, feeling empty inside. Every breath reverberates through his ribcage. "Nothing. We have nothing to help him. The best we can do now is... keep him comfortable, I guess."

She looks at Peter, her big green eyes growing soft and full of pity. "Oh, Peter. I'm sorry."

He shakes his head and looks down, towards the dirt. He ignores the fact that he can see Cameron's still legs. Peter opens his mouth to speak to him, to say *goodbye* to him, when a shout breaks them from their mourning.

"Wait!" Kiara shouts. She and a familiar older girl, maybe twenty or so, charge through the trees to their right. Kiara is waving a bottle of some unfamiliar liquid in the air, and she races towards Cameron, pushing Diana and Peter out of the way and grabbing Cameron's head.

"Move, please," Kiara says, giving Peter's shoulder a shove, sending him tumbling into the dirt. She tips the bottle towards Cameron's mouth, the dark liquid sliding slowly out of the top. Cameron's Adam's apple bobs as he swallows.

After it's gone, she sits up, pushing her hands onto her knees to help herself up. She brushes herself off, sticking the empty bottle into her bag and slinging it onto the ground against the base of the tree.

"What was that? That you gave him, I mean," Peter asks her, still semi-unsure of what just happened.

"I'm not a *thousand* percent sure, but the pharmacy label said it healed infections quickly," Kiara says, crossing her arms and looking at Cameron's still-unmoving body. "Let's hope it works," she says grimly, lowering her voice just enough.

Diana springs to her feet, her eyes locked not on Cameron, but on the taller, blonde woman standing to the edge of their camp. "Maya?" She asks. It comes out as an incredulous whisper, and Diana rushes over to the woman and flings her arms around her. The two start laughing, and Maya strokes Diana's hair affectionately.

Peter smiles, the realization and recognition dawning on him. "It's good she's here."

Kiara snorts, watching the sisters. "Yeah, no shit. Cameron would've died otherwise." Peter grimaces and she lays a reassuring hand on his arm, "I'm kidding. It'll be okay."

"Let's hope so," Peter whispers back.

Maya and Diana are still talking, clinging to one another's arms affectionately. Peter pats Kiara's arm and motions her to the charred remnants of what used to be their campfire that sits in the center of their camp. Kiara hands Peter her knife, and he digs through the ashes until he finds a piece of flint they've been using for the past few days. He chips the blade against the stone, over and over until a spark appears. Kiara quickly catches it on a clump of dry leaves, sticking them into the pile of kindling they had placed in the center of the ash pile. After a few moments, they have a small, plucky fire that lights up the midnight sky. Kiara crosses to the other side of the fire, sitting across from Peter, who sits in the dirt with his knees pulled to his chest. After a few minutes of silence, Maya and Diana join them. They sit with their backs to the border wall, right next to each other. In the orange light, Peter notices just how identical the two are: fair skin, blonde hair, and green eyes that twinkle in the light. Maya certainly looks a good four years older than the rest of them, but her eyebrows are thicker than Diana's and her skin is perfectly clear. If someone looked in from outside this motley picture, they wouldn't be able to tell the two apart.

"So, Peter," Maya says. "Nice to see you again."

Peter smiles at her. "Same here."

"Do we have any food?" Diana chimes in.

For the third time, everyone is quiet. Peter absentmindedly grabs their duffel, rifling through it but to no avail. He shakes his head at her, and Diana sighs.

"We need to get out of here, guys," Kiara says, "we're gonna starve just sitting around."

"But-" Peter says.

"Cameron!" Diana finishes.

"Exactly, he-" Peter starts, but he stops when he realizes Diana has sprung to her feet. She points at Cameron, and they all look over to realize he's stirring out of his sleep.

Peter stands up with Kiara, and the three of them rush to Cameron, the girls on either side with Peter kneeling by his feet. The two girls hold onto his shoulders, keeping Cameron steady as he opens his eyes slowly. Cameron's hand reaches up to rub his face, and when he removes it, his big, gray eyes lock onto Peter's.

"Hi," Peter whispers. His splintered insides piece themselves back together as a singular dimple appears in Cameron's cheek.

"Hey hey, superhero," Cameron says with a small smile. His voice is low and husky.

"Are you okay, Cam?" Kiara asks.

He reaches around to pat her arm. "Probably?" he says with a light chuckle.

Diana throws her arms around Cameron, and he grunts in surprise before hugging her back. After a moment, Kiara joins the hug, and Cameron is buried beneath the two girls who are laughing like ecstatic children.

Peter interjects as the girls pull away. "Let me check your infection, Cam."

"Ugh, really?" he laughs. "I just came back from the dead and you're checking my infection?"

Peter rolls his eyes and reaches for Cameron's shirt. When he lifts it up, Cameron sucks in a sharp breath, looking up at Peter. They lock eyes for a second, and Peter quickly looks back down when he feels his cheeks heating up, although he's not entirely sure why.

Cameron's infection is still dotting across his stomach, but it's cleared up enough for Peter to feel a little better. He reaches out and presses a hand against Cameron's forehead, and he's pleasantly surprised when he realizes that it's cooled significantly. Peter wipes his hands down his pant leg and smiles at Cameron.

"Good for now. But not entirely out of the woods," Peter says.

"Works for me," Cameron says back, his smile still plastered on his face. But after a second of silence, it falters.

"What?" Peter asks, worried.

"I-" Cameron trails off. "I want to make sure you're okay."

"Uh, that *I'm* okay? I should be asking you that."

Cameron smiles again. "I'm fine," he says, nodding.

"Do you need anything?" Peter asks.

"Yup. To get this revolt over with and be able to *eat* something."

Peter laughs. "Don't we all?"

Part Fifteen: The Scorpio

Cameron

A few hours after Cameron's resurrection, the group of five is spread out around the campsite, sleeping. Peter, being Cameron's delegated nurse, is awake, and, because it's pretty much impossible for someone to sleep while their ankle is being manhandled, Cameron is begrudgingly awake too.

They work in silence, so as to not disrupt the girls. Peter has never experienced such a quiet before, and he likes it. Cameron, on the other hand, is very much not enjoying himself.

"Talk to me," he says to Peter, as the brunette boy pours a little water over his ankle.

Peter looks up at him, and Cameron once again notes the dark curl that falls over his forehead. "Huh?"

Cameron rolls his eyes and wiggles his ankle to get Peter's hands off. Peter reluctantly lets go, and Cameron sighs. "I *dunno*, superhero. I'm bored."

Peter shrugs. "We have a lot to do."

"Yeah, but that's daytime stuff," Cameron whines. "Just talk to me. Please."

Peter sits back on his heels, huffing out a breath and glancing up at the night sky. "Okay. About what?"

"Anything."

Peter thinks for a second, and Cameron watches him far more intently than he should. Of course, Cameron can't be blamed for this. It's not exactly like someone can just... look away when it comes to Peter. Finally, and thankfully for Cameron's conscience, Peter speaks again.

"Tell me about your life."

Cameron laughs loudly, then claps a hand over his mouth. "Sorry," he whispers after a moment of collecting himself. "Nobody really just *asks* what life is like in Sector Three."

"Well, is it any different from life in Sector Five?"

Cameron scoffs half-heartedly. "Very different."

Peter sits criss-cross in front of Cameron. Any closer, and their knees would brush. "Did you have a job?"

"Can't work 'till you're twenty-one."

"Own a house?"

"Group homes until you're eighteen, if you can afford it."

"Well, what about family stuff?"

Cameron sighs. "No visitation of any kind from anyone outside the sector. Marriage is to Scorpios and Scorpios only, obviously, and each family is limited to one kid, in order to keep a 'consistent and manageable' population, since our sector is so much smaller than the others."

Peter whistles. "Damn."

"Yeah, tell me about it."

The two fall into a slightly awkward silence. Finally, Peter speaks up, and Cameron's stomach sets off fireworks at the sleepy tone his voice has suddenly taken on. "What happens if there's more than one kid?"

Cameron looks at the ground. "They just take the youngest and hang them. That's what happened to my sister. Didn't help that she wasn't a Scorpio, either."

Cameron swallows, his brain turning dark like it usually does when he thinks about his sister and his sector. It was just... uncomfortable to bring up. No one could understand, and even though the girls had consoled him, it still felt weird to be so vulnerable. Like they saw him differently. Or that he was bringing it up on purpose, even though Cameron knew Peter was just trying to make small talk.

"Hey," Peter whispers. When Cameron doesn't respond, he rises to his knees so he's about two inches above Cameron's bowed head. "Hey," he whispers again.

Cameron looks up at him, and sucks in a sharp breath when he realizes how close they are. "Hi," he whispers back, his voice cracking.

Almost instantly, Peter wraps Cameron in a strong hug, and Cameron, like he's *supposed* to fit there, melts into Peter's arms and sniffles as he takes in the smell of the woods mixed with cotton. He swallows hard, blinking back tears as his fingers curl into Peter's shirt.

"Sorry," Cameron whispers into Peter's shoulder after a quiet moment. He tries not to think about his arms around Peter's neck and Peter's hands around his waist.

"About what?" Peter asks, pulling away. Cameron instantly feels cold all around, like Peter left an emptiness behind. "You have no reason to apologize for feeling how you feel." He hesitates, looking purposefully into Cameron's eyes. "Don't apologize for being who you are, Cam."

Cameron wipes his eyes, nodding. "Yeah. Thanks."

A hint of awkwardness floats through the air around them as Peter clears his throat. "Yeah, um... don't worry about it."

A hesitant but familiar game of 'avoid eye contact with each other' follows, until the two boys lock eyes by accident and it's just like the first time they looked at each other. Weird and a little confusing, in more ways than one.

Peter swallows and looks away, but he senses that Cameron's eyes are still on the top of his head.

"Why are you staring, Peter?" Cameron asks.

Peter snorts, the awkwardness broken like a rusted chain link. "I'm *not!*"

"You *were.* You miserable asshole, you totally were. So, what's the verdict then? Were you counting my freckles? Ooh, or maybe looking at my dimples? People find the dimples very attractive-"

Peter rises to his feet, laughing. "Okay, okay!" he whisper-shouts, looking down at the ginger-haired Adonis sitting below him who's laughing just about as hard as he is. "*Goodnight*, Cameron," he says with a chuckle.

"Goodnight, Peter," Cameron whispers back. Peter turns to walk away, but stops when he feels the boy's ashy eyes on his back. He turns and stares at him, trying to keep a serious face.

"One hundred and twenty-eight so far," Peter whispers.

"What?" Cameron responds, looking confused.

Peter grins slyly. "Freckles," he whispers, "and you've only got one dimple, anyways." And with that, he turns and walks to his bed.

Part Sixteen: The Cancer

Peter

"Good morning!" Maya chirps as Peter's eyes flutter open.

Peter groans. "Ugh, Maya. Way too loud."

He sits up, stretching his arms over his head and looking around. Maya is perched over a small fire, cooking something that smells... really good, actually. Diana and Kiara are asleep under a magnolia tree, arms hooked around each other. Cameron is curled up in the fetal position, hugging a half-empty duffel bag to his chest and fast asleep as well.

Peter yawns and beckons Maya closer. "What are you cooking?"

She shrugs. "Well, *someone* was smart enough to bring food before she came, which was probably a good idea considering you guys were a week away from starving to death."

Peter chuckles, pushing up his shirt sleeves and running his fingers through his knotted curls. "Didn't answer the question, though."

She smiles, and Peter can't believe just how much she looks like Diana. He hadn't seen them side by side in eight years. "My mom taught me how to make easy omelets when I got to Sector Six. Just eggs, some chopped veggies, and a little bit of ham, if you have it."

Peter raises one eyebrow, asking the question, and Maya laughs. "Yes, we do have these ingredients, but today is gonna be the last day for actual meals, considering the only other things I brought were dried fruits, granola, trail mix, that sort of thing."

Peter stands up and stretches again. "Okay, well, how can I help?"

Maya waves him off. "No worries. It's the easiest thing, honestly. Best you can do is keep me company."

So, Peter sits down across from her at the fire, watching her crack eggs, put in vegetables, and stir them around in a small pan. They sit in a comfortable silence, and Peter feels happy that someone he cares so much for is back, right in front of him. It was a similar feeling he had when he saw Diana again, although not nearly as strong now as it was then.

"So," Maya says finally, "when was the last time any of you showered?"

Peter laughs, trying his best to stay quiet for the others. "Like... I don't know, a few days for me. Longer for those three, since they came from Sector One."

Maya crinkles her nose. "We should probably get on that, yeah? We can have two people go out and look for a stream or something today."

Peter nods. "We're lucky to have you, Maya," he says, looking up at her.

She meets his gaze. "I'm glad to be here. And I'm just pulling my weight, like everyone else." She pats the spot next to her. "Come over here and give me a proper hug, since I didn't get one before."

Peter grins and crosses to her, allowing himself to be enveloped in a warm hug. Maya squeezes him tightly, rocking him gently back and forth. After a long moment, she releases him and holds him at arm's length. Her eyes roam his face, and Peter notices that their normal greenness is covered by sparkling tears threatening to spill. "You've grown up so much," she whispers.

Peter sighs, smiling apologetically. "We all have."

Maya squeezes his forearms. "No, I mean *you*. Yeah, Kiara and Diana have, but... you've changed so much. You're not the little kid you were."

Peter doesn't show it, but he feels a little confused and sort of conflicted. What is Maya getting at? "Um... what do you mean?"

Maya shrugs. "You used to be so soft spoken, and shy, but now you're this brave, smart, kickass teenager." She smiles a little. "not that you weren't any of those things before. Now you're just letting us see those parts of you."

Peter smiles. "Well, I couldn't be this person without the others."

Maya shakes her head. "No. You think so, but this is just who you are. You can't give anyone else credit for you being awesome."

Peter scoffs playfully, but something about her comment rubs him the wrong way. Taking advantage of the others being asleep, Peter casts a wary glance around their camp before turning to Maya and lowering his voice. "Maya, are you sure about... all this?"

Maya smiles, and that simple gesture settles some of Peter's nerves. "Of course. We've been talking about this for years, Peter."

"I know, but..." he sighs, shaking his head, "I feel awful keeping this from Di."

"She doesn't need to know. If she does, it'll only hurt her."

Peter rubs a hand over his face, frustration mounting in his chest. "She's my best friend. If she gets hurt because of us, I'll never be able to live with myself."

Maya rolls her eyes, and Peter can't tell if she's joking or if she's actually getting upset. "And she's *my* sister. I feel the same way." She looks at Peter, and her voice is imploring when she finally speaks. "You get it now, right? What I was trying to tell you?"

Peter remembers the buzzing, electric feeling of warping the wall, the power that sparked to life within him, and he sighs. "Yeah. I get it now."

"You're special, Peter. So is Cameron. So are *nine* other people in this country. And they know it. You never understood this, but there are revolutionaries *everywhere.* This country is a powder keg, and all they need is a match." She jerks her head towards Diana, who is still sleeping soundly. Peter follows her gaze, chest constricting with guilt when he looks over at his best friend. "Peter, all they need is a catalyst. And *she* is it."

"She doesn't deserve this pressure."

"She's a leader. She's strong, she's brave. The country will have to turn to somebody."

"And why not you?"

Maya sighs, and Peter wonders if she's at all disappointed. "I'm already a criminal, Peter. I'm in too deep with the BOZ as it is. But Diana, she's got the heart to make things better." She gives Peter a stern look. "She just needs to only know so much."

Peter nods, and he reaches over and takes Maya's hand. "I feel awful."

"Don't. You're a Powerful One. You deserve to *feel* powerful."

Peter is so overwhelmed, the only thing he can do is hug her again. They're quiet for a little while, until a groggy morning voice interrupts them.

"Look at you two," Cameron says kindly. Maya and Peter look over to see him sitting up, cracking his knuckles. His Gray pants are stained with dirt, and his freckled arms are sunburnt just the slightest bit from all this time outside.

"Good morning," Maya says cheerfully, snuffing out the conversation from before. She crosses to him and tosses a bottle of water in his direction. Cameron, without breaking eye contact, cracks the top of it and starts to drink, listening intently to Maya as he does. "Breakfast is coming, and then we're gonna have some people look for a stream or something so you four can shower."

Cameron swallows and nods, wiping his mouth with the back of his hand. "Sounds great. Any idea for when we're going to head out?"

Maya shakes her head. "We need a solid plan first, and you need to be up and walking. A few days won't hurt us." She sits back down by the fire, and then she looks up at Peter as if remembering something. "Oh, Peter. I also brought this." She reaches into her bag and pulls out a roll of gauze and an alcohol wipe. She passes them to Peter, who looks down at them with an awed expression.

"Maya! You're the best." He launches himself at her and wraps his arms around her neck, hugging her tightly.

Maya laughs and pushes him off gently. "Yeah, yeah. Anything for you, sweetheart. Now I'm gonna finish breakfast and wake up the lazybones over there," she says, motioning to the girls, who are still out cold.

Peter stands, watching her walk over to them, and then turns towards Cameron, who's watching him intently from his seat against the tree. He really does look *so* much better, Peter realizes. His dark circles are fading, his cheekbones aren't so hollow, and he's fidgeting more than he was before, a sure sign he was on the mend.

Peter brushes himself off and plants his hands on his hips, smirking and raising one eyebrow. "You know, it'll be weird to see you up and walking again. You're more of a bother that way. I think I like it better when you can't move."

Cameron crosses his arms jokingly. "Very rude indeed, Peter. But you're the one to blame. If you hadn't catered to me so kindly, I would probably still be down for the count."

Peter laughs and crouches in front of him, holding up his new supplies. "Well, now that I have formal medical supplies, you can officially put 'Doctor' in front of my name."

Cameron rolls his eyes as he pushes up his pant leg. "Absolutely not. You're just the same old Peter to me."

Peter looks up at him as he begins to clean Cameron's wound. "Ouch. 'Same old Peter'."

Cameron chuckles softly. "You know what I mean. Same old smart, kind, captain-of-the-team Peter."

"Captain? No, more like a steward," Peter replies. "I'd rather clean up after you guys than be in charge."

Cameron shrugs, watching Peter work and causing him to feel a little nervous under his watchful gaze. "We still need you." When Peter looks up and their eyes meet, Cameron smiles gently. "I sure do."

Peter pauses. Normally he would deflect when Cameron complimented him, but today, he decided he'd do it differently. Something about today felt new, felt better. So he grins at Cameron and says, "Same goes for me."

Cameron smiles and glances down at the brand-new wrap around his ankle. His face lights up, and Peter feels nothing but happiness at the idea of making Cameron so enthralled. "This is awesome! God, you and Maya are my new favorite people."

Peter puts a dramatic hand over his heart. "You wound me, Cam. I can't believe I wasn't your favorite before."

But Cameron is only half listening, adjusting so that his back is flat against the tree trunk. He looks up at Peter, who is still kneeling in front of him. "Okay, I'm gonna try something, and I need your full help *and* trust."

Peter rolls his eyes. "When do I *not* go along with whatever scheme you guys cook up?"

"Very true. Okay, stand up."

Peter complies, putting his hands on his hips.

"Give me your hand."

Peter puts his hand out, and Cameron takes it, gripping his wrist. "I think I know what you're-"

"Pull me up."

"My god, Cam. I swear, if *I'm* the reason you hurt yourself all over again-"

"No, I'm feeling better today. Look, I'm up against the tree and holding on to you. I won't try to walk or anything, I just need to see if I can put weight on it again. Come on, superhero, help me out here."

Peter groans, but gives a tug on their locked hands, slowly but surely pulling Cameron to his feet. When he gets all the way up, Cameron leans against the tree trunk, all smiles. "Super weird to be up again."

Peter releases his hand carefully and takes a half step closer. "Can you stand up on your own?"

"I can try," Cameron replies.

Peter nods, and watches as Cameron slowly pushes himself off the tree and onto both feet. His eyes are squeezed shut, and his fists are clenched, the only indication that he's nervous. Peter waits with bated breath, heart pounding in his chest. Finally, after what feels like an eternity, Cameron plants both feet flat on the ground, wobbling a bit but gaining his footing nearly perfectly after a moment. Cameron slowly opens his eyes to see Peter standing before him with an incredulous expression.

"Oh my god," Peter whispers, letting out a huge sigh of relief, "Cameron, this is..." he trails off, looking Cameron up and down and grinning, "this is amazing."

Cameron grins right back. "Peter, I swear, if I could run, I would sprint around this whole campsite screaming my head off, right after I hug the living daylights out of you."

Peter blushes unintentionally. "Well-"

He's cut off by Cameron flinging himself at him, throwing his arms around Peter's neck. Peter, on instinct more than anything else, grips Cameron's waist to keep them both from toppling over. Both boys grow tense, feeling the awkwardness and falling quiet.

By the fire, the three girls are watching this intently, without the boys knowing. "Should we say something-?" Diana starts.

Maya shushes her. "No." She smiles softly at the scene in front of her. "Let them be."

Peter and Cameron are still locked in each other's arms, and slowly, they both relax, fitting in each other's hold a little better. Peter, being the shorter one in the embrace, nestles his face into Cameron's shoulder.

Cameron sucks in a sharp breath, but he reacts the same way Peter did, by ducking his head down next to Peter's ear and burying his cheek in his hair. Cameron tries not to note Peter's nose and lips pressed so close to his collarbone. Peter tries not to think about Cameron's fingers playing with the back of his shirt.

The world is quiet for a second, and the only sound Peter hears is Cameron's gentle breathing. It's just a normal hug, as one does, he tells himself. Nothing out of the ordinary.

Peter clears his throat and pulls away, heart flipping when he swears he sees Cameron's eyes flick down to his mouth before returning to his face.

"Um... we should probably eat," Peter whispers.

Cameron nods, running a hand through his hair. "Right. Can you help me over?"

The first and last thing Peter wants to do is touch Cameron again, but he nods and allows Cameron to thread an arm over his shoulders. When they turn around, both boys' eyes widen at the sight of the three girls watching them intently.

"Congratulations, Cam," Maya says finally. "I'm glad you're feeling better."

"Me too," Diana and Kiara rush in simultaneously.

Peter helps Cameron sit down, and then scuttles to a seat between Maya and Kiara. "So," Maya interjects, "I think I can hang back here with Cameron if you three want to go out and look for a stream," she says, motioning to Peter, Diana, and Kiara.

Everyone nods, and Kiara, Peter, and Diana eat quickly, putting the paper plates Maya has brought on the top of the fire per her instruction. They get up and exit the clearing quietly, leaving Cameron and Maya alone.

At least he can *breathe* again.

"Okay," Cameron huffs, "okay."

Maya snorts, snapping Cameron's attention to her. She's laughing quietly, or at least she *was*, and she's using her hand to cover her mouth.

"Sorry," she says, waving her hand, "but that was the most adorable thing I've ever witnessed."

Cameron suddenly feels defensive. "Friends can hug."

"No, not that," Maya says, waving him off. "The fact that you're verbally trying to calm yourself down *because* of the hug."

"I am *not,*" Cameron responds, crossing his arms. Normally, he'd get up and leave, but his now-throbbing ankle isn't helping with that.

"Yes, you are. Don't deny it, it's fine," Maya responds, tossing her own plate on the fire. "So, do you like him?"

Oh God, was this really happening? "What are you talking about?"

Maya rolls her eyes. "You can't be serious. Come on, Cameron, I know I haven't known you for long, but you can talk to me. As the older sister of the group, I'm sworn to secrecy."

Cameron groans. This cannot be real life. "I don't know where to start."

Maya shrugs as if it were obvious. "Well, do you have feelings for him, or is it strictly platonic?"

Cameron looks her in the eye and hesitates. "This is weird, because of Diana. Right?"

Maya stands and brushes herself off, shrugging again. "I figured you'd be the first person to realize I know probably twenty percent of what goes on in my sister's life, but if you don't want to talk, don't talk."

She starts to walk away, towards the bags, but Cameron fidgets and groans. "Okay, fine! Sit down."

Maya grins and sits again, crossing her legs at the ankle. She looks at Cameron expectantly.

Cameron wrings his hands together, mulling over what he should say. Finally, he sighs. "I don't know. I think... well, I don't know if he's..."

Maya raises one eyebrow. "...Straight?" She finishes.

Cameron nods. "Yeah."

"This might be a dumb question, but haven't you noticed that he's definitely at least a *little* into you?"

Cameron's face twists into a confused expression. "Well, I dunno, because there's this whole thing with Diana, how they were like childhood friends, and I feel bad for stepping on that."

Maya shakes her head. "Cameron, Diana and Peter have their own stuff to work out. But you shouldn't feel bad for *liking* someone."

"I-"

"You *do* like him. Don't you?" She asks, smiling gently. She already knows.

Cameron pinches the bridge of his nose and sighs, picturing Peter's smile, his sassy little eye rolls when he thinks nobody is looking, his face pressed into Cameron's shoulder. Cameron then looks up at Maya, who smiles softly and nods a little.

"Yeah. Yeah, I think I do."

Part Seventeen: The Aries

Kiara

Kiara, Peter, and Diana trek through the woods of Sector Five, under the shade of the magnolia trees. Kiara fidgets uncomfortably.

"Peter, it's so *hot*. How do you even stand it?"

He shrugs. "It's always hot. Diana probably understands."

Diana does in fact nod, stepping over a fallen log. "I don't think it's ever cold in Sector Seven."

The three get quiet again, and Kiara stops to listen to her surroundings. She hears rustling leaves from somewhere far away, and moments later, an airy breeze weaves its way through the group.

"Peter, do you think there are any streams close by?" Diana asks, her voice low and content. It's obvious that she's enjoying this nature walk, while Kiara, on the other hand, is not.

"I dunno. Whatever we do find, it's not like we'll have any type of soap or anything."

Kiara shrugs. "It'll be good to feel *slightly* cleaner."

Diana sniffs her shirt and scrunches her nose. "Yeah. What she said."

They continue to walk, Kiara and Diana on the ends and Peter in the middle, head turning every so often to survey their surroundings. Finally, he turns to the girls. "Actually, there might be a lake around here. Do you see the ground sloping?"

Kiara crouches, studying the ground. Sure enough, it's sloping downwards, and she wanders a bit further into the trees just far enough to see the shimmering reflection of a swampish lake. She turns around and waves the other two towards her, and they galavant down the hill to the water's edge.

"Sweet," Peter exclaims. "The water is pretty clear, too."

Kiara wrinkles her nose. "*This* is clear water for you two?"

Diana tilts her head. "I... I actually, uh, I don't think I've *seen* a lake in Sector Seven."

"Wait, what?" Peter asks incredulously. "Like, never?"

"Never. I live very, *very* deep in the suburbs."

Peter shrugs and bends down, dunking his hand in the water. He pulls it out and stands again, placing his hands on his hips. "Okay. Someone should go get Maya and Cameron, right?"

"Well, Cameron can't walk this far," Diana retorts, "so we need a different plan."

Both girls glance at Peter expectantly, and he sighs. "I... *guess* I can carry him again."

Kiara snorts with laughter. "Let's go get them."

So they walk back the way they came, reaching the campsite in about fifteen minutes. Maya is sitting around the campfire with Cameron, smoke curling gently into the air. Cameron spots them over his shoulder and his face lights up.

"You guys! I've been sitting here for like, a half an hour! Did you find anything?"

Diana laughs and hugs him from behind, wrapping her arms around his neck and sitting down next to him. "God, you're probably going stir-crazy just sitting here. Yes, we found something, but you're not gonna like how you get there."

"Peter has to carry me again, doesn't he?" Cameron asks, looking apologetically over at Peter.

Peter crouches next to Cameron, nudging his arm. "It's fine. You weigh a lot less than you think." He doesn't add that Cameron's weight has dropped significantly, probably from the toll his illness was taking.

"I'm not sure if that's an insult or not."

Peter shrugs and stands up again, holding out his arms. Cameron takes them, and Peter pulls him up, letting Cameron gain his footing by clinging onto Peter's elbows. Diana and Kiara brace him as well, and slowly, they let go.

"All good?" Kiara asks, eyeing the two boys.

Peter and Cameron don't answer, instead getting themselves situated again with Cameron on Peter's back. After some gentle adjustments, Peter nods. "All good."

Maya crosses to them and smiles at the predicament in front of her. She eyes her little sister. "You never mentioned this."

Diana looks up at the two boys. "I really didn't think we'd see it again, to be honest."

The five head into the woods, with Peter and Cameron slowly taking up the rear. Cameron has taken to smacking the tree branches he can reach, and unfortunately, causing most of them to fly back into Peter's face.

"Okay, Cameron, that's good," Peter mumbles, "hit someone else with those branches."

"Sorry," Cameron replies. "It's the first time I've been walking in days."

"*I'm* walking, Cameron, in case you haven't noticed."

Before Cameron can respond, they come across the lake. It's big and boggy, but the water gets deep pretty quickly. Kiara leans over the edge and realizes that about ten feet out, she can't even see the bottom.

"This... may be slightly awkward," Maya mumbles. She turns to the rest of the group, looking up from where she was peering into the depths of the lake. "Have we thought through the privacy situation?"

The rest of them think for a moment. "Boys and girls?" Diana questions.

"No!" Cameron and Peter hurriedly chime together, averting eye contact.

Kiara sighs, bending down and untying her shoes. "I don't even care anymore. In or out, but I'm going."

"Okay, the rest of us will wait. Don't take too long," Maya says. She beckons the others into the woods. "Give her some space."

The four head into the woods, out of Kiara's line of sight, and she pulls off the rest of her clothes, stepping gingerly into the lake. It's pretty warm for the late time of year, and she fully submerges herself, trying not to think about the murky muck under her feet.

She scrubs a hand through her hair and stands again, spotting her clothes further down the beach than she left them. "Diana!" she shouts. "Give me my clothes back!"

Peter emerges from the woods, shielding his eyes, and he passes her the clothes in question. "Sorry. It was Cameron's idea, Maya just executed it."

Kiara sighs, brushing away a water droplet that rolls freely down her nose. "It's fine. I expected as much."

Peter turns around as Kiara emerges from the lake and puts her clothes back on, cringing at the way the fabric clings to her wet skin. She taps his shoulder when she's done, wringing out her curls. "You're good."

Peter shrugs out of his sweatshirt, then his undershirt, and Kiara walks away before she sees anything else, going towards the voices in the woods. The other three are sitting on fallen logs and stumps, and the clearing is dark from the long, twisting branches of the trees around them.

"Hey, kid," Maya chirps. "Cold?"

Kiara shrugs. "Wet."

"A brilliant point."

Cameron yelps as a stick whacks him in the arm.

They sit in silence for a second, until Peter returns, water dripping from his curls. Kiara catches Cameron's eyes trace the movement and she smirks. Something is going on, and she was determined to get to the bottom of it.

"Who's next?" Peter asks, shaking water out of his ear.

"Me!" Diana shouts. She rushes off to the lake, and Peter takes her seat, leaning forward with his elbows on his knees. He grins at the remaining three.

"How are we feeling, Cam?"

Cameron swallows. "Pretty okay. I don't think I can walk to the water by myself, though."

Maya shrugs. "We'll help you. The biggest thing is that you heal so we can get back on the road."

"How long are we thinking that will take?" Kiara asks, looking towards Peter.

His gaze travels down to Cameron's ankle. "I dunno. The ball is in Cam's court now. He determines whether or not he feels well enough to walk, much less travel long distances."

Cameron looks down at his ankle as if it would tell him straight out. "I'm okay to stand. But not to walk," he says with certainty.

Peter nods. "Okay, so... there. If Cameron wakes up one morning and says we can go, then we go. If he says we need another two weeks so he feels better, we wait two weeks."

Cameron's gaze softens at him, and he looks around at the others. "You guys would seriously put this whole thing off for me?"

Kiara reaches across the circle and grabs his hands, smiling at him. "We'd do anything for you, Cam."

Maya places a hand over her heart as Diana re-enters the clearing. She senses the somber mood and pauses. "What's going on?"

"Nothing," Peter says, smiling at Kiara, "Maya, your turn."

Maya gets up and leaves, and the teens settle down again, sitting in a companionable silence. Diana squeezes water from her hair, Cameron looks up into the canopy of the trees, and Peter and Kiara whisper amongst themselves.

"Whatcha talking about?" Cameron interjects after a few minutes.

Peter turns beet red, clearing his throat. "Nothing!"

Kiara grins at his response. "Nothing," she echoes.

Cameron raises one eyebrow, and Kiara glances at Peter, who's looking at his clasped hands. Maya comes back then, and she grabs Peter, hoisting him up by the shoulder.

"Alright, Peter. Help me move Cameron."

So, Peter and Maya scoop Cameron up, bridal-style, and carry him to the beach. They set him down gently on his feet, with Maya clutching his arms tightly to keep him from toppling over.

Kiara and Diana trail the procession, and Kiara halts in her tracks when she realizes the next task. She clears her throat. "Guys, how will Cameron..."

Diana's eyes widen. "Oh, god."

Cameron groans. "I can take off my own pants. I'm not ninety years old."

Maya studies him, grimacing. "Can you keep your balance?"

Cameron rolls his eyes. "*No*, but I'm not gonna let you guys stand here and watch me fall over. Get out of here."

The other four start to retreat, until Cameron groans, turning his hips to face them. "Kiara, stay."

The other three leave and Kiara watches them go from her spot on the beach. "You don't want Peter to stay?"

He shakes his head. "He's been taking care of me for a while. He deserves to not stress," he pulls his shirt over his head and nods towards his feet, "can you grab my shoes?"

Kiara bends down, untying his shoelaces and carefully pulling his shoes off. "Anything else?"

Cameron sighs and unzips his pants. "Just grab my arms. Please."

Kiara complies and looks away.

"I'm sorry," Cameron says, "this is super awkward."

Kiara shrugs, face still turned away from him. "I literally couldn't care less."

He laughs, and Kiara stands to help him into the water. He sits and looks up at Kiara, and the two dissolve into laughter.

"You look like a little kid," Kiara chuckles.

"Come on, don't antagonize me like this!" He laughs, splashing water towards her.

"Okay, okay!" She shrieks, running away from him, further up the beach. "I just got dry!"

"You deserved it!" He hollers back, dunking his head underwater.

Kiara sighs and glances towards the woods, where she can just barely see the silhouettes of the others. She spots a familiar curly head, and smiles at Peter, even though she knows he can't see her.

Kiara turns to Peter as Diana begins finger-brushing her hair.

"Peter, I have a question," she whispers.

Peter's eyes are stuck on Cameron, who's meticulously examining his ankle. "Hm?"

Kiara shakes his arm and Peter finally looks at her. "I said, I have a question for you."

"Okay, what is it?" He sits back a little bit, crossing his arms and leaning further into Kiara.

She lowers her voice even further, sneakily pointing at Cameron. "Well, do you like him?"

"What?!" he practically shrieks. His face drains of color and his hand flies over his mouth.

"Whatcha talking about?" Cameron interjects.

"Nothing!" Peter exclaims, sounding much more suspicious than he intended.

Kiara smirks and looks between the boys. "Nothing," she affirms.

Kiara helps Cameron hobble out of the lake, and he pulls his shirt and pants back on pretty well on his own. Kiara gets his shoes on for him, tying them tightly as the others come out of the woods.

"Almost ready?" Diana asks, eyeing Cameron and Kiara.

"Yeah," Cameron says. Peter walks over to him, turning around so Cameron can get onto his back.

They begin to walk again, Peter slowing down every so often to readjust Cameron.

"You know, I really can't wait to get back into the Capitol," Maya says, eyes wandering as if her mind is elsewhere.

"What do you mean?" Diana asks, pushing a branch out of her way.

"It's beautiful there, no matter how awful those people are. You should see the archives. It was my favorite place when I worked there."

"What about when you went back home?"

Maya frowns. "Well, I had mom back home. Until she got sick. Because then, home was more stressful than work."

"I didn't know your mom got sick," Peter says.

Diana nods. "She died really fast, too. Only a few days after she got diagnosed. I just got a visit from a guard, and I didn't even get to go to the funeral, since it wasn't in Sector Seven."

Maya grabs Diana's hand. "It wasn't something you'd want to be around for, trust me."

Diana says nothing, just laces their fingers together despite the sour look on her face. Kiara clears her throat, breaking through the tension.

"Wanna play a game?"

"Sure," the others chime.

"Okay, so basically, I say something, and if you've done it before in your life, you put a finger down. First person with three fingers down wins."

Everyone responds by putting up three fingers, looking out of the corners of their eyes at Kiara.

She thinks for a moment. "Okay, put a finger down if you've ever... snuck out past sector curfew."

Everyone but Diana puts a finger down.

"What? Even you, Peter?" she practically shrieks.

He shrugs, smirking. "Only once. It was important, anyway."

He doesn't elaborate, although Diana looks at him with a confused expression. "Next," Kiara says, clapping her hands together, "put a finger down if you've ever kissed someone."

Maya and Cameron both put a finger down.

"I'm at one already, this isn't fair," Cameron says, waving his index finger in the air.

"Tell me about it," Maya says, nodding solemnly.

"Put a finger down if you've met your BOZ leader."

Everyone puts a finger down. Diana frowns. "Ki, *everyone* does, when they turn twelve."

Kiara grins at her. "I know. I just felt bad for you."

Diana gapes dramatically at her, and Kiara laughs. "Wait, do I put down two if I've met both of mine?" Maya asks.

"You've had two?" Peter responds, sounding shocked.

Maya nods. "Oliver and Archer Hill. His dad was there when I was twelve, but when I worked at the Capitol, it was Oliver."

"Imagine being on a first-name basis with your BOZ person," Cameron says wistfully from atop Peter's back. "Can you even imagine me walking up to Mister Myers and calling him 'Gerard'?"

Peter chuckles. "Unfortunately, I think you're the only Scorpio who *would* do that."

Cameron scoffs playfully, and Peter blushes.

"This means Cameron and I win!" Maya interjects. She reaches over and shares a fist-bump with Cameron, and Diana rolls her eyes.

"I'm more concerned about the fact that Peter is seventeen and Diana is sixteen, and neither of them have kissed anyone."

"Cameron, not all of us can be six feet tall and look like a supermodel," Diana retorts sarcastically. Cameron just strikes a flexing pose.

"Thank you, darling. Glad to know *one* of you appreciates my beauty."

Kiara glances at Peter, but he doesn't say anything, instead just becoming *very* interested in the trees around him.

The five reach their campsite, and Maya crosses immediately to the fire. "I'm thinking of a quick snack and a nap."

"Seconded," Peter says with a yawn. Kiara watches him gently lower Cameron onto the ground, helping him sit by his bed.

Diana is sitting by the fire, chin in her hands. Kiara sits next to her. "Hey."

"Hi," she responds without looking up.

"Is everything alright?"

A sigh and a shrug. "I guess. It's just... I'm realizing how little I know about Maya."

"What do you mean?"

"Well... I don't know. Just that she has this whole life, so far away from mine, and it feels like she's some stranger."

Kiara chews her lip, trying to think of the best response. "Well, isn't she? I mean, of course she's still your sister, but the worst thing about the Split was that we inherently *became* strangers. But the beautiful thing about this motley camp is that the more time passes, the more we realize we're not strangers, we're still family."

Diana nods slowly, absorbing her words. Finally, she looks at Kiara out of the corner of her eye. "But do you think Maya feels the same way?"

Kiara looks over at Maya, where she's reviewing a map with Peter, up against the tree next to a snoozing Cameron. "Maybe. I don't think talking to her, just you two, would hurt anything," Diana follows her gaze towards her sister and her best friend. Kiara nudges her arm gently. "I don't think it would hurt to talk to either of them, actually."

Diana looks towards Kiara, raising one eyebrow. Her mouth is set in a gentle frown. "What do you mean?"

"Have you taken the time to sit down and rehash things with Peter yet?"

She hesitates, remembering the feeling of Peter's lips against hers. "No."

"Okay, so do that, if you feel so inclined. We need to be a fully-functioning team if we're going to get through this. And, not to mention, these are the two people you love the most."

"Four," Diana responds instantly.

Now it's Kiara's turn to look confused. "Huh?"

Diana turns to face her. "You keep saying how Peter and Maya are the two people I love the most," she motions around the camp one-by-one, to Peter, Maya, Kiara, and Cameron, "but it's all four of you. You guys are becoming my family now, and I love *all* of you the most."

Kiara just looks at her for a second, until Diana leans forward and wraps her in a strong hug. "I love you, Di."

"I love you too, Ki. Thank you for your advice."

Kiara pulls away and looks her in the eye. "Giving advice is what I'm best at."

"And kicking ass," Diana fills in.

Kiara chuckles. "*And* kicking ass."

Part Eighteen: The Cancer

Peter

That evening, after dinner, the group is sitting quietly in various parts of the campsite. Never before had Peter been able to sit in this comfortable a silence, not since he was in school and would hide with Diana amongst the trees.

Peter was sitting under a tree, sharpening one of Kiara's knives. Next to him, an arm's reach away, was the border wall, and Peter would occasionally hold the blade up to see it better in the eerie light.

They were immersed in an eerie blue darkness, the fire having gone out and no one bothering to relight it, but the glowing border light illuminating the space enough to see. Maya was seated near Cameron, both reviewing maps and lists that had been made. Kiara was dozing near the largest of the magnolias, and Diana was braiding together three long strands of dry grass, her hair down around her shoulders, having just tried the same style on herself.

Suddenly, a twig snaps from somewhere in the forest.

Every one of the five people in that clearing freezes; even Kiara's eyes fly open. Peter watches as they all react in the same way: eyes flitting around the treeline, breathing steady and slow, hands slowly creeping towards the nearest weapon, and not the slightest sound.

The sound of a voice and the crackling of a handheld radio cuts through the darkness, and Peter listens as carefully as he can, trying to ignore the thumping of his own heart.

"I'm near the wall. No sign of them yet, over."

The gruff voice belongs to a man, and Peter watches as Kiara swiftly and silently grabs the lowest magnolia branch and pulls herself into the tree, moving into the canopy and disappearing from view.

Just then, Peter spies the silhouette of the guard come into view, and he's acutely aware of how visible he is, framed by the border wall. But he could fight while the others moved under the cover of darkness, hiding themselves from danger.

But Peter was frozen with fear, his fingertips cold and tingling, as if he wouldn't be able to bring himself to take hold of the border wall and use it to harm someone.

Peter had told Diana his nightmare was hurting someone. He hadn't expected it to come true so soon.

But with Cameron and Maya out of his reach, and Diana moving mechanically to follow Kiara into the trees, it didn't seem like Peter had any choice.

One move, and Peter would become visible to the guard, the harsh glow of the wall being the only protection from the man's gaze. The sound of footsteps grows nearer, and Peter's hand snakes closer to the wall, fingers inching through the coarse dirt.

Kiara's knife lies abandoned on the ground.

Just as the man shouts some garbled, incoherent noise, pointing in Peter's direction, he grabs a piece of the wall and leaps to his feet.

It isn't as though Peter really thinks. No, all he does is watch as time seems to slow, robotically going through the motions he knew best. His hand, the one now glowing blue, tingles and ignites with power, and Peter feels it thrumming through his veins. He plants his feet, squinting in focus, and takes a deep breath.

The guard's gun is drawn, arms outstretched, the barrel pointing towards Peter's chest. He should be shaking in fear, and yet, he was instead shivering with power, framed by the endless blue wall behind him.

Peter watches as the guard's finger lands on the trigger.

It's unclear who shoots first.

Peter's projectile hits the guard straight on, aim unwavering, and the bullet from the man's gun strays, embedding itself in the border wall six inches from Peter's head.

The only thing that brings Peter down from the intense high of his power is the sound of screaming and the sharp, raw smell of charring hair.

Peter blinks, stumbling backward as he takes in what he did, his friends appearing in his swimming vision. He feels nauseous, he feels violated, he feels *evil*.

The Peter who had told his friend that his biggest fear was hurting someone? That boy was no longer a piece of him.

"Peter," Diana says, stepping into his line of sight, between him and the guard. "Peter, breathe."

Peter is mumbling something, inhaling shakily between gags, as he watches over Diana's shoulder as the other three move the guard's body, his death creation dissipated with one press of Cameron's palm.

Diana's hands are on him, and he yanks himself away, as if he'd hurt her just by meeting her gaze.

Finally, he looks up at her, and her gaze is frighteningly resolved. "Peter," she whispers, "you saved us. It's okay."

"I killed him," Peter manages at last.

"We're safe."

Peter lets her words sink in as he allows himself to be enveloped in a hug, the pair sinking to the ground a safe distance from the wall and the burnt patch of dirt a few paces in front of them.

You saved them, Peter tells himself as his breathing begins to even out, *it's okay.*

He squeezes his eyes shut and tries to ignore the anxious repetition of *you killed him* that's ricocheting through his skull.

"Peter?" a voice whispers. "Peter?"

He opens his eyes to see Kiara standing over him, gaze concerned. He almost laughs. He couldn't remember the last time his stone-faced Aries friend let down her resolve in such a blatant manner.

He had been sleeping restlessly in the dirt, back turned towards the wall and the place where he'd killed that guard a few hours before.

The others had started a new fire, and they were still awake, with Cameron, Maya, and Diana looking towards Peter worriedly. It was obvious that Kiara had lost some sort of bet as to who had to go wake him up and ensure he wasn't losing his mind.

"Do you need something?" Peter whispers, trying and failing to not sound rude.

Kiara opens her mouth, then closes it again. "Are you hungry?"

Just the thought of eating makes Peter want to throw up, which sets his nerves off even more. "No."

"You haven't eaten for hours."

"I know, Ki."

She sighs and sits in the dirt in front of him. Her curly hair is matted, her ebony skin streaked with mud.

But she still looks brave, Peter thinks, she still looks strong. Stronger than him.

"Peter, you can't let this eat away at you."

He shakes his head, refusing to meet her gaze, instead anxiously drawing lines in the dirt in front of him. They were even in shape, length, and depth, and the routine movement stilled some of his anxiety.

Kiara doesn't speak and doesn't seem perturbed by the fact that he ignored her. Instead, she watches as he draws a perfect line with his index finger.

Then, she uses her own fingers to mess up his rough drawing, skewing the dirt and ruining his work.

"Ki," Peter warns with a soft groan. He knew exactly what she was doing.

She doesn't respond, so he draws another line. She messes up that one, too.

Peter's frustration finally mounts and he glares up at her. She's waiting with a stern look that makes Peter swallow his remark.

"Perfection isn't real, Peter," she says, holding his gaze. "This revolt will not and cannot be perfect. The more you strive for flawlessness, the worse things will hurt when they go wrong."

"I killed a man, Kiara," Peter argues, brushing his dirt-covered, shaking fingers down his pants. "You don't know how that feels."

"No, but I probably will," she replies, shutting him up, "and I know that as awful as I may feel, it's a sacrifice I'll have to make to protect myself. To protect *you*. And I would kill a hundred people if it meant keeping you safe."

Peter pauses, absorbing her words. With a shaky inhale, he glances down at his ruined drawings. They looked disastrous, but with Kiara's... help, he supposes, the lines weren't perfect, sure, but they were still *there*. They were there, in some backwards way.

He looks up at his friend and smiles gently. "Let's hope it doesn't come to that."

Part Nineteen: The Taurus

Diana

"Maya," Diana whispers, grabbing her sister's sleeve, "can we talk?"

Maya stands and brushes herself off, nodding. "Sure. Let's take a walk."

Diana bites her lip, looking around at the others. Peter is sleeping restlessly on the bare ground, using a bag, presumably Maya's, as a pillow. Cameron is next to him, and Kiara is further away, under a tree, also fast asleep. "Should we leave them?"

"Well, do you want them in this talk, too?"

"No," Diana states finally.

"Okay, then. Let's go."

So the sisters walk through the woods slowly, and after a moment, Diana notices they were unconsciously walking in the direction of the lake. She continues with Maya, gazing up at the night sky and willing her thumping heart to calm down.

They reach the beach, and Maya sits, digging her bare toes into the sand. She looks up at Diana, who's still standing awkwardly above her. "What's up?"

Diana takes a deep breath, clearing her throat. "Maya, I feel like..." she trails off, looking out to the lake, squinting to see the opposite shoreline.

Maya raises one eyebrow and nudges Diana's ankle with her sandy foot. "What?"

Diana plops down next to her, looking her in the eye. "We're... disconnected. At least, that's how I feel. I just haven't seen you in so long, and now it feels like there's a wall between us. We were sisters when we were kids, but now we're just... team members."

Diana stops rambling and looks over at Maya, who is sitting quietly, knees pulled to her chest. The nighttime breeze ruffles her blonde hair, and she reaches into the sand, digging out a flat rock and skipping it once, twice, three times over the water's surface. Finally, after a long, agonizing lapse, Maya glances at her little sister out of the corner of her eye.

"Di, I don't really know what to say."

"Maya, I'm sorry, it's just how I'm feeling and I-"

"No, wait," Maya interrupts, holding out a hand that causes Diana's mouth to clamp shut, "Diana, I *get* it. But why didn't you tell me sooner?"

"Well, look what we're doing! Look at what's going on around us! We haven't had the *time*."

"Diana, if it means this much to you, we should've *made* the time. I *want* to work this out with you. But I can't do that if you're not going to communicate with me. I'm sorry for not thinking about this sooner. Because you're right, we haven't caught up at all since I got here."

Diana takes a deep, shaking breath, and sighs. "I'm sorry. You're right, this should've been the first thing we did when we saw each other again."

"Okay, so tell me about what you're feeling."

Diana huffs. "I dunno. I miss you."

"I missed you too."

"Well, I miss you now."

Maya grabs her sister's hand. She smiles through the darkness at Diana. "Di, guess what?"

"What?"

"In probably a week or two, this whole thing is gonna be over. And then, when we win this whole revolution, we'll probably get to go back to living together." She thinks for a second. "Where do you think we'll live, anyways? Would we go back to Sector Six, or Sector Seven?"

Diana smiles a little, shaking her head. "I want a high-rise in the Plaza. I've always wanted to see the inside of one of those things."

Maya shrugs. "It depends on the BOZ member."

"How would you know?!"

She smirks. "I've seen inside Oliver's, *once*. I was his intern, and I just had to run some files to his place."

"Was it super fancy?"

"Sort of. Everything was so shiny, but the actual apartment just felt... empty. He obviously lived alone, they all do, so it felt lonely in there."

Diana squeezes their laced fingers. "It won't feel like that for us. It'll be full of life, and laughter, and Peter and Ki and Cam will all have guest bedrooms to stay in if they want."

"Well, wouldn't they just live with us?"

Diana shrugs. "Well, I dunno. Kiara probably wants to live by herself. Cameron will live with us, probably, and Peter's gonna want to go back to Sector Five."

Maya nods, looking back out towards the lake. "Okay, well, we'll have five rooms, just to be safe."

Diana grins. "Yeah."

They're quiet for a moment, until Maya reaches out and wraps her arms around her sister's shoulders. They hold each other in the dark stillness for a long while, until voices from behind them make them turn around abruptly.

"No, guys, they have to be at the beach, I'm telling you!" Cameron whisper-shouts.

"Oh my god, what happens if they got found out?" Peter groans.

"Or lost?!" Kiara practically wails.

The three are wandering blindly through the underbrush, not having seen Diana and Maya on the beach yet. Diana watches their shadows bicker, until finally, the silhouette she assumes is Peter uncups something from his hand.

A ball of the border material lights up their huddled faces, and the three look up from the blue glow to see Maya and Diana staring at them from their seats on the beach. Diana swears she's never seen relief so purely and truly flash across anybody's faces the way it did those three, just then.

"You're okay!" Cameron shouts, causing violent shushing noises from Kiara and Peter. But all three of them rush to the girls, with Peter helping Cameron shuffle along, tackling them onto the sand in a crushing hug. Diana huffs out a breathless laugh from underneath her friends.

"We're okay! We just went for a walk," Diana says, sitting up and pushing them gently off her lap. "Why are you guys all awake?"

"I woke up and noticed you two were gone, and I sort of panicked," Peter explains. "I woke up the other two to ask if they had seen you, and they both said no-"

"So we *all* collectively panicked," Cameron says with a chuckle.

Diana looks towards Kiara, who's yet to say anything. But she's staring wide-eyed at something up against Maya's pant leg. Diana looks, seeing that the baseball-sized clump of the border wall Peter had dropped was pressed against her thigh. It should be burning a hole right through her skin, through her clothes.

But nothing was happening.

Maya follows their gazes, gasping when she notices and shoving the ball away with a wild, *bare* hand. She leaps to her feet, along with the other four, who are staring at her like she has two heads.

"Maya, what's going on?" Diana asks, pointing at the ball that's still resting on the beach. "That should've killed you!"

"I don't know, I, uh, I dunno, I must've moved quickly enough!" She says, voice rising nervously. Her fingers rush to the locket around her neck.

Peter bends down and scoops up the ball, squeezing his hands together and snuffing out the light. He looks at Maya seriously, and Diana bristles at their heated gaze.

"Maya."

"*What*, Peter?"

He hesitates, glancing Diana's way, and then sighs. "You have to tell them."

Diana swallows the rising lump in her throat. "Tell us *what,* Maya?"

Maya swallows, straightening her shoulders. She looks so serious, so tired. So unlike the Maya they know.

"This whole thing was my idea."

Cameron's eyebrows knit together. "No, Peter came up with the revolt."

Maya shakes her head. "No, *I* did. When I was seventeen."

"Seventeen?" Diana whispers incredulously. "How did Peter know about this?"

"She told me," he juts in, looking down at the ground. "We visited when I was fourteen. Maya filled me in on everything, how she found out about the powers working with Oliver, and how I was in the book. So was Cameron."

Cameron looks at Peter with a betrayed expression. "Peter, you knew who I was the whole time?"

Finally, Peter looks up. His face breaks into a hurt look when he meets Cameron's soft eyes, and his voice wavers. "No. *No*, Cameron, I swear. When Maya told me, I didn't want to listen. I didn't think anything was wrong."

"Maya, is this true?" Kiara asks.

"Yes," Maya affirms. "I told Peter. I even showed him the book, I snuck it out of the archives. I told him everything, but he didn't listen. He didn't *want* to listen, and I don't blame him."

Diana rubs her hands over her face. "Maya, I don't understand. What do you mean, you 'told him everything'?"

"The BOZ isn't what you think. The representatives are each picked to protect the Powerful Ones from each sector. They aren't around to rule, they're around to ensure nothing happens to their charges. Why do you think Gerard Myers got removed?"

Cameron's eyes widen. "He lost me."

Maya nods. "Exactly."

"But that makes no sense," Kiara interjects, "why does it matter if they're in charge of the Powerful Ones? Why do *we* need to revolt?"

"Because," Maya insists, "when I worked there, the very first year I did, Oliver told me their plan. The BOZ was planning to gather their eleven Powerful Ones and make an army."

"Why do they need an army if we're alone in the world?" Diana practically shrieks.

"I don't know, okay?! All I know is that the kids I saw when I worked there don't deserve to be soldiers! *Peter* and *Cameron* don't deserve to carry out the crazy massacres they have planned!" Maya is on the verge of tears now, and Peter and Cameron cast a forlorn look at each other. "Diana, I couldn't tell you. It was too dangerous. Hell, even Kiara got roped in."

"What?!" Kiara asks, voice rising as well.

"Ki, did they give you a Tracker when you turned twelve?"

Kiara clenches her jaw. "No."

"How about when you were fifteen?"

"*No*. What does that matter?"

"Because when I turned nineteen, I got the boot from the Capitol. They thought I had been fraternizing with the Powerful Ones, turning them against the BOZ. Henderson knew about Kiara's connection with Diana, her connection with me. So, Kiara got cut off, and Peter got me taken off as a contact too."

"Yeah," Peter says, realization dawning on him. "I did."

Diana sighs, sniffing back tears. "Maya, this isn't fair. Why didn't you say anything?" She whirls on Peter. "Why didn't *either* of you say anything?"

"Diana-" Peter starts.

"No. You know, I went along with this whole thing because I *believed* in you, Peter. Because I believed in *both* of you. I thought, 'you know, maybe everything could be normal, and we'll all be alright'. Maya, what happened to living together? What happened to five rooms in the Plaza?"

Maya crumbles, tears streaming down her cheeks. "Di, we can still do all that-"

"Maya, you pleaded with me, not *ten minutes* ago, that I needed to communicate with you, and yet, the whole time, you were hiding this huge secret! Your intentions are good, but you need to *talk* to me, Maya.

Honestly, I sort of wonder what else you're hiding from me."

"Diana, I'm not hiding anything from you."

"Really? Have you noticed your dates don't line up when you talk about Kiara's Tracker? Or that you seemed awfully close with this Oliver guy? Or how about when you touched the border wall and *didn't get burned?*"

"Diana, I don't know what to tell you," Maya says, voice setting in a hard tone, signifying the end of the argument. "I don't *have* all the answers, okay? And I'm sorry we lied, I am, but I can't take back all the years I hid this from you. You have to believe me when I tell you that I have nothing else to get off my chest. I'm not hiding *anything.* I want to be honest with you, I *wanted* to tell you, but I couldn't."

"Why?!" Diana shouts, opening her arms wide and gesturing to the beach around them. "Maya, *why* couldn't you? *What* kept you from telling me when I was pouring my heart out to you just now? Or telling Kiara when she came to get you? Or telling Cam when you stayed behind with him while the rest of us found the lake? You have no excuse for not saying something."

Maya opens her mouth to say something, but pauses, gazing at Diana with glimmering green eyes. "I know. I'm sorry, Diana."

"You are my sister. And Peter, you're my best friend. It doesn't feel good to know you guys were hiding this from us."

"I'm sorry, Diana," Peter mumbles. "I never wanted to hurt you."

"Yeah, well, you did," Diana says, voice finally cracking. "You both did."

And with that, she turns and walks away, back towards the campsite.

Part Twenty: The Scorpio

Cameron

Finally, around three hours after the group's big fight, Maya, Kiara, and Peter were asleep. They were all spread out, which Cameron was certain was intentional. Diana was sitting by the fire, alone, head in her hands.

As much as his sign implied otherwise, Cameron hated conflict. It hurt him to hurt others, and seeing his friends upset was something he just couldn't live with. As much as he didn't *want* to involve himself in this family fight, he felt like he was obligated to help as much as he could.

So he limps over and sits down next to Diana, nudging her with his arm. "Hey. Are you okay?"

She looks up at him with a sigh, motioning to her puffy cheeks and red eyes. "No."

"I'm sorry about this."

"It's not your fault."

"It isn't yours, either."

Diana falls quiet, nodding. She looks back over to the fire, and Cameron does the same. The orange flames flick into the night sky, smoke curling in tendrils around them.

"What do I do now?"

Her voice was so weak, so small. "What do you mean?" Cameron asks slowly.

"Well, I can't go on like this. *We* can't. We're not a team anymore."

Cameron nods slowly, and Diana watches him do so. He looks down at her, and they make eye contact.

The next thing Cameron knows, Diana is sobbing into his chest and she's wrapped up in his arms.

"Di, hey, it's okay," he whispers gently, "it's okay."

She doesn't respond, so he lets her cry. It's like comforting those kids during the Scorpio escape all over again, when Cameron was the one who told them their family didn't make it across, or that they would never go home again. Cameron felt things too deeply, and his heart aches as Diana begins hiccupping from crying so hard, her sobs muffled by his chest.

"I just don't get it," she whispers, voice creaky like a rusty hinge.

"I know. I don't either," he replies. She starts to cry again, and he squeezes her a little tighter.

Diana looks up at Cameron after a moment. "Are you mad at him?"

"At... who?"

"At Peter. For not telling you."

"I'm not mad, I'm disappointed. In *both* of them."

She nods, looking away. "Yeah."

Cameron looks over to where Peter is sleeping. "If you'll excuse me for a second."

He stands, and Diana grabs his wrist. The two share a look, and Diana nods. "Try to talk to him."

Cameron smiles sadly and nods. "I will."

Diana gets up and begins to get ready for bed, and Cameron crosses to Peter.

"Get up," he whispers, nudging Peter with his foot.

Peter startles awake and sits up in a flash. His frantic hazel eyes scan the clearing before landing on Cameron's legs and traveling up his torso, and Cameron fidgets under Peter's gaze despite himself. Finally, the two boys lock eyes.

"Get up, *please,*" Cameron says again, crossing his arms over his chest.

Peter scrambles to his feet and finally they're eye-to-eye, or as eye-to-eye they can get considering the height difference.

Peter's eyes are full of worry, and Cameron feels his tense shoulders soften a little and some of his anger melt away.

Not all of it, though.

"Let's go."

"Go where?"

"On a walk."

"Are you gonna murder me, or something?"

"I dunno, maybe. Now let's go."

They start off towards the woods, walking shoulder-to-shoulder. Though they weren't in the friendliest of situations at the moment, it seemed as though the two almost needed to walk side-by-side.

After a long moment of silence, Cameron speaks without taking his eyes off the woodlands ahead of them. "Why did you do it?"

"Not tell Diana?"

"Not tell *anyone*. What was so important that you could betray the girls like that?"

Peter shrugs, jostling Cameron's shoulder a little. The two are still keeping a steady pace through the underbrush. "I don't really know. Maya told me I shouldn't. I wanted to, but I'm not an idiot. I knew what it would mean for everyone I cared about if something happened and I got found out." He glances at Cameron. "You have to believe me, Cam. I didn't know about you having powers, either. I didn't even know about *mine*. Maya showed me the book, tried to show me the Cancer section, but I didn't want to know. I didn't want to live the rest of my life knowing some person, maybe in my own neighborhood, had to carry that huge secret."

"You didn't know that person was you?" Cameron whispers, turning to look at him and stopping.

Peter pauses as well. "Yeah," he affirms, voice laced with sadness.

They stare at each other for a long moment, and Cameron pulls his bottom lip between his teeth, tilting his head as if considering something. He looks up at Peter after an agonizing moment of silence. "Okay."

"Okay, what?"

"Okay, I believe you. And I forgive you, too. I don't think what you did was right, but I understand why you did this."

Peter's eyes grow wide. "You do?"

Cameron rolls his eyes and huffs out a chuckle. "Yeah, did you not just hear me?"

Peter laughs and shakes his head, looking down. The two fall into a lapse of silence until Peter's head snaps up and he looks at Cameron frantically. "Oh, my god!"

"What?!" Cameron says, putting out his hands either to block something or catch him if he happened to fall over. "What, what? What's going on?"

Peter's pearly white teeth shine in the moonlight as he grins at Cameron. "Look where we are!"

Cameron looks around, growing confused. They were just in the middle of the woods. "I don't get it."

"We're away from the campsite," Peter responds, so giddy about something he was bouncing from foot to foot.

Cameron raises one eyebrow. "Yeah?"

"And you walked here. *By yourself.*"

Cameron pauses, and then gasps as it hits him. He looks at Peter and his mouth falls open. "Oh my god. I *did,* didn't I?"

Peter nods rapidly, barely containing his excitement. "You did!"

Cameron gasps, then begins to laugh, gravitating towards Peter as if pulled by some invisible force. Peter lets Cameron pull him into his arms, and the two wrap each other in a strong hug, laughing and nearly falling over from their joy.

"Thank you," Cameron gasps, his whisper-shout tickling Peter's cheek.

"No, I- of course, of course," Peter whispers in response, "I'm... just glad you're okay."

Cameron nods against the top of Peter's brunette curls, nestling his face further into Peter's temple. "Me too."

Peter lets them stand in silence for another moment, then pulls away, holding Cameron at arm's length and studying his face. "Should we tell the girls?"

Cameron thinks for a moment. "I dunno. Not now, at least."

"Well, why not?"

"Peter, it's the middle of the night."

The two laugh at each other again, seemingly fueling their joy just by being around each other. Cameron takes a deep breath, looking into Peter's eyes.

"Can we go back?"

Peter smiles softly and nods. "Yeah. We can."

And so they walk back together, in the dark forest, surrounded by nothing but trees and each other.

Part Twenty-One: The Aries

Kiara

Nobody has ever gotten ready for the day without talking for this long, Kiara thinks.

All five people in this clearing are dead silent, drinking water and packing up bags. Cameron is crouching by the fire on his newly-healing ankle, covering the embers with dirt. Maya and Diana are packing up separate bags, on separate ends of the campsite. Peter is leaning against a tree, sketching something on their map, and Kiara's just watching it all.

She clears her throat after a moment. "There's something I forgot to mention."

"What?" Diana asks, looking up from where she's aggressively shoving clothes into the duffel bag.

Kiara squeezes her eyes shut and grimaces. "We're plastered all over the Plaza."

"What?!" Cameron whisper-screeches. "Like, people are seeing posters with us on them?"

"Uh, yeah," Kiara says, "plus they're offering a reward."

"*Shit*," Peter whispers.

"How much money?" Cameron asks.

"100,000 dollars," Kiara mumbles.

Peter mumbles another curse word.

"No," Diana says. Her mouth is hanging open, and her eyes are as wide as dinner plates.

"Yes. All four of us." Kiara motions to Maya. "She'll probably be there too, as soon as people notice she's gone."

"So how the hell are we gonna get through town?" Cameron asks.

"I have an idea, actually," Maya chimes in hesitantly.

The four of them turn to her. "What?" everyone except Diana choruses.

"Well, Peter, you were talking last night about how Sector Five people are always sick. So can't we just... go? It's six in the morning, and everyone spends their days inside for the most part anyway. So how many people have really seen these posters? And Peter's a sector citizen. If we're caught, he can just say he disappeared to go catch us, and then we have a one-way ticket to the Capitol jail, which is right around the corner from where we need to be anyway," Maya says plainly, shrugging.

"Holy *fucking* shit," Peter whispers to no one in particular.

"She's right," Kiara says begrudgingly, turning to Diana.

Diana glares at Maya, and for a moment, Kiara is worried she'll shoot down the idea. But then she turns away, lifting her chin, and says, "As long as you're sure about it."

They exchange worried glances. Finally, Kiara shrugs. "Let's go, then."

So they walk through town in the shadows of the buildings, stopping with bated breath when they hear the slightest noise. By the time the five get to the station, they're breathing heavily, and they duck behind a nearby building that has a good view of the entrance.

"How do we get past the guards?" Peter asks, gesturing to the men stationed outside the door.

Kiara starts to roll up her sleeves, but Cameron puts his hand on her arm. "Wait. How far are we from the nearest border?"

Peter cranes his neck. "No idea. Like, a quarter mile?" He points to the east, "it would be over that way."

Cameron turns to him. "Let's go then. I have an idea, and we need a border to help. Follow my lead."

So Cameron heads straight into the path of the nearest guards. The girls run to stop him, but he holds out a hand. "No, stay back. Trust me." So they slink back into the shadows.

Peter reluctantly follows Cameron's lead, and the guards eventually spot the pair. One points, and yells in a gruff voice: "Those are the boys from the posters! Get them!"

"Slow on the uptake, aren't they?" Cameron whispers, rolling his eyes. The guards race towards them, and about twenty yards away, Cameron grins and raises an eyebrow. "Run for it!" He shouts to Peter. He pivots almost impossibly fast, turning and running almost diagonally from where the girls were hiding. Peter's breath catches and he spins on his heels to catch up.

"Where?" Peter asks frantically.

"Follow me! Quickly!" Cameron says back.

So the boys take off running through the streets, Cameron leading and Peter hot on his heels. Cameron can hear the heavy breathing of the guards behind them, and soon, Peter catches up to him.

"Plan?" He asks, breathing hard.

"We just need to get to the border," Cameron says, "then I'll show you."

Peter shakes his head, his breathing almost as loud as the four sets of pounding footsteps. "You're lucky I like you, Cameron."

Cameron smiles. "Trust me, I know."

Peter nods, and they weave around buildings and lamp posts until they get to an alley behind a row of buildings. The border shoots up in front of them, leaving about two feet of room between the back of the buildings and the imposing wall.

"Okay, Cam. Now's the time to explain, please!" Peter yells to Cameron, panic mounting in his chest. He tries to stave off the lingering guilt from the previous fight he'd had, and he tries to focus instead on what he was doing for the others, Kiara's words from before echoing through his mind.

They skid to a halt right in front of the border, arms out and flailing to brake themselves. "Grab it!" Cameron shouts to Peter.

Peter reacts instantly and unquestioningly, reaching a hand in as the guards round the corner and unholster their guns. Peter whips around and throws the ball at one of them, just like he practiced on the tree, enveloping him in a blue column. Peter reaches behind himself with his left hand and does the same to the other guard, and as soon as the border goes up around him he fires his gun. Peter and Cameron flinch simultaneously as Cameron reaches out to Peter, both boys turning into one another as they duck their heads with eyes squeezed shut.

But the border goes up before the bullet can be fired, and silence settles around them. Then, one guard screams from inside the shield, and Peter just knew his insides were becoming enveloped with the burning sensation the border wall was leaving. Cameron grabs Peter's hand and pulls him into a side alley, away from the pained shouts of the guard and away from Peter's looming regret.

They're both breathing heavily, and Peter leans against the wall when they get safely into the shadows, rubbing his eyes to dispel the images of those blue columns from his mind. The two stand side-by-side, chests rising and falling rapidly in a weak attempt to catch their breath. Cameron looks at Peter out of the corner of his eye, only to notice Peter is doing the same. Cameron smiles at him, and Peter returns it, nudging Cameron with his elbow.

"Good job." Peter runs a shaky hand through his hair. "We make a good team."

Cameron exhales, and smirks at him. "You did most of the work."

Peter tilts his head and the gesture sets off butterflies in the pit of Cameron's stomach. "Well, I wouldn't have done *anything*, if someone hadn't forced me to run a quarter mile without even knowing the plan."

Cameron chuckles. "For the record, I didn't really know the plan either."

Peter's eyes go wide, and Cameron laughs out loud, causing Peter to do the same. When they're done, Cameron notices Peter's moved closer, and they're literally inches apart.

"Cam..." Peter says, his eyes flicking down to Cameron's lips ever so briefly.

"Yeah?" Cameron whispers back, willing himself not to panic.

Peter hesitates for a moment, then steps back and clears his throat. "We should go back."

Cameron nods rapidly. "Uh-huh. Yup. Yes, go back."

Peter smiles, waving Cameron out of the alley and back towards the station.

They get there in a matter of minutes, jogging fast enough through alleys to get there quickly but not so fast they'd draw suspicion towards themselves, strategically avoiding the path they already took.

"Are you guys okay?" Diana asks worriedly, reaching out and taking each of their wrists in her grip.

Peter and Cameron share a look, some unspoken... something, passing between them. Cameron quickly looks away, and Maya motions them towards the door.

"Doesn't matter, let's go. It's only a matter of time before they call for backup."

The five head in, reveling in the silence of the station. There's no one there, no guards, no tellers, no passengers. Just them. The tall wooden ceilings of the old building echo their footsteps, and the light from the moon filters in gently through the windows.

"What do we do now?" Diana asks.

Peter motions towards a pair of benches. "Wait for our train?"

So they sit. Well, most of them. Cameron plops down with Kiara, while Maya lays down on the second bench, their drawstring bag propped under her head, and Peter stands in between the two benches. Diana paces near the edge of the platform, where the tracks drop down about two feet below them. She keeps peering into the dark tunnel, checking for the train.

"Di, can you sit down? You haven't eaten in a day. You're going to pass out," Cameron says, motioning to the bench in between himself and Kiara.

Diana ignores him, then startles. "Cameras! We never checked to see if this place had cameras!"

Maya chimes in from where she's laying with her eyes closed. "Of course they have cameras. But it would take the people at the Capitol at *least* two hours to get someone out here to stop us, and by then, the train will have gotten here and left with us on it."

Diana nods with satisfaction, sitting next to Cameron and leaning her head against his shoulder. Cameron hugs her from the side, and she lets out a long sigh, so long it makes Cameron chuckle when it finally stops. Diana doesn't move for a few minutes, and they sit quietly, waiting for the train. They sit. And sit. And wait, until eventually, the train screeches into the station, coming to a halt in front of the group. Cameron peers into the tinted windows of the front room, where an Old American conductor would have sat. The monorails now were controlled by a system of computers, so they very well may be the only people on the train.

Cameron starts to stand, then realizes Diana is snoring against him. He smiles and gives her a little hug, remembering their tired night, and scoops her into his arms bridal-style and carries her through the sliding train doors to set her down on one of the cushioned benches. She doesn't stir at all, simply drifting into a deeper sleep as the rest of them get situated. Peter and Kiara are holding onto the handrails attached to the ceiling, gazing out the windows. Maya is across the train car from Diana, but she's in the same exact position as Diana is, curled into a fetal position and fast asleep. Cameron lays at Diana's feet, sticking the lumpy duffel bag under his head and draping his old, dirty, Orange sweatshirt across his chest for warmth. Cameron sighs contentedly, and soon he's falling into a gentle sleep.

"Quicker, Cameron. Hurry along." Cameron's mother says. She's holding his hand, pulling Cameron quickly across the crosswalk. They stop in an alley, where a sheet has been hung in between the two buildings as a makeshift roof. A

trashcan sits in the middle, a small fire going inside of it. A stack of pillows lean up against one of the walls, and on the other side sits an old, decrepit chest with a padlock draped across the middle.

Cameron pulls himself up into a seated position atop the chest, watching his mother as she sits on the pillows and unwraps his baby sister from her swaddle. These days, Lacey needs to stay hidden. At least, that's what Cameron's mum tells him. Since Lacey isn't a Scorpio, she shouldn't be here. But Mum doesn't trust the schools, so Lacey has to hide here until she's grown up and can leave on her own. Mum removes the swaddling cloth and Cameron smiles when he sees her round, apple-cheeked face. Mum wraps her quickly in the swaddling cloth, attempting to keep her warm against the frigid and seemingly never-ending Sector Three winter. Cameron pulls his old jacket tighter against himself, realizing just how cold mother looks in her day dress. She cut up her coat to make diapers for Lacey, and she doesn't own any other clothes to avoid spending too much money. Cameron recalls her boss last week throwing a handful of change at her feet and slamming the door in her face. As a thirteen-year-old, Cameron didn't know much, but he figured that's what 'fired' meant.

"Is she cold, Mum?" Cameron asks.

"Aren't we all, dear?" she says back.

Cameron falls quiet, but suddenly, the crisp, cold silence is broken by shouts from the street. Before his mother can stop him, Cameron hops off the chest and races to the opening of the alley.

A man has just been thrown into the street by some of the guards and is now being kicked over and over by a gaggle of them. Bystanders are glancing over quickly, then hurrying off to avoid being the next target.

"I didn't do anything!" the man shouts.

Cameron grabs the arm of a passerby who is hurriedly walking away from the scene. "What did he do?" Cameron asks.

"Crossed the street before the walking light went green," they reply, pulling themselves out of Cameron's grip and continuing down the street.

Cameron watches the scene unfold, with the man whimpering in the gutter and the guards beating him senseless. Eventually, one pulls out his gun, and that's when young Cameron knows to turn around. The gun sounds, and he squeezes his eyes shut as the noise rattles his frail bones. Cameron stares up at the sheet billowing in the wind, and after a few minutes, he turns back around to stare at the spot where the man once was.

Everyone has cleared away, but the snow is dotted with blood.

Cameron wanders back to his mother. "Mum, I want to leave."

She stares at him. "What do you mean?"

Cameron crosses his arms. "I hate the BOZ. I want to go somewhere else."

She stands and crosses over to Cameron, and lightning fast, she slaps him across the face. "Do not ever say that, Cameron. The BOZ is the only thing that will keep you alive."

Cameron touches his cheek, numb with shock. His lip quivers, but he bites back his tears, gritting his teeth and turning his head away from her to stare at the ground.

Lacey starts to cry, and his mother rushes over to her and holds her against her chest, muffling the sound. Even babies crying can be dangerous.

Cameron looks back out at the bloody snow in the street, and he vows that nothing will stop him from helping people like that man.

Even the BO℥ can't do that much.

"Cameron? Wake up. We're there," Peter whispers.

Cameron opens his eyes to see Peter kneeling by his head, and Cameron smiles despite himself. "How long was I out?"

"Like, an hour, not super long. Nobody wanted to wake you, though."

"Because he has crippling morning anger!" Kiara shouts from across the train. She's now seated next to a still-sleeping Diana, and Maya is sitting up across from them, shoulders still tense.

"Not true," Cameron says, laughing.

"Well, morning anger or not, we're still there," Maya says, reaching over to shake her sister awake.

Diana sits up with a start. "What?!"

"Nothing. We're there."

Diana nods and crosses her arms, and anger electrifies the air between the sisters.

The five of them stand, letting the train become bathed in silence. All at once, the weight of this colossal task sits on their shoulders. Cameron swallows hard, taking in each of his teammates: Diana and Maya's matching green eyes with hazel rings toward the middle, Peter's dark hair that curls up at the end, Kiara's high cheekbones. Cameron swears to himself that he will do whatever he can to keep them safe.

Even if it costs him his life.

Part Twenty-Two: The Taurus

Diana

Diana takes a deep breath. No one on the train moves, and it's like they're all sharing a brain. Her head is screaming: *Get a grip, Diana.*

But she's scared.

"Holy hell, I'm scared." Peter finishes the thought for her. He breaks into a grin, hand over his heart, and after a second, everyone is laughing at his random, uncharacteristic outburst.

Kiara reaches down and squeezes Diana's hand. "You alright?" Kiara whispers to her.

"No. But it's okay," Diana whispers back, "you?"

Kiara shrugs. "Well, it's easy to be okay when you have basically no clue what's going on."

Diana giggles under her breath. She releases Kiara's hand and starts toward the doors. They're yet to open, and Diana remembers they're sitting in the middle of the most heavily guarded building next to the Capitol. She places her hand on the window, feeling jittery, then turns to the rest of the group.

"Okay, everyone. This is it," Diana says. Everyone looks at her, and Diana realizes she has their full attention. "This is what we've been waiting for. As soon as we step out of this train, the countdown starts and we're on the clock. Remember: first the Trackers, and then…"

"We do what we have to," Cameron says quietly.

"Yeah," Diana replies, "but whatever happens, we need to be there for each other. I can say that I love every single one of you from the bottom of my heart, and no matter what happens, I believe in all of you. I know we can do this if we keep our heads and don't give up," Diana looks around at each of them in turn. "So, let's kick some ass."

Kiara nods. "There's that Taurus passion."

Cameron grins. "*Vive la France*, bitches."

Everyone nods resolutely. "Okay," Peter says. "Shall we?"

So, Peter and Cameron each take a door, pulling them wide open. Before the group can step out, though, three guards charge in, guns drawn.

"God, I knew this would happen," Maya says.

They all fall back quickly. One guard closes the doors behind them, and they spring forward to grab at the kids. Kiara pulls out the two knives from her pack, throwing one to Diana and the other to Maya before rolling up her sleeves. Cameron springs forward, grappling with one of the guards and wrenching his gun out of his hands.

Another guard spins around, and Peter races forward right as he lunges to grab Cameron. The momentum launches them both to the floor, and they grapple with each other for a moment before Kiara lands a sickening kick to the guard's face. He loosens his grip on Peter, long enough for Peter to kick him in the gut and scramble back to his feet.

Maya runs forward and plunges her knife into the slit in the guard's armor, right at the base of his collarbone. He goes limp, and Maya yanks the knife out and shoves him to the ground. Peter runs forward and grabs his gun and baton, throwing the gun to the side and gripping the baton tightly.

Cameron is still wrestling with the other guard, and Diana rushes forward to help him. She grabs the back of the guard's chest-plate, yanking him off Cameron and shoving him into the wall. Cameron wipes blood off his lip and punches him across the face, hard, hard enough that it hurts. The guard starts to move, and Cameron shouts, "Hold him, Diana!"

So Diana pushes against the guard's chest with all her might, as Cameron lands swing after swing on his jaw. After a few more punches, the guard slumps forward, and Diana lets him drop to the ground. She turns to face Cameron, whose lips are covered in blood and whose knuckles are red and torn. Cameron makes eye contact with her, wincing and shaking out his hand. "Damn, that hurts," he says with a small laugh as Diana smiles. "One more to go?" he asks. She nods, and they all rush the third guard. Maya grabs one of his arms, wrenching it back so hard he lets out a pained shout while Peter rams his other shoulder with his baton, and the guard goes down. Suddenly, he pulls out his gun, and Kiara shouts, "No!" before throwing herself onto him before anyone can stop her.

They all react instantly, trying to pull Kiara off him, when the gun lets out a loud crack, the signature sound of a bullet firing.

Kiara is standing there, holding the gun. She's staring down at the guard, who's lying there, dead from a gunshot wound to his chest. Her shoulders are shaking, and the gun clatters to the ground, the noise echoing off the walls of the empty train car.

Peter breaks the silence. "You... *killed* that person."

Cameron sighs and points to another guard. None of them are recognizable anymore, all crumpled up in their uniforms and caked in blood. "Maya killed that one."

"Oh god, I'm gonna be sick," Kiara whispers, turning away from the guard.

"Guys," Maya interrupts.

All four teenagers look at the older girl, who's standing further back from them. Her jaw is tense, and her voice is thick with emotion. She blinks rapidly before continuing. "Don't do this. Don't villainize yourselves. You didn't have a choice."

"It's not like we won't have to again, probably," Cameron mumbles.

They all nod slowly, as if stuck in some trance. Finally, Diana exhales a relieved breath and hugs Kiara. Diana turns to face the rest of the group, and smiles when she takes in everyone's minor injuries. It certainly could've been worse: Cameron's lip is bleeding and his knuckles are torn, the space around Peter's left eye is rapidly turning red, and Maya's shirt is torn at the hem. Kiara is no worse for wear, besides a tousled hairdo, and Diana is okay, except for the fact that she feels like the wind has been knocked out of her.

"Okay," Diana says. "Maybe try this exit thing again, before they send in reinforcements?"

Everyone nods, and they wrench the doors open, running out of the train and sprinting across the platform. They dodge through crowds of people, who barely have time to turn around before they've run past. The group approaches the front doors, and Cameron motions to Maya, who nods. Two guards stand watch, and Maya and Cameron grab the arms of each one while Kiara shoves the doors open. Peter and Diana run through, Maya and Cameron behind them, and Kiara taking up the rear.

They're outside now, and there are even more people out here than there were inside.

"Where do we go?" Peter asks.

"The Capitol," Maya says, pointing, "around the backside of the building. That's where the staff entrance is."

So they take off again, sprinting through the open Plaza. Even at eight in the morning, the place is starting to fill up. The group has to slow their pace as they get to the center of the Plaza, as a man dressed in Yellow grabs Cameron's arm.

"Hey!" the Gemini says. "This is one of the kids from the posters!"

Cameron whips around, socking him in the face, and the man crumples to the ground. Peter and Diana both halt in their tracks, staring, and Cameron rolls his eyes as he shakes out his hand. "You had one job, and that was to *keep moving*. The bar is literally so low for you guys right now and yet you're still limbo dancing in hell," he groans softly and grabs Diana and Peter's arm, dragging them onward. "So let's *move*, please."

So they continue until they reach the fountain in the very center of the Plaza. It's the place where Diana first got the idea to find Peter, and she slows down as she stares at it, a plethora of emotions threatening to take over.

Kiara tugs on Diana's arm. "Let's go, Di. We'll have time to reminisce later."

So they continue running, until they get to the Capitol building. They run around the back, where the dome of the building is casting a long shadow over the ground due to the slowly rising sun. The five sit against the wall, as close as they can, next to a dumpster and the stairs to the back entrance. Kiara taps Peter on the shoulder, eyes fixed upwards.

"Give me a boost, Peter," she says, pointing at the security camera monitoring the back entrance door.

Peter gets down on one knee, threading his hands together to give her a step-up. Kiara steps into his hand, and he pushes upwards, lifting her into the air high enough for her to grab the camera there and rip it off the wall. He sets her back down, and she stomps on the camera before tossing it into the dumpster and sitting down next to the others.

"Okay," Diana pants, "quickly catch our breath, and keep going?"

Everyone nods tiredly. So, they sit against the wall in silence, panting for breath. At the far left of their little line, Cameron grabs Peter's hand. Peter reaches to his right and grabs Diana's, she grabs Kiara's, and Kiara grabs Maya's at the far right end. They all give each other's hands a little squeeze, in a silent show of alliance.

Maya stands and approaches the keypad on the door. In a few swift motions, she slides the cover off, exposing a keyboard of numbers. She types out a code, and Diana watches as the numbers blink green, confirming her older sister was right.

Maya whispers to herself, her tongue poking out of her mouth in deep focus. "Four... six... two... seven."

A soft *click* breaks the silence, and everyone sighs in relief.

Maya, with a smug smirk, turns the metal doorknob and pushes the door open gently, motioning with her hand. "Everyone in," she whispers.

The five all stack nearly on top of one another to get a peek into the atrium. It's empty, all polished floors and tall ceilings. A huge spiral staircase sits to the side, and a hallway stretches down another.

Peter points to a set of large wooden double doors, stretching nearly as tall as the ceilings. "What's through there?"

Maya follows his finger. "The meeting room, the congress floor. All the BOZ members' offices are upstairs, but when they meet together, it's in there. Down the hall is the elevator to the basement and kitchen, and the entrance to the archives."

"The archives," Cameron says. "That's where this book is, right?"

Peter clears his throat awkwardly. "Um, yeah."

"How many of them are here right now?" Kiara asks.

Maya considers for a moment. "I'd say all of them, really. They all walk over together in the morning, with all their guards."

"But it's early," Cameron protests.

"They meet every morning at eight. So they're probably in there now." She jerks her head towards the double doors.

"So what you're saying is, *now* is the best time to get the hell through this atrium," Diana states plainly.

"Probably," Maya affirms. "Okay. Cameron and Diana, you guys need to find somewhere to send a message to the Trackers. Peter and Ki, can you find the book?"

"What will you do?" Kiara asks.

"Find food and clothes. There has to be something in the basement."

"Okay," Cameron says, grabbing Diana's hand. "Where are we going?"

"Upstairs," Maya responds. "Go, quickly."

The two take off through the atrium, footsteps pounding on the tile. They hurry up the stairs, Diana skipping every other one to keep up with Cameron. Peter watches them go, a cold knot settling in his stomach.

"Do we go that way?" Kiara asks, pointing down the first-floor hall.

"Yes," Maya says, "be careful."

So Peter and Kiara enter the Capitol, walking hurriedly down the hall, glancing over their shoulders to make sure no one was walking with them.

Part Twenty-Three: The Taurus and The Scorpio

Cameron

Diana and Cameron race to the first door they see at the top of the stairs. Diana peers into the window in the door, pointing to a few blinking lights.

"There's a computer system in here," she says. "This has to be it."

She jiggles the handle, but it won't budge. "Shit, it's locked." She continues grappling with it, the metallic sound clanking down the hall towards the doors of what Cameron can only assume are BOZ offices.

"Move," he says, grabbing Diana's arm and pulling her gently away from the door. Cameron leans down and pulls the utility knife Kiara gave him out of his pocket. He shoves the tip of the blade into the lock, wiggling it around until he hears a soft click. He tries the handle, but it doesn't budge.

He presses the hilt of the knife against the window in the door, testing the strength of the glass. He rolls his eyes as he comes to his next solution. "Kill me now," he says, to himself more than anyone else, before pulling his arm back and smashing the window with the hilt. It shatters a decent-sized hole in the window, and Cameron reaches his hand in, trying to dodge the jagged glass to the best of his ability. He grasps the lock, turning it until the handle finally rotates, and he pulls his hand out and pushes the door open, only *barely* cutting his finger on a piece of glass. He winces and sticks his finger in his mouth, shaking his hand out and opening the door to reveal the dark control room.

Diana

Cameron pushes the door open, allowing Diana to step inside before he does. Cameron shuts it behind him, groping around the wall for a light switch, locating it on the wall and bathing the room in warm yellow light. The room is packed with monitors and computer screens of all shapes and sizes, blinking greens, reds, and yellows.

"Which computer is it?" Diana asks. "I can try to look at the wiring if I know which one to use."

Cameron heads to the biggest screen, a huge computer that sits against the back wall and is surrounded on either side by a rectangular monitor and a panel labeled 'Trackers'. He points an index finger towards it confidently.

Diana rushes to the keyboard in front of the computer screen, tapping keys at random to turn it on. Once it blinks on, displaying the Capitol logo and a box to enter a password, Diana yanks open the panel and studies the wires.

"Okay, so I don't know the password, but there needs to be some wires I can pull to get past the firewall," she says.

"Tell me what to do," Cameron says.

Diana points him towards the door and the window. "Cover those somehow. I'll let you know when I'm in."

Cameron nods and heads to another table on the other side of the room, and Diana turns back to her task. "Okay," she says to the panel. She scans the plugs, realizing that a black wire is plugged into the wall and crossed over to a second outlet, and a yellow one is the same way. It must be rigged to the computer security system, she realizes. Diana sends up a quick prayer to the computer gods, then yanks out the black wire.

Cameron

Cameron heads towards the door, searching for something to use to cover the window, which covers the right side of the wall, big and rectangular, looking out into the hallway. He stands on the table in front of it and gropes at the top of the windowsill, realizing there's a blind, which he yanks down, putting a big monitor on top of it to hold it in place.

Then the door. The window still has a hole in it, obviously, and unlike the big window, there is no blind to cover it up. Cameron remembers his sweatshirt in his bag outside, cursing under his breath that he agreed to leave it behind. He searches the spotless room for a discarded blind or sheet, knowing he'll come up empty. Sure enough, he does.

"Motherf-" he groans, reaching his arms over his head and pulling off his shirt. He drags over a chair, opening the door enough to stick his shirt in and closing it again so it drapes over the window and stays in place. Cameron hops down, puts the chair back, and wipes his hands, crossing his arms over his bare chest.

Cameron heads back over to Diana, who's hard at work rewiring the whole panel. She's crossed over a black wire and a yellow wire, pulled out a red one completely, and is now studying the hole a blue one was plugged into, leaving it dangling from one end.

She speaks to Cameron without looking up. "You all set?"

"Uh, yeah," he says, "anything else?"

"Yeah, can you-" Diana turns her head to look at him, eyes widening when she sees Cameron's half-naked form. "I don't even want to know."

"We had no blinds for the door! I needed to use something," he replies defensively.

Diana smirks, shaking her head and turning back to her work. "Can you shut the lights off? I'm almost done with this, so I'll give you a thumbs up when you can hit them. I just don't want to draw suspicion to us, considering it's brighter than a carnival in here."

Cameron salutes her, heading to the light switch and waiting for her cue. Diana works for another moment, replugging in the blue wire over a green one. Then, she turns and gives him a thumbs up. Cameron flicks the switch, bathing the room in darkness besides the irregular blinking of the devices. Diana flicks a switch on the panel, and the computer screen blinks.

Diana

The computer screen lights up, and Diana gasps with excitement. She scrolls with her finger until she reaches a settings screen, hitting the 'default' button. A tab opens with all the people who have Tracker access, and Diana cuts every device off except for the computer she's working on, clicking again and again on every guard icon to deny access. Then, she opens a box that shows the default messages. Now able to alter the settings, she deletes the guard button in its entirety, leaving all the country's people unable to call for the guards with one swift motion. Then, she adds 'Revolution' in its place, hitting the button that allows people to send custom messages.

Then, she goes into the 'send message' tab. She hits 'select all citizens' and a six-figure number appears on the screen. She clicks the 'type message' bar, and launches into the message they had agreed upon on the train.

Citizens of New America:

The Board Of Zodiacs is hiding something: a select few individuals in New America have powers to warp and destroy the border walls, and the BOZ plans to take advantage of them. Our group is planning to lead a revolution against the BOZ, to uncover their secrets and create a stronger government once and for all. If you want to join us and take up our cause, meet us in the Plaza as soon as possible. Do not be afraid of these messages being seen by the government, as we have a revolution official on call in the official Tracker center at all times. Be brave, New America. Ignore the prejudiced ideals of the Board Of Zodiacs and join our cause to create a better future for everyone.

Make the right choice.

Diana leans forward on the table, taking a deep breath to steel her nerves, and Cameron puts a hand on her shoulder. "You okay?" he asks, squeezing gently to remind her he was there, real.

"Fine. Just nervous," she replies after another deep breath.

He nods. "Well, all we can do now is wait."

Part Twenty-Four: The Aries and The Cancer

Peter

Kiara and Peter enter the large library, marveling at the high ceilings and endless shelves. The room is circular, and the shelves are built straight into the wall. The library is two floors tall, with staircases on either side of them leading to the upper level. The place is warm and inviting, if not a little daunting, with a musty smell of old leather and paper.

"Wow," Peter says.

Kiara whistles. "You can say that again."

"Okay," Peter says, brushing his hands together, a physical manifestation of his anxiety, "let's find this book."

They head through rows of shelving, and as they pass giant tomes and atlases, Peter runs his fingers over the dusty spines. They eventually reach the very back row, and Kiara treks to the far right, reaching a shelf that looks exactly the same as the other ones. Peter, on the contrary, goes all the way to the left.

They stand in silence as they scan the shelves, until Kiara calls Peter's name from across the vast room. "Second shelf, right there," she says, pointing.

Peter hurries over to her, and sure enough, the book he saw so many years ago was there.

Kiara smiles, reaching up to the shelf in question. There are about ten books in the row, all of which are leather-bound and as thick as Peter's thumb is long. They all look the same, but one is clean and polished while the other nine look as if they haven't been touched in years, outfitted with dust-covered spines and faded leather.

Kiara, standing on her toes, grabs the clean book and studies the front. "What's the title again?"

Peter thinks for a moment. "'*Powerful Ones in Regards to The Board Of Zodiacs.*'"

Kiara nods, keeping her eyes on the cover of the book. "This is it."

She looks up at Peter, and he gulps. "Can we read it, you think?"

Kiara shrugs. "It's here for the taking."

So, Peter takes the book from her and opens the front cover, flipping through until he gets to the table of contents. There's thirteen chapters, the first one being an introduction to 'The Abilities Of The Powerful Ones'.

The other twelve chapters are each of the zodiacs.

"Woah," Kiara says, eyes skimming the table of contents. "Flip to a random chapter."

So Peter flips to page 134, the Aquarius chapter. The first page looks a little like this:

Chapter One: The Waterman
Aquarius

The Aquarius zodiac is arguably the most powerful sign, as observed regarding their Power, and the Powerful One born into the Aquarius group must be protected and monitored at all costs. This Powerful One has the ability to turn water into the border material, simply by cupping the water in their hand and concentrating on the execution of this task.

"Woah," Peter says, "I forgot about all this."

"Keep reading!" Kiara says. It doesn't seem like she heard the second part of his shocked whisper.

So, Peter flips the page. The next page has a heading and then is filled with lines, where names are scrawled in two different handwriting styles, each signature dating back years.

Board Of Zodiac member, Protector of the Aquarius Powerful One:

Orion Oswald
Barbara Oswald

"Barbara Oswald," Kiara says. "She's the current BOZ member, head of the Aquarius sector."

Peter nods, continuing to the next page. In neat handwritten print, a name and serial number is entered. This time the heading is different.

Aquarius Powerful One

Amy de la Rosa, 922
Katie Courier, 670
William Chance, 289

"Interesting," Kiara says. "This must be the person with powers in Sector Four," she taps the book with her finger. "Go to the Scorpios."

Peter flips through until he reaches chapter ten, and the setup is exactly the same.

Chapter Ten: The Scorpion
Scorpio

The power associated with the Scorpio sector is the ability to drop border walls as he or she pleases. The Powerful Scorpio can also raise a wall at the base of a felled wall or the origin of a felled wall.

"Names," Kiara commands.
So Peter flips the page, and the text is the same as before.

Board Of Zodiac member, Protector of the Scorpio Powerful One:

Celina Myers
Gerard Myers

"Gerard Myers got kicked out of the BOZ. Remember? As punishment for the escape?" Kiara states.
"Yeah, you're right," Peter says. But his eyes are stuck on one name on the next page.

Scorpio Powerful One

Lola Rivers, 003
Fredrick McDonald, 682

And finally:

Cameron O'Connor, 102

"Holy shit," Kiara whispers. "It's really real."
Peter scrambles to chapter six, scanning the list of Cancer names, until he sees:

Peter Simon, 629

Peter traces his fingers over the print, his heart hammering in his throat. He leans back against the wall, looking at Kiara.

She's staring back at him. "That's... you, right?"

Peter laughs dryly. "Well, that's my number, and my name, so..."

Kiara whistles. "*Damn.*"

"This is important, this is actually *real*," Peter says, trying to ignore his fluttering heartbeat. "We should show the others."

Kiara nods. "Let's go."

Walking out of the archives, Kiara looks around cautiously and Peter clutches the book to his chest, moving as one unit down the hall.

They head through the building, and as soon as they reach the center of the room on the upper level, Diana and Cameron rush out of the control room and come face-to-face with Kiara and Peter. They stop short as they meet each other, and Peter flushes when he notices that Cameron has somehow... lost his shirt.

"Did you find the book?" Diana asks.

"Yup," Peter says, handing it to her. He had dog-eared Cameron's page and his own, and Diana flips to Cameron's as the other two gather around her.

Cameron's eyes widen at the mention of his surname. "O'Connor? Who's name is that?"

Kiara giggles. "It's your last name, Cam. They used them all the time in Old America."

He nods, considering. "I guess I can get used to it."

They flip to the Cancers, observing Peter's name and the list of others. "*Cool,*" Diana whispers.

"Peter Simon," Cameron states. His delivery of Peter's name makes him smile a little, and Peter quickly looks towards the ground.

"Okay, guys," Kiara says. "What's the plan?"

"I guess... we wait to see if anyone sends us messages. And wait for Maya to get back," Diana replies. Her delegation was second nature to the group now, it seemed, exemplified through their immediate compliance.

So, they head back into the control room and make themselves comfortable. Diana and Cameron sit in two of the desk chairs, and Kiara sits on a table next to where Diana was. Peter sits on a table in the center of the room, eyeing Cameron's bare chest, and Cameron catches Peter looking.

"Like what you see, superhero?" he asks teasingly.

Peter grins. "*No.* I was just wondering if you wanted my sweatshirt."

Cameron blinks at Peter. "You're wearing layers?"

"Yeah. I got Di's message and knew I was in it for the long haul." Before he can answer, Peter pulls his sweatshirt over his head, revealing a plain Gray long-sleeve shirt underneath. He throws the sweatshirt to Cameron, and he smiles before putting it on. Peter smiles back. "Looks good."

Cameron smirks in his regular fashion, but Peter is almost certain he sees color creep across his cheeks. "Thanks."

Kiara turns away from the door, her grumbling stomach audible from across the room. "Come on, Maya," she says to the empty hall.

They wait a little while longer, until Maya comes charging into the room, arms full of clothes and food. She uses her foot to slam the door behind her and turns to the group with a grin.

"You guys, that was close. They were leaving the floor right after I left the elevator. I swear Miriam Miller nearly saw me."

"What did you get?" Diana asks, voice laced with coldness, presumably still from their late-night fight. Maya, in all her typical outspoken glory, hesitates for a moment before answering.

"Sandwiches." With that, she throws a wrapped sandwich at Cameron, who catches it with a gasp.

"Oh my god, Maya, I love you," he says, unwrapping it and digging in with vigor.

Maya passes out the rest, and then holds up a Pink shirt.

"Oh, god, no," Diana says, swallowing the food in her mouth before continuing. "No. I'm not wearing that."

"Why not? Actually, everyone should change. Makes it easier for them to confuse you with other people, since you won't be in the same clothes as on the posters," she flings the shirt towards her little sister. "Show a little Libra nationalism."

Kiara starts to chuckle when a White sweatshirt hits her in the face.

Maya passes out clothes for all of them: Cameron is in his Gray pants with a Navy Blue short-sleeve top, Peter is in Black pants and a Sky Blue top, Kiara is in Brown shorts and a White sweatshirt, and Diana is in Black leggings and her Pink short-sleeve.

"What about weapons?" Cameron asks, mouth full.

Maya shrugs. "I don't know where they are. I'm certain the BOZ would keep whatever weapons they have well-hidden."

Peter stands and brushes himself off. "I want to see the meeting floor. Maybe there's some stuff about this Powerful One army in there."

Cameron wipes his mouth and rises as well. "I'll go with you."

"Just... be careful," Diana says warily. "If you see people, get the hell out of there."

Part Twenty-Five: The Cancer and The Scorpio

Cameron

Peter and Cameron hustle through the hallway, heading down the stairs in silence. When they reach the bottom landing, Cameron peeks around the corner.

"I can't see anyone going in or out," he says.

Peter points to the oak doors leading to the meeting floor. "Through there, then?"

Cameron shrugs. "I guess so."

So they head to the oak doors, pulling one open just a crack to peek into the giant congressional floor.

The sight is amazing. A giant floor of chairs sit facing a huge podium on a raised stage, and behind the podium sits twelve throne-like chairs, each one a different color. All of them are occupied:

A man in a Red suit,

A woman in an Orange dress,

A man in a Black suit,

A woman in a Navy Blue skirt and blouse,

A man in a Gray suit,

A younger man in a Yellow suit,

A man in a Forest Green suit,

A woman in a Purple dress,

A woman in a Pink dress,

A man in a Brown suit,

A woman in a White suit,

And a man in a Sky Blue button-down.

They're talking, but the boys are too far away to hear them. Without thinking, Cameron sneaks into the room and crouches behind the closest chair in the audience. He's facing away from the door, and after a few tense moments, Peter crouches next to Cameron.

"What the hell are you doing?" he whispers frantically.

Cameron grins at him. "Listening, obviously."

So they creep forward, row by row, until they're about ten rows away from the BOZ members. The boys are close enough so that they can hear them, but they've still not spotted the pair, so Peter and Cameron are safe, at least for now.

Cameron tilts his head towards them to listen, peeking through a crack in the chairs in order to check which member is speaking.

"They're going to revolt, Barbara," the man in Red growls.

The Navy Blue woman shakes her head. "Even if they do, George, they've got multiple Powerful Ones on their side. We cannot rightfully kill those we've sworn to protect."

The man in Red shakes his head, yanking his tie to tighten it. "What do you think, Cara?" Henderson asks.

The woman in Purple perks up. She's young, maybe ten years older than Maya. She looks a little overwhelmed, and her eye twitches when the Aries leader addresses her.

"I think... I think that the Pisces are yet to interfere, so I have no comment," she remarks, turning her head towards the floor.

The Red Man stomps his foot on the ground, slamming his hand against the podium. "Are you all out of your goddamned minds?!" he howls. "Your subjects are missing, three of which have powers that could crush even the strongest of armies. They have been disturbing the peace all over New America, and now they could revolt. Do you think that people will side with us when they see we've been hiding these powers from them?"

The room falls silent. Cameron holds his breath, watching the council members' every move. George Henderson is the only one standing, and the others look like shamed children. The Aries leader crosses over to the man in the Black suit, staring at him until the man in Black looks up at him.

"Gerard," he starts, voice low but demanding, "you've just been welcomed back. Do you *really* want to take their side when I have been here longer than any of you?!" His voice starts to rise, and he shoves a finger in the man's face, startling him and the other eleven people in the room. *"Answer me,"* he growls.

The man in Black licks his lips, grinding his teeth together, and then he stands, facing Henderson head-on. "I don't blame the rest of you," Myers says to the rest of the group, although he's keeping his eyes on the Red Man, "but I have to side with George. My population was *decimated,* due to the ignorant actions of one problematic teenager. One *powerful* teenager, who I swore to watch and guard."

Peter gasps quietly. "He got kicked out because he wasn't keeping a close enough eye on you. Just like Maya said."

Cameron nods, still focused on the scene, but his stomach churns with fear and bitterness.

"Oh, seriously, Gerard, get over yourself," the woman in White groans. "Cameron O'Connor got away because you weren't doing your job, not because he's too powerful to control."

"As if you have anything to say about doing your job, Brewer, coming from the one who can't control her own protesting citizens-"

"Brewer was doing a perfectly fine job-" the woman in Pink interjects.

She's cut off by the man in Gray. "Miller, you shouldn't even *have* a say, considering your charge went missing because of your mother."

"Only the members who actually *have* a good rein over their charge should get a say," the Forest Green man says, shrugging.

"Oliver, thoughts?" Cara King asks, voice trembling nervously.

The youngest person in the room looks up, eyes widening behind his Yellow glasses. Peter watches his Adam's apple bob as he swallows, and he studies his slightly slouching posture. "I... um, I-"

"Of course he's stuttering all over the place, just like his father did," Gerard Myers mumbles.

Oliver rises from his seat, ever so calmly, and crosses to Myers. In the blink of an eye, Oliver Hill raises his hand and slaps the Scorpio leader across the face, and then returns to his seat as if everything were perfectly normal.

Myers' hand flies to his cheek, and he sputters before turning to Henderson. "Are you just going to let him do that to me?!"

Henderson smirks, seated regally in his throne. "Gerard, you'll find that I don't give a damn about what happens between you and Oliver. I *do* care, however, about what the hell we're going to do about Peter Simon and Cameron O'Connor running loose together, and being in touch with our other charges," Peter doesn't miss the pointed look he gives Oliver Hill, although Henderson doesn't elaborate. "Even our best security cannot find them now, and every sector has been combed thoroughly. It isn't like they can just disappear."

Myers groans loudly, pulling the focus to him. "I'll tell you one thing. This boy Cameron has caused nothing but trouble since he escaped, and now he's met other Powerful Ones. All together, they're virtually unstoppable." He turns to the other eleven people. "But we *can* stop them. And I will not rest until Cameron O'Connor and this band of delinquents are dead."

Cameron sucks in a breath, turning away from the BOZ members, who are now chittering nervously. Peter looks at him, and Cameron blinks rapidly to try to quell the tears threatening to pour from his eyes. It doesn't work, and soon he's crying quietly. Cameron goes to swipe at his eyes, but Peter grabs his hands before Cameron can raise them and give away their position.

Peter

Peter takes Cameron's hands. "Stop!" he whispers. "You're gonna wave them right over to us."

Peter guides him carefully back to the hall, where he quickly and quietly slumps against the wall around the corner from the doors that lead to the meeting hall.

"Hey," Peter says, his voice at a somewhat-normal level now, "talk to me."

Cameron turns to Peter with wet cheeks and puffy eyes. "I've put you all in danger."

Peter tilts his head teasingly. "Technically, this was *Diana's* idea..."

Cameron laughs a little, then shakes his head. "I know. But you heard them. They're planning on fighting us, no matter what. Doesn't it scare anyone that the man who swore to protect me is siding with that psycho Aries guy?"

Peter nods, understanding what he isn't saying. "It scares me a lot."

Cameron studies Peter's face. "I'm really, really, scared."

Peter looks at him. "I know. It scares me that *you're* scared. You're never scared."

"You don't know that. You don't know me."

Peter looks away from him, sort of hurt by his reflexive attack. "I do, though. Honestly, Cameron, I think I know you better than anyone else in our group. I have trained with you, I have traveled with you, and most importantly, I've completely bared my entire soul to you, not even really by choice. So, to be frank, I think that putting up all these walls and trying to shut me out is the wrong thing to do. Because I have done nothing but care for you this whole time. And that's all I'm trying to do. Help you," Peter stands up abruptly, looking down at him.

Cameron brushes at his eyes, standing up as well and turning to face Peter. Peter tilts his chin up just slightly to try to get to Cameron's height, out of instinct more than intention. "That's not what you said."

"What?"

"You said help. But before you said care."

Peter rolls his eyes. "Sorry. So *sorry* that I'm trying to talk a little sense into you and you're not catching anything."

Cameron flinches at his words, and Peter almost apologizes, but Cameron fires right back before he can say anything at all. "And I'm sorry that I'm concerned that I've put people I care about into immediate danger and all *you* care about is how deep our little bond is. Sorry that I'm actually worried about the fact that every single one of us could very well be dead tomorrow, and I cannot do *anything* to help you guys."

Peter blinks. "I-"

Cameron shakes his head, new tears rolling down his cheeks. "Don't. I'm going to find weapons. Please, don't follow me."

And then he leaves.

And Peter doesn't follow.

Peter walks back up the stairs to the control room, his head hung low. Cameron had disappeared around a corner, and when Peter reaches the top stair, he turns back around to try to look for him. But the other boy was already gone.

Part Twenty-Six: The Taurus

Diana

Peter mopes in with his head hung low, shutting the door quietly behind him. The three girls rush to meet him.

"Where's Cameron?" Kiara asks. "You were supposed to stick together."

Peter nods. "They're here. The whole BOZ. And the Aries leader was mentioning killing all of us. He's trying to snuff out the revolt before it even starts."

Kiara's jaw tenses, a barely noticeable movement. "What did he look like?"

Peter shrugs, looking back down the corridor through the broken window. "I guess old. White hair, really nice suit. I only assumed he was an Aries because he was head-to-toe in Red."

Kiara takes a step back. "God, no," she whispers.

Diana looks at her, studying her face quizzically. "What?"

Kiara looks at Diana, and her brown eyes are glistening with tears. "This guy is bad news. He- he's a major creep, and he won't hesitate to kill us. We need to be more careful."

The rest of them are silent. They're angled away from the door, with Diana at the front of the group, Maya to her left, and Peter closest to the door, like they're blocking Kiara from the world outside and anyone dangerous who may apprehend her. After a moment, Peter whispers. "How do you know that, Kiara?"

Kiara shakes her head gently, allowing a fresh batch of tears to roll quietly down her cheeks. "What?" she replies, her voice matching his low, quiet pitch.

Peter takes a step forward, raising his hands ever-so-slightly as if approaching a startled animal. "That he's violent. 'A creep'."

Kiara doesn't speak, staring at Peter as if he had asked her a question in a foreign language. After a tense moment, he nods, frowning, almost understanding, and Kiara breaks down, shoulders shaking. Although she's crying, Kiara doesn't move, keeping her head high and standing still, hurt but not beaten, broken but not unfixable.

After looking between the two of them, something clicks into understanding. Diana steps into line with Peter. "Kiara, did he-?"

Kiara shakes her head. "No. He didn't do anything *specifically,* but when I was twelve-" she can't continue, instead stepping backwards away from her friends and gripping the table behind her to balance herself.

Maya steps forward. "You don't need to tell us, Kiara," she says softly.

Kiara wipes the back of her hand against her eyes, squaring her shoulders and looking at the others with a fire in her eyes. "He did hurt me. But it could have been worse, much worse. And I'm almost certain he's hurt other girls from my sector, too. That's why I *cannot* let him win."

The other three nod, and Kiara exhales heavily. Diana feels something heavy settle in her chest, a burden that was once only Kiara's, now willingly everyone else's. She can't tell if it's a good thing, but she feels some kind of relief at the idea that her friend was no longer shouldering this alone. The three stay where they are, stock-still, until Kiara speaks again.

"Guys," she begins, her voice thick in an attempt to keep from crying any longer, "if Henderson is serious, which he must be, we need to be prepared. How are we going to fight them?"

"Good point," Peter says, swiftly allowing the subject to change. "Is there an armory? We talked about this before-"

"Yes," says a voice from behind them.

They all spin around, seeing Cameron leaning in the doorway. Kiara rushes into his arms, and he hugs her back. Diana joins the embrace, allowing him to squeeze their shoulders and lighten their moods just a little.

They break apart, and Diana notices that Peter has come a little closer, but he's keeping his distance from Cameron. They share a brief awkward and bitter look, then Cameron turns back to the girls.

"There is an armory, next to the kitchen. Huge place, down in the basement. Guns and batons, but mostly swords and knives, older weapons. I say we go down there and take what we need."

"How do you know that?" Maya asks.

Cameron shrugs like the answer is obvious. "I went searching around, stumbled upon the place."

"You what?" Peter asks, eyebrow raised in either shock or anger.

Cameron cuts him a cold glare. "Lighten up, I'm fine."

The girls watch as the two face off. "Well, you may not have been. If something had happened-"

"-Nothing did happen." Cameron interrupts. He looks towards the girls, pointedly avoiding Peter's gaze. "Shall we?"

Diana nods. "Let's go."

So, they head out the door of the control room, hurrying down the hall in a cluster. Peter and Cameron are on either end of the group with Diana leading, and Maya and Kiara follow next. Soon, Cameron comes to walk next to her.

"Where are we headed?" Diana asks.

"Downstairs," he says, leading them back to the first floor and then into a small room that sits about ten yards away from the entrance to the congress floor. He pushes it open, revealing a medium-sized elevator, and Cameron ushers them in, allowing the doors to close behind them. Without pushing any buttons, it jerks downwards. Everyone stumbles at the jolt: Diana grabs onto Maya, she grabs the wall, Kiara sticks her hands out to balance herself, and Peter grabs Cameron's arm and then quickly separates himself from him.

When the doors open again, they're in a room with high ceilings and marble walls and floors. If not for the musty smell, one wouldn't know they were underground. Right ahead of the group is a door that says 'To Kitchen'.

But to their left is a room marked with four large pillars, two on either side of a huge door. Cameron grabs the silver handles and gives it a tug, and it hisses open to reveal a vault-like armory. The walls are lined with glass cases full of all kinds of futuristic-looking weapons, and above them hang swords, bows, and guns. Lining the far back wall are armor stands with all types of armor: chainmail, leather, steel, and one made of a peculiar Black substance that emits a purplish shine. Some things are obviously much older than others, and some things look as if they were recently handled.

"Woah," Peter says, running his hand cautiously over the dusty blade of a large sword.

"Guys, look," Kiara says. She motions to the wall on the right, where twelve swords are fanned out in an arc-like shape. Each is slightly different in shape, color, and hilt, and each has a gold plaque underneath, the obvious centerpiece of the room.

Cameron crosses to the wall, studying the first sword. It's not very long, perhaps about a foot and a half, and the blade is straight steel with a wooden hilt painted sky-blue and engraved with swirling patterns.

He reads off the plaque beneath it: "The Sword of the Virgos."

Cameron moves on to the next sword, directly to the right of the Virgo one. This one is slender and long, about three feet, with a blade that is thin but looks deadly sharp, and an amber handle, giving the hilt an Orange color. Cameron reads: "The Sword of the Leos."

Peter moves to the other end of the arc. "Each zodiac must have a sword."

Maya stands to his left, examining a steel sword with a Yellow stone handle. Diana can only assume it's the one for her sector. "But why? Can't anyone just use them?"

"No," Kiara chimes in from behind them. She's reading from an old book propped on a pedestal next to the swords. She reads aloud: "Each sword found in the armory is fit specifically to the powers of each sector. For example, a Pisces will fight much more powerfully than normal with the assistance of The Sword of the Pisces," she turns to Peter and Cameron, "so you guys should take the ones from your sectors, since it'll increase your abilities. Think of it as a good-luck charm, but… painful."

Cameron and Peter share a look, then Peter shrugs. The two go up and down the wall, looking for their swords. Peter finds his first, a steel blade that measures out at around two-and-a-half feet. The hilt is silver, with the Cancer symbol stamped into the handle. The end of the blade is pointed finely, and it emits a bright glare when the light catches it. He takes it off the wall and passes it from one hand to the other. "It's heavy."

Diana goes up to him, studying the sword. "It's *so cool*."

Cameron groans from somewhere near the right side of the arc, and they turn to face him. "You've got to be joking," he says. His sword is only about a foot long, the blade thick but sharp. The hilt is obsidian, giving it the signature Scorpio Black. There are no markings or runes in the hilt or the sword itself, and it's decidedly less flashy than the others. He takes it off the wall and turns to face his friends, waving the sword in the air. "It's so tiny!"

Kiara laughs. "It's suited to you. Whatever the size, it'll work for you in battle."

Peter snorts. "That's what she-"

Diana elbows him. "Shut *up*, Peter. Gross."

Maya is still studying the other ten swords. "What about the rest? Shouldn't we just take ours, just to be safe?"

Cameron shakes his head. "The others belong to the Powerful One in each sector. What if you messaged them, Di, and told them to meet you here to get their swords? It might help to dole them out the way they're meant to be."

Diana nods. "I can do that when we get back up there. For now, Ki, Maya, and I need weapons."

So the three girls scatter, Maya grabbing a set of throwing knives off a glass case, Kiara grabbing a set of brass knuckles, and Diana taking a good walk around before settling next to a glass case with a peculiar-looking weapon inside. Cameron comes up next to her and peers into the case.

"What is that?" He asks.

Diana reads off the plaque. "A prototype guard weapon. It says it was recalled for being too overpowered. There's a button on the hilt there that can switch it from a knife to a baton."

Cameron looks out of the corner of his eye towards Diana. "Do you want it?"

Diana smiles and nods. "Obviously. But I don't know how to use it."

Cameron uses the hilt of his sword to smash the glass case, gingerly removing the weapon and handing it to Diana. It's the length of her forearm, and when both weapons are concealed, it looks like a thin black cylinder. She presses the first button, and a foot-long baton springs from the top. Cameron jumps back, then moves close again. "Press the other one," he instructs. Diana does, and the baton conceals itself and a sharp steel blade replaces it. She presses the second button again, and it goes back down into the handle, allowing her to safely tuck it into her pocket. Cameron grins at her. "See? Now you *do* know how to use it."

"I like it," Diana affirms.

Cameron nods, then looks towards the others. "Okay guys. Next step: message the other ten people with powers. Then, we should split up. We need someone monitoring how many people show up at the Plaza. We also need to do something to rally everyone before we just start fighting people. Like Diana, you could speak."

Diana nods, heart thumping at the prospect. "Yeah. Okay, sure, I guess. But how are we going to do that without alerting guards? They're everywhere."

Cameron nods in Peter's direction. "That's my next idea. Peter and I could probably find a way to get the guards in one place, then trap them with the borders."

Peter points at his own chest. "Me?"

Cameron rolls his eyes. "No, the other Peter. Yes, you. Let's split up. Di, control room. Maya and Ki, you go together and find windows where you can monitor the monorail station. And Peter, you and I will head to the closest border."

So the five of them head to the elevator. When they reach the first floor, they split up, with Kiara and Maya heading to the main entrance, Peter and Cameron sneaking out the back door where they first came in, and Diana hastily heading up the stairs back into the dark control room. When she gets there, Diana loads up the message board and opens the book Kiara gave her. She scans the list of names, messaging each person who was most recently listed per sector, and once Diana has sent out the same message for each, she refreshes and waits for responses. A few come in, and she smiles when she sees all are affirmative answers. Diana grabs food out of the bag and starts snacking, drinking water for what would be the first time all day.

She turns to look at the computer screen, then turns back to face the door, leaning against the table. When she looks up from her food, though, she sees a woman dressed in Navy Blue with straight blonde hair standing in the doorway, having entered completely silently like some sort of spirit. Her face is old, with wrinkles written across her features, but her dark lipstick and eyeshadow makes her look powerful, not to mention dangerous.

Diana jumps and pulls out her weapon, recognizing her as Barbara Oswald, the leader of the

Aquarius sector. She scrambles to push the second button on her weapon, and the knife blade shoots out the top. But Barbara Oswald's eyes give no sign of fear, and she simply shuts the door quietly behind her before turning to face Diana.

"You kids really thought you could break a window on a door and no one would notice?" she asks. "You're lucky it was me who came in here, and not Henderson or Meyers or Davis." Her eyes bore into Diana's, and Diana puts down her food and holds the knife in front of her, taking a shaky step towards the woman. She doesn't move, simply stands and straightens her blazer. Diana is appalled by her lack of fear, so she stops in her tracks and stares at her.

Oswald continues slowly forward, running her fingertips over the monitors and tabletops. As she walks, she speaks softly but with the affirmation of a veteran politician.

"So, Diana Florence Monroe. I've heard a lot about you and your band of rogues. A ragtag group of kids, you are, huh? Who would've thought five different signs could get along so brilliantly, enough to stage a revolt to overthrow the leaders of the government," she stops talking, landing about two feet from Diana, who's still quiet, and Oswald smiles at her apparent confusion. "Scared?"

Diana bites the inside of her cheek, willing herself to speak. "No. Confused. What are you doing just standing here talking to me? Go ahead, drag me back to the rest of them. Torture me, kill me."

Oswald smiles. "I have no intention of showing you off to the rest of my colleagues."

Diana steps back, anger bubbling up inside her chest. "Then what are you waiting for? If you're going to kill me, you may as well do it now before one of my teammates gets back."

Barbara Oswald takes a menacing step closer to Diana, studying her unwashed face and unruly ponytail. Then, she laughs. It's a kind sound, and paired with her bright, sudden smile, Diana's confusion grows. "What?" she asks, praying the waver in her voice comes across angrier than it sounds to her.

"I'm not going to kill you, Diana. In fact, I came with information for your benefit."

Diana raises an eyebrow. "Yeah, right. And why should I trust you? Cameron said you were talking with the other BOZ members about killing the five of us."

"Well, your friend is correct, we were discussing it. But I'm sure your friend Cameron could also vouch that I spoke *against* the slaughter, as I hear some people in your group are Powerful Ones." She stops wandering and turns back to face Diana, challenging her to rebuttal.

Diana studies her, noticing her confident expression. But it also doesn't seem like she's lying. In fact, for some unknown reason, everything in Diana is telling her to believe this woman. After a moment of tense silence, she responds. "Fine. What is it?"

Oswald's face betrays a small smile, and she nods slowly. "Good girl. I'm sure you're aware that the Plaza will be very heavily armed, per usual?"

Diana rolls her eyes and crosses her arms. "Yeah, why?"

"Well, I know I and a few other members are against this display of violence, on either side, so we've decided to have no part in this revolt. But although we don't believe in your gang of hoodlums, we also don't want to support the mass murder of a bunch of children. So I propose a distraction."

Diana blinks. "What kind of distraction?"

The Aquarius smiles again. "I propose that the leaders of the five opposed sectors rally the guards in the Capitol and the Plaza for some type of rendezvous in order to keep them away from you and your little battle."

"Who, besides you, is on our side?"

"Well, Miss Diana Florence Monroe, you have the support of the leaders of the Aquarius, Pisces, Sagittarius, Libra and Gemini sectors."

Diana nods, surprised. "Have you discussed this with them?"

She nods. "In fact, Mister Boone from the Gemini sector, Miss Brewer from the Sagittarius sector, and Miss Miller from the Libra sector are wholeheartedly behind the five of you."

"And the Pisces leader?"

Oswald grins. "She's more or less with us. Shy as a newborn puppy, that one, following my every move. So what I say goes."

Diana smiles, her opinion of Barbara Oswald slowly gaining traction by the minute. "And you? What do you think?"

Oswald smiles again. "I think that I have no affiliation for either party, but I see more of myself in you five than I probably should."

Diana bites her lip, suddenly bashful. "Thank you, Miss Oswald."

She nods. "Of course, Miss Monroe. I wish you and your friends luck."

The woman crosses to the door, setting her hand on the knob and pausing, turning back around to face Diana. "And for the record," she starts, "feel free to call me when you're rebuilding the government."

Diana nods, and she leaves, shutting the door behind her and bathing the room in silence once more.

Part Twenty-Seven: The Cancer

Peter

As Cameron and Peter sneak out the back door, Peter studies the morning sun.

"Looks like almost ten," Cameron says quietly.

"Yeah," Peter replies, letting the two of them fall into an awkward silence.

"How are we gonna get through to the wall without being seen?" Cameron asks, not looking at Peter.

"I... don't know. You have your weapon, right?" Peter asks.

Cameron holds up his sword. "Unfortunately, yes."

"Okay, so... let's just go."

He scoffs. "Genius."

Peter turns to face him. "Do you have a better idea?"

Cameron's jaw sets tensely. "No."

Peter nods, motioning for Cameron to follow him. They slink through the alleyway, hands on the hilts of their swords. When they reach the end of the wall blocking them from the rest of the Plaza, the boys make a run for the next building. When they reach the wall, they squeeze behind the building and study their surroundings. There's a border heading to god-knows-what sector about a hundred yards from them, and Peter starts to head over when Cameron grabs his arm.

"One second," Cameron pants. "You're literally running. Slow down."

Peter rolls his eyes. "You'll live."

Cameron smirks. "You never know."

He brushes past Peter, peeking into the alley opening and waiting until people pass by before heading behind the next building. Peter follows until they reach the border, where the pair halts and studies the luminous material.

"Question," Cameron says.

"Hm?" Peter replies, not taking his eyes off the wall.

"How do we travel with it? If I were a civilian, I would be a little confused to see two teenage boys traveling with giant pieces of the border wall."

Peter bites his lip. "I... didn't think of that."

Cameron walks the length of the wall, running his fingers over it but not leaving them there long enough to drop the wall. Peter looks down at his sword, fiddling with the hilt, until something pinches his finger. "Ow!"

Cameron startles and turns back to Peter, crossing over quickly until he's standing at Peter's side. "What?"

"My sword, it pinched my..." Peter trails off when he sees the hilt of his sword. Upon pressing the Cancer symbol, it seems like he opened up a hatch that shows the hilt of the sword is hollow. Peter presses the symbol back in place, closing the hilt and returning it to normal. Then he presses it again, opening the hatch once more.

"Wait. Leave that open," Cameron says. He motions towards the wall, then back towards Peter. "Use that to put the wall material in."

Peter gasps. "You're right," so he reaches into the wall and places the material into the hilt of the sword, repeating until the hilt is completely full and glowing blue in his hands. Peter closes it and grins at Cameron. "Smart."

Cameron smiles back. "Genius." It seems obvious that he's not speaking about himself.

"What about you? Can yours do anything special?" Peter asks, breaking the silence that settles around them.

Cameron smirks. "Under the wrong circumstances, that could sound *super-*"

Peter groans and laughs. "Stop, I meant your sword."

He frowns, holding it up. "No. It's so *boring.*"

Peter holds out his hand. "Can I see?"

Cameron nods, handing Peter the sword and leaning back against the wall. He stands a few paces away, studying the blade. It looks superbly *normal*, so Peter moves onto the hilt, which is made of obsidian, smooth and shiny. Once again, he can't see anything special, so Peter hands it back to Cameron. "I'm sure it does something?"

Cameron shakes his head dismissively. "Maybe. Let's head back."

Without waiting for an answer, Cameron starts back towards the looming Capitol building, leaving Peter alone again.

Part Twenty-Eight: The Aries

Kiara

Maya and Kiara head down the hall, until they reach the grand front entrance. There are two large windows that look out on the steps that lead to the door, and they station themselves in front of one. Hanging by the windows are large blackout curtains, and Kiara tugs on one of them, admiring the thick fabric that seems to stretch all the way to the ceiling.

"These are sweet," she says.

"Yeah, no kidding," Maya replies. "Good to hide in too, in case someone comes down the hall," she says, jokingly wrapping the curtain around her shoulders like a cape.

Kiara grins. "I never thought of that."

Maya smiles. "I could tell."

So they hunker down next to one of the big windows, peering out at the monorail station. The sun is in the middle of the sky, the bright air giving the outdoor forum a beautiful glow. But from inside the Capitol, one could practically feel the sense of foreboding in the air. People walk around shopping and talking, but when Kiara looks closer, she can see the sideways glares, the tense looks, and the conspiratory glances cast towards the Capitol. Everyone has obviously received their message, and if not, then they're just being *super* weird.

Maya notices, too. "I guess people got the message."

Kiara nods, starting to reply, when she hears footsteps on the stairs. The girls turn around to see Barbara Oswald headed towards them. Maya and Kiara freeze, and Kiara can feel Maya stiffen next to her. Barbara laughs as she approaches and waves her hand in a motion of dismissal. "No need to gape, girls. I'm just on my way out." She pauses for a moment, "by the way, the rest of the members have gone for lunch. The place is clear. Tell those other two Powerful Ones to meet me in my office in thirty minutes," then, she walks right past them, out the front door, and down the stairs.

"What the hell?" Maya whispers.

Kiara shrugs. "Guess she's on our side."

Before they can turn back towards the window, they see Diana coming down the stairs. "Hey," she says. "Did Miss Oswald catch you, too?"

Kiara and Maya both nod. "Where are you going?" Kiara asks her.

"To let in the Powerful Ones from sectors One, Ten, and Eleven. They're here to grab their weapons."

"And you're going to explain their powers to them?"

"Yeah, I read up on each of them. The Aries one is sick. This kid can turn the border wall into fire."

"Damn," Kiara says. "And they couldn't have chosen me?"

"Tell me about it," Diana chimes.

Diana waves, then heads off towards the elevator. After a few moments she returns with a slender sword, its wooden hilt painted Red, a sword even smaller than Cameron's that has a hilt made with Brown crystals, and a steel sword that's average length with a long White quartz handle. She holds them out in front of her, smiling at the other two, then slips out the back door.

"She better be careful," Maya says, turning back to the window. She points at the monorail tracks that dash across the sky from behind the station. "Look how many people are coming."

Sure enough, the monorails are flying in and out of the station, and as the sun starts to lower, people pour out the doors dressed in all different colors. They split in different directions, but there are clumps of people who mingle, talking discreetly to one another.

Kiara turns towards Maya. "I think we should group back up."

Maya looks at her. "We've only been here fifteen minutes."

Kiara nods, biting her lip nervously. "Yeah. But look at all these people. They're here for us," Kiara meets Maya's eyes, and she nods. "Tomorrow. It's gonna be tomorrow, isn't it?"

Maya nods, her mouth set in a grim line. "Yeah, I think so."

Part Twenty-Nine: The Scorpio

Cameron

Peter and Cameron reach the door as Diana is waving a group of three people into the building. She stops her small group and approaches the pair.

"Hey, guys," she says.

"Hey," Peter and Cameron chime together.

"What's going on here?" Peter asks.

Diana motions to the three people behind her. One is a taller boy, maybe eighteen, with dark skin and curly brown hair. He's dressed in Brown, and he's holding a sword that looks even wimpier than Cameron's, which the ginger boy seems to notice with delight. The second is a young girl who can't be much older than twelve, with strawberry blonde hair tied in two pigtail braids. She's in Red, holding a long, slender sword that almost matches her height. The third is a girl dressed in White, with black hair in a slicked-back bun. She has a beautiful sword clutched in her left hand that Cameron is jealous of, and she looks around twenty years old.

"Peter, Cameron, this is Marcus, Katie, and Olivia. They're the Powerful Ones from sectors Ten, One, and Eleven. I gave them their swords and a little run down about their powers, and then I decided that they shouldn't just walk back into the open. So they're gonna stay with us until the battle, and, as the others show up, they can hang out too."

Peter nods. "Okay, great. Nice to meet you guys. Let's head upstairs."

As they walk, Diana converses easily with the three strangers, whereas the two boys hang back, tagging along in awkward silence. Eventually, Peter musters up the courage to tap the strong-looking Capricorn on the shoulder.

"So, uh... Marcus," Peter begins, "what can you do?"

Marcus doesn't bat an eye at Peter's question, and, to Cameron's surprise, he smiles as he answers. "I can double whatever border material I'm holding." He holds up both hands. "Something to do with my zodiac symbol?"

"His symbol is half-human, half-animal, so two separate entities," Diana chimes in. "Everyone's has to do with their symbol." She stares at Peter and Cameron, who wear joint expressions of confusion. "For the most part."

"Like mine!" the little Aries chimes in. "Mine doesn't have anything to do with a *Ram*, but I'm a Fire Sign!" She puts her hands on her hips triumphantly.

Diana and Peter laugh at her. "Katie is right," Diana says. "Like Olivia, as a Sagittarius, she can turn the wall material into a spear that only *she* can hold."

"I don't get it," Cameron whispers to Peter.

Peter leans in to whisper to Cameron, and his hair brushes Cameron's cheek. "Sagittarius' symbol is The Archer."

Cameron nods, and then withdraws from him, the distance between them stretching into nothing short of tense.

When they get to the control room, the group hunkers down beside tables and in chairs. Diana doles out food, and the three other kids eat hungrily while Peter and Cameron snack slowly, perched on tables across the room from one another. On occasion, Peter catches Cameron's eye, and Cameron quickly looks away.

It's not that Cameron is mad at him or anything. It's just that something Peter said when they argued in the hall was actually true. "*I know you better than anyone else in our group.*"

Peter does know Cameron, and he knows that the deeper a relationship they build, the further into Cameron's past they'll have to go, and that's the last thing Cameron wants to show him. So, keeping Peter at arms' length until the battle where Cameron can finally sever ties completely will have to do. That's how he was raised. People come in and out of your life briefly, and the shorter those paths intersect, the less chance you'll wind up hurt.

Kiara and Maya enter the control room then, looking dejected. Without trying to alarm the other kids, Peter, Diana and Cameron cross over to meet them just inside the door. Kiara's brown eyes are downturned, and she looks forlorn, and Maya is chewing her lip, eyes darting around nervously.

"What did you see?" Diana asks them, her voice just above a whisper.

Kiara meets her gaze. "There are *so* many people."

Everyone is quiet. "When do you think we should pull the trigger on this?" Peter whispers at last.

"Tomorrow," the other four whisper simultaneously.

Everything falls silent again, and all they can hear is the gentle whir of computers and the quiet murmurs of the other three Powerful ones.

"So, this is it, then," Cameron says, looking at the floor.

"Tomorrow we revolt," Diana whispers.

Part Thirty: The Cancer

Peter

Peter and Cameron race down the spiral staircase, out of breath.

"Jesus, she's gonna kill us!" Cameron huffs.

Peter just nods, panting too hard to reply.

They were officially five minutes late for their mystery meeting with Barbara Oswald, the Aquarius leader, and Peter was more than a little nervous to see her reaction. Diana had sprung this on them earlier, and Peter felt like he was about to be subject to an ass-kicking by the most powerful woman in the nation.

The two reach the bottom of the staircase and slow their pace to a walk. Peter spots Cameron looking around at the walls and ceilings of the huge atrium, and Cameron catches his eye with a grin. Thankfully, Peter felt like the consequences of their argument, although not completely resolved, were slowly starting to lessen.

"I think I'd like to live here."

Peter laughs. "*In* the Capitol?"

Cameron shakes his head and grins, and just like that, any final remaining tension from earlier that day was dissolved. "No, just around. But I like this place. This whole building, I mean."

"Interesting you say that, considering the people who work here want you dead."

"Yeah, but you have to admit that it's beautiful. Just... peaceful, when it's empty. Imagine, just working late, and it being all dark in here, and echoey. And you could slide down that whole banister and no one could tell you you can't."

Peter smiles softly at his vision. "That would be nice."

Cameron nudges Peter with his shoulder. "Well, when I take Myers' spot, I'll invite you around sometime."

"Bold of you to assume I don't get to take Mister Lee's place."

Cameron shrugs. "You have to get more assertive, Peter," he says sarcastically. "More presidential."

Peter straightens his shoulders and tilts his chin up, putting on the best 'presidential' pose he could muster and dropping his voice low. "Excuse me, Mister O'Connor, this is the Sector Five leader calling. How is the snow up north?"

Cameron snorts with laughter and mimics Peter's tone. "Oh, very well, thank you. Has your whole population been wiped out by southern disease yet?"

Peter laughs, making his voice normal again. "Not quite."

"Boys," Peter and Cameron spin around to see Barbara Oswald standing there, arms folded over her chest. "What are you two doing?"

"Meeting you?" Cameron questions hesitantly. Peter smacks his hand gently, biting back a laugh.

"Well, you're awfully out in the open for two magical renegades, aren't you? To my office."

She begins to walk away, and Cameron and Peter reluctantly follow. She leads them back up the stairs and down the hall, to an office marked with a gold nameplate. 'Oswald' shines out in delicately engraved letters, and she pushes the door open, revealing a huge, well-furnished office.

"Damn," Cameron says.

Peter nods, taking in the industrial place. The chairs and sofa are all Brown leather, and the walls are dark Navy Blue, the same color as Oswald's sector. A large metal light fixture hangs from the ceiling, and a mahogany desk sits in the center of the room. Oswald motions the boys to chairs, and they both sit at the same time, obediently following her every order, even the wordless ones.

She crosses to the desk, sitting down and appraising them carefully. "So. You two are the Powerful Ones, hm?"

The boys stay quiet, and she continues.

"Well, actually, I called you here just to talk. I don't need to see what you do, I already know. In fact, I was there when Cameron got his powers transferred as a young boy."

"You were?" Cameron asks. "What happened?"

Peter smiles gently at Cameron's curious tone, angling his chin towards the floor to ensure the older woman didn't see his amusement. He looks back up as Barbara begins to speak again.

"Your predecessor was an old man named Fredrick. He came to us, saying he saw a young, ginger-haired boy playing in the schoolyard, and he asked if said boy was a Scorpio. Sure enough, Cameron, you were. So, the old man transferred his power to you, and then we wiped your memory of the event. And Fredrick was killed."

"Woah," Peter whispers.

"I didn't even know him," Cameron whispers in response, staring at Oswald. "Why would he give it to me?"

"Nobody knew. Luck, I suppose," she replies. She turns her piercing gaze on Peter. "You, on the other hand, I have no idea about."

Peter clears his throat. "Sorry?"

"I have no idea who gave you your power. I assume Lee knows, as incompetent as he is."

Cameron grins. "I like her," he whispers to Peter.

"Same," Peter replies.

"*Anyway*," Barbara says sharply, pulling the attention back to her and immediately snapping the boys back into full focus, "I wanted to talk to you boys about creating a distraction for the guards."

"Like what?" Peter asks.

"Like you two sacrifice yourselves."

Cameron chokes on air and coughs. "What?!"

Barbara waves her hand dismissively. "Not actually. I gather the regiments on duty, and you two turn yourselves in. They'll come flocking like sharks to blood and you boys will use your powers to trap them like you did outside the train station."

"You... know about that?" Cameron asks.

"Of course I do, it was brilliant. Which one of you came up with that?" Cameron does nothing, so Peter points to his partner. Barbara smiles at Cameron, and it's part reassuring and part unsettling. "Good job, Cameron. How would you, Peter, feel about transporting a large amount of border material to a meeting spot?"

"Sure," Peter replies.

"Good," Barbara says, nodding at their submission. "You two will make fine allies."

"Miss Oswald, I have a question," Cameron says, leaning forward in his seat and setting his elbows on his knees in a nonchalant and confident way that makes Peter's heart flip.

"Yes?"

"Correct me if I'm wrong, but you seem like the type of BOZ member who might try to make an army out of powerful children."

Peter's eyes go wide, and he wonders if Cameron knows he just signed a death warrant.

Oswald just smirks. "How is that a question, Mister O'Connor?"

"I guess it isn't. But I'd just like to know if you're one of those who wants us to just surrender and become soldiers."

Oswald considers this, standing up and beginning to pace the room slowly. She speaks without looking at the boys. "Well, I'll admit that originally, when George pitched the idea, I didn't see any problem. What was the point of having Powerful Ones if we weren't using them?" She pauses, the slightest and shortest of hesitations. "But then, I met William."

"Your charge," Peter inputs softly, remembering the typed name from the book.

"Yes. He was very young, I can't remember his exact age at the time of his transfer. He was so afraid, and the transfer really hurt him. When he woke up from the operation, he was crying. None of the other children I had seen had cried; you didn't, Mister O'Connor. But William Chance cried like the little child he was, and when he opened his eyes and saw me, he held out his arms for a hug. Who was I to refuse? So I hugged him, and he *thanked* me. He whispered 'thank you' in my ear, and wiped his tears and left, back to the school."

She pauses, and Peter studies her face. Her pale skin is etched with wrinkles, from years and years of stress and sadness. Her body language is strong and straight, but her fingers are shaking.

"And?" Cameron prompts gently. His right hand lands on the leather armrest of his chair, and Peter's eyes trace the lines of his fingers.

"And then I changed my mind. I pictured William, crying after killing the country's most dangerous criminals with his own small hands. And I changed my mind."

The boys are quiet. Then, Peter nods. "Thank you."

Barbara looks up at them, eyes betraying her shock. "For what?"

Peter shrugs. "For helping us. For understanding we're not weapons."

Cameron nods from next to him. "Yeah. Thank you."

Oswald looks at them intently, then nods slowly. "You're... welcome," she clears her throat and brushes off her skirt. "Anyhow, you two should probably get back. You know when to meet me?"

"No," both boys chorus.

"Ah," she says, hesitating. She's obviously in a rush to get them out of there. "Tomorrow morning, 5am, on the congress floor."

Cameron begins to groan, but stops himself, instead nodding rapidly. "Yes, ma'am."

Peter stands and crosses to the door, smiling gently at the woman. "Thank you, Miss Oswald."

She sits again at her desk and smiles back at him, her expression showcasing the slightest, almost unnoticeable glimmer of respect. "Just Barbara is fine."

Part Thirty-One: The Taurus

Diana

After a couple hours of waiting, the computer room is filled with thirteen people: Peter, Cameron, Maya, Diana, and Kiara, and eight other Powerful Ones, armed and ready. Excluding Peter and Cameron, they were still missing one person, the Powerful One from Sector Six. The Libra Powerful One had apparently been gone for years, and nobody was expecting them to show up anytime soon. The missing Gemini, though, they *were* expecting to show. Or, at least, they *had* been expecting them.

"Where are they?" Diana asks, pacing the floor. She points to Kiara after a moment of nervous walking. "Check the book, find their name, and I'll message them."

Kiara flips to the page where the names would be and holds up the book with a concerned look. "It's torn out."

"What?" Diana asks, exasperated. She turns to look, and sure enough, the two most recent names under the *'Gemini Powerful One'* header had been ripped out of the book, the edges of the page frayed and thinned.

"So do we go without them?" Peter asks.

"What about their sword?" Cameron counters. "Do we just leave it in the armory?"

Diana shrugs. "We don't have a choice, it's almost dusk, we have to get ready. And no, Maya should take the sword, since she's a Gemini. Maybe it'll still work for her."

Maya shakes her head, rubbing her locket between her thumb and index finger. "I shouldn't," she says. "It's not mine."

"Are you sure?" Kiara asks. "It couldn't hurt."

Maya ponders this, then tilts her head nervously. "I really shouldn't. It would be wrong to take it. And besides, I don't have powers, so why would I need to amplify what's not there in the first place?"

"You do you, I guess," Diana says, snuffing out the conversation.

"Excuse me, Diana?" Marcus, the Capricorn, asks, approaching the group cautiously. "Is there a bathroom nearby?"

"Down the hall," Maya says flatly, tearing her gaze away from Diana.

"Who needs the bathroom?" Diana asks, turning towards the other Powerful Ones. A majority raise their hands, and Diana nods, turning to Maya. "Lead the way, Maya."

So they head down the hall, a band of kids sneaking through the walls of the nation's most important building. Maya motions them to a door in between two offices. "Through there."

They all take turns, with Peter and Cameron leaning against the wall outside in a makeshift security. As the kids finish up and begin to clump up in the hallway, Diana notices all the Powerful Ones are still in their sector colors, and Maya is too, even though she brought new clothes for the others.

"Maya!" Diana calls, as they head back down the hall in a group. She races to catch up with Maya, who's leading the pack and turns when she hears Diana. "Maya, why didn't you change clothes earlier?"

Maya shrugs nonchalantly. "I just forgot to grab some clothes for myself, I guess."

Diana raises an eyebrow. "But it was your idea."

Maya turns to face her. "I know, Di. I just didn't feel like it, is all."

"Ooookay," Diana says, half-convinced. Maya smiles at her a little, and the tension diffuses, only somewhat. Diana walks back to Kiara, who's talking to the little girl from her sector.

"Hey, Di," Kiara says when Diana joins them. "This is Katie."

"I know, we met earlier," Diana says, leaning down to the little girl. "Hello, Katie."

Katie grins at the older girl, and Diana notices she has two dimples in the apples of her cheeks that pop out when she smiles, similarly to Cameron. "Hello, Miss Diana."

Diana smiles back at her. "Just Diana is fine."

Kiara nudges Diana, smiling from the corners of her mouth. "Katie was telling me about her life in Sector One. She moved into the new buildings, and I had never gotten the chance to see them, so she was telling me all about it."

Diana feigns a look of shock. "Really! Well, tell us more, Katie," she prompts.

The little girl smiles again, wringing her hands together as she speaks. "Well, they moved all of us first-years to the new section, because we're closer to the central part of the sector."

Kiara looks confused. "What do you mean, 'first-years'?"

"That's what they've started calling the newest shipment of kids. Since this is my first year in Sector One, we're the youngest of the kids."

Kiara nods, looking pensive. Diana pokes her in the side. "What's the matter, Ki?" Diana taunts. "Feeling old?"

Kiara smiles halfheartedly. "No, it's just-" she turns to Katie, who's looking up at her worriedly, "Katie, are you... scared to be here, all alone?"

Katie looks taken aback. "Um," she starts, "I guess. I've been alone for a little while now, but I do remember my teacher at school." Her little bottom lip quivers just slightly. "She was very nice to us, and she cried every time a kid was taken. I had a brother who was..." she trails off, thinking for a moment. "He was an Aquarius, I think. When he was taken, a year before me, my teacher kept me late and talked with me about it through the whole night." She smiles at the memory. "She was the closest thing I had to a mom."

Katie turns to look at Kiara and Diana, eyes widening when she sees them gaping back at her. Kiara crouches and opens her arms, and Katie wordlessly steps into them. Kiara whispers into her ear, and Diana has to crouch next to them to hear what she's saying.

"It'll be okay, Katie. Maybe you guys can see each other again after this is over, yeah?"

Katie nods, smiling again. "I'd like that."

Diana ushers Katie back with the other kids, and Kiara and Diana break off from the group and shut themselves in a bathroom nearby, Kiara pulling her dark curls into a braid and Diana giving her blonde locks a good finger-brushing before putting them up in a ponytail. Once they're done, they study each other in the mirror, and before the other can say anything, the two girls pull each other into a bone-crushing hug.

"I didn't even realize until now that this might be goodbye," Kiara whispers.

Diana shakes her head. "No, don't even think that. It'll be okay."

Kiara squeezes Diana tighter. "No, we have to." She pulls away, looking into Diana's eyes. "It's possible. And I just wanted to thank you before we go."

Diana smiles, her eyes welling. "For what?"

Kiara hugs her again, then pulls away, turning to leave. "For letting me know I wasn't alone that day."

The girls leave together in silence, clutching hands, wiping tears, and hoping for the best.

Part Thirty-Two: The Cancer

Peter

Hours later, the Gemini Powerful One still hadn't shown up. A few BOZ members had come back, so leaving the room was strictly off-limits, and Marcus and William had found a way to barricade the door, only letting in certain people who knew the special knock Cameron came up with. Maya told Peter and Cameron to hold down the fort while she went back to the bathroom, and Kiara and Diana split off together, chasing down food, so the boys were alone with the other Powerful Ones. The other eight people are sleeping or chatting amongst themselves, whispering nervously, the looming sense of foreboding overshadowing this lengthy waiting time. Cameron is sitting on a table, fiddling with his sword.

Peter crosses over from where he was standing by the window. "Hey," Peter says to him.

Cameron doesn't look up. "Hi."

Peter hesitates. "What... are you thinking about?"

Cameron looks up at him, gray eyes unreadable and clouded with so many different emotions. "I don't know."

Peter nods awkwardly, motioning to the seat next to Cameron on the tabletop. "Can I sit?"

Cameron looks back down at his sword. "If you want."

So Peter pulls himself up next to him, taking out his sword and studying it with the rigor in which Cameron is looking at his own. After a moment, Cameron looks at Peter and smirks, chewing his lip to keep from laughing.

"What are you doing?" Cameron asks.

Peter looks at him, trying to keep a straight face, and puts on his 'presidential' voice from earlier. "Well, you're looking at your weapon very intensely, Mister O'Connor. I figured if I looked at mine like that, I may see what you're seeing."

Cameron laughs out loud now, covering his mouth to keep from bothering the others. After a moment he settles, shaking his head. "I just wish something would happen. The others are so cool." Without context, Peter wondered if Cameron's words were really about his weapon, or if he was talking about something else.

Peter looks at his face, at the sadness etched into his forehead, and he takes Cameron's sword gingerly from his hand, forcing Cameron to look at him. "Honestly, I don't think it's the sword. I think you're worried about your own abilities."

Cameron's expression doesn't change, but his eyes give off a glint of surprise. "What?" he whispers.

Peter continues carefully. "I think the sword is a... metaphor of sorts. You think it can't do anything, but mine and the others' can. I think the only reason you're worried about the sword is because you're afraid that not having the advantage of a powerful weapon will make you weak. You think that the swords amplify power, but you have nothing there to amplify."

Cameron is quiet for a while, and then he nods, eyes falling to his clasped hands. "You're right. God, all I wanted was to do something useful. But compared to the rest of you I'm basically helpless."

Peter stares at him, mouth agape. "What on *earth* do you mean? Cameron, you're the glue that held this group together. You're the reason we even figured ourselves out at all. You're the reason the girls even got past Sector One. You're the reason we have weapons," Peter waves their swords in the air, grinning. At this point, Cameron is smiling. "I can go on, if you want."

Cameron shakes his head, grinning. "No, it's okay." He looks at Peter, his hand resting close to the other boy's. "Thank you."

Peter smiles back. "For what? I should be thanking you for leading us through this."

Cameron looks at Peter for a second, leaning forward just slightly until Cameron's face is close to his. Peter feels Cameron's hand touch the tips of his fingers, and Peter's breathing quickens. Cameron's eyes bore into Peter's, and Peter swears they flick down to look at his lips before returning to meet his gaze.

But then Cameron gives him a hug. *God, Peter. You're so stupid.*

Peter pulls away first, and rubs the back of his neck sheepishly, pushing himself off the table as the other three girls walk in. They join the boys at the back of the room, and the computer dings with a new message. Diana pushes through to check it, and the rest of them crowd around to look at the screen.

Hi, I'm Lilian. I wanted to send you a message of support the day before the revolt. I am in the Plaza now, outside the Capitol, waiting for you. I believe in us.

They all exhale at the same time, Diana leaning against the table and rubbing her eyes. She looks tired, she looks fearful, and Peter doesn't know what to say. Diana looks at all of them, steeling her shoulders. "Okay. I need to prepare for a speech."

Peter grabs her shoulders. "No, we need to *rest*. You're no use in battle if you can't keep your eyes open."

Diana nods, and excuses herself to lie down. Maya squeezes in under a table across the room, and Kiara pulls herself on top of the table. Cameron catches Peter's eye before turning away quickly and lying down a good distance away from everyone. Peter finds a table in the center of the room, slides under it, and lets his eyes drift closed.

Part Thirty-Three: The Aries

Kiara

After about thirty minutes, Kiara looks to her left, seeing Peter asleep on the floor beneath a table. She strains her ears for a moment, hearing Maya and Diana's almost identical snoring. Kiara sits up quietly to see Cameron asleep on the right side of the room, and the eight other kids scattered across the left side are all still and quiet.

So Kiara slips off the tabletop and heads for the door, grabbing a utility knife on her way out. She shuts it quietly behind her, then heads for the large staircase that will take her to the ground floor. When she gets to the bottom, Kiara peeks her head towards the window, showing that the sky is just starting to turn purple, signaling the impending rise of the sun, the impending start of their revolution.

Kiara turns away from the window and heads towards the BOZ chamber, shoving open the huge doors without a care in the world. She's relieved to find it empty, and she strides to the front, where twelve chairs are lined up beside a huge podium, six chairs on either side. The chairs are plush and grand, and Kiara resists the urge to recline in one. Instead, she approaches the chair closest to the podium, directly to the left of it. It's the same as all the others according to its design, but one feature makes her blood boil.

It's Red.

Kiara runs a hand over the plump fabric, gritting her teeth as she takes out her knife, and before she can think, she drives the blade into the arm. Kiara tears it apart, releasing stuffing and thread. She scratches the wood and chips the paint, reveling in the satisfying feeling of dragging him down a peg.

When she's done, Kiara steps back, panting. She turns to leave, then notices that the Purple chair to the left of the defaced Red one is crooked. She straightens it, putting it back in its rightful place, and then casts one more look at the Red chair, heading back up the stairs and into the control room.

Kiara falls asleep with a smug smile on her face.

Part Thirty-Four: The Cancer

Peter

Peter wakes up to someone shaking his shoulder.

"Hey," Cameron whispers, prodding Peter with his fingertips. "Sorry to wake you."

Peter rubs his eyes and scoots over to make room for him. "No, don't worry about it." Cameron slides in next to him, shoulder-to-shoulder in the corner of the room. "What's up?"

Cameron shrugs. "I dunno. I'm just... nervous, I guess," he casts an unreadable look Peter's way. "Needed someone to talk to."

Peter nods, biting his lip. "Yeah. I'm nervous too."

Cameron looks at him out of the corner of his eye, and Peter studies his gray irises and flaming hair. "No brilliant words of advice?"

Peter shrugs. "There's nothing to say that could help. I won't tell you that it will all be okay, because it might not. But deep down, we both knew that from the beginning."

Cameron nods. "Yeah, you're right, I guess." He looks away, eyes scanning the room.

Peter admires the side of his face. "All I can say is just... remember why you're doing this. Remember all the people you're doing this for." He lowers his voice barely above a whisper. "That's what I'm doing."

Peter watches Cameron swallow, and slowly, he turns his head so he's looking Peter in the eye. Peter's heart leaps into his throat when he feels Cameron's fingers up against his. First his pinky, then his ring finger, and soon, Cameron and Peter's fingers are so, so close to intertwining. Peter looks down at their hands, but Cameron's whisper spurs him to look back up at the other boy.

"Hey," Cameron starts. "Is this okay?"

Peter clears his throat. "Um, yeah," he pauses, chest rising and falling heavily, and then looks back down at their hands. He takes a long, deep breath, counts to three, and then locks their fingers together completely, so they're properly holding hands. Peter feels electricity shoot through his body, and he looks back up at Cameron, whose mouth is hanging slightly open at the blatant show of affection. Peter smiles a little through the darkness and wonders if Cameron's heart was racing just as his was. "Yes. It's okay."

Cameron smiles back, swallowing hard, and pulls Peter a little closer. Fleetingly, Peter wonders if Cameron is going to press his lips against Peter's own, but with a *thunk* of his heartbeat, he realizes that he doesn't need to. He knows, deep down, that he'd still feel exactly the same, that he'd never ask for anything more than this.

Peter sighs contentedly and sits there quietly, the cold on his right side smothered by Cameron's warmth on his left side and his head on Peter's shoulder. Finally, after a long moment of peaceful silence, Cameron's whisper cuts through the dim room.

"Peter?"

"Yeah?"

"What are you gonna do after this?"

"I dunno. Go back to Sector Five, I guess."

A beat.

"Hey."

"Yeah?" Peter replies.

"I know you want to move somewhere else, and just run away where nobody knows you. But *I* want you to know me. Okay? I want to know you forever. It doesn't... I don't care how, alright? As long as I know you."

Peter doesn't respond, because he has nothing to say. Somewhere deep down, he wants to tell Cameron that he wants to know him forever too, that he wants to know him better than anyone has known him before, but he doesn't need to. Peter knew that Cameron understood how he felt, and he realizes with a smile that Cameron had always been very good at understanding Peter, even when he didn't say anything at all.

Cameron whispers again after a very long moment filled with no sound other than the whirring of computers.

"Can I stay here the rest of the night?"

Peter squeezes his hand, leaning his forehead on top of Cameron's head, tightening his grip on their joined hands. "Yes. Please stay."

Cameron nestles further into Peter's shoulder, and Peter makes up his mind right then and there, thinking back to the question Kiara asked him those few days ago.

"Well, do you like him?"

Peter looks down at their hands, running his thumb over Cameron's.

Yeah, Peter thinks, *I do.*

Part Thirty-Five: The Scorpio

Cameron

Cameron wakes up to Peter prodding his shoulder.

He goes to rub his eyes, pulling at his right hand, but it doesn't budge.

He looks down to see his fingers, nails bitten down and skin weathered, laced with Peter's, holding his hand like there aren't other people in the room.

Cameron looks back up at Peter quickly, and Peter smiles gently at him.

"Good morning," the brunette boy whispers.

"Hi." Cameron looks around to where the other kids are still sleeping. Like it was perfectly natural, he squeezes Peter's hand and pushes himself up a little further. "Why'd you wake me up?"

Peter chuckles softly. "Trust me, I didn't want to, but we have to go meet Barbara." He releases Cameron's hand from his and gets to his feet. He holds out a hand to help Cameron up, and Cameron takes it.

The two sneak out of the control room, heading to the landing of the stairs. Neither one speaks, and they're all silence and hands in pockets, looking around at the dark Capitol. They reach the top of the stairs, and after a brief moment of hesitation, Peter pushes himself onto the flat banister, sliding down the railing and landing somewhat shakily on the first floor.

He looks up at the top of the stairs to see Cameron staring down at him like he'd grown an extra head, not just disrespected the nation's Capitol building.

Peter shrugs. "You said so yourself, you wanted to slide down the railing when no one was here." He motions around with his arms. "Well, no one is here."

Cameron's shocked expression morphs into a grin, and he seats himself atop the banister, sliding down just as Peter did. He lands next to Peter with a small stumble, smiling triumphantly, and Peter laughs, the sound echoing off the walls of the atrium.

Cameron's chest warms at the sound, and he can't help himself, grabbing Peter's hand in his and locking their fingers together again. Peter looks down, growing quiet, and Cameron's heart thuds nervously against his ribcage.

But then Peter gives their hands a squeeze and tugs Cameron towards the doors of the congress floor, running his thumb along Cameron's.

Peter releases Cameron's hand to open the doors, and there, sitting in a large, Navy Blue chair, is Barbara Oswald.

She looks up at them from under a pair of round, Navy Blue glasses that probably cost more than the accumulation of everything Cameron was wearing right now. "Hello, boys."

"Hi," Cameron says, reluctantly following Peter to the front of the room. He notices a Red chair, identical to Barbara's, is completely destroyed at the center of the group. He points at the chair. "What-"

"Your little friend," Barbara interrupts, following his gaze. "The warrior queen."

"Kiara," Peter whispers with the smallest of smiles.

"Ready to go?" Barbara asks, standing and promptly changing the subject.

"Go... where?" Peter asks.

"To the location I've sent the guards. They all know you're revolting, everyone knows. Hell, people have been camping out in alleyways since yesterday morning."

Cameron grins. "Really?"

"Really. Anyway, they think I'm gathering them to hand you two over. They're planning to see you tied up and unarmed."

"So they think," Peter says with a smirk.

Oswald smiles right back, quirking an eyebrow. "Exactly."

So the trio leaves the floor and heads back into the atrium. The boys veer left, towards the servants' door, but Oswald goes right, towards the huge main entrance. "This way," she says, and Peter and Cameron quickly pivot on their heels to follow her.

Barbara Oswald pulls open the main doors, welcoming the dawn sky and morning chill. Cameron is shocked at her confidence: the enemy of their entire revolution, entering the world and screaming for attention without saying a word.

They walk through the Plaza under the early dawn sky, and it's all Cameron can do to just take in the sight around him. *Nobody* is there that early, and yet, in the twilight alleyways he can see people, so many people, with tents and small fires and gear. They watch as the boys pass through with Barbara, who's striding confidently through the very center of the hub.

They reach a large, nondescript building behind the BOZ apartments. The place is made of wood, almost like a bigger version of the rickety shacks Cameron lived near in Sector Three.

"Is this, like, a secret guard hideout?" Peter asks.

"A lounge?" Cameron adds, only half-joking.

"More of a meeting house. An unmarked, untraceable location," Oswald answers, crossing to the keypad on the door.

Cameron nudges Peter. "*Watch this,*" he whispers. Then, before Peter can stop him, Cameron blurts out, "Four, six, two, seven."

Barbara stops in her tracks and turns around slowly, facing him. "I'm *sorry?*"

"That's the code," Cameron says, unwavering. "Four six two seven."

"And how on *earth* would you know this?"

Cameron shrugs and Peter feels like throwing up with nerves. "Doesn't matter, but I know it." He crosses in front of Oswald and punches in the code, pulling the door open with a satisfied smirk. "Might want to change that, by the way," he calls over his shoulder as he enters the dark building.

Oswald turns to Peter, who just shrugs. "He's always like this, before you ask," Peter says plainly, before entering behind Cameron.

The room is vast and echoey, and Peter clears his throat as they stand side-by-side in the darkness. "Where are the-"

A loud *bang* sounds as the room illuminates, and the boys jump and spin around to see Oswald standing next to a large breaker switch. She smirks at them. "Sorry to scare you, but I figured doing this in the light would be easier."

"Doing what?" Peter asks at the same time as Cameron whispers, "Oh god, she's gonna kill us."

Oswald rolls her eyes. "I'm not killing *anybody,*" she says as she waltzes past the boys. Cameron hears her whisper under her breath, ever-so-quietly, "I have people who would do that *for* me, anyway."

Before Cameron can respond, Oswald opens a large set of barn doors at the back of the warehouse, revealing the border wall.

"I'm... really confused," Cameron whispers.

"This is where we first put up the wall," Oswald explains, her voice echoing off the ceilings. "It's a ten-by-ten square, tested by the original twelve founders. The guards don't know it's here, because it's locked with-" she pauses, glaring at Cameron, "the code."

Peter tries to ignore Cameron's *adorable* grin from next to him.

"Anyway, this is the version that made it to the rest of the country. So, Peter, here's your power source."

"Sick," Peter whispers, crossing to the wall. He runs his fingertips over, comfortably, calculatingly, as if he'd done it a thousand times before.

"So I very much should not touch this," Cameron says, from the safe distance away where he and Peter had been standing before.

"You very much should not," Barbara affirms.

"Wait, what?" Peter says, turning around. "But I need his help."

"How so?" Oswald questions. "Your powers essentially contradict one another's."

"No, watch," Peter says, grabbing Cameron's wrist and dragging him towards the wall. "Do the thing, the one Kiara taught us at the campsite."

Cameron nods and starts to crouch at the base of the border, when Oswald speaks up. "Boys, I'm not sure about this. This wall is the source of the borders around all twelve sectors. If you destroy this, Cameron, we have nothing to go from anymore."

Cameron begins to respond when Peter pipes up. "He won't, actually. Cameron is probably the best

Powerful One I've seen so far, and I've met all but two of them. And one of them is also me. So, he won't destroy it."

He glances down at Cameron to see him looking up at him, smiling gently. He looks at the border, and Peter follows his gaze. "Ready?" Cameron whispers.

"Ready," Peter responds, looking closely at the wall to avoid Cameron seeing his petrified expression. "Twenty feet?"

"Twenty feet," Cameron repeats.

So, Peter begins to back up, counting in his head. When he hits twenty, he stops, landing around the middle of the room. He's a good ten yards from Barbara, who's holding her lip between her teeth nervously. "Okay, Cam," Peter calls to Cameron's back, "go."

Peter sees Cameron's hand touch the wall and he squeezes his eyes shut.

When he opens them again a heartbeat later, he's holding a piece of the wall and the rest is still there, framing Cameron's body as he stands again, brushing his legs off. Cameron and Peter lock eyes, and Cameron grins at Peter, giving him a gentle nod that means much more than he could put into words.

Kiara had told them that day at camp to think of each other to get their powers to work this way, and as Cameron smiles at Peter, he flexes his fingers into a fist and back again, remembering Peter's hand in his all night.

Peter smiles back at Cameron, and the two stand there until the moment is splintered by Oswald. "God almighty, boys," she says, face breaking into a grin, "you two will make history."

Part Thirty-Six: The Taurus

Diana

Diana and the girls wake up when the other eight Powerful Ones start to stir, right as Peter and Cameron re-enter from their meeting with Barbara Oswald. Diana had fallen asleep under a table, and she stretches a little to get the ache out of her back. She rises and sees Maya and the other three, talking in hushed tones: Maya is fiddling with her locket, Peter is casting glances at Cameron, and Kiara keeps looking out the window, as if waiting for someone.

When Diana approaches, they turn to her, voices quieting, and wordlessly, Kiara hands Diana a small stack of index cards with words scrawled on them in Peter's familiar handwriting. Diana scans the cards, realizing that this is the speech she's set to give in just a little while, written by Peter, who probably knew her thoughts better than she did, at least at this very moment. Diana nods at them, each person giving her a small touch or look in support but no one saying anything. The room is heavy, and each face wears a passive, almost dejected look. There was no turning back now, and it seemed like the revolt in its entirety was hitting each person in its own separate manner, all at once.

Diana steels her shoulders, feeling her weapon in her waistband, and pushes the door open, leading their group down the stairs. When they reach the bottom landing, the oak doors of the congress floor shove open and the Board Of Zodiacs exit, all twelve standing assembled in a triangle, watching the kids pass without stopping them.

Diana reaches the front doors, taking a deep breath and looking back at her companions. Maya nods at Diana, looking down at her feet. Diana follows her gaze, and she shuffles out "I love you," before smiling at Diana. Diana gives her a nod, but she can't bring herself to return the smile. Kiara is looking straight ahead at the front entrance, and Peter and Cameron keep looking at each other, although neither of them say anything. Diana grabs the handle, each of her companions puts their hand over Diana's, and they push the door open together.

The light of the morning briefly blinds her, and Diana blinks against the brightness. She steps up to the edge of the top stair, and when her eyes focus, Diana notices the sea of colors in front of her – people, and a lot of them at that. Diana's companions each take a spot next to her, with Cameron and Maya on her left and Peter and Kiara on her right. The other eight Powerful Ones line up behind them, and the BOZ members cluster to the far left of them, spreading down the stairs in color order. Diana catches the look of Barbara Oswald, and she motions to the crowd, making Diana notice that there are no guards. Their secret diversion must have worked, and Diana smiles as she catches Cameron and Peter's eye. With the crowd standing in silence, Diana clears her throat, takes a glance at her cards, and starts to speak.

"Good morning, citizens of New America. My name is Diana Monroe. I'm sixteen, and I am a Taurus. Next to me are my companions: Cameron, Maya, Peter, and Kiara. They are not Taureans. They are a Scorpio, a Gemini, a Cancer, and an Aries," Diana pauses to gauge the crowd's reaction, waiting for cries of outrage, but all look wildly passive, and she can't tell if that's a good thing or not. "I started on my journey to find my best friend, Peter, after we were separated four years ago. But instead, I found

Cameron and Kiara as well, and we discovered something shocking: Cameron and Peter both had powers." Diana's voice wavers, and Peter catches her eye, giving her a nod that spurs her to continue.

"This girl is lying!" Someone interrupts her before she can speak, and Diana turns to her left to see the BOZ member from her sector pointing an accusatory finger at her. Before he can storm up to Diana, a man in Brown grabs his arm, holding him back. He must be the Capricorn leader Barbara was talking about, and Diana mouths a subtle "thank you" to him before continuing.

"I figured I would get this same reaction from some of you. Peter and Cameron are going to demonstrate their powers for you all today, to prove that we're telling the truth." Diana motions to Peter, who unsheathes his sword and releases the hatch in its hilt. He pulls out a clump of the border, the material shaping itself into a ball in his hand, and he hands his sword to Kiara, who takes it silently. Peter looks at Diana, and she nods, allowing him to take aim at her and throw the ball in her direction. When it hits Diana, it materializes into a column, surrounding her in a protective shield. After a few scattered gasps from the crowd, the shield drops, and Diana looks down to see Cameron kneeling where the base of the column once was. They hurry back to their spots in line, and Diana steps forward once again to address the now shocked and still silent crowd.

"As you can see, these powers are very much real. And Peter and Cameron are not the only ones," Diana motions to the other eight kids, standing behind them, and smiles a little when she sees young Katie, her hand resting on the hilt of her sword. "These ten are called the Powerful Ones. One person per sector. But there is another secret the government has been keeping from all of you," Diana pauses to flip to the next card, "the Board Of Zodiacs was not created to run this government, but instead called together to protect these Powerful Ones. And from recent events, they have not been succeeding."

The BOZ member dressed in Black scoffs, "How so? We've done a fine job."

Diana glares at him, then motions to Cameron. "I'm glad you bring that up, Mister Myers, because you are a prime example." She turns to face the crowd. "Gerard Myers was kicked out of the BOZ when my friend, Cameron O'Connor, helped four hundred Scorpios escape the abuse and neglect of their sector. I would argue that Mister Myers' allowing Cameron to escape could not be called protection, nor could the horrifying conditions he put his charge through. So we are here to ask you, citizens, to revolt. Now is the time to create a new government, one filled with peace, trust, and honesty." Diana looks towards Maya, willing her voice not to break. "How many of you want to see your families again? How many of you want to see the person you love again?" Diana's voice starts to rise as she sees various strangers in the crowd: the young boy who can't be more than thirteen, the old man whose wrinkled brow is set in resolve. "So join us, New America, in creating a better world for each and every one of you!"

Her final words ring over the packed Plaza, and then, to Diana's dismay, everything falls silent. She takes a deep breath, wondering what to do next, wondering if this was the end of the revolution itself. Diana feels Peter fidget nervously next to her, and she glances towards him as he whispers: "What do we-?"

He's cut off by a gunshot. Instinctively, the group of five tightens around each other: Diana steps back into Maya's arms and everyone else grabs for whoever is next to them. Someone lets out an anguished cry, and Diana turns, nerves jolting and heart pounding, to see that someone in the crowd has shot Gerard Myers. Wildly searching the mass of people, she can't tell who pulled the trigger, but it's too late anyway. Blood seeps into his Black suit, and he claws at his chest. To Diana's horror, the rest of the BOZ stand there motionless and watch him crumple, blood trickling from his mouth, as life drains from his eyes.

Everything is quiet again, but only fleetingly, for then chaos erupts all around them. People shout, metal scrapes against metal, guns fire, and pained cries are heard all over. Diana turns quickly to the other kids, giving them a reassuring look. "Listen up, guys. Be careful, think on your feet. Avoid large crowds." She motions them into the fray, and they rush into battle together. Diana looks to the other four, her closest friends, her family. "I love you guys. We can do this, alright? Remember, guards and BOZ *only*. The only citizens you should fight are their supporters, no one else."

They nod, Cameron and Peter unsheathing their swords, Kiara sliding her brass knuckles on, and Maya pulling out her knives. They glance Diana's way before rushing into the crowd, and Diana starts after them until she hears someone cracking their knuckles behind her.

"Well, well," a male BOZ member in a Sky-Blue suit approaches Diana, grinning like a maniac. "Is this what you wanted?" he asks, motioning towards the swirling crowds. He pulls out a dagger, and before Diana has time to think, he lunges at her. Diana barely jumps out of the way before he comes at her again, and this time, his blade slices through the air an inch from her eyebrow, and Diana grabs his wrist with her free hand, yanking him towards her. She hits the second button on her weapon, and a knife blade shoots from the top. Before she can stab him, though, he switches his dagger to the other hand and grazes Diana's forearm with an erratic swing.

Diana gasps in pain, and he smiles again. She grits her teeth and extends her arms, motioning as he did as anger boils her insides. "This?" she begins, "this is what the *nation* wanted!" She switches the blade to the baton, dodging his next swing and pounding the baton against the back of his head. He stumbles forward, and Diana slams the baton against his jaw, connecting with a sickening crunch. He falls forward, and Diana takes a deep breath before driving her heel into his face, over and over, until his crooked jaw and unmoving form is a satisfying enough stalemate.

Diana turns back towards the fray, noticing that the number of bodies on the ground is sickeningly high, but not nearly as scary as the sight of those still alive. Everyone is still fighting, but her friends are nowhere to be seen. Diana only has time to briefly scan the crowd when a strangled shout drifts her way, and she quickly turns to see little Katie, a knife driven down into her collarbone, collapse on the ground. Diana doubles back quickly to kneel by her side, shoving her way through others to get to the child.

"Katie!" Diana shouts, her hands groping at the wound wildly in a futile attempt to stop the bleeding. "Katie, it's okay. I'm right here."

Katie coughs, blood trickling from her lips. "Miss Diana," she whispers.

"Yeah?" Diana asks, tears streaming down her face. Diana removes her hand from around the knife, stomach plummeting when she sees the wound. There's no part of the blade left visible, and Katie's bones protrude under her skin as she struggles to breathe. Blood trickles from the cut, and Diana knows better than to take the knife out.

"Miss Diana, is it going to hurt?" The child is sobbing now, and as she sucks in her sharp breaths, blood seeps from the injury, slicking Diana's hands.

"Wh-what?" Diana asks, her panic growing as the din of the battle that surrounds them grows louder.

"Is it going to hurt when I go, Miss Diana?"

Diana gasps as she comprehends, swiping at her tears with the back of her bloodied hand. Diana takes a shaky breath to try to calm herself before doing her best to console the dying child. "No, no, Katie. It won't hurt," Diana puts her arms around Katie and cradles her as best she can without touching or getting anywhere near the wound. "It's as easy as going to sleep."

Katie nods, lip quivering in the same fashion it did in the hallway. "Can I close my eyes now, Miss Diana?" She clenches her little fist around Diana's hand. "It hurts very bad."

Diana nods rapidly. "Yes. Yes, Katie, you can close your eyes. I'm here."

Katie nods, just barely, and her eyes flutter closed as her breathing shallows but doesn't stop just yet. Diana lowers her forehead to hers for a brief moment of respite before a shout breaks her from her mourning.

"Diana!" Kiara's voice cuts through the din of battle. Diana's head jerks up to see Kiara waving her over, and Diana goes to stand up when she remembers Katie. The child is still breathing, despite how shaky the breaths are. "No, no," Diana whispers to no one. There's not enough time for her to help everyone. There's not going to be enough time.

"I'm sorry, Katie," Diana whispers, setting her back on the ground, "I'm so sorry."

Diana stands up and rushes to help Kiara, but when she sees the scene playing out unfold in front of her, time, although fleeting before, seems then to slow to a standstill.

Maya is sparring with a guard, fists flying, and she glances Diana's way as the guard pulls out a gun. Peter notices and shouts something, the sound garbled, as he flings a ball of the border Maya's way, swallowing her up in a protective forcefield. The guard fighting Maya falls against it, shouting a painful shout as he burns. Diana notices his charred hands and face, and he slips to the ground in a blur. Before Diana can blink, though, Cameron comes running into view, another guard with a gun hot on his tail. Cameron spins around to look at him, right as the guard raises the gun and takes aim at Cameron's chest. Cameron, face twisted in fear, trips over his feet, falling backwards and putting his hands out behind him to stop his impact. He catches himself on Maya's shield, his touch hovering there long enough to drop the border around her. Cameron lands on the ground with a sickening thud, rolling over onto his side, while Maya is standing, caught off guard, with nothing around her but wide open space.

She's a prime target.

Then, the bullet meant for Cameron tears through her abdomen.

Maya crumples to the ground astoundingly fast. Cameron is curled on the ground, forehead to concrete, his twitching fingers the only indication that he's still conscious. Peter is off to the side, and after a brief moment of evident panic, he races over to Cameron, rolling him over and yanking him to his feet. Diana can't move, she just watches her sister fall, her hands scratching at her stomach.

As Diana rushes to Maya, she sees Kiara take out the remaining guard, her knife dancing across his throat, and Diana turns away from the spray of hot blood, her stomach threatening to heave once again. Then Kiara rushes to where the rest of them are now kneeling by Maya's side. Diana helps her into her lap, her hands groping to cover her terrifying wound. Deja vu spins through Diana's head, and she pushes the thought of Katie, still alive and trembling, out of her head. The blood seeping through Diana's fingers mixes with her salty tears, dripping onto Maya's face as her eyes widen and she starts to gasp for breath. Her Yellow shirt is turning an eerie shade of Brown as the blood pumps steadily with each passing heartbeat. Maya is gasping for air, and Diana uncovers her hands to see that there is nothing she can do.

"Maya. Maya, look at me," Diana says, grabbing Maya's face with her bloodied hands so she can look into her eyes, "it's okay. You're gonna be okay. I love you, Maya."

Maya smiles at Diana, not quite looking at her but instead looking through her, at someone who's not there. She whispers, her voice coming out hoarse and pained. "Smile."

Without thinking, Diana smiles, her despair surely etched into her features. To her shock, though, Maya grins back, attempting to reach out a hand to wipe Diana's tears but being unable to do so, so Diana meets her halfway and leans into her touch. Maya whispers again, her voice fading almost as quickly as the color from her cheeks. "I haven't seen you smile in so long. I love you too."

And then, she closes her eyes, allowing her body to spasm in Diana's arms once, twice, before she stills. Diana removes her hands from Maya's face, staring at her bloodied palms. She takes a shaky breath and lets out a choked sob, and then someone lets out a scream akin to a dying animal. Diana only realizes it was her when Peter, Cameron, and Kiara rush to her side, wrapping their arms around Diana, stroking her hair, whispering comforting words. But Diana hears and feels none of it, registering that her only family left has been ripped from her the same way she was eight years ago.

"No, no, no!" Diana screams. She clutches Maya's saturated shirt with both hands as Peter threads his arms around her waist, pulling her away gently. "No, Maya, no!" She struggles against Peter's hold and Cameron crouches to add another set of strong arms to the mix. "No, I never got to say I was sorry! No, Maya, please-"

Peter finally pulls Diana away, instantly swallowing her up in a hug. She tucks herself into him, right in his lap, and she pounds her fists against his chest as she heaves out a broken cry.

He holds her in silence, tucking his nose in her hair, whispering something indiscernible. Cameron wraps his arms around both of them, and swallows against the lump in his throat as he realizes that Peter is shivering just as badly as Diana is. Kiara watches them, and then sets gentle hands on Peter and Cameron's shoulders, pulling them to their feet.

Part Thirty-Seven: The Cancer

Peter

Kiara ushers the boys away from Diana, who is still crying on the ground next to her sister.

"Guys, go, seriously. Track down as many of the other Powerful Ones as you can and get a headcount on how many are still..." she trails off, casting a look at Diana. Kiara looks back at Peter and Cameron. "I'll take care of her."

"What are we gonna do when we find them?" Peter asks Kiara, prepared to follow her instruction. He supposes if the general is down for the count, the soldiers must turn to the lieutenant.

Kiara shakes her head. "We have to give up the fight. We can't keep losing people like this. Find the rest of the Powerful Ones, get them somewhere safe, and find the BOZ so we can surrender." She shakes her head, as if anticipating their disappointment, "it's not worth the lost lives."

"Kiara, we can't," Cameron argues, "we'll spend the rest of our lives rotting in jail."

Kiara's head snaps up to look at him. "I'd rather be in jail than dead, Cam! With the blood of innocent *children* on my hands!"

Cameron's mouth clamps shut, and both boys are quiet. Cameron and Peter nod solemnly at the lashing, and Cameron steps forward to whisper to Kiara, hostility forgotten. "I recommend not moving Maya's body. It'll take up too much time, trust me. Just get Diana somewhere safe."

Kiara nods, then motions them back into the crowd. Cameron sticks close to Peter, and Peter can feel his warmth against his side.

"What do we do?" Peter whispers, looking at Cameron in his peripheral vision.

"Help someone," Cameron responds, voice at a normal volume.

Help. What a weird word, Peter thinks. It seemed as if *nothing* they had done so far today had helped anybody.

"But we can't help all of them," he replies, motioning to the vast crowd.

"We can help one person," Cameron replies. "One person is better than nothing."

Peter nods, swallowing the truth of Cameron's words. He takes a deep, shuddering breath from next to him, and finally, after a moment of scanning the mass of people, Peter points out towards a kid in Purple.

"Isn't she the Powerful One from Sector Eight?" he asks.

Cameron nods. "She looks like she's struggling."

Sure enough, the girl has just finished what seemed like a big fight, for she's hobbling on a hurt ankle towards the side of the building, where she leans against the wall, wiping blood from her face.

Without answering Cameron, Peter starts towards her, tapping her on the shoulder. She's probably around thirteen or fourteen, and she looks frightened. "Do you need help?" Peter asks.

She nods rapidly. "Please. There are two guards over there, but I think I twisted my ankle. I– I can't fight them on my own."

Cameron appears next to them, seemingly calming her down with his presence alone. "Let's get you inside."

Peter turns to Cameron. The ginger-haired boy's cheeks are dusted red from the exertion, and Peter swallows, trying to drink in the image. "Be safe."

Cameron smiles softly, and the one dimple reappears. "You too, superhero."

So Cameron disappears with her in his arms, heading towards the back door of the Capitol. Peter, after a very evident consideration of whether he should *follow* him or not, eventually rushes towards two straggling guards, swallowing one up with the last of his border material. He turns to the next one, now-empty sword in hand, and the huge guard charges for the teenager. Peter sidesteps as fast as he can, swinging his sword around and hearing it slice cleanly through skin. His stomach churns, but he forces himself to spin around and swing again with his eyes closed. When Peter opens them, the guard is on the ground, a garish shoulder wound bleeding heavily. Backing up a few steps, his head clouding with sudden guilt, Peter takes that as his cue to leave, and he spins around to look for Cameron.

Except Cameron is nowhere to be seen, and Peter's heart starts to pound when he realizes that he should have been back to him by now. Almost upon thinking this, Peter feels an empty, cold, space next to him and his already-turbulent head fills with even more horrifying thoughts.

Cameron, cornered by a guard.

Cameron, stuck in a BOZ office, shouting for help.

Cameron, injured and unable to get out of the way of impending danger.

Suddenly, this whole revolt feels like more than Peter can bear.

He thinks about yelling for him, but decides against drawing more attention to himself. Peter decides to go *look* for him instead, so he runs towards the back of the Capitol, towards the entrance they used before, feet pounding against the concrete, and his blood rushes through his veins a little slower as he heads towards the semi-familiar surroundings. As he rounds the corner, Peter swears he could feel his heart leap into his throat as he takes in the sight in front of him.

Cameron is sitting in the shade of the wall, legs pulled to his chest, breathing heavily. Peter runs to stand in front of him, running a shaky hand through his tangled hair.

Relief, Peter realizes, is the feeling that courses through him. He was so worried, and now, here he is, his whole tall frame and red hair and freckled cheeks, right in front of him. He's right there, and he's *okay.*

"Cameron. You're insane," Peter says, his voice rising at the end of the phrase as frustration takes relief's place.

Cameron looks up at Peter with an endearing smile, although his eyes are red and rapidly welling with tears. "I know. Isn't it great?"

Peter opens his mouth to respond, but he pauses as something hits him. Something that he doesn't really know the name of just yet but he's certain exists as he stares down at Cameron. "I lied," he blurts out.

Cameron blinks, face growing concerned. "What do you mean?"

Peter sits next to him, keeping about six inches between them. He takes a low, deep breath, and lets the cool wall pressed against his back relax his muscles before he finally speaks. "When we fought in the Capitol. I said I cared about you."

Cameron winces instantaneously. "And that was a *lie*?"

Peter nods, too blinded by what he's trying to comprehend to realize his slip of the tongue. "Yeah. Yeah, I said 'I cared', but I feel a lot more than that, I think," his words rush out at once, and it takes a minute of courage-building before Peter can look over at Cameron.

He's nodding slowly, chewing his bottom lip, and Peter's stomach does backflips. "So you like-"

"And I dunno, but I think that's maybe why I don't like Diana the same way I used to-"

"Peter."

"I know this really isn't the time, but-"

"Superhero, just listen!"

Peter swallows his next words, thankfully, and looks over at Cameron.

The ginger-haired boy is staring right at him, and Peter's breath is ripped from his lungs as he studies his gray eyes.

Cameron exhales heavily, mumbling something under his breath and turning away from Peter.

"What?" Peter asks nervously. He thinks he definitely just blew it. Did he misread the situation? He couldn't have, every time he remembers Cameron's fingers tangled with his he feels his stomach alight. "I'm sorry. I shouldn't have said anything, I was trying to say that it's not the right time for it, *especially* with-"

Cameron turns back towards Peter, who is suddenly hyper-aware of the limited space between them. Actually, he's caught by surprise so badly that his mouth clamps shut and he feels his neck and cheeks get hot. He notices Cameron's gray eyes are sparkling with a look Peter has never seen before, and Cameron's voice comes out barely a whisper. "I *said,* 'it's about time'."

"For... what?" Peter whispers, unable to stop his heartbeat from thundering.

Cameron reaches out naturally, as if this happens all the time, and runs his fingers down Peter's shoulder, his bright eyes following the movement. Peter swallows, leaning into the movement, and his breath escapes his lips in a gentle sigh. The noise causes Cameron to look up, and he smiles as he studies Peter's face. "For you to finally admit you have feelings for me." His fingers land on Peter's wrist, and as he intertwines his fingers with Peter's, Peter finds himself unconsciously pushing into the contact, and Cameron squeezes his hand. "It's just..." he trails off.

Peter ducks his head, forcing Cameron to look at him. "What?" he whispers.

Cameron meets his eyes and smiles. "It's just *you*."

And with that, he leans in and kisses Peter, removing his hands from Peter's grip and cupping Peter's cheeks. Peter inhales sharply at the contact, and his whole body explodes with heat as he pushes through the fog and registers that he's *finally* kissing Cameron and god, it feels *perfect*. Peter pushes further into the other boy, and a noise that sounds like the word *superhero* escapes Cameron's lips in a hushed whisper. Peter can't help but smile, and he chuckles against Cameron's lips, causing Cameron to grin as well. Their noses and teeth bump by accident, and Peter pulls away.

Peter rubs his thumb over Cameron's cheek, and Cameron touches a loose curl of hair on Peter's forehead before retreating away from him. They sit in silence next to each other for a moment, both of them breathing heavily from nerves more than anything else. Cameron looks at Peter out of the corner of his eye, and Peter holds his gaze while he reaches out his hand, allowing Cameron to thread his fingers through Peter's again and tug him a little closer. It's almost like now that they're touching, they can't seem to get close enough.

"So what does this mean now?" Peter asks him, placing his free hand on Cameron's knee. It's a simple gesture, a respectful one, but it makes Peter's stomach flip and Cameron's cheeks heat up.

Cameron gives his hand a squeeze and places his free hand over Peter's, the one resting on his leg. "I think it means we're... together." He glances Peter's way with a sly grin. "If you can handle that, that is."

Peter leans in and gives him another quick kiss, smiling against Cameron's lips. "I was hoping you'd say that."

So Peter sits with Cameron for a moment, reveling in his presence, so comfortably close to his own. Neither of them speak, and it seems like this little corner of the world is bundled in silence compared to what lay on the other side of the building. After a moment, Peter pulls himself to his feet, tugging Cameron up with him.

"We should go back. Kiara probably needs help, and Di..." Peter says, letting his voice trail off. Finishing the sentence meant making it real.

Cameron nods, eyes cast to the ground. Peter pulls him a little closer, ducking his head to look at Cameron's face. "What's wrong?" Peter asks.

Cameron meets his eyes. "I think it's my fault, Maya dying. I... if I had caught myself before I fell, her shield would–"

Peter corrals him into a hug, hoping it's at least a little comforting considering the few inches Cameron has on him. He clutches at Peter's back, and Peter whispers in his ear, trying to console Cameron as best he can.

"You didn't do anything. It was just a... scary ripple effect. Please, Cam, don't blame yourself for *anything*. It was an accident."

Cameron nods, but he squeezes Peter a little tighter nonetheless. All Peter's thoughts of going back to the others disappear, and as he stands there holding Cameron, breathing in his scent, Peter realizes he has wanted to be in this exact position since that night when they stood watch together. He buries his forehead in Cameron's collarbone, and Cameron tucks his chin near Peter's temple.

They're interrupted by Kiara and Diana rounding the corner, and neither of them even blink at the sight of Peter and Cameron together. The boys split apart, but Kiara waves her hand dismissively.

"No, please, continue," she says sarcastically, "but preferably after all this?"

The boys nod awkwardly, and Cameron swallows before forcing himself to look at Diana. Her eyes are puffy, and her breath is ragged, but she's standing, fists clenched. "Di," he starts, "I wanted to apologize–"

Diana cuts him off by holding up her hand sharply. "No. You didn't do anything wrong," her voice wavers, and her words are thick with grief, but her tone was still that of their leader, that of the strong Diana they knew.

He nods, looking once again at the ground. "Can you ever forgive me?" His whisper is less of a question and more of a plea: *forgive me, forgive me.*

Diana walks to him, silently wrapping her arms around Cameron's neck, pushing herself onto her tiptoes. He leans into her hug, and she whispers: "There's nothing to forgive. You couldn't have known what would happen. Hell, you couldn't have known she was even in there. But we have to keep going." She pulls away from him, taking something from her waistband. It's Maya's locket, its chain glinting in the sun, and while they all watch, Diana opens it to reveal a slip of paper, old and yellowed. "She never let anyone touch this. But I figured... anyways, look what's inside," Diana unfurls the paper, revealing an identical line with a name and date, the same ones on the pages of the book about the Powerful Ones. This name is written in a neat signature font, one Peter had seen in the tome from the archive. Diana hands the paper to Peter, and Cameron leans close to read it. Peter sucks in a sharp breath when he sees the name:

Maya Monroe, 762

Part Thirty-Eight: The Gemini

Maya

Maya sees her sister and Kiara exit the control room and go towards the stairs. She hurries to the front of the room, to where Peter and Cameron are talking to the other kids.

"Hey, boys," Maya starts, hoping her frantic heartbeat doesn't translate to a shaking voice, "I'm gonna run to the bathroom, okay? Keep an eye on everyone."

They nod, although Maya barely catches the movement as she doubles back and walks as quickly as possible down the hall. She rounds the corner, out of the others' sight, and is met with twelve doors, each leading to the office of a BOZ member.

Maya knows exactly what door she needs.

She goes further down the hallway until she reaches the sixth door. She knocks forcefully on the wood and jiggles the locked knob, repeating the process, anger mounting, until the door finally swings open.

"Ah, Maya. I figured I'd see you here eventually," Oliver Hill says as he opens the door.

"Can I come in?" Maya asks coldly. She crosses her arms over her chest and enters without waiting for his answer, kicking the door shut behind her.

Oliver sits back down at his desk, kicking his feet up onto the table, and Maya leans against the wall and studies him for a moment. He's tall, certainly, and his eyes are bright blue. His hair is dirty blonde, a few shades darker than her own, and Maya doesn't fail to note his expensive Yellow suit, leather shoes, and luxury eyeglass frames.

He's a lot different than the kid Maya knew in school, that's for sure.

"Maya, can I help you with something?" he asks, smiling at her, her name sounding like a taunt from his lips. Maya scowls at the familiar gesture, then crosses to his desk and leans on the front of it, propping herself up with her hands and bringing the two even closer.

"Actually, yes. Oliver. I want you to extract my power."

He laughs immediately. "Maya, you're twenty. You're in no way going to die soon."

"I'm sure you heard about the revolt happening tomorrow," Maya fires back.

He rolls his eyes, bringing his feet off the desk and leaning closer to Maya. "Of course. And why is that relevant?"

Maya smirks. "Well, I'll be fighting in it."

His eyes widen in a brief moment of shock, but he quickly regains his composure. "Why don't you want your power to fight, Maya?" He gets closer still, and their bodies are now inches apart. "I know your mother didn't give it to you just so you could throw it away."

Maya takes a step back, pacing the office, and Oliver gets up and crosses to the front of the desk, perching himself on top of it. "My mother didn't even want me to have her power, Oliver. She was going to give it to Diana," Maya turns to face him and extends her arm, palm up, "Get rid of it."

Oliver studies Maya for a moment, grabbing her hand and tugging her closer. Maya allows herself to be pulled to him, and Oliver drops her hand when Maya is about a foot away from where he's sitting. "Maya, you know I can't," Oliver lowers his voice, as if someone outside the door could hear his words of betrayal, "I care about you too much to let you put yourself in danger like that."

Maya swallows hard and takes a step away from him. "Oliver, if you cared that much, you wouldn't have accepted this position in the first place." She waves a hand around, motioning to the office.

Oliver scoffs, his facade turning ice-cold once again. "I had no choice, My. It was-"

"Your father, I know," Maya looks him in the eyes, softening her voice as much as she can bear, "Oliver, please. I can't play this game anymore."

Oliver sighs, running a hand over his face. "At least choose someone else to give it to, Maya. I can't get rid of it altogether. If Henderson found out, I'd be killed."

Maya steps closer to him, shaking her head. "You know I can't do that, Oliver."

He sighs, standing up to face her. "You're just as stubborn now as you were eight years ago."

Maya smiles. "Trust me, I know," Maya takes one of his hands in hers, "Oliver, why don't you join us? I know Oswald is on our side. You have the chance to do so much good," Maya tilts her head up to look at him, "I know you, Oliver. You're better than this."

Oliver nods slowly, then squeezes his eyes shut, thinking hard. When he opens them, he wraps his arms around Maya's waist and pulls her flush against him, leaning down and kissing her softly, the same way he used to. When they part, Oliver cradles Maya's face in his hands, stroking her cheek delicately. "I loved you, Maya Monroe," he says sadly, pulling himself away from her.

His melancholy words are all the answer Maya needs, and she nods solemnly, stepping back and walking to the door. Maya turns back around to face him before she goes. "I loved you too, Oliver Hill."

He's seated once again, and his beautiful face is a perfect picture of regret. "I'm sorry," he whispers, just loud enough for Maya to hear.

Maya nods again. "I know."

And then she leaves.

Part Thirty-Nine: The Cancer

Peter

"Maya was the Powerful One this whole time?" Cameron asks, looking back up at Diana.

She nods. "I can't see why she hid it from us. She must have found out when she worked at the Capitol."

"I think I know why she hid it from you, actually," Kiara says. "The Gemini power was *ridiculous*. Crazy dangerous. I read about it in the book. I think she wanted to keep you safe by not making you guilty through association."

"What was it?" The others speak at once.

Kiara sighs. "She could use the border material to warp someone's soul."

"What the hell does that mean?" Cameron asks after a beat of confused silence.

Kiara chews the inside of her cheek. "She could destroy someone's soul, creating a... zombie, essentially. All she would need to do is touch them, and hold their hand there until they..."

"Died," Diana finishes.

Kiara nods. "Helpful for bringing someone back from a fatal injury, or something of the sort," Diana's shaky sigh is just loud enough for Peter to hear, "so she probably realized how much power she had and didn't want to endanger you."

"That's dark," Cameron says. "None of the other powers require someone having to *die* in order to use them."

"But why does it matter if Maya hid hers? Wouldn't the BOZ just pick someone else anyway?"

"No," a voice says from behind them. From around the side of the building comes Barbara Oswald, she's walking towards the four, and wiping her bloodied hands down her skirt. They all take a step back, but she holds up her hands in a gesture of surrender. "I'm not here to hurt you. I figured someone should tell you how the powers get passed from person to person." She motions to Peter and Cameron. "These two already know."

"How?" Diana asks sharply. Peter prays her cutting tone was aimed at Barbara, not at himself and Cameron.

"The Powerful One, the current one, will come to the Capitol sometime before their death, when they start to grow old and weak. Their protector, their sector's BOZ member, will then ask them who they want the power transferred to. They can choose anyone in their sector. Then, we extract the power from them and transfer it to the chosen person."

"What do you do with the old person when the power is extracted?" Diana asks.

Barbara appraises her carefully. "Well, we can't let them walk free, can we?"

"What?" Kiara whispers.

"So you were going to kill Maya anyway?" Diana asks, her voice thick with emotion.

Barbara nods, then motions to Cameron and Peter. "And these two as well."

Peter feels Cameron's hand wind its way around his.

Diana shakes her head, turning away from Barbara to face Kiara, Cameron, and Peter. She looks as if she's about to be sick. "We can't keep fighting, guys. Not like this."

Barbara studies the back of her head. "Whatever do you mean, darling? You've won."

The teens all stare at her. "What do you mean?" Cameron asks, his words sharp and direct. "Kiara told us to shut this whole thing down."

Barbara motions towards the back door of the Capitol. "There are six remaining BOZ members. They've agreed with me that now is the best time to surrender."

"So she's really, really gone, then," Diana says, her voice small and fragile. Cameron reaches for her with his free hand, placing a gentle hand on her shoulder.

"But I still don't understand why Maya hid her powers, even if her BOZ member knew it was her," Kiara says, taking a step forward.

"Well," Barbara starts, "there were some... concerns about hiring Maya to work here when she was about seventeen. The BOZ member who represented the Geminis had just been switched."

Peter nods, remembering. "Yeah, Oliver Hill. He took the spot from his dad."

"Correct," Barbara says, "Oliver was very young for the position, only seventeen."

"Wait," Cameron interjects. "That would mean he went to school with Maya, right?"

Barbara nods. "Well, not only did Hill go to school with Maya, when they were both nineteen, after Maya had been working for about two years," she studies Diana before continuing, "Oliver asked Maya to marry him."

Diana gasps. "She never told me that."

"I don't blame her, it was a disaster. Oliver was mad for her, and she too was in love with him, any fool could see that." Barbara shakes her head in a genuine motion of sadness. "But Maya turned him down. She felt like she was betraying her people by being with Oliver, especially after he told her about the powers. She felt like a citizen and a BOZ member being together was... wrong."

"She was right," Kiara scoffs quietly.

Barbara continues, undeterred. "Maya quit soon after. It was the talk of the Board for months. George Henderson-"

Kiara bristles at the name,

"-chastised Hill repeatedly, but the poor boy was heartbroken. He was ready to give up his spot and run back to Sector Six to find her."

"What happened?" Cameron whispers, his creased eyebrows signaling he was thoroughly engrossed in the story.

"Well, Carla Monroe came to Oliver to switch over her power. She was the current Powerful One for Sector Six, and she was getting very sick. So, she was advised to pass it down."

"Wait," Diana interrupts. Her voice is as shaky as her hands, balled at her sides. "My mother was a Gemini. She... was sick. And her name was-"

"Carla," Oswald supplies. "Yes, Diana. Your mother was the Powerful One. She was planning on giving you her power, until she realized when you were born that you weren't a Gemini. So, she gave it to Maya instead." Her gaze softens on Diana. "Why would a mother abandon a child unless the child betrayed her first?"

Peter holds up a hand to pause the conversation. "So there's no way Oliver Hill could've been with Maya, right? That would never work out."

Barbara nods. "Once Maya became the Powerful One, she came back to the Capitol and talked to Hill. I remember watching her walk out of the building, poor thing. I've never seen someone look so dejected."

Diana exhales, but it comes out as more of a heaving sigh, and she looks at Barbara Oswald with a tearful expression. "Can I speak to him? Oliver Hill? Please, I just want to know what happened between them."

Oswald shakes her head. "I would say yes, Diana, but Mister Boone of the Capricorns just found his body." She shakes her head. "Poor child was mutilated, torn nearly to shreds by a wild mob of rioters."

Cameron and Kiara, normally pillars of unyielding strength, both cover their mouths in shock. Peter wipes away a tear threatening to drip from his chin, and Diana shakes her head, already looking numb and broken. "How many people in total, Miss Oswald?" she whispers.

Barbara shakes her head. "A lot," she responds. She uses her finger to lift Diana's chin, forcing her to meet her eyes. She points in the direction of the other three, motioning Kiara, Cameron, and Peter to get closer. "I know what you kids are thinking. I am telling you right now, you did *not* kill these people. They made the choice to join you. There are no winners in battle, no matter which side comes out less scathed than the other. And there is no undoing what has been lost. But all you four can do now is go out there and show these people they were not wrong to stand behind you." She puts a strong hand on Diana's shoulder. "Do you understand?"

They all nod.

Diana sighs, then speaks after a moment. "So that's it, then. The Gemini bloodline is gone."

Barbara shakes her head. "That wouldn't be the first."

"What?" Peter asks. "How many more have been killed?"

"Five."

Kiara sighs in defeat. "Who?"

"Sectors One, Four, Seven, Ten, and Twelve."

"That only leaves five," Kiara says, her voice quiet.

"No, it leaves six," Barbara says.

Everyone's gaze turns to her, and Kiara's eyebrows knit together with confusion and concern. "What do you mean?"

"Maya's power has been removed," Barbara starts, "which is a miracle in itself. She was recognized by one of our members, who brought her body somewhere safe where the power could be extracted." She pauses, and her eyes meet Diana's fleetingly. "Enough remains, in fact, where it could be given to a new carrier."

Peter steps forward, his brows furrowed as if he were trying to puzzle out this problem in his head. "So you need another Gemini."

Barbara tilts her head, like he was only half-right. "We need *anyone*. If nobody carries the power, it can be saved, or destroyed, which is the more likely scenario." She hesitates for the briefest moment. "The Gemini power in the wrong hands may prove detrimental."

They all quiet, and Cameron glances at Kiara, whose eyes grow wide. "Don't look at me," she says, holding up her hands. "I don't want it."

"I do," Diana says then, looking up to see everyone's gazes on her. "I'll do it."

"Diana, you understand the risk of this," Peter says, placing his hands on her shoulders and staring into her eyes. "You are the most wanted person in the nation. Giving yourself another target on your back may not be a good idea."

"Or it is," Cameron says, stepping up beside Peter, "and it's a *great* idea. Diana isn't only the most wanted, she's also the biggest leader. If she has her sister's power, nobody will argue that she's worthy of taking it on."

They're all quiet; no one has a reply, and when Barbara turns wordlessly towards the door, they follow, and she leads the four back through the wrecked Capitol building. Chairs from the congress floor have been dragged into the atrium and torn to bits, wood and marble from torn up flooring lies strewn everywhere, and windows are smashed, the broken bits of glass glinting in the light. As she steps over a Red, torn-up, throne-like chair, Kiara smiles triumphantly but doesn't say a word.

Out on the front steps, the scene hits them like a ton of bricks.

There are ruins everywhere: upturned stones, more shattered glass, bodies twisted every which way, mutilated. Men, women, and children are lying everywhere. Blood has seeped into the concrete ground, drying and staining the marble steps of the Capitol. The battered and bloodied BOZ members are standing in a group to one side, and Diana puts on a brave face as she steps forward. There are about half the number of people as before, maybe less.

"Citizens of New America," Diana starts, her voice cracking, "we've won." Her voice has no ring of happiness, and instead, she sounds almost dismayed.

The crowd roars, and a straggling citizen starts to rush at Diana. The Taurus leader grabs his arm and holds him back, although he looks equally distraught.

Barbara Oswald and George Henderson step forward, with Henderson holding a contract and a pen. As he hands it to Diana, a burst of smoke appears, clouding them in the fumes. They stumble backwards, and Cameron grabs for a hacking Diana whose eyes are red and watery from the fumes. When the fog clears, the Red

Man has Kiara in a headlock, a long knife produced from the folds of his jacket held dangerously close to her throat. Kiara is unarmed and standing incredibly still. She's realized at the same time the others have that he put on a front to get close to her, and a single movement will send his blade through the delicate skin of her throat.

When Kiara meets his eyes, Peter can see the other realization that dawns on her.

They're too far away to help.

Part Forty: The Aries

Kiara

Kiara feels George Henderson's arm tighten around her throat.

"Don't move, 333," he says, his breath sour and hot in her ear.

"Screw you," is all Kiara can manage before he tightens his arm even further.

Kiara glances over to the others, realizing that her friends are all frozen in place. *Good*, she thinks. If they got any closer they'd certainly be killed.

"I've waited so long to do this," Henderson says, "and now I have an audience."

Kiara gasps out her words, seeing spots dance in her vision. "So do it, you ass."

But he doesn't move, instead flinging Kiara around so they're facing the crowd. "Citizens of New America, these are children. They cannot rule you! *I* am the only one fit to lead the Board Of Zodiacs. They are weak!"

With that, he flicks the blade outward in a sweeping motion to the crowd, giving Kiara her in. She stomps on his foot as hard as she can, ducking when he brings the knife back to where her throat had just been. Kiara rolls out from under him, jabbing her elbow upwards to block his flying slash. The blade streaks painfully all the way down her forearm, and Kiara grits her teeth against the flash of pain. She grabs his arm, wrenching it upwards and brings her foot up hard into his crotch. He doubles over in pain, and the tight, white-knuckled grip Kiara has on his arm causes him to drop the knife. It skitters across the concrete, landing by

Cameron's feet, who knows better than to get in Kiara's way, so he kicks the knife back towards Kiara, where she traps it under her foot. She's still clutching Henderson's wrist, and Kiara spins him around by his arm in one fluid motion, shoving him to his knees with her other hand. Kiara puts him in a headlock, allowing him to scrape his nails over her arm while she grabs the knife from the ground. Kiara shoves him away from her, holding his weapon over the same spot of his throat that he had her trapped by just a few moments before.

To Kiara's disgust and horror, he just grins. "What are you gonna do, Kiara? Kill me?"

Kiara's mouth falls open, but it soon twists into a snarl. "What did you just call me?" Her voice is cold, and doesn't sound like her own.

"Kiara," Henderson says, drawing out every syllable, "do it. If you kill me, you're no better than I am."

Kiara nods, savoring the truth of his words. She kneels down next to him, hoping the silent crowd can't see the knife in her hand trembling. "I'm *not* you. I will *never* be like you."

Henderson grabs her wrist, yanking the point of the knife close to his throat. He grips Kiara's wrist tightly, leaving her right hand immobile, so she shifts over and kneels on his other hand, putting all her weight on it so he can't disarm her. "You're the scum of our sector, girl," Henderson spits, "and I will not rest until your little friends are dying slow, painful deaths and you are chained to a pole, watching."

Kiara's anger reaches a boiling point. "What do you have against me?!" She practically shouts. "What did I ever *do* to you?!"

He gets up close to her face, shoving Kiara off and rising to his feet. Kiara gets up to meet him, their physical aggression towards each other momentarily forgotten in the swirling rage. "You and your friends have done everything in your power to unseat me. You have ripped my entire livelihood from beneath my feet, and you, as an Aries, should have had mercy on your own kind!" He takes a step towards her, and Kiara sees her friends move a little closer.

"That has nothing to do with me. What did *I do*?" Kiara asks, allowing him to close the distance between them even further, leaving about two feet in between the two of them. Kiara has to tilt her head up to meet his gaze, and his sickening grin has been replaced with a twisted snarl.

"Look around you, Kiara. You're the only one in your little motley crew that's worth a single moment of anyone's time. You can fight. You're the only one with a shred of diplomacy. Let me ask you, Kiara. Is it worth putting the whole country in danger just for your friends?"

"I don't want to hurt anyone…" Kiara says, trailing off and letting a dejected expression fall over her features. She glances at her friends, and sees that Cameron is clutching Peter's hand and Diana is standing in front of them, all wearing matching looks of disdain, disappointment, and betrayal.

George Henderson takes a step closer to Kiara, his smile returned, stretching his lips and showing his repulsive teeth. "*That's right*," he growls.

Kiara allows him to take her arms, feeling her skin prickle at his predatory advance. But Kiara lets him get close. Close enough. She meets his eyes, her expression unwavering, and he nods, seeming to understand.

If only.

Kiara raises one eyebrow, letting her next words ring over the Plaza. "Except you."

And with that, Kiara drives her knife into his forearm.

Part Forty-One: The Cancer

Peter

"She did *not,*" Cameron whispers from next to Peter, who just nods, his eyes transfixed on the scene.

"You will *burn* for this, 333!" the injured Aries leader shouts, ripping the bloodied knife from his arm and throwing it down at her feet. He roars in a mixture of pain and fury, and Kiara wrenches him towards her by his collar.

"Go, you asshole. Get you and your lackeys out of here before I change my mind and put that knife somewhere *way* more uncomfortable," she growls, shoving him away as the building tension finally severs.

Henderson slowly backs away from Kiara and races back towards the monorail station, disappearing through the double doors. Only when she sees his train disappear into the sky does Kiara let herself fall to the ground, landing on the marble steps, consumed by exhaustion and the flaring pain from her cut arm. Before Cameron, Peter, and Diana can rush to help her, though, Barbara Oswald waves her hand and two BOZ members, the Capricorn leader and the Taurus leader, walk towards her and help her stand next to Diana, giving them an almost united look, the line between BOZ and Revolutionaries blurred.

Diana strides forward, addressing the crowd once more, surveying the damage around her with a pained look.

"Citizens. Like I mentioned before, the Board Of Zodiacs has decided to surrender to the revolutionary forces. But I have a different proposal in mind."

Cameron groans under his breath. "How long are we gonna be standing on these godforsaken stairs?" he asks. Peter smiles despite himself and brushes his knuckles over the palm of Cameron's hand, which is hanging by his side.

Diana continues, undeterred. "I want to go back to what we had. Go back to the presidency, and the Cabinet. So an election will be held to allow the people of New America to place four of the remaining BOZ members in a government position with the rest of us."

To Peter's surprise, Diana is met with raucous applause, and she smiles, albeit painfully. "Well then, it's settled. I'd like to personally thank each and every one of you, no matter what side you fought on. A bill with my exact plan for New America will be put in the hands of every single one of you by the end of the week. Thank you, everybody. And know that as your leaders, we will do everything we can to lead with empathy and kindness towards all of you." She steps back with a wave, and the crowd roars again.

"Talk about the people's leader," Peter mumbles, fighting a smile. When Diana turns around as the crowd disperses, she races into a group hug, and Peter, Cameron, and Kiara all wrap their arms around her. Diana pulls back, tears and blood spattered on her dirty face, and her eyes meet Peter's.

Only six words come to his mind. "Thanks for coming to find me," Peter says with a grin.

Part Forty-Two: The Taurus

Diana

Diana mumbles a curse word under her breath as the needle pierces her flesh.

"Are you okay?" a voice asks from above her.

Diana glances up from the floor to look at the person speaking. She's a nurse, a young one, who looks slightly frazzled, as if she hadn't known about this quick power transfer thirty minutes ago.

Because it hadn't quite been fathomable thirty minutes ago.

Diana is seated on the Congress floor, with no one but the nurse in her company. The room had been tidied up just enough so that some medical equipment could fit, and two dilapidated chairs were put out for Diana and her caretaker.

"Yes. Fine," Diana says back.

The nurse nods, pushing with her thumb on the trigger of the syringe. Slowly, Diana watches the blue liquid inside lessen as more and more makes its way into her veins.

Diana waits with bated breath, closing her eyes and focusing on her inhale. Somewhere, in some unidentifiable part of her body, something feels different. Something in her was thrumming with energy, a tiny ember that she felt could ignite into a flame if she just barely stoked it. She doesn't know how- and she recognizes the irony- but she feels closer to Maya than ever before.

With one quick jab of pain, the nurse pulls the needle from Diana's arm and sits back on her heels. The two make eye contact before Diana forces herself to look away;

something about her flushed cheeks and puffy eyes seems less powerful than she wants it to be. "How are you feeling?" the nurse asks.

Diana pauses, pulling a long breath of air into her lungs. She clenches her fists, watching her fingers furl, dirt and dried blood caked under her nails. She felt no different and yet she felt completely changed. She looks back at the nurse, nodding her head in the slightest gesture of resolution.

"I feel fine."

Diana had never seen such destruction before.

She'd heard of it. She'd heard of the death, the fires, the grief that crashed like a tidal wave over the world during the American Destruction. She'd tried not to imagine how it must have felt for those people, to go to sleep wondering if they were going to wake up. To send their children to school or their spouses to work questioning if it were the last time they'd touch.

Diana had felt more in the past week than ever before. But now, she felt nothing.

Nothing but the shaking of her fingers, the smell of smoke and curdled gunfire, the sharp iciness of the marble wall against her back. Her eyes felt saggy with the weight of tears both shed and unshed, her chest felt hollow with a feeling she'd grown all too familiar with in all too short a time.

She felt the physical. But nothing else.

Someone enters the deserted atrium then, and Diana doesn't dare move at risk of alerting her emotions.

"Diana?" Kiara's voice is husky and crackly, like a piece of crumpled paper in a fist.

Diana looks up, meeting her gaze. The other girl in front of her is standing as she always is: chin upturned, brown eyes alert, shoulders straight. But Diana saw the invisible, saw that Kiara was fighting the crushing weight that was pushing on those shoulders.

Kiara sits down beside Diana and the two make no sound. They both study the mess they'd caused: a beautiful, grand building, torn to pieces by rage and bare hands.

"Did they talk to you already? And give you her power?" Kiara whispers. She doesn't look at her friend, and Diana is grateful for it.

"They did," Diana responds, answering both questions at once. She isn't whispering, and her voice bounces between the cracks and crevices of the room. If Diana from a week ago heard this voice, she wouldn't recognize it.

"The presidency, then?" Kiara mumbles. Diana realizes with a look out of the corner of her eye that Kiara's fingers are moving; she's turning a chipped piece of tile between them. "It's yours?"

Diana just nods, her eyes welling with tears that burn and cause her to push off the wall and pace to the center of the room as if trying to escape the onslaught. "If I want it. I haven't given them an answer yet." She places her hands on her head and looks towards the ceiling, consciously reminding herself to inhale.

"Di?" Kiara's voice isn't concerned, like everyone else's was. Instead, it's more imploring, like she knew that Diana was holding something back that was poisoning her insides.

"There's never been a female President, Kiara," Diana says. With that, the tears start falling freely again and Diana wonders how she even has any left. She turns back to Kiara, words spilling out of her, words that Diana couldn't stop if she tried. "There's never been. There's never, *ever* been a girl who's been in charge. And do you know who it should've been?"

"Maya," Kiara replies immediately.

Diana nods, a frustrated sob escaping her lips. "God, she would've been perfect. And when they said it could be *me*, I-" she lets herself inhale again, breathe out another shaking cry, "-I turned around to tell her. I grabbed her hand and looked at her smiling at me."

Kiara nods, the dust on her cheeks streaked with tears, but she doesn't say anything.

"She wasn't there. I turned around and I was completely and entirely alone. But now, all I can think about is how in all those books we were shown at school, there was only ever men. And then there was Henderson, who created so much evil, but he *didn't* actually create it. He inherited it.

"And the only thing I could picture was how Maya would've said that a woman *should* be in charge. And now there could be, but they want a woman who isn't strong enough to do it," she turns to Kiara, and the two hold eye contact for a moment before Kiara breaks down in tears, burying her head in her hands. Diana wipes at her cheeks and speaks over the sound of her friend's sobs.

"You, Kiara, might be the strongest person I know. You *and* Maya are the strongest people I know," she corrects herself, walking to Kiara and kneeling in front of her. Kiara looks up, and Diana takes her arm, directing their gazes to the already-soiled bandage wrapped around Kiara's forearm, crimson crusted on the seams and the outline of stitches bulging against the fabric, done by some amateur nurse. When Diana speaks again, her voice is hard with determination and just barely hysteric. "*This* is not what makes you strong. Everything you've been through is not what makes you strong. It's the fact that you have pulled yourself through all of those places where you think 'there's no getting out of this' and the fact that *you* keep *me* afloat, too. *Your* strength is what makes me strong. And there is no way *any* man could do what we do for each other, Ki. Whether I agree to their terms or not, I will always, *always* try my hardest to be there for you."

"We destroyed everything," Kiara sobs, scratching almost maniacally at the bandage on her arm. "Look at what we did." She gestures around the room, and Diana refuses to look. Kiara meets her gaze, taking Diana's cheeks in her hands. "You *are* strong enough for this. You are strong enough for *anything*, Diana."

"Promise me we'll hold each other up," Diana says, lip quivering dangerously again. "I can't even try to be the woman in charge of everything without you."

Kiara shakes her head, moving to clutch Diana's hands in hers. "You can be in charge of *anything*, Diana, as long as you try. But I will be with you the whole time."

Diana chuckles sadly, and the sound is out-of-place in this hurricane of emotions. "Maybe it's overdue, a female President," she mumbles.

Kiara snorts with sarcastic laughter, and the girls pull each other into a hug, burying their faces in neck and hair. "You could say that again," she whispers to the room.

Part Forty-Three: The Cancer

Peter

Peter was seated in silence with Diana, Barbara Oswald, Kiara, and Jasper Davis. An eclectic bunch, surely, but a relatively passive one, at least for the moment.

Davis, Kiara, and Peter were on the Congress floor, but not really *on* it. Instead, they were seated in the chairs that were normally meant for the audiences, rather than in the big upholstered seats onstage. Those remained completely abandoned, except for Diana and Barbara, who were partaking in a hushed conversation. Barbara was in her Navy Blue chair, and Diana sat in the Orange one, although she'd never met Charlotte Michaelson and had no connection to any Leo. The three who were not seated onstage were listening to the conversation in front of them as if watching a play. However, unlike in the theater, the air was filled with tense silence and the lingering smell of smoke.

"I am imploring you to think about this logically, Miss Monroe," Barbara says, voice stern.

"I am. Besides, was it not your idea in the first place?" Diana replies. The way in which she held herself scared Peter just a bit: her spine was straight, her puffy eyes were alert, and her tone was even. He'd only seen this Diana a few rare times before now.

"Of course it wasn't," Barbara answers, quirking an eyebrow in a gesture that Diana mimics, maybe accidentally. "Giving you Maya's power was my idea. This was suggested by the other remaining Board of Zodiac members."

Jasper Davis, seated in between Peter and Kiara, scoffs quietly as he shifts in his seat. "Yeah, sure," he mumbles sarcastically.

Kiara grits her teeth and takes a calming breath. "Shut up," she whispers to him without taking her eyes off the production taking place in front of her.

Barbara turns to the three there, in the front row, and in what seems to be an epic breaking of the fourth wall, she locks eyes with Peter. "Mister Simon, if you would?" She stands and motions for Peter to join them, and he rises, followed by Kiara and Jasper, who don't follow him to the stage but stand nonetheless.

Barbara motions for Peter to take a seat, but he doesn't, leaving Diana dwarfed by the two people on either side of her as she remains in her spot, fingers clenched and white against the arms of the chair.

"Mister Simon," Barbara begins, her tone almost sickly-sweet, "please give *your* opinion on this matter."

Everything in Peter is telling him not to speak, but he does anyway, his fear and adoration of Barbara Oswald being a more convincing argument. "Diana, I trust you. But don't you want to wait?" She doesn't respond, her jaw set, eyes fixated on nothing in front of her. Peter glances nervously at her before continuing. "Think of everything we've- *you've* gone through, Di. You could take some time, and no one would blame you for that. Don't you want to grow up a little?"

Before Peter has even closed his mouth, Diana seems to snap, her gaze flinging to Peter's and full of rage, although not aimed entirely at him. When she speaks, or yells, more like, her tone is commanding and that of a leader. "I did! I *have*," she corrects, voice cracking as she tears her gaze from Peter's. "I have done more growing up than any sixteen-year-old deserves to do in one week. In one *lifetime*. There are kids our age..." she trails off, eyes growing misty, and Peter swears he's the only one who notices before she blinks away her tears, "there are kids *younger* than us who have lost any opportunity to grow up at all. So now I will devote my life to making sure that the ones who come after me get that chance. I have the opportunity now to *help* people. To make a real difference. And I will not let that slip away."

The others say nothing, and Peter realizes, looking around, how Diana stunned them all into silence without even rising from her seat. She doesn't meet his gaze, but staring at the side of her face, settled into a stoic expression, something like resolve settles in Peter. He looks up at Barbara, hanging onto the small shred of confidence that was glimmering in his chest.

"You heard her," he says, pushing on even as the others look at him with a shocked expression. Barbara raises one eyebrow, as if daring him to continue. "If she wants to be the President, let her. You were outvoted by the rest of the Board of Zodiacs, and they offered her the position. It's her right to accept it or not."

Barbara nods slowly, and after a beat of agonizing silence, she holds out her hand. Without a word, Diana takes it, allowing Barbra to pull her to her feet. The two stand there for a tense moment, Diana's hand still clutched in Barbara's, and slowly, Barbara bows her head.

She stays that way for a long moment, and when she rises, she mutters two words that shatter the silent air around them and sends a shiver down Peter's spine.

"Madam President."

Part Forty-Four: The Scorpio

Cameron

"You wanted to see me?" Cameron asks, gently pushing open the door of Diana's brand-new office. He takes a moment to look around the space, still wrecked from the day's events: a bookshelf has been pushed over, its contents scattered across the room. Both large windows on the back wall are surprisingly intact, but the curtains are shredded. The large desk in the center of the room is scratched and chipped, and Diana is leaning against it, her back to Cameron.

She speaks without turning around or lifting her head. "They want to make me the President."

"Oh." Cameron's shock comes out a whisper.

Diana finally faces Cameron then, and he's greeted by a familiar sight. Diana sniffles as she wipes away a tear, barking out a bitter laugh. "Yeah. The BOZ members who are still around want *me* to lead *them*."

"That's good, though. Right?"

Diana huffs out a breath, looking around the overturned space. Cameron's heart thumps in his chest, and he's nervous for no reason at all. "I lost the only family I had not five hours ago. And they're most concerned with inaugurating a child."

Cameron bites his lip, turning over her words. "It'll be weird for you, probably. Working with them."

"It will," her green eyes land on Cameron then, and he swears he can see a glimmer of an idea behind them. He's seen this Diana before, the calculating leader from their travels. "But I won't be doing it alone."

"What do you mean?"

"Cameron, my entire life was rerouted in the span of half a week because of you guys. I'm not going to let you all scatter to the ends of the earth again."

Cameron blinks. "What are you proposing, then?"

Diana doesn't smile, but the tears stop coming for a brief moment. "Back in my sector, Mister Davis always had a guy he traveled with. Sort of like his second-in-command." She takes a step towards him. "That gave me the idea to give you, Ki, and Peter different jobs, ones that'll keep you around." Her voice wavers, and she shrugs half-heartedly. "If you *want* to stay around, that is." Her voice grows small, and Cameron places both hands on her arms. "Please, Cam. Stay around. I... without Maya, I don't know if I'll be able to go on without you."

"I will." He finally pulls her into a hug, and Diana sighs shakily into his chest. "Of course I'm staying."

Diana pulls back after a long moment of silence, and the pair makes silent eye contact again. "I haven't quite figured out what the others' jobs will be. But I did get some information on ours." She crosses behind the desk, pulling out a piece of lined paper. There are notes scrawled on it in what Cameron realized was Diana's unfamiliar handwriting. "When Presidents used to take office, they'd always have a Vice President, someone who they knew they could trust. Someone who'd take on the presidency if they needed to." She levels a pointed look at Cameron. "I want you to do that."

"What? You want *me* to take *your* place?"

"Only if something bad happens to me, or I can't be President anymore for whatever reason," she sighs. "Cam, you-"

"Why *me*? Why not Peter, or Kiara? You've only known me for a couple days-"

"Cameron." Diana's tone is firm, and Cameron stops talking. They hold each other's gaze for a moment, and something serious and unsaid passes between them. "I need you to do something for me, alright?"

Cameron shakes his head softly, out of nerves more than refusal, but Diana continues, unrelenting. "I chose you because if the country has to look to someone, to anyone else, it would be you. They already do. But someday, they might have to look to you for *this*, and I know you'll be ready."

"Diana, I..." He trails off, looking down at his hands, which are wrung together nervously, "I can't."

"You can," she takes his hand, unfurling his clenched fingers. Carefully, she places something gold and shining into his open palm. It's a small pin, engraved with *S. Security, II.* Cameron looks up at Diana to see her holding one of her own, engraved with *President, I.* His mouth falls open slightly as a colossal mound of emotion overwhelms him.

Before he can say anything, Diana speaks again, her voice a whisper. "I also chose you because *I* believe in you." In one fluid motion, she closes his fingers around the pin. The two make eye contact once again, and both nod at the other, the smallest of movements. Diana smiles, so slight that Cameron isn't sure it's even real. "I believe in you."

Part Forty-Five: The Taurus

Diana

As the sun sets on the Plaza, the biggest crowd ever gathered there assembles over the course of an hour. The citizens leave a wide berth around the fountain in the center, where fifteen feet of concrete are dug up on both sides, revealing broken dirt beneath. Small easels sit in a row, two on one side and three on the other.

At the front of the crowd are scattered and somewhat familiar faces: the woman who raised Jason the Virgo, Katie's brother, Marcus' girlfriend. Their heads are bowed and some are crying.

Just as the sun sinks behind the golden dome of the Capitol building, eight figures begin to descend the stairs. They're all dressed in Black, but there are three others behind them who are in their sector's colors.

Peter, Cameron, and Kiara walk towards the fountain first. Kiara is crying, as is Peter, and Cameron cradles a thick manilla envelope in both hands. As the crowd watches, he approaches each easel, placing photos of the fallen on them. Katie, grinning widely in a sparkly Red dress and tights, William, holding a flower that matches the Navy Blue clothes he's dressed in, Marcus in all Brown, hugging his friends.

The four BOZ members approach next. Barbara Oswald kneels next to William Chance's grave, bowing her head and gently running her fingertips across the coarse dirt there. Mr. Boone goes towards the crowd, holding out his arms for Marcus' girlfriend to step into. Ms. Brewer takes the hand of her charge, Olivia, and holds her tightly, two people who just happened to be lucky. Ms. Miller just stands there, hand on Cameron's shoulder, the perfect picture of two people who fit together under strange circumstances, people who have no one left.

The last person to approach is Diana. She's in a Black dress, with Black tights and shoes. Her blond hair shines in the golden light, and the sunset illuminates her wet cheeks. She holds the last picture: one of her and Maya hugging, small children grinning widely at each other and completely lost in their own happiness. Slowly, with mechanical precision and not the slightest inkling of an emotion, Diana sets the picture onto the easel in front of the last hole.

As soon as the picture leaves her hands, Diana sinks to her knees, sobbing so hard her shoulders heave. For a long moment, the only sound that bounces across every corner of the Plaza is that of the President's distraught cries. Slowly, her friends walk to stand next to her, placing gentle hands on her shoulders. Peter gets to his knees next to her, dirt digging into the pristine Black pants he has on. He takes Diana's hand and whispers something to her, rising to his feet and helping her up after him.

Diana looks across the rows of people, who are staring at her the same way the stars gaze at the moon. Diana clears her throat, releasing a slow breath. "We have decided that this fountain will be renamed, and devoted to those Powerful Ones who were lost, and in the memory of everyone else who left us too soon yesterday."

At this, she looks around, the rubble and destruction from the events of yesterday's revolt still spread everywhere. She wipes her eyes and crosses to the first row of holes, the one with two photos. As she speaks, Diana kneels and tosses a handful of dirt over the coffins resting inside. "Katie, Aries number five hundred. In the time I knew her, Katie was the most hopeful human I had ever met. And... and I'm sorry I won't be able to watch her grow up." She moves to the next person, "William Chance. Survived by leader Barbara Oswald, who would like everyone to know that William was like a son to her, and she hopes he is in a better place now, with his mother and baby brother." Barbara comes up behind her, pulling something from behind her back and placing it into the hole: a single Navy Blue lupine flower, that she covers up with a sprinkling of dirt.

Diana moves across to the other side. All eyes are on her, and no matter what side people fought on, everybody in America is united at this very moment. "Marcus was a Capricorn, survived by his leader Mister Boone, and his girlfriend Grace." Diana crosses to Grace in the crowd, who is still being held up by Mr. Boone's kind embrace. "He wanted you to have this, I think. It... it was in his pocket," she whispers, pressing a small, circular something into her palm. Grace nods, smiling gently.

"Thank you. For protecting him," Grace whispers.

Diana nods sadly, voice strained. "Of course. I'm so sorry."

She forces herself to walk away, to the next grave. "I only met Andrew once, before we knew who the other person was. The day we met, he was being dragged away by guards, just a little kid." She gazes up to the sky, toes nearly touching the edge of the dirt. "Andrew, I'm sorry I wasn't brave that day. I'm sorry I didn't help you." She looks back to the crowd. "I don't know his last name. I don't know his family. But I do know that if I can be as brave as Andrew once was, I'll be okay."

She goes to the next one. "Jason. You know, I always thought that the Virgo Powerful One had the best power. Anything they wanted, in the palm of their hand. Jason could've had riches, or power, and instead he used his power in his last moments to save Jesse." She motions to the Powerful One in Orange, the Leo, who survived. Jesse is staring straight ahead, lip quivering, "Jesse told me that Jason found him inside the Capitol, locked away in an office, cornered by a guard. And just as the guard spotted Jason, he turned the material into a weapon for Jesse to protect himself. The guard killed Jason, but Jesse was able to save himself thanks to Jason's help." She places a handful of dirt gently into the hole. "So thank you, Jason, for saving one of your own."

Finally, she reaches the last grave, the one she'd been pulled away from before. Her grief is only indicated through her eyebrows knitting together and her chin wobbling, and she swallows hard against the lump in her throat. She kneels in front of the picture, looking down into the dirt pit in front of her, where a coffin made of shining wood rests in the ground. She manages a whispered, "Oh, Maya," and then begins to cry, gripping the earth beneath her as if to clutch onto her sister once again.

"I didn't know Maya for that long a time," someone says from behind her, shattering the quiet. Diana looks up to see Cameron step forward, nodding at her gently, a silent show of support, an affirmation that Diana could rest for a moment. "And I'll forever feel guilty for the part I played in her death. But one thing I did know about Maya was that she loved her sister. Diana and Maya shared a bond that shocked me, because I never knew that you could love another person that way." He reaches down and takes Diana's hand. "Maya taught me to be a better person. She taught me to love deeper. And for that, I'll forever be grateful to her."

Kiara steps forward then. "When I went to go get Maya, about halfway through our journey, I didn't really think it was worth risking my life for someone I barely knew. But without Maya, none of us would be standing here right now. Her information, her wit, and her bravery saved all of us yesterday. And I know she helped more people than just us. She was always kind, and never gave up."

Finally, it seems as if the whole country turns to look at Peter, whose eyes are welling with tears. "I... I don't really know what to say." He clears his throat, but doesn't move. "As a kid, Diana was my best friend. But Maya, Maya was like a big sister to me." He turns to look down at Diana. "I want you to know that we love you. *Maya* loved you. She *always* will." He reaches out a hand to her, and Diana takes it, allowing herself to be pulled to her feet. Peter holds her at arm's length, looking into her eyes. "She made all of us better people. And nothing will feel the same anymore now that she's gone. But Maya would want us to keep moving forward," his gaze softens a bit, "and she would want you to lead us. And I want you to know that we are all behind you. *All* of us, especially Maya."

Diana takes a deep breath, saying nothing. Eventually, she looks up at Peter, who's looking down at her with just a hint of uncertainty. Without a second thought, Diana wraps her arms around his neck, hugging him tightly and burying her face into his chest. Peter reacts just as he did when they were kids, wrapping his arms around her waist and tucking his head next to hers. Slowly, gently, Cameron and Kiara join the hug, and the four of them hold onto each other in the middle of the Plaza as the gathered crowd begins to applaud, more family now than friends.

Epilogue: Six Months Later

Diana

Diana is interrupted from reviewing one of Peter's proposals when a thick folder lands on her desk. "Thank you," she says without looking up. She puts down the paper in her hand and takes her feet off her desk to flip through the folder, when Kiara peeks her head into the office.

She's in a Red suit with a White undershirt and Black sneakers. Her hair is down around her shoulders, and she instinctively tugs her long sleeve past her wrist to cover the long scar left from George Henderson's assault six months ago. This is her first time back at the Capitol, having gone back to do George-Henderson-caused damage control in Sector One during the months following the revolt.

"Nice digs," she says, admiring the space. She's right, the office has had a revamp since she was last there. They were all given offices on the second floor of the Capitol building, old BOZ offices left over from the officers that were killed. Diana's belonged to Cara King, who was found buried underneath some rubble, having been crushed by the debris. She chose it because it was clean and stark, a contrast to many of the other available offices. Peter got Mr. Garcia's, and he was *still* finding loose papers all over the place. Cameron had chosen Oliver Hill's office, leaving four unused. The desk was Diana's favorite part of the room. It was large and sturdy, made of a light oak wood, and polished to a pristine shine. Bookshelves of the same material were built into the walls, and two big windows behind her peered out over the Capitol steps.

"Thanks," Diana says, pushing the folder aside. "How are you feeling?"

Kiara shrugs, tilting her head in a *so-so* mannerism. "Okay, all things considered. I noticed no one took his office."

Diana shakes her head. "Locked it up. Only Peter, Cam, and I have the key."

Kiara nods. "What about you?"

Diana assumes she's talking about Maya, and the events surrounding her funeral. The fountain in the Plaza was ultimately renamed in Maya's honor, and although the ceremony had been difficult, Diana felt better now, getting closure and making sure Maya's legacy would live on.

"Fine," Diana replies after a beat.

Kiara nods, looking back out into the deserted hall, probably for Cameron and Peter. The boys had quickly and excitedly assumed government jobs like Diana had, taking offices across the hall from each other. They worked closely with the remaining members of the BOZ, the four who had been voted to stay in a leadership role. Ms. Oswald, Mr. Boone, Ms. Brewer, and Ms. Miller had responded well to working with the four kids, and the citizens agreed through an almost-landslide vote that they were the four to keep. George Henderson had run off, and Mr. Davis, the Taurus leader, refused to even consider changing his alliances, so he was locked up in the Capitol jails, along with the small handful of citizens and old guards that had continued to give them grief.

The changes made had been small at first but were slowly growing into a snowball effect. The guards had been removed and were now being trained as a police force, only responding when called by a citizen, the monorails ran anywhere, the assigned clothing decree was lifted, and with Cameron's guidance (and magic), the border walls were slowly but surely coming down and the population was starting to become integrated. The proposal Diana had been reading, written by Peter, was about revamping the school system. All it needed was the unanimous signatures of the eight leaders. They all generally operated as equals, but their titles and specific tasks were different. For example, Cameron was Secretary of the Security Department, and Peter the Secretary of the Education Department. Diana's official title was 'President'. Kiara had opted out of working at the Capitol, claiming she was not one for a desk job, so Oswald stuck her with the title 'Citizens' Liaison' and sent her around the country, checking up on everything from the police force to construction.

　　"Where are the boys?" Kiara asks, making herself comfortable in one of the large leather chairs in the office.

　　"Lunch. They decided to pop out after our meeting with Boone about the Integration proposal," Diana says, standing up and crossing to her. She sits down in the chair across from Kiara, but she ushers Diana back to a standing position.

　　"Your clothes! I've never seen a more stylish seventeen-year-old," she says.

　　Diana grins. The fashion *had* been a huge upgrade, and with the help of Ms. Miller, the old Libra leader with quite the flair for dramatics, the three Capitol regulars were always looking sharp, no matter the time of day. Today, Diana was outfitted in an outfit similar to Kiara's, except her pants and blazer were Navy Blue while the undershirt was White. Diana's shoes were a pair of sensible dress sneakers, because while Miller put up a stink and insisted she wear heels to give her short frame a boost, Diana refused, claiming that desk work was no place for stilettos. Her hair had been washed and cut almost immediately after her position was awarded, and now it resided at her shoulders, with wavy layers that never seemed to go away.

Their house was a lavish penthouse apartment for the four of them in the Plaza, and the floors below them were occupied by Oswald, Miller, Boone, and Brewer. They each had their own rooms, and Kiara's remained mostly untouched, considering she spent most of her time traveling. Diana had claimed the smallest room, even though it was still the size of her living room in Sector Seven. The furniture was modern and clean, with a bright color palette that made one temporarily blinded when the sun shone through the floor-to-ceiling windows and hit the marble countertops.

Kiara grins. "They're not here, so we can gossip about them."

Diana sits down next to her, throwing a hand over her heart dramatically. "*So cute.*"

Kiara giggles. "Right?! Peter was so shy at first, but it's adorable how Cam brought him out of his shell."

Diana nods. "Peter apologized to me about our past together."

Peter knocks on Diana's door frame. "Can I come in?" he asks.

Diana is standing with her back to him, looking around her new room in their apartment. She nods, turning to face him and motioning to her bed. Peter takes a seat on the foot of the bed, clearing his throat and looking around.

"How are you doing?" he asks.

Diana thinks about it. How is she doing? Maya's funeral had been yesterday, and the revolt itself a day before that. "I'm okay," she responds, sitting at her small desk and spinning her chair around to face him.

"Barbara and the others seem to like us," he says with a small smile.

Diana smiles back. "Like us? Peter, they love us. You especially."

He laughs, and the room goes quiet. After a second, he looks at Diana. "Can I talk to you?"

She nods. "About what?"

He sighs. "Cameron."

Diana bites her lip, picturing the two. "Are you guys okay?"

He nods, a smile dancing across his lips. "Yeah, we're... good. I just wanted to apologize to you."

"Um, why?" Diana says, her eyebrows knitting together in confusion.

He wrings his hands together. "Because I didn't know if you had feelings for me. And I know when we were younger, we were sort of..." He trails off, letting the statement hang in the air.

"Peter, can I be frank?" Diana asks.

He finally meets her eyes. "Please."

Diana crosses to him and sits next to him on the bed, keeping some space between them. "You were my first love, Peter. But when we started to get the ball rolling, I think I realized that maybe I didn't need someone else to show me how good a person I can be. Then you found Cameron, and I know that was scary and new, but it let both of us discover new parts of ourselves. And I think that's a really beautiful thing. And I couldn't be happier for the two of you, because honestly, you guys were supposed to be each other's people from the start."

He's quiet for a second, his finger tracing the embroidered pattern on Diana's comforter. "I couldn't have said it better myself. And I suppose I owe it to you for us even meeting." He looks her in the eye. "You're still my best friend, though. Forever. You don't get a choice in that, no matter how sick of me you might get."

Diana laughs for what might be the first time since Maya's death. "I wouldn't want it any other way."

Peter hugs her, and Diana smiles into his shoulder before pulling apart. After a comfortable minute of silence, she smacks his leg gently. "So, how is it with the both of you?"

Peter smiles and falls backwards onto the bed. His cheeks turn pink and he covers his face with his hands, and Diana laughs, shoving his leg playfully. "It's really great," he says. He uncovers his face and looks at Diana, still sitting up above him. "I'm actually really surprised with how quickly it felt... comfortable. I'm just... really happy, Di."

Diana smiles, heart welling with pride. "I'm glad."

Kiara smiles. "Who knew that a Scorpio and a Cancer-"

She's cut off by the boys charging through the doorway. Peter puts out his hands on either side of the doorframe to keep from falling, and Cameron races in right after him, ducking quickly under his extended arm and making it successfully into the room. Cameron puts his hands on his legs and gasps for breath, and Peter is panting equally as hard. Their clothes are wrinkled and disheveled, Peter's curls are ruffled, and Cameron's ginger locks are sticking to his sweaty forehead.

"Did you guys run here?" Diana asks, instinctively crossing over to Cameron and taking hold of his collar to fix his top button that had come undone in their mad dash to her office.

"Yes," Peter huffs out. His eyes scan Diana's office, and they land on something on her desk. He strides over to it, grabbing the manilla folder from before and holding it up with an expectant look. "Did you read this?"

"Uh, not yet," Diana starts, "I only got it like ten minutes ago."

"Who dropped it off?" Peter asks.

Diana thinks back, realizing she didn't see whoever dropped it on her desk. "I don't know. I never saw them, I was reading your proposal. Why, did you guys get the same thing?"

Cameron pipes up from the doorway. "There were folders at home with our names on them."

Kiara side-eyes him. "Why were you home? I thought you were at lunch."

Peter coughs, and Cameron's cheeks flush a dark red. "No reason in particular," Cameron says, running a hand through his hair and straightening his button-down.

Diana points at him. "Gross." Then she looks back at Peter. "What's in them?"

He motions to the folder. "Read for yourself."

Diana plucks it from his hands, sitting down at her desk. The others crowd around her, and she opens the folder to a piece of paper with a bunch of fuzzy, black-and-white photos. The first picture is an aerial view of the ocean.

Diana holds it up in front of Peter. "This is just the ocean."

"Correct," he says. "Keep looking."

The next picture is a ground view of a giant castle that sits atop a cliffside. Kiara whistles. "That's sweet. Where is this place?"

Peter says nothing, just points at the next photo. A town, made up of tight row houses made of brick, streets lined with cars, and most importantly, people. But they aren't in a zodiac color.

"What is this, Peter?" Diana asks, her concern growing. She flips to the last picture, a professional-looking photographical portrait of two people, a man and a boy about their age. They're dressed like royalty, the man in a crown and long cape, the kid in a military-looking uniform adorned with badges made of silver and gold. The man looks around forty, with dirty blonde hair that's graying slightly. His eyes are cold, and his hand rests menacingly on the hilt of the flashy sword hanging by his side. The boy, although not smiling, seems much nicer. He's sixteen or seventeen, and his dark hair is a few shades darker than the older man, who Diana assumes is his father. He has full, dark eyebrows, which are a contrast against his only somewhat-tan skin, but his eyes are what Diana notices. They're so dark they're almost black, and even though the photo is faded in color, she could see a charming, humorous glint in them. His build is strong, and one thing is for sure about the both of them: they have power, and money.

The heading under the photo reads, *King Cornelius Percival Rutherland of Alynthia, posing with son Prince Lucas Rutherland of Alynthia.*

"Royalty?" Kiara whispers.

Diana flips to the next page quickly, trying to forget Lucas Rutherland's dark, haunting eyes. The paper underneath the photos is a description of a kingdom called Alynthia, and she reads aloud.

"Alynthia is an island kingdom nestled in the Eastern coastline of North America. Although small, Alynthia is known for its large, merciless army. The Alynthian Palace sits atop the cliffs of Alynthia, looking over the Atlantic Ocean on one side and their kingdom on the other. Cornelius Rutherland, the first King of Alynthia, showed up on the unclaimed land two years after the American Destruction, the year the Board of Zodiacs was created in New America. Seven months after he established the kingdom, his son, Prince Lucas Rutherland, was born. The kingdom has stayed hidden for almost seventeen years, due to the King's evasion of American officials."

Diana can practically hear her heart pounding in her chest. She looks out the window, towards the east, as if she could see Alynthia from where she stood. She shuffles the stack of papers around, feeling sick when the photo that lands on top is the one of Lucas Rutherland and his father. She looks back up at her friends: Kiara is looking pensive, staring out the window towards the same place Diana was looking; Peter is clutching Cameron's right hand with his left, and they're discussing something in a whispered tone Diana surely could have heard if the blood was not rushing through her ears.

Diana stares back down at the desk, saying to no one in particular, "So, what does this mean?"

The room goes so quiet you could hear a pin drop. Finally, Peter taps the knuckle of his index finger onto the space right above Lucas Rutherland's head.

"It means we're not alone."

Chaos erupts around them and everyone talks at once. Without Diana noticing, Cameron takes the picture from the top of the stack, studying it intently. "Wait. Guys," he says after a moment. Everyone turns to look at him, and he holds up the picture, pointing to one of the many gold pins running down the King's chest. "Look familiar?" he asks.

The other three crowd around, and Diana gasps when she sees the engraving on the pin Cameron was pointing to. Her stomach drops when she sees the same pin on the Prince's chest. "Is that...?" she whispers.

"The Libra symbol," Peter responds. He backs up a step, rubbing his forehead. "Wait. Didn't Miller's mother lose her charge when she first started as the Libra leader? And then Miss Miller never got a new one, since the old one never passed on their power?"

"Holy shit," Kiara says, clearly understanding something that Diana did not. Kiara looks at Peter with wide eyes. "We need to talk to her."

"What are you talking about?" Diana asks, feeling somewhat idiotic for not following.

Peter looks at her, and his eyes hold a seriousness she has never seen before. "Cornelius Rutherland ran away from *somewhere* and established his kingdom, right? This happened the same year the BOZ was created. It just so happens that that same year, Miller's mother, the first Libra leader, lost her charge. Remember when Miller almost got booted from the BOZ because she had no Powerful One?" He points at the pin on the King's jacket. "Well, here he is."

Diana's eyes widen as all the pieces click into place. "So you're saying..."

Cameron nods. "The King of Alynthia is the lost Libra Powerful One."

Peter's mouth sets in a grim line, and he moves his finger to point at the Prince. Diana swallows, almost knowing what Peter is going to say before he speaks.

"Now the power has an heir."